THE PROMISE OF THE CHILD

VOLUME ONE OF THE AMARANTHINE SPECTRUM

TOM TONER

Night Shade Books
New York

Night Shade books may be purchased in bulk at special discounts for sales promotion, corporate gifts, fund-raising, or educational purposes. Special editions can also be created to specifications. For details, contact the Special Sales Department, Night Shade Books, 307 West 36th Street, 11th Floor, New York, NY 10018 or info@skyhorsepublishing.com.

Night Shade Books® is a registered trademark of Skyhorse Publishing, Inc.®, a Delaware corporation.

Visit our website at www.nightshadebooks.com.

10 9 8 7 6 5 4 3 2 1

Library of Congress Cataloging-in-Publication Data
Toner, Thomas.
 The promise of the child / Thomas Toner.
    pages cm – (Amaranthine spectrum; volume 1)
ISBN 978-1-59780-845-3 (hardback)
I. Title.
PR6120.O445P86 2015
823'.92–dc23

2015013632

Illustrations by Patrick Knowles
Cover design by Claudia Noble

Printed in the United States of America

"Smiles form the channels of a future tear."
Byron

"It was true that as one watched life in its curious crucible of pain and pleasure, one could not wear over one's face a mask of glass, nor keep the sulphurous fumes from troubling the brain and making the imagination turbid with monstrous fancies and misshapen dreams."
Oscar Wilde

PROLOGUE

Praha: 1319

Eliška watched the rain outside while she waited, the windowpanes already misted with the steam from her sodden furs. The chestnut leaves brushing the glass were a rich emerald green against the dark sky, fat and luscious from a fourth summer of unceasing rain. Somewhere in the square a peddler was shouting, his calls softened by the downpour.

She let her eyes wander to the desk before her, carved from light wood and heaped with papers. Thick black and red seals of office dangled from some like dried scabs, snapped where the knife had slit them. If she stood from her chair she might perhaps see some of what was written, but she knew better than to think of disturbing anything on that wide table, instead looking to the shelves, her eyes settling on the fireplace. The dank day made it feel much later than it was, but the flagstones in the hearth were clean and swept, the andirons resting on them still unused. There would be no fire tonight in this fine, high-ceilinged room, not even if its master worked at his desk until morning.

On her walk across the mostly deserted Judith Bridge, she had seen a woman leaning against the parapet, vomiting into the swollen river. Two stray hounds on the far side had stopped in the driving rain to watch her with ears pricked, their eyes bright. Eliška had hurried on, her escort clapping his hands to shoo the animals. The dog packs had a taste for children, but it couldn't be long before they started after larger prey in this starving city. People blamed the rotten meat thrown into the shambles for encouraging the packs, and perhaps soon they'd need to be hunted in the narrow streets like boar in a woodland.

Hearing the muffled bells of St Vitus sounding across the Mesto, she looked back to the window, watching the scrape of damp leaves against the glass.

"Princess."

The voice in her ear was pleasant, conversational, but she gasped nonetheless.

"Do not stand," the man pleaded, holding out a ringed hand and smiling down at her look of alarm. He glanced over her furs and tutted. "You are wet."

"*Bonjour à vous*, Aaron," said Eliška softly, composing herself and running a hand over the fur at her throat. She knew it pleased him when she practised. "I walked."

Her husband's principal exchequer, acting ruler of Bohemia in all but name, nodded and smiled brightly, glancing out at the square. "I would have sent someone if you'd written ahead." He went to his desk and papers, sparing them a cursory glance before moving to the window. Eliška knew the glance was contrived to be casual, but those eyes took in everything; they'd have spotted a single moved or shuffled document, any item out of place. Not for the first time, she wondered if it might be a test, leaving his private correspondence for all to see while they waited in his office, and whether the sheaves of paper were even important at all.

At the window, the man stopped, taking in the view between the trees. "Praha looks splendid even in this rain, don't you think?" He turned to her, that face always somehow difficult to recall, kind and avuncular, just beginning to run to fat from years of sitting behind great tables.

"As lovely as Paris?" she asked him, trying her best to smile.

He laughed lightly, a breath from his nostrils. "Very nearly."

Her eyes lowered to the newest chains of office around his shoulders, globular garnets winking from their links. John had rewarded his advisor well for his years of service, as had his father before him. The town house he kept on Seminárská was no indication of Aaron's true wealth—the man could have had a palace carved from blue Carrara marble or splendid quarters in the castle on the hill if he so chose—but this modest building had served as the advisor's sole residence since her husband's coronation in 1310, before the years of famine and damp had scoured the city.

"They say the rain will continue all summer," she said, sitting back in her chair and watching his reflection in the glass as their eyes met. "But Gascony and Aragon will be spared this year."

Aaron's reflection continued to watch her, a spirit peering in at her from the window. He shook his head.

"Not England. I have a letter from King Edward; he writes that there was no bread for him with his supper when he stopped at one of his towns in June. No bread for their own *king*. Bohemia is not yet that desperate."

Bohemia. Perhaps when it is, you shall take your leave.

Eliška glanced to the thickly embroidered rug covering most of the pale floorboards beneath her chair, as if in contemplation. There might be letters from more illustrious men than Edward on that table, had she the courage to look earlier. A certain Pierre, a friend of Aaron's and a fellow Frenchman, wrote to him often. Pierre went also by the name of Pope Clement, when it pleased him.

"Have you been there? To England?" she asked, gesturing with a nod to the table and its clutter.

Aaron's eyes followed hers to the table. "Not for years and years, Princess—though I would venture to say it was a finer place when I did, under the rule of his father." He raised a hand above his head briefly. "Tall men are often more adept at governance, for some reason, and the Scot Hammer was exceedingly tall."

Eliška had travelled abroad just the once, to meet her new husband at Luxembourg when she was barely fourteen; Aaron himself—fresh from assisting the Emperor in the wars against Florence—had arranged the union, and she remembered at first quite enjoying his company in a foreign court of strangers so far from home. He had made her feel safe, always sparing her the time to talk in confidence, no matter what the hour, and sometimes even making her laugh at a point in her life when she had thought she could not. Indeed, as she looked around the chamber, it occurred to her that there might be nowhere in the land safer than where she sat now, in this rain-battered town house. Thieves and rapists roamed the outlying districts of the city and her days finished well before the sun had set. Even her lonely rooms in the castle might not be nearly so impregnable as this dark chamber with its lingering stink of wax and varnish. Anyone at court could tell you who really ruled the city, but those who valued their noses kept their mouths shut and their eyes closed. They said Aaron the Jew kept no lovers, that he never slept; some claimed he seldom ate a morsel, the whispers among the diplomats he entertained monthly suggesting that he did not even deign to *touch* things. Eliška's eyes still went to the man's hands—pale and long and veined with blue—whenever they met, despite her best efforts. The more she thought about it, the more ridiculous such whispers sounded, as if her husband's court were filled with children. Of course she had seen him eat, and drink. He had touched her shoulder just then, had he not? She couldn't remember.

Whatever the prejudices against the king's secretive atheling, his statesmanship and vision were legendary, and under his guidance Praha was promising to rival Rome one day as a seat of enlightenment. Heaps of silver Groschens stamped with the collared lion of Bohemia tumbled in daily from principalities as far-flung as Berlin and Frankfurt as the city vied to become, against the designs of countless kings and princes, capital of the whole empire. The princess might even admit— privately, of course—that her husband's absence barely obstructed Aaron's designs at all. Unlike John, the softly spoken chancellor seemed to live for his adopted city, and as far as Eliška knew, Aaron hadn't left it since her father-in-law the Emperor's death in Buonconvento a few years before.

But she was not so naïve as people thought, this princess, with her round, mole-speckled face and sleepy eyes. If Aaron came and went at leisure, or kept many wives, or visited all the brothels in the Holy Roman Empire, nobody would ever know. As with the affairs of state, he managed his own business behind bolted doors and heavy tapestries, in cold chambers where no fire blazed in the hearth.

He was watching her again when she looked back to the window.

"And so you are here to discuss Václav, Princess." He looked at her properly at last. "Begin."

Eliška felt a blush rise to her ears. She had tried to keep something from this man and he had embarrassed her—albeit momentarily—for it.

"Yes," she admitted. "My son is unwell."

Aaron nodded as if it were old, familiar news, his eyes going to the floorboards at his feet. "As I said, you ought to have written in advance—I am busy today."

"You could come tomorrow." She heard the young girl in her voice as she spoke but no longer cared. "Can you?" She kept her gaze on her hands, feeling his stare running the length of her body.

"Yes, perhaps." He sighed. "In the afternoon. Don't let any physicians touch him until I am there."

She glanced at him, relief fading the blush. Whether good magic or bad, she was glad of the chance of it. "Your . . . payment this time, Aaron?"

The man turned his head briefly to think, a few strands of iron grey, thinning hair catching the day-dark light. There were no moles on his chalky skin or blemishes of any kind save the creases around his eyes. "He's to come here a year earlier than we agreed. When he is seven. I may choose to take the prince travelling with me." Aaron looked sharply back at her. "Are we agreed?"

A year earlier was small coin. Eliška knew her reputation as a methodical, industrious girl, and knew she had no choice. She would lose her son either way.

"He is yours, Aaron. Bring him back to me when he is great."

Aaron smiled broadly, his eyes suddenly kind. "The *greatest*, or not at all."

Chapel

A white chapel guarded the tiny crescent port, looking north-west to the strait between the islands and into the deep blue waterway where the fishing boats came in. Sotiris only remembered the building from the front, never from any approaching angle. Shallow stone steps led downwards from its locked door to the urchin-caked rock beneath, sinking into the darkness of the sea. He had never seen inside; the single square window was always too grubby and the Ionian light too bright, even at sunset. Only smudges of colour revealed themselves if he looked away across the water, back to the port. Pale blobs of yachts or catamarans bobbed, becoming clear only for an instant before memories of their form were muddied by all the intervening time, and houses on the harbour-side were little more than far-off parcels of yellow and white and pistachio green.

The chapel was one of the places his mind took him on walks, guiding him along the grassy hillside that fizzed with twilight cicadas and down to the locked door. When he tried to look up at the side of the building, gaps in the recollection pulled him quietly to its front. Memory was crude, cubist, unyielding.

The chapel and its island had become a sort of stage, a setting upon which things he sometimes read and heard could play out in his mind. He didn't know if other people thought like this and it had never occurred to him to ask.

Sotiris's remembered walks to the chapel were almost certainly more fiction than anything else. The memories were pickled, viewed through the oily layer of whatever preserved them, altering their colour, texture, even their form. But they had fared well, considering. He counted again, briefly. Those memories of the chapel were almost twelve and a half thousand years old.

A tourist boat with an outboard motor glides into view. He should have heard the raw-throated engine—he knows the boat well, even if its shape and colour are vague—but it is strangely silent, as if much further away. The boat passes only a few yards below him in the strait, headed for port. There are people standing on board and he recognises all of them but one: the man at the centre of the group, a glass in his hand.

Sotiris knew perfectly well that he was dreaming, that his sleep had found the well-thumbed scene at the front of his thoughts that night and offered it up once more, but still he was frightened.

He places his hands on the wall, the chapel at his back, and peers over as the vessel passes beneath. The figure is in shade, then obscured by a bunch of yellow parasols they must have found for their guest's arrival. Raising his eyes and staring back to the little coloured blocks of houses beyond the yachts, he keeps thinking, *Why doesn't the boat make any sound?* It's as if it doesn't want to be noticed, perhaps trying to reach the port without any fanfare. But the people at the colourful harbour-side already know it's coming—they're there, they're waiting.

Then the tour boat passes the chapel and leaves the shade, sun warming the parasols and colouring the motor smoke. The depths it's heading into are almost green. He sees the guest again, mingling, charming, carried onwards to Sotiris's island. He glances over his shoulder, the chapel twisting, and wonders if he can run back in time along the hill path to Vathi. It was possible, just about; but the people waiting at the harbour by the rusted bollards and benches and nets would shoo him away like the local leper. They didn't know. Sotiris straightened in his dream, turning from the harbour and trying to wake. The truth was that he really didn't want to be there when the boat came in; he didn't want to see their guest close-up.

It wasn't a man, the image that mingled and charmed on the top deck of the boat; that's what those people waiting couldn't understand. It was a mirage, a skilled deception, a glamour. It hadn't come to help them.

Fortress

Through a fog of roving hail the machines dropped, at first nothing but far-off grey specks revealed now and then in the blustery white sky. By the time the colossal brick-red fortress at Nilmuth had noticed their approach, the specks were already angling their descent, the scream of their fall reaching the watchers below. The hundred and five craft fell in a diamond shape, the outermost machines slowing as they reached their target and elongating the formation to a narrow spear. From miles around the descent and attack would look slow, like a flock of ravens mobbing a dying beast, and their speed was only given away by the popping bursts of supersonic detonations impacting through the fleet as they met the highest spires of the fortress.

The first machines, selected for their bulk, detonated as they hit the spires, rupturing stone and metal. The second wave followed a moment later, their beak-like forms burrowing through the next layer of towers and into the depths of the fortress. Bodies and masonry thundered past the third wave of machines, a gulch of flame blackening their already dark hulls as they hit gas tanks and piping. They fell deeper, rigged to explode at a certain depth to allow the passage of the next, more vital wave, eventually blowing apart the inner foundations of the great central spire. The machines that came after were self-powered, bellowing their exhausts through the smoke to slow their descent and extending skinny arms to claw for purchase on the citadel's rock flanks. They lodged in the ruins of the spire, rubble and stone still falling like rain around them, and popped hatches in their undersides to disgorge dozens of tiny figures.

Tzolz glanced up through the dripping sleet at the war machines circling the gaping breach in the fortress, lumps of wet rock the size of horses still falling among his team and denting the reinforced hulls of the landing craft. He checked his spring rifle again, looking around to the assembling mercenaries still funnelling from the hatches, and moved wordlessly through the debris to a ruined corridor, his armour-plated feet crunching over the dismembered bodies of the Vulgar who had lived at this level. Teeth and fleshy shards of bone littered the rubble like seeds, some sticking to the polished metal of his boots.

His squad took point, crowding past him to the edges of the doorway to hurl tiny Oxel scouts. The fairylike Prism species whistled to each other and scampered in, their bulky flight-suits clinking with dangling bomblets. As he waited, Tzolz looked back through the dripping chasm at the vacuum-suited Lacaille knight still sitting in the open hatch of the furthest craft, the heavy helmet making any expression unreadable. Rusted pipes and chunks of material still dropped like snow into the breach and Tzolz backed further into the doorway.

A series of detonations signalled the depths of the Oxel's explorations and he turned quickly, shaking the moisture from the weapon and hoisting it to his shoulder. Ahead, the dark and smoky corridor had been widened, doorways to adjoining chambers blown in by the tiny scouts, and he diverted two teams in either direction with swift hand movements, taking the central passage himself with three more. Their spies had indicated that the Shell was frequently moved for its security, resting at irregular intervals in an iridium-lined chamber in the guts of the structure. If the agents valued their skins they'd have made their way out of the country to the harbour at Untmouth by now, knowing full well what awaited those who remained in the fortress and the fallow lands surrounding it. Tzolz flicked his lights on, illuminating the rest of the corridor with a caustic white glare that sent shadows bouncing across bare stone walls and elaborate hanging braziers. At the end of the section of corridor there began a succession of spiral ramps once necessary for vehicular access, one of which would take them down into the lower levels. After three ramps they would hit a shaft, the spine of the fortress, where a drilling team was to meet them.

He waited, holding up a gnarled finger. Crude microphones on his breastplate tasted the silence, hearing the distant explorations of his five other teams as they swarmed through the fortress, the grumble of detonations and the groaning of the structure all around them adding to the distant moan of the wind through the chasm at their backs. No conversation between his units was permitted, and so at last he heard them, whispering in their little high-pitched voices. Tzolz allowed himself ten more seconds, finger still raised, understanding Vulgar more than adequately. He pointed slowly at the leftmost opening of the many-branched corridor ahead of them and his three mercenaries converged on it, their thin shadows looming like skeletons across the wall. At the edge of the doorway he turned off his lights and listened to the darkness, the voices—inaudible to a normal Prism ear—louder in his helmet now. He knew exactly where they were.

He unclipped a bomblet from a canister on the belt of his suit, pulling the firing pin and counting, then stooped and rolled it swiftly down the spiral ramp. A few seconds later, one of the voices hesitated, obviously turning as its volume fluctuated, and Tzolz muffled his auditory channel. The blast shook the spiral passageway, shrapnel spinning and clattering from the entrance. Tzolz flicked on his lights and dashed through the curling smoke, leaping the last of the passage and landing among the disoriented Vulgar platoon, the small figures illuminated harshly in his strobing gaze. He rammed his rifle's bayonet into the closest Vulgar, spinning and knocking an armoured elbow into another's head. Their screams filled his muffled earpiece, the little creatures realising at last what he was, and he snarled inside his helmet, pulling the bayonet free and scything it through another. They were poorly equipped and shoddily dressed despite being caught at home, and Tzolz began to wonder if he might be able to reach his quarry long before the fleet caught up to his small force. He aimed quickly and put a bullet through one more, his troops crouching at the foot of the ramp and firing into the flickering blackness. When the screams had stopped, he leaned against the wall, breathing quickly, his lights taking in the heaped bodies at their feet. His squad began searching the defenders' elaborate but ill-armoured clothes, long, dark fingers investigating pockets and flaps, taking what valuables and compatible ammunition they could find.

Tzolz bent to examine one of the Vulgar, his lights blazing across the pale elfin face. It coughed, retching once, and then tried to turn its head away from the light. He caught its chin with one hand, squeezing its jowls together, and turned it back to him, sliding up his reinforced faceplate. The small Vulgar's eyes widened as they focused on him, pupils shrunk to pinpoints in the glare. Tzolz looked into the creature's eyes as its broken body attempted to struggle, then back to his team, who were ready to continue. He slid the palm of his three-fingered hand over its face, forced his thumb into one of its eyes and pushed, watching the white flesh depress until it gouted blood. With a wet crack, the Vulgar's skull crumpled in his hand and its movements ceased.

Venturing further into the fortress, the tunnels below became more lived-in, with tapestries cloaking the walls and dividing living spaces, the homely smells of sour ale and poorly maintained plumbing adding to the sense of warmth in the dim light. Tzolz removed his helmet, tossing it onto a loaded dining table in some servants' quarters, and loosened his chest-plating. Like many of his team, his genitals were partially exposed, and the removal of his armour only served to make him look more gangly and naked. Such things mattered not to his breed, one of the wilder, more basic Prism races that dared to delve into the Firmament, and the added bulk would only slow him down from here on in. A small timepiece set into his shoulder-plating told him they had less than an hour before battleships stationed in the inland sea would be within range of the fortress and his means of escape. He looked around the large dining hall once more as he pulled on his gauntlets, taking in the dimly glowing logs in the hearth, some scattered to smoke on the tiles by the force of his arrival, and the shelves stacked with bottles and jars, small squealing animals in cages and stinking yeasty cheeses. The Oxel scouts were already raiding the larders, gorging themselves on the hanging lengths of dried, salted meats, but his squad stood around the room still as statues, their thin faces watching him intently in the firelight. There was only one thing his mercenaries really liked to eat, and they would soon have it.

*

At the shaft, Tzolz stopped, the blackness complete around them. They had travelled in darkness from the abandoned servants' quarters down and down until his ears popped. Only the sound of running water had told him they were finally upon it, the great spine of the citadel. He switched his suit lights back on as his feet met soft mounds on the floor, and he looked down to see that they were walking once again on casualties, pieces of all the Vulgar that had fallen from the higher levels during the attack. Most had tumbled straight down the shaft, but some had hit the sides and bounced, ending up lodged like detritus in the corkscrew corridors that made up the shaft's sides. Two levels below them, the drilling team were waiting in silence, their hungry, reflective eyes visible in the suit's weak light. Further below them, the bricks and stones turned to solid rock, cold granite slabs that glittered with running water. At his signal they began their work, dragging heavy drills to the sides of the shaft and pulling chains to start them.

The noise of grinding filtered up along with the drifting cloud of pulverised stone, turning the air around Tzolz's group into a milky soup wherever he shone his suit lights. The team stood, waiting, their faces haggard and obscene in the mist like sunken corpses in a moonlit pool, the portable generators within each soldier's armour issuing their own small whisps of coiling smoke. Running among their feet the Oxel played, one tripping and falling into the chasm before its fellows could stop it. Tzolz watched the body tumble, screaming, until it was lost in the darkness.

The drilling team shut down their machines, the mist swirling in the updraught from the shaft and dissipating. Tzolz's crew bent to look, some grabbing their spring rifles and training them on the hole that had suddenly been revealed in the chasm wall, a weak light pouring from it. Tzolz waited, sighting his own weapon on the caved-in portion of wall below. The edges of the hole crumbled further until a portion of the wall suddenly sloughed away completely, dropping into the shaft in a cloud of dust and stone and unveiling a cross section of tunnels and levels swarming with shrieking Vulgar soldiers. They squealed to each other and fired into the drilling team, Tzolz's men dropping as many as they could before bolts and sparkers started raining into the level on which they were crouched. The Vulgar squad was mostly composed of trained Loyalists, but the motley armour indicated hired help as well, with not a few Zelioceti and even Wulm mercenaries among their number. Tzolz lifted his rifle to cover his head and made his way down the open passage in the side of the shaft, shots chipping the stone around him. They were surely too far away for any great accuracy, but still he made a last dash for the safety of a stalled drill lying canted on its side. Fizzing sparkers whined and bounced from its casing as he dropped behind it, brushing at a smoking dent in his shoulder-plating. Glancing up at his squad, he could see that two were dead, the third taking a bolt through the eye as he watched. The remains of the drilling team had pushed into the hole and were climbing the ladders in what appeared to be sleeping quarters. Tzolz followed their progress along the flimsy-looking wooden bunks and up into the next chamber, some leaning from the level they were on to shoot up into the mass of screaming Prism scampering this way and that along their bunks. He checked his clock, knowing before he did so that there was no more time for fighting. He clawed at the drill, bringing it up to his chest with a wheeze, and held it there like a shield as he made his way to the hole.

A Wulm dropped into his path just as he reached the ladders, shoved from its level by the panicked Vulgar loyalists. It shook itself and stood, squealing as Tzolz threw the drill aside and slammed his rifle into its small head. The long-eared Prism's face crumpled in a froth of blood and it rolled, tumbling into the chasm. He looked up at the drillers clambering above, some taking bolts and falling, then back along the open tunnel he was in. There were bodies piled against the rustic wooden door at the far end, its edge burned away by some sort of incendiary explosion. He kicked it open in a storm of splinters, bringing the rifle up and felling a Vulgar as it ran for the next chamber, then made his way to an apparently undefended lower passage. As he jogged, Tzolz realised he was limping and glanced down to see that the meat of one calf had been mostly torn away by a clawed bullet. He ground his teeth and ran on.

Corphuso watched the Amaranthine as she touched the machine's edges, running a finger almost tenderly along the coils that made up its outer lobes. She hesitated, her ancient mind lost for a minute in some distant reverie, and tapped the structure with her finger, as if trying to gauge the exact blend of the fine amalgam of alloys from which it was made. The tap of her finger produced no sound, the architect noticed, and was pleased.

The flotilla would be underway, he knew, sailing up the fjord and into the canals that led to the fortress's surf lands. From what they could hear, deep in the base of the under-chasm, the attack had lost momentum, perhaps—Corphuso dared to hope—already totally intercepted at the serving levels. The mighty citadel of Nilmuth hadn't been breached in five hundred and seventy years, despite centuries of sporadic civil war across Drolgins. Now a freeVulgar mercenary army from Untmouth protected the fortress at all times, stationed in the vastness of its broad foundations, and a fleet of destroyers—a gift from their secretive allies the Zelioceti—kept watch over the port. Only brute force had gained the Lacaille access today, but they hadn't enough time to reach the treasure they were digging for. Corphuso smiled nervously as he watched the Immortal examining the Shell, wondering again just what he had made, and how it would change things forever.

"Are you pleased with it, Amaranthine?" he asked, observing how little she appeared to notice the distant rumbles of conflict in the levels above them.

Voss looked up at him, her hand remaining on the structure it had taken him twenty-four years to build. She was dressed in the exquisite finery the Immortals always wore whenever he saw them, priceless jewels dripping from every cuff and piccadill. "I think it is a marvel, Corphuso. A blessing, but also a curse."

He looked at the glimmering machine. "I expect, as ever, the blessing shall be yours, the curse ours."

She smiled, the expression so rare on her pretty face that he couldn't help but instantly smile back. "You shall be a Prince of the Firmament now, Corphuso—you can leave the cursed behind at last."

The architect sat down, glancing briefly at the Vulgar soldiers standing to either side of the doors. They were wizened, ill-looking things, their skin shiny and liver-spotted in the glow of the fire. If they had heard what she said, they made no sign. It was true—he wanted to leave the Investiture, but he had never told a soul. The Prism worlds were places of pestilence and fear, where the short-lived suffered and scavenged and fought. His successes had left him far wealthier than most, his large family married into the courts of Moonkings and

Princelings across the Prism Investiture, but he was now bound to the counts of Nilmuth as they fought over his invention themselves, and all but a prisoner in the fortress. His dearest and yet most secret wish had always been to leave all this filth and terror behind with enough money and influence to be granted a place among the Immortals in their Firmament, and perhaps—were there any hope of such a thing—to become an Amaranthine himself.

"I am bound by duty to my kingdom, and by its loyalty to the Firmament, Amaranthine," he said carefully, glancing again at the soldiers. "It is not for me to decide my fate, nor would I wish to."

The Amaranthine looked into his eyes, the smile lingering at the edges of her mouth. He wondered how many liars she had known over her long, long life, and how many she had seen shamed.

"Quite so, Corphuso," she replied at last.

He took up a heavy book awkwardly, leafing through the dense Vulgar print to the engraved pictures, noticing from the corner of his eye how she still looked at him. He was waist-high to the Amaranthine, nothing but a dwarf in her eyes, but some deep Vulgar sense of pride always allowed him to forget his small stature. Gradually he became aware that the sounds in the fortress had changed, almost disappeared, while at the same time deep, resonating grumbles were seeping through the thick walls from the lands outside. The soldiers looked at each other, then at the architect.

"It's the flotilla, Architect," one said excitedly. "It must be!"

He stood, putting down the book to listen. The Amaranthine had returned her gaze to his machine, apparently uninterested in their good fortune. Detonations, distant and yet obviously enormous, popped and thudded high above the fortress. The Lacaille invasion force was fighting back, apparently. They must want what he had very badly to risk returning fire on an armada of sixty-one Lumen-Class Zelioceti destroyers. For what felt like the millionth time, Corphuso deeply regretted forging the thing the Amaranthine was stroking, wishing he could take it all back. Supposedly a machine of life, it had become an inevitable tool of death.

Some other noise returned his attention and that of the soldiers to the thick doors of the under-chasm library where they were sheltering. Someone or something had run the last of the steps and was now outside the door. The Amaranthine looked up suddenly, taking her hand at last from the Shell.

A weighty oaken slat cracked and sizzled as the door was fired upon from outside, two more shots blowing the double doors in. The two soldiers fell under the flying debris as someone opened fire into the chamber, rolling in the mist to find cover. Corphuso crouched and knocked the table, scattering the stack of books he'd been absently looking through during the siege, pieces of the chair he had been sitting upon a moment earlier raining down around him.

Looking across the floor from under the table, he caught a glimpse of his attacker ducking behind a column. He felt hot sweat prickle down his neck and chest, staying very still. So, the Lacaille were now employing the very breed they feared the most. He hoped they suffered for it in the end. He saw the bony, elongated Prism male, genitals exposed, hideous face partially hidden in shadow, slide the bolt on its rifle and peer around the column.

As it did so, the air turned to fire.

Corphuso rolled and covered his face, waistcoat and cloak shrouding him like blankets as the library was engulfed. For what felt like a small lifetime roaring heat pelted the table, flowing around his small hiding place and sucking away all the air, then suddenly it was over as quickly as it had started, the fire dissolving into sooty smoke.

He peered out from under his smouldering clothes to where the Amaranthine stood, the charred flagstones describing a perfect semicircle of blackness around her feet. Corphuso glanced back to the column, the shelf of books behind it still aflame, but could see no sign of their attacker.

Voss, the Immortal, patted the unharmed machine at her side, the spiral of hollows in its shell gleaming iridescently in the smoke-thick air like polished opal. "I suspect it's time to take your treasure elsewhere, Corphuso." She smiled again. "Come. You need no longer worry about appearances—the Firmament expects us."

PART I

Cove

Lycaste watched as the fish darted about his ankles, standing as still as he could. Garishly painted and about the length of his smallest finger, he had seen this kind many times but couldn't remember their names. He crouched slowly for a better look, reflections darkening the water. One of the fish had something, a worm or parasite like a long white thread, dangling from its eye. Where the thing was attached, a milky cataract had formed.

He reached in, startling them away, and took a cupped handful of water to splash on his neck and forehead. He liked the salt on his face, the sting of it on his cheeks when he looked at the sun. Today, of all days, he needed time, silence. Silence to think, perhaps, silence to hide away. But that wouldn't be possible. Lycaste shook his head and started back, gazing at the outcrops of the bay beyond and feeling the water dry on his hot, rust-coloured skin.

Even in the sheltered bay he wouldn't swim, his overactive imagination seeing shadows move, staining the perfect turquoise around the far-off crags. His friends swam nearly every day, but they'd long since stopped asking him to join them. Huge migratory sharks had been spotted out there, coasting silently between the baking rocks. Fat, pearl-coloured monsters five times the length of him; what they ate or where they came from he couldn't say.

It was later than it seemed, time to go in. He wandered up the stony beach, his feet skipping on hot pebbles as he looked for patches of cooler sand to walk on. Lycaste's estate included the small cove, his orchards taking a weak hold at the edge of the beach, a thin strip of mottled eggshell between rich swathes of sultry green. Further down towards the next bay the water became a light, chalky blue as it washed against the suddenly white pebbles of a separate beach. He preferred his land, his colours.

He saw Sonerila and the boys sitting beneath a Midsumnal wine tree, chopping bulbs from its silver lower branches and dropping them into a basket. Lycaste crept close, hidden now and then by the sculpted topiary.

"Just the largest ones," the servant said, taking the scissors from the taller boy, Papaver. "Just enough to fill the basket."

The boys sorted through the bulbs while she watched.

"That's enough. You can take the smaller fruit home with you."

"Why does he always eat alone?" asked the younger of the brothers after a moment, sitting and staring out to sea.

"He doesn't always eat alone."

"Pentas doesn't join him any more."

Sonerila looked at him, finally placing her scissors into the basket beside the pile of pale silver bulbs. "Take these to the solar—leave them on the table."

Lycaste watched them carry the bundle into his house while he rubbed at the sand on his long legs.

"Why not just give everything away, Sonerila?" he suggested, walking out from behind the tree.

Her elongated face turned to him without surprise. Sonerila always had a talent for knowing precisely where he was at any particular time; perhaps that was why his mother had chosen her to stay on. "A reward for their help. I get precious little from anyone else around here."

He moved out of the shadows to examine a manicured tree. "They came for the gossip."

"And I gave them fruit instead."

"You should have given them these." He held out a branch dangling off-white berries. "They're turning."

Sonerila looked at him, her long head dappled in shadow. "*Is* she coming tonight?"

He sat and stretched out on the grass, arms behind his head in poor imitation of ease, then considered the helper, half his face in bright sunlight that forced him to squint. "I hope she will. I don't know."

The bird smiled just as a lady might, pretty dimples forming at the corners of her beak. "How could she refuse a face like that?"

Lycaste smiled back, shading his eyes and looking past her. The boys were trotting down the slope from the house towards them, their purloined wine packaged up in waxed paper parcels from the kitchens.

"Hello, Master Lycaste."

"Catch anything today?" he asked them, always unsure how to talk to children beyond a certain age.

"Three big fish on Lesser Point, for Master Impatiens's table." The boy and his brother exchanged glances. "Old Jotroffe was there again. Papaver's taller than him now."

"And how is he?" asked Sonerila.

"Strange, as usual. He swam with us, kept asking about the sharks—if we'd seen any recently."

Lycaste looked between them. "You swim at the Point?"

"All the time."

"And have you? Seen any?"

"No, just porpoises. Hey, want to buy anything? We brought the cart."

Lycaste shook his head. The cart was always full of junk. The quality objects they hauled from estate to estate were nearly always gone by the time they reached the beach, all the best stuff taken. Lycaste was beginning to doubt there was even anything decent in there at the start; the one time he'd found a usable plastic figure for his palace they'd hiked the price. The boys hoped to start work in Impatiens's export business in a year or two, possibly with the prospect of travelling to the next Province every now and then as things progressed. Perhaps then they'd stop ripping him off.

He glanced up at the sunlight shining through the emerald leaves, already masking their chatter as his thoughts turned to the previous few days. Of all the help kept on, Sonerila was his favourite. She was always there to comfort him, to give him the best advice. Once the boys had gone he'd be able to talk to her properly; she would know what to do.

*

The house was half-submerged in the garden itself, a few acres of sculpted trees rising smoothly up the stepped sides of a grass-covered hummock. Five bell-shaped towers grew from the low hill, peeling white stone structures strung with lanterns and ruddy bougainvillea. The flowers hummed in the breeze as the evening ripened, enhanced chambers in their bracts hauntingly reverberating to different chords.

Backing off the beach, the estate gave way in each direction to rolling hills and groves of subtropical jungle, now wild again after generations tamed. Lycaste strolled through the orchard towards one of the white towers with Sonerila at his side, listening. The screams from the woodland to the east were loud this evening, echoing from the broad, curved walls of the closest towers.

He slowed and turned. Something didn't feel right. A sensation he hadn't experienced since childhood: someone was observing him, watching him as he walked. Heat on the back of his neck, almost physically creeping across his skin. Lycaste looked up at the hills, as if expecting to see someone in the darkness of the undergrowth, but the day was late, the shadows grown deep.

As he neared a slim archway at the base of the tower, his body darkened quickly, like glass suddenly polarised. The tone of his skin settled on a matt charcoal before switching rapidly through a tight spectrum, the colours churning together over his body like mixing paint. After a second, his skin evened to a milky blue, mirroring the fading light in the sky. Lycaste paused to look at his hand, watching the last of the colour tinge his fingers, then went inside.

Impatiens called it a *doll's house* whenever he saw it, but it was much more than that. Lycaste pulled out his favourite chair and sat down, taking up his paintbrush from its pot of water and a section of the extension he had begun building last month. He turned it in the evening light, looking for the unpainted window frames he remembered needed doing, waiting for the lamps to awaken around him. At his side stood dozens of stoppered blue jars and bottles filled with trinkets and tools, most of them gifts from the birds whenever they went into Mersin. He dabbed at some white paint, applying it carefully as the lights woke up, beating to the rhythm of his heart and relaxing into a rich glow. He finished a window frame and sat back.

The whole piece had taken him seven years. It reached almost to the ceiling of the large chamber, an idealised house fit for a Province prince. Inside were hundreds of figures and animals, all individually painted and with full Melius names and stories of their own. Lycaste reached in and picked up a few of the earliest figurines, scrutinising each one in turn and laying them in a row with some others. His painting skills had improved slowly over the years, and these had begun to look a little crude, as if a child had made them. Briza, Drimys's young son, occasionally asked if he could help Lycaste with his work, but the boy was absolutely forbidden. He'd caught the child playing with the house once, in the days when he still left the door to the chamber unlocked, and banned him from the whole top floor of the tower. This was his, and only his.

Lycaste carefully moved the figures to one side, counting them under his breath as he did so, to make space for the extension, which he placed on a folded square of stained white linen. The prince needed more space in his palace for all his new pets, a number of which Lycaste had just made. He reached under the table for the metal tray of powdered colourings, pausing to look at them as he put them on the table. They were a gift from her, after he'd finally found the courage to show her this locked-away place.

He barely heard the knock on the door. Impatiens pushed it open an inch and peered in.

"How's your doll's house, Lycaste?"

"It's a palace," he muttered, dipping his brush in the water pot.

"My mistake." Impatiens surveyed the model for a moment, as if looking for something. "Did you find my—"

"Yes, thank you." Lycaste dug in a drawer and handed him the skeletal, rather mummified body of a lizard he'd found set upon the miniature dining table one morning, the tiny figures arranged around it as if at a great feast. "I've made my own food for the table." He indicated the painted bowls and cups, some tiny coloured beads and woollen balls placed inside them with tweezers.

"They must get fairly hungry, locked away up here."

Lycaste wiped his hands and went back to his painting, ignoring the man.

Impatiens sighed and rubbed his great bushy beard, listening to the rattle and clatter of preparations downstairs. "It sounds like your dinner party's happening without you. Coming down?"

Lycaste nodded, reluctantly setting aside the paintbrush and practising his breathing techniques. Old, familiar butterflies rose to dance in his stomach at the thought of having to entertain guests, fluttering more manically still as he glanced at the paint tin, knowing she might have already arrived.

"You can't swim at the Point."

"The Lesser Point, they said."

"Still—"

Drimys pushed his plate away, leaning back and staring at the vaulted white ceiling of the dining room. "You don't think the boys were just trying to impress you?"

Lycaste glanced at both men and shrugged. He'd done little more than pick at each of the many courses of his supper, relieved and yet disappointed that only two guests had arrived after all. "They told me they saw Jotroffe out there again."

"Now there's an odd creature," said Impatiens, leaning to cut into the vast block of fruit-studded cheese in the middle of the table. "Even looks strange, doesn't he?"

Lycaste could only agree. He'd met the man many times, usually when he was out walking, though the hermit appeared to take care never to make a habit of trespassing, despite the boundaries of Lycaste's land being exceedingly poorly marked. Jotroffe was extremely short, like a child, willowy and slender, though almost certainly not young; anyone who spoke to him could see that. His face was deformed, unfinished somehow, like seeing your reflection in a small concave mirror. His speech, though understandable, took a very long time to form, the words following each other with an agonising slowness that could snare unwary travellers into a whole afternoon's conversation.

"The last time I saw the fellow, we talked about the weather for most of the morning," muttered Impatiens, spreading the cheese carefully onto a biscuit, "then finished with a good long session on whether walnuts were superior to cashews. His eventual opinion? After all that? That they were 'most assuredly of equal merit.' Astonishing."

"It was 'optimum fingernail length' when I met him at the port," said Drimys, burping gently into his hand. "No more than three inches of white among polite society, I'm reliably informed."

"Was he always like that?" asked Lycaste, still regarded as an outsider by most residents of the Province despite having lived by the beach for almost twenty years. He looked at his own long nails, polished and clipped that evening in expectation of Pentas's arrival.

"Ever since I've known him," Impatiens said. "They say he bored the crew of a ship from Brindisi into throwing him off here, but he won't ever tell you his own story. *That* I'd wait all day to hear."

Lycaste stirred the remaining food on his plate with a long fork, mushing it all together. "Do you think he's just trying to get home?"

"I can't imagine they'd want him back," Impatiens said and rubbed his whiskers, apparently remembering something. The eyes in his great, gnarled face lit up. "Did you see what those boys gave me today?" He stood, walking into the next room and producing a brace of fish from a basket. "I don't recognise them." He slapped them on a salver in the middle of the table, a large iron hook still fastening the catch together. Lycaste thought they looked like the deep-sea creatures sometimes caught in Mersin, all teeth and eyes.

"What did you give them?" asked Drimys, pulling one from the hook and peeling its lips back to see inside its mouth.

"They owed me." He took the remaining fish from the plate and stretched its fin back to expose the spines, letting it flop back into place. Its wide, pale eyes were frozen in a startled expression. "Might be worth something up in Karaoz."

Lycaste detected the onset of merchant-speak, laying down his fork and folding his unused napkin carefully. Soon they would be discussing pounds or ounces or similarly opaque things, the stuff of grown men to which Lycaste—who had never really understood trade at all, having inherited everything when he came of age—felt hardly able to contribute. As far as he saw it, his gardens grew plenty of whatever he required, from delicate cuts of grown meat to fruit, plastics and metal ores. If anything needed to be bought for the house the helpers did it, leaving Lycaste written receipts of trade that he barely looked at before they were filed away in a cupboard somewhere.

He went to the wall and rang a small bell on a chain to let the birds know there was work to be done. Those two would talk all night, forgetting Lycaste was there entirely.

"It must be deeper out there, at Lesser Point. Could be as good a place as any to start," Drimys was saying.

"Start what?" Lycaste asked, ringing the bell again. Something about Drimys's expression had caught his attention.

"The fish only grow large enough at the Points," Impatiens said, lifting one of the creatures from the platter again and miming a little dance, wriggling its fins. Both of them began to laugh.

"What are you talking about?"

Impatiens and Drimys fell silent after a moment, considering him. "You wouldn't like it," said Impatiens, putting down the fish.

"Like what?"

He turned to Drimys, who was avoiding eye contact as he refilled his glass. "Shall we tell him?"

Lycaste was losing his patience. He pulled on the bell a few more times and waited for an answer.

"How strong is your boat, Lycaste?" Drimys asked, glancing up finally.

He looked at them both, uncertain if they were playing a joke on him. The two men appeared serious enough in the dim light. "It hasn't fallen apart yet. Why? Do you want to take it out?"

"It can hold three, can't it?"

"I think so."

Impatiens glanced at Drimys again. "I say we take him along—it's *his* boat."

His friend and business partner looked unconvinced.

"Look, Lycaste—" Impatiens gestured for him to sit "—we've come up with a sort of adventure. Use of your boat, if you grant it, should in fairness get you a place on the crew."

"We never discussed who's captain," said Drimys suddenly.

Impatiens frowned. "I think you'll find we *did*. I've a much greater knowledge of the coastline." He turned his attention back to Lycaste, shaking his head. "Anyway, it's Midsummer. There's a lot of fish about. That means those sharks should be back."

Lycaste stared at them, unsure again. "All right."

"It'll be dangerous," said Drimys, sitting forward.

"Yes," said Impatiens, "but we're going to take precautions, we're going to plan this down to the smallest detail."

"Plan *what*?" asked Lycaste, exasperated. He looked at their expectant faces. "You mean to catch a shark? The way the boys catch fish at the Point?"

"Exactly." Impatiens raised his blond, tangled eyebrows. "You can be armourer." He glanced back at Drimys, who was shaking his head. "*Chief* armourer," he added.

"But nobody's seen one for a year or more," Lycaste said, knowing that might not be true. "You think they're out there now?"

Drimys pointed at Impatiens. "Like my most esteemed partner said, it's Midsummer. They're out there."

Lycaste stuck a finger in his mouth, worrying the nail. "I don't know about this."

Drimys smirked at Impatiens as he arranged his cutlery. "I told you he'd say that."

"Why do you need my boat?" Lycaste asked. "Can't you use Ipheon's?"

"His needs mending," Impatiens admitted sheepishly, looking at his empty plate. "Just think—we'd be famous. People would come from miles around to see!"

"Why would I want people to come from miles around?" The idea terrified Lycaste more than any shark could.

"I forgot—you get that sort of attention already. But we have a business, Drimys and I. We're gentlemen of prospects. It would be excellent publicity, at the very least."

Lycaste met Impatiens's eye, something he rarely did with anyone. "I don't need more people at my door."

Impatiens nodded solemnly, his gaze flicking to the table. "You won't even lend us your boat?"

Lycaste rose from his chair. "Excuse me."

He walked slowly, weaving through the whispering fruit trees, sometimes craning his neck to look at the spray of cold stars and the green half-moon that had begun to rise over the hills, its light staining them with artificial colour.

Pentas's absence struck him as more loaded a gesture than anything she could have possibly said, and he'd felt the weight of her scorn with each glance at the empty place-setting. He reached the edge of the water—green-tinged waves that bled to black lapping gently at the stones, still warm when he dipped his foot in—and looked up nervously from the sand, knowing before he did so that there would be no one to see. He carried on along the beach with one foot in the water, deliberately going in the opposite direction from where she might be—as if the reverie might subconsciously carry him to her.

Lycaste had contemplated leaving, perhaps returning to Kipris Isle for a year or two, but he could hardly show his face there, either. His eyes moved unseeing across the jungle of indifferent stars, wondering where he could go. There were trade ships docked in the ports of the Tenth Province that might take a wealthy traveller anywhere within the Nostrum—Fouad, Tripol, even past Tunizerres and as far as the Westerly Provinces—but such a journey would be long and likely fraught with danger. Lycaste knew he hadn't the stomach for travel, just as everyone said. After five miles he'd be pining for home, trembling and sick from the sea.

The moon had now risen fully, its dense whorls of cloud shrouding whatever mysterious things went on up there. His feet met grass and he looked up to see that he was back in the orchard, walking slowly through an irregular grove of young trees. He hadn't known love could be so draining, so demanding. The stories he read had never explained what it did to you when it left, how much it stole as it drifted away.

He would have seen Eranthis sooner if her skin had not flushed a bottle-green to match the moonlight, and the resemblance to her sister was just enough to shock his heart into life—the way she carried herself, the angle of her neckline, the exact curve of her bare shoulder. Even before he saw her face.

"Lycaste."

"Eranthis. I thought you were . . ."

"You were hoping for someone else?"

He resumed walking slowly back to the tower, the sounds of low conversation coming from the lighted doorway. His entire life had been spent surrounded by nudity, people clothed only in the formal colours they assumed when etiquette required. He cared for Eranthis, of course, almost as fondly as you could care for someone who was not family—but the similarities between the sisters were all too noticeable, and he found it hard to look at her now.

"She's confused, Lycaste. She thought she could trust you more than other men."

He hesitated, turning back. "Of course she can trust me."

"Pentas has been through so much. She needs you—just not in that way." Eranthis came closer in the moonlight, her features, more yellow than red without added colour, were stronger than Pentas's. "I know you have . . . difficulties, that it's not always easy for you to understand people or feel things for them, and that now you do feel something at last it's not returned in the way you'd like—"

He shook his head. "That's her business."

"Give it time. All things heal with time."

Lycaste looked off to the hills as he contemplated such an empty statement. "It *is* hard, for me," he said at last. "My parents on Kipris always wanted another son, someone different." He glanced dejectedly back at her. "I thought I'd be used to rejection by now."

"Nonsense." Eranthis smiled. "I've never known someone so in demand. Perhaps you should open the door when the bell rings once in a while. Perhaps happiness is waiting on the other side."

He nodded solemnly, thinking that he just wanted to be home, in bed, anywhere else. Eranthis took his hand and walked him towards the gentle light of the doorway.

"She counts you as her finest friend—can't that be enough for now?"

He smiled and looked away, opening the door for her as he knew a gentleman should. She didn't understand what it was like to be shy, to have one's entire life governed by self-consciousness. In Eranthis's mind there were always others out there for Lycaste, potential suitors just a letter or a smile away. But he knew that was not so. He had found his love, even if she did not want him in return.

Inside the butler birds were drying bowls with sheets of linen, passing them to one another to be stacked. Holcus, Borago and Sonerila were each excellent—and expensive—examples of some pedigree breed Lycaste could never remember the name of, their ancestors no longer present in the world. Where wings had presumably once been, there were now four flightless twig-like arms complemented with a multitude of clawed fingers, their legs long enough for them to reach waist-high to most Tenth people. Lycaste had grown up among creatures like them and he took the birds and the services they provided for granted. They were *people*, in the accepted sense—along with anything able to converse—and their large grey eyes could appear unsettlingly human in the right light. Briza, Drimys's little boy, treated the birds like aunts and uncles, entirely unconcerned with any differences between their species.

The boy had joined them, and Lycaste watched him carefully as he sat down, anxious in case the child dropped anything. He carefully positioned himself as far from Eranthis as he could.

"Tell him to use a plate if he's going to eat something," he reminded Drimys, pouring a final digestif and staring morosely into the darkness of the drink.

"It's all right," said Impatiens, preparing to leave. "He has a task— we gave him the silver to polish." He touched the boy's shoulder. "He has something for you, don't you, Briza?"

Briza smiled shyly and placed a small plastic figure on the table. "Sorry for touching your dolly house, Lycaste. This is mine—you can have him."

Lycaste took the figure and examined it. It was a wolf, standing on its hind legs like a man. The plastic was yellowed and sun-faded, but he thought with a lick of paint he could find a place for it somewhere. He glanced back at the boy, trying his best to smile.

Virginis

Looking up at the vaulted walls unfolded something in the observer's mind, expanded it somehow. Sotiris never tired of gazing upwards, and had never sat or spoken to anyone without taking time to glance around him just once more as he considered the business before him. A person, no matter how philosophically minded, could stare into the ink of the Void without comprehension, pupils unmoved by what they hadn't been constructed to parse, but looking at this was different. It was like peering inside one's own eyeball, scooped of its vitreous jelly and with only the raw nerves left clinging to the inner surface. Above him arced millions of square miles of islands the colour of autumn leaves, birthed by one enormous river delta that bled across the world in mint-green tributaries. Cloud patterns whirled and drifted, a great storm hanging like a bruise across one of the small inland seas above; there would be ships crossing that glittering bay, tiny galleons too small to see tossed and blown in the gale. Stationed at the centre of the world upon a network of colossal buttresses three thousand miles above, between him and the storm, was the small, silent Organ Sun. It was dim enough to look at, its tides of fire peeling apart at a thin black band running down one side to cast an amber shadow across a wedge of the Vaulted Land a few thousand miles over Sotiris's shoulder, high on one mountainous continent.

The dream still lingered, faint in his thoughts. As always, he'd awoken before the boat reached the harbour, but it was closer than it had ever been now. Close enough for the crew to start uncoiling heavy ropes and stand with them, smiling and waving. That was new.

Hytner, slumped back in his chair, was looking at him.

"I did suggest that we stop at Henry James."

Sotiris sat up straighter, rubbing his eye with a knuckle. "Which book were we talking about?"

Hytner picked it up from the table, tapping the title. "*Portrait of a Lady.* Didn't you read any of it?"

He tried to remember but came up blank. "Weren't we on Dumas? Have we skipped some?"

Sotiris's friend stared back, apparently mystified. "Last year, Sotiris. We read Dumas when I came to see you in Cancri."

"Ah. Cancri. That's right. I was at the September House." He scratched his neck and frowned incredulously. "Almost a year ago."

Hytner continued to stare, playing with the carnelian buttons of his frilled collar. "Is something the matter?"

"Something the . . . ? No, nothing's amiss. Keep going." He pointed at the book in Hytner's hand. "What did you think of it?"

His companion sighed, slapping the tiny jewelled book resembling an ancient pocket Bible back on the table. "I gave up at eighty pages."

Sotiris smiled, stretching into his chair and watching the contented movements of the bees around them in the meadow. One drifted close enough for him to see its silver shell, beaded with orbs of fabulously expensive blue lapis: even the insects here were pampered beyond measure. Such things were of course modest in comparison to those in his home Satrapy—there the bees' robotic counterparts were each made from a single lump of gold, hollowed precisely to make a functioning drone capable of mindless pollination. But that was Cancri, where the concept of understated opulence simply did not exist.

He watched a speck rise and drift away from the surface flames of the sun, thinking about the harbour. Across the lawns, clothed Melius acolytes were playing something with bats and balls. Beyond them rose the Virginis cathedrals, great geometric shapes in the curved haze. He heard the umpire of the game announce something, watching the play come to a brief halt.

"That was out," said Hytner faintly, leaning forward as if he meant to interrupt their play. He squinted, raising the flat of his hand to shade his eyes. "He's allowed it, though."

The two of them looked at each other as the Melius resumed their game. Eventually Hytner let out a long breath, the delicate cream lace around his chin trembling. "I suppose you've heard from your *friend* by now? What mischief is he preparing down there? Or are you not allowed to tell me?"

Sotiris smiled at him and shook his head. "I have received no letters from Maneker, though I know you won't believe me."

Hytner returned his gaze to the game. "So he departs for the Old World and doesn't even tell his dearest friend." He hesitated, battling some internal dialogue. Sotiris could almost hear it. At last he gave in. "What kind of Amaranthine has he become? What could they possibly have done to him to turn him so quickly?"

"He has been persuaded," said Sotiris with a shrug, aware that the leisurely morning of idle talk was now at an end. "Just as the Devout were." He watched Hytner bridle at his words.

"The *Devout*, indeed," he spat. "If only His Venerable Self could be made to see that this edict should be reversed—have Maneker put away somewhere, a Utopia. At least exiled, removed somehow, and his followers punished for such presumption." Hytner shook his head. "This new business with the Prism should count for something."

Sotiris blinked sleepily in the sunlight, brushing another of the glinting bees from his armrest. "You think the Satrapies are in enough danger to warrant overturning an edict?"

Hytner's eyes narrowed. "You don't? The Prism ridicule our borders, Sotiris, pilfering what they like when our attention is engaged elsewhere. If it weren't for the Vulgar and Pifoon standing armies, the Firmament would be overrun in months, if not less." He leaned forward. "Perhaps not even the Vulgar can be trusted any more, since the rumours of some new . . ." He searched for the words. "Some new *killing* device being developed at Nilmuth persist." Hytner regarded him gravely. "These primates grow too big for their cage. Its bars must be strengthened."

Sotiris raised his dark eyebrows. "I don't believe the Prism—as they are now—could arrange a decent invasion force for all the treasure in the Firmament, let alone develop anything new that we haven't foreseen or manufactured ourselves." He spread his hands. "If you are so convinced, then surely all the more reason to let the edict stand, perhaps—why not allow this Pretender to try his hand at wielding the Firmament's might? Why be so eager to crush him before we've seen what he can do?"

Hytner compressed his lips to a thin, pale line before he spoke again. "If you were not the most dependable of Perennials I would consider that a treasonous comment, Sotiris. Treasonous beyond belief. His Venerable Self can only be protected by a Parliament of peers now, he's too—"

Sotiris sat up slightly, exasperated. The man's silence lingered irritatingly in the air. "Say it," Sotiris replied at last. "Go on. He's mad. *Insane.* Destined for a Utopia himself before too long." He stared at his friend. "I know it, you know it, twenty thousand Amaranthine damn well know it."

The other Perennial closed his eyes, massaging his brow. "You have to take sides this time," he said softly. "You can't keep avoiding these questions."

They stared at each other, the whispering meadow appearing to amplify the sounds of the game across the lawn. Respect for Sotiris in the Firmament was a bright constant, long-lived and hardy like the artificial sun glowing overhead. He had a good many friends among Perennials on both sides of the debate. Neutrality, while on paper perhaps a cowardly trait, had ensured that he kept them. He took in Hytner, dressed in all his Virginis finery. He, of course, didn't have that problem.

Hytner glanced away in frustration. "This supersedes friendship, Sotiris."

Sotiris shook his head, following Hytner's gaze. A visitor, still some way off, was heading towards them across the meadow.

"You won't be allowed to hold on to neutrality for ever," said Hytner when he received no response. "They won't talk to you like this, they won't give you a second chance."

"*They* are still a minority, Hieronymus. I think you forget that in your panic. This Amaranthine, whoever he may be, however old and powerful he may say he is—though of course I severely doubt his claim— is still just one man on the Old World, with a few devout followers. The kingdom of the giant Melius is where they shall stay; they would never risk coming here, into the greater Firmament."

"Not yet, at least. But give them time. This . . . Aaron, he has been quick about his work. Gliese, of all places, has already been offered to him—straight into his hands, should he want it. You think he won't accept the capital as a coronation gift?"

"He *can't*. Not until his claim has been tested."

"All right." Hytner leaned forward again, very close. "And what if he speaks the truth, if he is the Eldest? What are we to do then?"

Sotiris stood from his chair. "Then all follows the natural order, and we must be thankful."

Hytner remained seated but turned to watch the man approach. It was Stone, dressed in the apparel of the Devout, the sect that harboured the man now seeking the Amaranthine crown. His sleeves were rolled down despite the mildness of the morning, their heliotrope studs twinkling as he waved away some of the bees congregating in his path.

"Must be hot in that," said Sotiris quietly.

"What have you come here for?" growled Hytner as the Amaranthine approached. "I'm afraid illiterates aren't welcome at our book group."

Stone sneered. "Quiet. My message is for Sotiris, and Sotiris alone. Leave."

"Leave? You see, Zacharia, this is why nobody likes—"

"Leave." Stone withdrew his hand from his pocket, holding it poised against his thigh.

Hytner glanced at Sotiris coldly and rose from his chair. "I've no desire to spend any more time in such hopeless company." Shaking his head, he walked away through the buttercups. "We are ruined, all of us. You'll see, Sotiris."

Stone watched him go with cold eyes, his fist clenched. Like all Immortals, he looked perpetually young, frozen at the moment when his cells took their last breath of mortality. The look suited some, but not Stone; his body had changed at twenty-two, his face remaining forever unfinished.

Sotiris took his hand without fear. "What is it?"

Stone's face relaxed. "It isn't good news. It's your sister."

He tensed, moving to the table. "What about her?"

"You'll have to come with me." Stone took hold of his arm carefully. Sotiris looked for Hytner, retreating across the meadow.

"Come," the man repeated.

Sea Hall

"Sotiris Gianakos."

He stooped to a bow as he was led before the Perennials, his gowns whispering as they dragged behind him on the gleaming floors. Some were decades younger than he, children Sotiris might have chastised for being a nuisance at dinner. Here, in the golden Sea Hall of Gliese, they were his equals. Sotiris's eyes traversed the vaulted cloisters of pocked gold as he took his seat, past pillars studded with globes of black opal to the map of the Firmament beaten in glittering relief across the vast dome above them. His skin still tingled with the shock of Bilocation—its atoms having bridged the gulf of a light-year in a matter of seconds—and he rubbed his hands together like a traveller come in from the cold as he returned his attention to the seated figures.

Stone had taken Sotiris as far as he could, too immature by half a millenium to be present alongside him now. On their way in, crossing the polished floors of beaten silver cobbled with chunks of apple-green jadeite, they had passed a weeping Melius, tall and awkward, his coloured skin blistered from dozens of lashes.

"Perennial Parliament," Sotiris said, his Unified—the language of the Amaranthine for more than ten thousand years—crisp and formal. "I have received news of events."

The cries of the distant Melius grew too thin and distant to be heard as twelve pairs of ancient eyes looked at him. Finally an Immortal, clothed in a shimmering blue hooded gown, stood from his chair.

"Sotiris, your sister is dead. The Terziyan Utopia protects her Immortal remains and awaits your presence." The Amaranthine hesitated. "I am sorry to have to bring you this news." He sat, collecting his cane from its perch at the side of the golden chair and studying its tip.

Sotiris waited for anyone else to speak in the Sighing Silence. The halls, open to the cold grey sea, reverberated like a conch when the storms swept across the Vaulted Lands and over the inlet upon which they perched.

He supposed he had known the moment Stone came for him that something had happened to her. The Insane lived only as long as fortune favoured them. To dwindle to madness and travel to a Utopia was to realise that death would follow, sooner or later.

"I would know, Perennial Parliament, the manner of Iro's fate."

The Perennial who had spoken—one Christophe De Rivarol—shuffled in his seat. He looked among his contemporaries, none of whom appeared to wish to speak. "Word was carried from the Old World by an Amaranthine pilgrim who had been visiting the aristocracy of Vilnius Second. I have it on good authority that she drowned. You must know that it was not unpleasant."

Not unpleasant? he wondered. Sotiris could think of few more unpleasant ways to die.

"Thank you, Christophe." He regarded the assemblage of Perennials. "I know that you all cared for her as I did, and that she was beloved in the Utopia. It is no great tragedy that she died in a place she called home and after many, many years of life."

A murmur of approval percolated from the seated Amaranthine.

"Will you take sluice, Sotiris?" asked De Rivarol with something like relief, directing the attention of a pantaloon-clothed Melius to the gleaming jug at his side. The Melius moved silently to take the jug and approached Sotiris. He accepted, watching the creature pour in a flamboyant yet precisely controlled manner, and took a swig of the water. It was speckled with a silt of tiny rubies cut into the shapes of mythical creatures.

"The Parliament assumes you will apply for leave to visit the Old World," said another Amaranthine, sliding a huge bound stack of gilded papers across the table beside him.

Sotiris looked at the man, then at the stack. "I should imagine so."

The Amaranthine nodded briskly at the Melius, who lifted the papers and presented them to Sotiris. The giant's massive, too-many-fingered hand then flourished a long plumed pen, cut from the black feather of a Gliese magpie. Sotiris studied the copperplate script for a moment, leafing through the declarations of intent.

"The Devout are aware of your loss, Sotiris. They will gladly accommodate you during your stay if you desire it."

He glanced back at the Amaranthine. Trang Hui Neng, fully twelve thousand, five hundred and twenty-eight years old, was third in line to the Immortal Throne by the old claims. Sotiris had never liked the man, though they had managed to remain icily cordial for many hundreds of years. It was no great secret that Hui Neng supported the Devout and their Pretender, this fabled Aaron the Long-Life, wishing to see him enthroned as the new Firmamental Emperor before the year was out. Sotiris failed to see how such a position might hasten Hui Neng's own ascent to the throne, or benefit any of the influential Perennials who shared his views. The current Emperor's mind had faded some time ago, much like that of Sotiris's own dear sister. It would surely not be long before he was taken to the Old World to live out his final days, and the ritual of succession could begin anew.

"I shall bear that in mind," Sotiris said, touching the nib of the pen to the paper.

"Very well," Hui Neng said, watching Sotiris sign the declarations. "It may be prudent not to tarry in the Utopias. The pilgrims there say that the conflict brewing on the Old World is already spreading to the Upper Provinces."

He ignored the comment for a moment, perhaps designed to stir up some detail of his plans during his time on the Old World. Hytner had been right; even with news of Iro's death they were playing him to see which way he would fall.

"You wish me to visit the Devout," he said vacantly, "perhaps to see my old friend Maneker—is that it?"

Hui Neng and De Rivarol smiled at each other. "Only once your mourning is complete, of course," De Rivarol said. The sea winds wailed for a moment somewhere within the acres of golden cloisters beneath the dome, and Sotiris smelled the tang of salt in the air.

"You have not heard from him, I suppose?" Hui Neng asked, motioning for the papers. The huge Melius muttered under his breath and strode forward again to collect them and the pen from Sotiris's hand.

"Maneker?" He shook his head. "Have you?"

"We have not," Hui Neng said coldly. "There are Amaranthine who would see him captured, returned to the Firmament and perhaps humiliated for questioning the order of succession." He spread his hands, indicating the quiet, seated figures. "We know you do not share their views, my dear Sotiris. We know you understand the importance of hearing this Immortal's claim before judgement is made."

He looked levelly at Hui Neng. "I adhere to the wishes of the Most Venerable Firmamental Emperor, and those of the Satrapy Parliaments."

Hui Neng's eyes met his, then dropped to his hands. "You have been given the eastern sea chamber, should you wish to rest before your onward journey. We would like to extend once more our immeasurable condolences."

"Thank you," Sotiris said, looking among the assembled Perennials, one of whom was a radiantly beautiful female Amaranthine whose name he could barely remember. He stood, nodding to her and placing a hand on the back of the ornamental chair. "What will become of the Melius I passed at the doors?"

De Rivarol raised his eyebrows. "Thieves are thrown into the Orifice Sea. It is the law."

Sotiris considered the back of the chair, nodding. "I see. Well, I should take my leave." He glanced with a weak smile at the Parliament. "It has been a long day."

Sotiris made his way alone through the long golden halls, pausing at a junction as he tried to remember the way. A Melius servant had been assigned to help him but he had sent it back, preferring to be alone.

He stopped at a slanting patch of grey late-afternoon light, leaning to look through the circular open window to the shore below. Waves heaved and tore at the brown rocks beneath, hurling surf high into the wind. Sotiris gazed at the scene for some time, listening to the waves' booming sigh as he took in the haze of Vaulted Land arcing above the furious sea.

At length, he turned from the window, continuing in the dim golden light to the entrance of his chamber, where clean white linens had been stacked on a gilded footstool in anticipation that he would wish to bathe.

Sotiris pushed open the door and went to sit on the vast four-poster bed that dominated the chamber like a golden sarcophagus, dumping the linen on the blankets. As the door swung shut, his breath caught slightly. He placed a hand to his eyes, fingers tightening at his brow as he held his breath. Finally—when he was sure the sound wouldn't carry in the empty halls—he allowed it free in a trembling sigh, pressing his hands against his face as he wept.

Witness

Hytner glanced back. Two empty chairs sat at a table stacked with Sotiris's books and two cups of pure water. He followed Stone's foot-marks in the dew to the edges of the meadow where it joined the river. Their reading sessions were at an end, apparently; Sotiris could come back and get his own books.

"*Fine.*" Hytner sighed, folding his arms and contemplating his next move. And to think he'd actually expected Sotiris to come to his aid. To leave without even saying goodbye—well, he'd finally given an answer, even in such abrupt form. Stone would doubtless be taking Sotiris to Maneker now, to see the great treasure of which the Perennial had been awarded stewardship. Hytner was honest enough with himself to admit that he envied Sotiris his connections, that if it weren't for his own prin-ciples of honour and tradition he would be right there in the front row, queuing for a chance to see this impossibly ancient Amaranthine and be rewarded in turn for his new loyalty. He suspected a few of the oppos-ing Satrapies in the Firmament—among them the Virginis Parliament near where he stood—secretly felt the same, cheated out of the prize, bitter. But he was also deeply frightened. Maneker had drawn a clear line by accepting the Sixth Solar Satrapy of Gliese for himself and his Pretender, and to find oneself on the wrong side was to incur a penalty. Open opposition was evaporating already, disappearing almost as quickly as Sotiris had.

He looked up, some movement in the sky catching his attention. There was nothing but the Organ Sun, roaring silently far above.

And then it went out.

He gripped his elbows in total blackness, the six-thousand-mile-wide cavern around him an empty space uncorroborated by any of his senses. Where the sun had been, a large green afterimage now floated in the dark, darting with his eyes. Inner Virginis, the Firmament even, had been reduced to the nothingness between his hand and face. Then, just as a mild panic was convincing Hytner he should head for the surface, the sun reignited, a weak fire spreading through its crystal depths. He glanced around him at the now evening meadow, apparently unchanged, and then back at the artificial star. He could see its outline, the strange material from which it was made. As he watched, a guttering sliver of molten light tumbled from the structure, swirling as it met the opposing gravity before falling like rain upon one part of the world. Then the sun itself moved, slipping away from its buttress supports as they crumbled and dropping towards the land, every shadow lengthening suddenly.

Hytner saw, but never heard, the sun detonate.

Elcholtzia

Lycaste awoke blinking to bright rays of sun shining in through the front arch. A wasp was droning angrily somewhere high under the domed ceiling, trapped and bumping into the chalky walls.

He sat up and rubbed at his face, realising he'd fallen asleep in his upholstered chair in the dining room again. From outside, beyond the hum of the flowers, he could hear distant screams and laughter. People on his beach, low adult voices mingling with Briza's clearer yelps.

Lycaste walked out into the vibrant garden, sumptuous heat hitting him as he left the cool tower. A small part of him was angry that they still used his beach without his permission. Impatiens's house across the bay overlooked a cove similar to his own, and there was no apparent reason why they couldn't play there instead. At least people were still asking permission before they picked fruit from his trees, though he wondered how long it would be before even that little pleasantry was discarded.

Impatiens saw him and raised a hand. He, Drimys and Briza were further down the beach towards the caves, where the pebbles became coarse brown sand. No one was coloured this morning, their bodies blazing red against the beach. Dozens of sticks had been planted in the sand for some sort of game but now stood forgotten. Instead they were building a large sandcastle, which to Lycaste looked rather like an unfinished model of his own house.

As he left the grass it returned, that feeling of being observed. There was someone watching him, he was almost certain of it now. He scanned the orchard, the hills, his tallest tower. He put a hand to his glistening brow and surveyed the patches of shade between the wild palms in the distance, seeing nothing but blackness among their messy, dried tangle. Had the watcher been there last night, marking him then? Lycaste rubbed at his neck self-consciously and trudged quickly down the slope of clattering pebbles towards the sand, keen to be hidden by the bank of grass that separated the orchard from the beach.

Impatiens walked up to meet him, breakfast still clinging to his beard. "Can we have a look at that boat, Lycaste?"

He had begun to hope his friend would have forgotten about the whole thing. He pointed to the caves, where a small, upturned boat lay in shadow at the edge of the rock. "It's down there, though don't get your hopes up—it's probably not seaworthy any more."

They walked to the shade of the cave and looked down at the boat. Its bowl-like hull, notched along its middle with a smooth, straight groove, was almost perfectly hemispherical, somehow able to repel the water as it slid forwards, like a magnet thrust towards its twin. Lycaste had only recently begun to wonder how it worked, that water-repulsing material; it felt like plastic but surely could not have been. A few years ago he'd painted it a jolly lemon yellow and it was badly in need of another coat. He eyed it critically while Impatiens went to the far side. The boat looked so small now; the thought of what they were planning to do with it felt ridiculous. They heaved it over and pushed it towards the waterline, displacing a dazed and seething profusion of black crabs.

"It won't fit more than three," said Lycaste as they entered the water, its surface parting and struggling away from the front of the craft to leave a clearly visible air gap between the hull and the green swell.

Impatiens nodded and continued wading. "You, me and Drimys." They were now waist-deep in the lime waves, guiding the sides of the boat as it rose gently with each sucking swell. Lycaste was ready to hop in, imagining the beast as he vaguely remembered it—a creamy white streak, a distant ragged fin. Impatiens strode on, churning the sand around his calves into a tropical murk.

"What does a chief armourer do, exactly?" Lycaste asked.

"Chief armourer fires the harpoon."

He quickly pulled himself aboard as the waves breached his chest, considering the idea for a moment and finding that he was excited despite himself. He reached over the edge to help Impatiens in and they sat watching the cove glide by, his boat manoeuvring through its own vacuum by the softest pressure of a hand laid upon its stern. The rocks were in shadow, the tall caves set within them drained by the morning low tide. The two friends had explored most of them over the years, walking miles along the coast and naming them like pioneers; Lycaste always deferred and let Impatiens decide, it was his friend's talent. Serious, rather unimaginative sorts of names were picked to begin with: Cape Lycaste, the Cove of Sorrows, Stinger Reef. Their final discovery, the novelty having worn off by then, had consisted of a tiny beach piled inexplicably with sun-bleached animal bones. They had named it Scary Bay and abandoned all further searches, vowing to each other that they would never go out that way again.

"Where are we heading?" Lycaste asked, feeling decidedly unsafe inside the small bowl.

"Anywhere. Over to the next bay. Come on, Lycaste—show me how fast it goes."

"You know how fast it goes." He knelt and leaned on the stern, gradually tipping the half-sphere until its rim almost touched the gliding surface of the sea. The waves flew apart at the boat's approach, the warm wind drumming faster in their ears. He heard Impatiens laughing distantly.

Lycaste ground the heel of his palm to the right, carving a white tide of repulsed water, and swung them back towards the shore, now far-off.

"Let's have a go." Impatiens slapped his hand on the stern before Lycaste could answer, rocking the boat away from the shore again and raising another plume of spray. He leaned with all his weight and they raced out into the open sea, Lycaste anxiously watching the beach recede through the strands of his wind-blown hair.

The rich green waves began to slop more forcibly, repulsed from the hull in a roiling, slapping current and broad, foam-crested wings. Impatiens eased the pressure and they slowed, silence flooding back as the water calmed around them. Lycaste looked down into the clear sea; it was very deep now. Schools of dark fish swam far below, broken by shimmering refraction. Anything could glide eerie and unnoticed beneath them. He glanced over at Impatiens, who was also staring rapt into the depths, sparkling reflections playing on his face. A hot breeze tousled his long blond hair across his eyes, breaking the spell, and he sat back, thinking.

"We'll need bait."

Lycaste wondered for a moment what might attract the creatures they wanted to find. "I have a crop of bloodfruit from last year."

"Fermented?"

"Some of it."

From time to time in the hottest months, his flesh trees ran with sticky red sap. This unsettling phenomenon usually meant they were overripe; the fruit Lycaste was thinking of would be perfect. Their flavour even had a little kick to it. He nudged the edge of the boat deliberately with his toe and it began to move, turning parallel to the far-off beach.

"Has anyone ever been eaten?" he asked after some time, rather hoping Impatiens wouldn't hear his question.

Impatiens laughed, nodding enthusiastically.

He hesitated. "Who?"

"It was a woman, I think. Her name escapes me—it was a very long time ago, though, Lycaste."

Lycaste nodded, shading his eyes and peering back to shore, clearly marking the two red shapes as they played in the sand. The hills bore down lushly above them, wobbling in the rising heat. He could make out single browning palms standing lonely on the slopes.

Lycaste thought again of his observer. Someone was up there.

"Have you seen anyone new around lately? In the Province?"

Impatiens turned and stared at him, uncomprehending. "Someone we don't know, you mean?"

"Yes."

His friend picked some bright yellow paint from the side of the boat, thinking. "I went to see Elcholtzia three days ago. He would have mentioned someone—you know what a chatterbox he is. Why do you ask?"

Lycaste bit his lip, feeling slightly foolish. "I don't know, I thought I might have seen a new person," he said, hoping the small lie would validate his fears.

"Where?"

"It doesn't matter, it was probably just one of you walking about." He wanted to change the subject now he'd gone too far, but Impatiens leaned forward, interested. New people didn't turn up very often.

"What did they look like?"

"I don't know. I'm fairly sure it was one of you now, thinking about it," he said quickly, looking away.

Impatiens sat back, disappointed. He stared down into the depths again as they sailed back to shore and began to trail his hand in the water, as if daring something to come. He gradually sank it lower and lower, entranced by the sea-floor below them. Finally he looked up and lifted his arm out. "Let's go for a walk later, up into the hills. You can ask Elcholtzia about your stranger."

When they landed at the beach, Drimys was stretched out, asleep. Briza had covered about half of his father's body with sand but tired of the game when he'd got no reaction. The sandcastle was finished and Lycaste strolled up to it, wondering if it was indeed meant to be his house. The five towers were there, the central one a little taller than the others. He wandered around to the front where he could see the gaping entrance, part of which had caved in since it had been dug. Lycaste sat down next to it and patted the entrance back into place, but it fell in again as soon as he took his hand away. The sun had dried it out, he saw: running his hand along the top of the mound, the powdery outer layer of sand swept away in his palm. Maybe this was what would happen to his own home, in time.

He looked up the long strip of beach, speckled brown against electric jade, wondering what it would all look like in a thousand years. Would his house that he loved so much even be here any more? Perhaps some enterprising person would have built something else on top of it all, after Lycaste was long dead and with no sons or daughters to inherit what once was his. He smoothed his hand over the hump again, scouring away the dry sand, and clambered up stiffly. It was because of the things she'd told him, this new fascination, this new fear. He'd never heard of anything quite like the idea of ghosts until Pentas brought it up one evening, an age-old belief from the Seventh Province. The Seventh was a far-flung place to someone with such limited knowledge of life as Lycaste; he thought the people there must be very strange indeed to have come up with such things.

Ghost. He played with the word quietly on his tongue, looking out across the beach to the caves.

This had been his uncle's land, once. Only upon his death had Lycaste been permitted to visit and claim what had been left to him, the sole child born to the family for two centuries. Trollius, who had once owned the very sand between Lycaste's fingers, had never been kind to his nephew on the rare occasions when they had met, boisterous and unfeeling in the presence of Lycaste's timidity. He remembered a strong mutual dislike between them.

Disappointing to his uncle as he was, Lycaste was the only heir; the estate was his at twenty-five to do with as he pleased. Despite his indifference to his relative's death, Lycaste fancied absurdly that they were closer now than they'd ever been. Trollius had lived in the house by the beach for more than a hundred years, and although Lycaste found it hard to imagine the rancid old man appreciating anything, he must surely have enjoyed the very things that Lycaste found so continually breathtaking. Sometimes Lycaste would sit at his favourite spot, beneath the tall windows of the third tower, its vista encompassing the sea and the hills as well as the far-off blue haze northwards. Not even the highest tower could show you all that, its own view obscured by its position between the other four outposts. In the evening, the sun's rays slanted crimson into that top room as the flowers wailed, and he wondered if his uncle in all his years had ever felt the same peace and contentment as Lycaste did, sitting quietly and alone in that airy chamber.

Sometimes, after the westerly sunset was nothing but a slit of neon in the lambent blue, he slept up there, hidden in his nest above the world, closing and locking the heavy antique door so as not to be disturbed. They were arms, his towers, arms that swept him up and carried him to safety from the noise and the questions and the demands. They suited his own hermitic temperament elegantly, but perhaps his uncle had never bothered much with them. Too many flights of stairs, perhaps; he had hated stairs. If Trollius's ghost still lived here—he imagined his uncle's spirit shaded blue, like the sky—then Lycaste would be safest at the top of some stairs.

They met where the path forked about half a mile from Lycaste's home, climbing into the low hills away from the sea. The dusty track was more like a parting in the grasses, weaving in and out of the dense shade of the trees. Followed for long enough, it would take them out of Lycaste's estate and through a number of others, eventually joining a rocky causeway and leaving the Province entirely.

"I saw Pentas last night, you know," said Impatiens after their conversation had lapsed sufficiently. "After I came home from your dinner."

Lycaste listened to the pause, hearing the thick buzz of cicadas all around them. "How was she?" he asked at last.

"I cannot understand," his friend replied after a moment's thought, "just why you have fallen in love with that girl—of all the people you might have chosen. She really is nothing remarkable—I hope you don't mind my saying so." He looked up from the ground at Lycaste. "Her older sister, on the other hand, strikes me as a much finer catch."

"Eranthis?" Lycaste smiled sheepishly. "You think—?"

Impatiens laughed, a harsh bark that startled the cicadas. "Not a chance, dear fellow. She's known you quite long enough to have seen through the mystery by now, I'm afraid."

He glanced down again, feeling foolish for playing into Impatiens's little joke. "I know you think I don't understand what love means, but I know what I feel, Impatiens."

The older man's face softened. "I'm sure you do. Make yourself better for it, Lycaste, and choose another. It's not as if you're short on offers."

Again the same advice, as if everyone but him knew for certain how Pentas felt.

"So many people make such long journeys to come here, to the Tenth, to seek my betrothal . . ." Lycaste smiled apologetically, trying to find the right words. "But there's only one person I want. Can't they see I'm not about to change my mind?"

"You had better, for all our sakes," sighed Impatiens. "Now stop *dwelling* on it, handsome fool—you'll give yourself a headache."

The sun beat the backs of their ruddy necks as they reached the top of the first hill, stopping in the shadow of a copse of thin palms to look back at the view. The cove was partially hidden—only its encircling arms of rock visible beyond the hazy white towers of the house. Lycaste sat looking down into his gardens, thinking of how everyone called him handsome or beautiful to cheer him up, and how it had only just begun to feel like praise after all.

He studied the orchard and wondered if this was the very place his stalker came to watch. It couldn't be—the far side of the garden beyond the house wasn't visible from here. He let his gaze run along the hills until it swept the sea near where he thought the caves must be.

A huge shadow was moving ponderously beneath the jade surface down there. He tapped Impatiens lightly on the arm, but the other man was too busy rummaging in his satchel and didn't look up. Lycaste punched his shoulder lightly.

"Ow! What?"

"Look!"

Impatiens followed his pointing finger, his eyes widening. The shadow turned, sickle-shaped in the waves, moving towards the edge of the outcrop.

"It's heading out of the bay," Impatiens whispered. He suddenly stood, as if somehow it would give him a better view, and picked up his bag.

Lycaste didn't like the look of this. "What are you doing?"

Impatiens ignored him, staring. "It's big, it's a big one. Look, when it stretches out . . ." He waved his finger at the cliff. "He's half as long as the rock!"

"It's not a shoal of fish, is it?" Now Lycaste was standing, nervously clasping his elbows in each hand.

"No, that's definitely . . . there's the fin." They saw a slip of white puncture the green. The shadow disappeared under a rocky arch and they both walked forwards into the sunlight, shading their eyes to see. It reappeared and followed the curve of the outcrop. Unless it changed course it was going to disappear from view soon. Impatiens began to run along the hill.

"I think it's only a lot of fish, Impatiens," Lycaste called out. "Let's just stay here."

They hadn't made any weapons yet. He watched Impatiens, suddenly afraid that the man would go rushing off to get the boat anyway.

But Impatiens was already walking slowly back to the ridge. "Gone," he said, sitting down again.

Lycaste sat down, too. "I thought you were about to run down there and jump in the water."

His companion said nothing at first, settling his eyes blankly on Lycaste. "It's all right if you don't want to be part of this. I'm sorry if it felt like I was forcing you last night. Drimys and I can manage just as well without you, I expect."

Lycaste didn't know what to say. "I don't think we're ready yet, is all."

Impatiens sighed. "And you never will, Lycaste. I'll find someone else. Don't worry yourself."

He fell silent a moment, considering this. "You think I'm a coward."

"It's not that. You're . . . sensitive."

Lycaste flushed. "I'm not afraid."

His friend took a long look at him. "If you can do this, you know, you can do anything."

"You think so?"

"When we catch that shark—and we *will* catch it—love and all its mysteries will appear easy to you, nothing in comparison to the ordeal we'll have been through." He spread his hands, one tufted, unruly eyebrow raised wickedly. "You never know, Pentas might even change her mind after seeing the great hunter with his prize."

Lycaste exhaled long and hard, unable to avoid picturing the scene. He knew he was playing into Impatiens's hands, as he always did. "Well, if you put it that way," he slipped a fingernail into his mouth, chewing at its ragged edge. "Perhaps we could try tomorrow."

"Someone," Impatiens said, beaming, "just became a man."

Lycaste smiled dutifully. The two looked at each other and back out to sea, Impatiens grinning, his mind already visibly leaping ahead to the possibilities.

"And lots of people will want to come and see it?" asked Lycaste finally.

"Hundreds!"

"Where will they stay? Mersin?"

"Who knows? Who cares? We'll be famous!"

It was true that the last thing Lycaste wanted was fame, for he had more than enough of that already. As far away as the Fifth Province, Lycaste was known as *the Great Beauty of the Tenth*, someone so uncommonly handsome and angelic in features and form that he received callers to his house on the cove at least once a year, come to see if his face was as perfect as the rumours insisted. He had received more offers of marriage in his fifty-one years than everyone he knew combined, rejecting as a matter of course every single one of them. He had always seen his coveted reflection as a curse, not a gift, and hardly any use now that he'd managed to drive away the only girl he'd ever loved.

They set off again slowly, Lycaste following dejectedly behind as his mood darkened once more, and descended into a shaded valley. Abruptly stopping in a clearing of wild flowers, he realised he'd lost his friend altogether. It was those long legs of his; at very nearly ten feet tall, Impatiens was larger than any other Melius man Lycaste knew. He wasn't worried; the path had diverged but he knew to follow the slope of the ground upwards to Elcholtzia's house, high on the next hill.

The sighting of the shark had got him thinking. He received more suitors at his door than passing sharks, and yet here was one, the very day after he had been told of the plan. He began to wonder whether Impatiens knew more about the creatures' movements than he let on.

Lycaste continued on up the hill, clinging at rough branches as the ground steepened, but could see nobody ahead in the shadows. He brushed the dirt from his hands and listened, quite used to being forgotten by now. It happened so often that he barely registered it, sinking into his own thoughts as his friends ran ahead or debated some abstract notion that he hadn't a hope of understanding.

As his breathing subsided he began to hear it: soft murmuring, like a secret conversation in some dark corner. Lycaste crouched in the undergrowth, smelling sweet sap and soil. The light was blocked by more than just tree branches at the edges of his vision. Gesturing, clothed forms whispered to one another.

He'd been spotted. The creatures of the woods were discussing him now. Branches cracked and snapped as they moved, perhaps trying to see him better. Lycaste kept his gaze on the slope; he didn't want to appear nervous. They'd seen him often, and he was fairly sure they knew who he was by now. A friendly wave was often the best way to acknowledge their presence, for they never approached. Of course it had occurred to him that they could be the ones watching him in his orchard, but there was no evidence that they were at all bothered about the lives of the people sharing their land. Still, he hardly enjoyed their company; it was like peering from the window of a brightly lit room into the darkness of night, unknown things looking back at you.

Sounds to his left, on the slope not far away. He slowly resumed his scramble up towards the rise, lifting his arm and waving once as he climbed. The voices stopped briefly at the tiny gesture, then continued. Listening hard, Lycaste fancied he could, as usual, hear pieces of recognisable words in among the whispers. The rhythms were all wrong, though; he couldn't separate individual sentences from the mutterings around him. One of the words sounded all too familiar, though no doubt reconstructed wrongly by his racing imagination. *Pentas.*

As he reached for another dry branch, a thin red arm grabbed his wrist, startling him. Impatiens grinned, hoisting Lycaste up as the ground turned to loose soil.

"You took the difficult route," he said softly, glancing over Lycaste's shoulder.

"Are they following?"

"No."

The ground levelled as the trees thinned, bathing them in the afternoon sun. The two men staggered out under the livid blue sky and saw that the flowers here were ordered and arranged. The mumbling from the jungle was replaced by the grumble of bees clambering heavily in and out of gaudy flowers. They had reached the edge of Elcholtzia's garden, in the clearing atop the highest hill.

A sandstone path led them through the rows of colour to a gate set in a low white wall. Just ahead was the observatory, curling southwards like a wind-bent palm. Rugs, tapestries and linens hung from the crenellated balconies of the top floor, fluttering and drying in the sun, draping down over the rear garden where the building bent back on itself. It was not, as far as either of them could discern, actually an observatory for it observed nothing, but that was how Elcholtzia grandly referred to his house on the hill. The white structure in which he lived had been almost entirely sculpted by the wind, with a sparing hand guiding it only as it deformed in the Mediterranean breeze. As with all buildings, it had been grown; implanted in the ground where its stone-like material had replicated faster than a living thing, sinking hollow capillary roots into the rock for water pipes and pouring with a whisper in every direction. It required only a firm grip or scaffolding to mould the stone as it knitted together, and within a few days you had a fine translucent shell in which to live, the sun glowing through it like the delicate skin of an ear. Extensions were added by notching the material, injuring its surface so that the thin bone of the structure reacted, growing soft and pliable again as it spread to fill the wound. Elcholtzia had grown the observatory himself years before the others arrived, when their Province was so lonely that you wouldn't see another person all month, and its S-shaped form was quite unique on the rugged slope.

With one last peek at the shadows behind, Lycaste made his way up the path, ducking occasionally as fat, downy bees droned past. Elcholtzia appeared at the doorway beyond the gate, a streak of deep orange aglow against the dazzling white walls of the misshapen building. He appeared like that with every visit, as if warned of their approach. Each time the old man stood unsmiling, waiting for them to pass through the gate, watching that they closed it properly.

"Gate?" he asked them as they approached.

"Shut," muttered Impatiens for what could well have been the thousandth time. Watching them while they embraced, Lycaste took in how the old man had changed. His gristly frame now looked even more delicate, skin stretched over bone. Elcholtzia moved to Lycaste and patted him with a scrawny hand, thanking him for coming in his dry, uninterested voice.

Inside the antechamber it was very cool, the chill air suffused with a faintly unpleasant smell both sweet and sour. Lycaste tried to think what it reminded him of, but Impatiens got there first.

"You must try to air this place. It smells like death."

The old man took them across the sunken cylindrical main chamber of the place to the steps, passing through long shafts of sunlight churning with golden motes. He stepped around a pool of greasy residue in the middle of the floor and pointed to the warped, painted ceiling high above. It was swarming with black flies. Just below them dangled a haunch of scarlet meat, half-illuminated in the glow of one window.

"Lamb. For my visitors."

Lycaste glanced at Impatiens, who was looking at the residue on the floor. It was smeared in oily sweeps, as if something had slipped in it. Diminishing marks paced around the tiles and faded back to the front door. The whisperers in the jungle sometimes ventured to the edges of the cove to forage, but he had never heard of them coming into anyone's house before.

Impatiens stared the longest, perhaps wondering at the profitability of importing real flesh. "Where did that come from?"

Elcholtzia swung open a pair of tall wooden doors that led to the stairway and the angled upper floor. "I have it delivered. They won't eat my grown stuffs, for some reason." He regarded Lycaste solemnly. "How are you enjoying the telescope, Lycaste?"

He'd forgotten all about it, there had been so much on his mind. The thing Elcholtzia had given him lay unused in the third tower, a slender tube like a rolled-up piece of paper. Elcholtzia had demonstrated its use to him as if instructing a stupid child.

"It's wonderful, Elcholtzia, thank you. I haven't had much time to use it properly, though."

"You've been too busy?" He smiled thinly at Impatiens. "Have you looked at anything in detail yet?"

"The Greenmoon," Lycaste lied.

"Ah, and what did you see?"

Lycaste cursed the man, always trying to teach him things as if he were not yet grown-up, catching him out when he'd not learned his lessons. He thought of what he knew about the moon. "I saw lots of trees."

"Extraordinary—so you found a patch of clement weather?"

"I'm sorry?"

"Nothing but pea soup every time I've looked, not a break in the clouds for the last four months or so."

Lycaste feigned poor memory. "Maybe it was just clouds, not trees."

Elcholtzia nodded. "You should use it, Lycaste," he said. "It broadens the mind."

Lycaste felt his face grow hot. "I will, I promise. When I have the time."

"When you have the time," Elcholtzia repeated emptily, and led them into the first-floor chambers. They had to stoop to avoid hitting the wooden beams. Lycaste wondered why the man had sculpted his home so badly; everyone thought Lycaste so unintelligent, yet he would never have built his own house like this.

It smelled altogether cleaner up here, locked away from the death below. The air was spiced and smoky, the floors warm and boarded with smooth white wooden planks. There was no sound save for a muffled clicking that came from another room.

"Is the fire lit, Ez?" Impatiens asked, wandering to the next room to make tea. Lycaste watched his friend leave, afraid to be left alone with the old man. Impatiens almost never called Elcholtzia by his full name, an honour Lycaste himself had not yet earned. He thought it a strange name, suspiciously foreign-sounding. It had a bulkiness to it, an ugly, inelegant rhythm better suited to the villain in a stage play.

"Yes, I like the fragrance," Elcholtzia replied, tilting his narrow head so that his voice would carry to the kitchen. "My mother used to claim inhaling smoke was bad for the liver—what nonsense."

Lycaste sat on some stained and ancient-looking cushions in a bright circle of sunlight that fell across the floor, shifting further back as the old man looked at him.

"Now then," Elcholtzia said to him, "what's this I hear about you and Pentas?"

Lycaste's colour drained.

"Don't go white." Elcholtzia wheezed a laugh, waving a hand dismissively. "I've heard it all from Eranthis anyway."

Impatiens returned with steaming ceramic bowls of tea on a tin tray, placing them in the sunny spot with a rattle. "You must see that you hire servants in the new year, Ez, I can't be making things and carrying all the time." He looked between them. "What are you saying to poor Lycaste? Don't interrogate him—he's shy enough as it is."

"And he'll *remain* shy unless he's trained not to be. You cosset him, Impatiens."

Lycaste took a bowl, burning his hand and wishing he were somewhere else.

Impatiens sat down, shaking his head. "I'm his friend, not his mother."

"Someone should write to that dear, maligned lady and send her an invitation," said Elcholtzia. "I'd very much like to meet whatever produced Lycaste here. Are your parents as good-looking as you, Lycaste?"

He put the tea down, fingers smarting. "They're handsome enough."

Elcholtzia studied him. "I daresay not as much as you. Another suitor arrived here not long ago. Wanted to know which house was yours."

Lycaste rubbed his burned skin and looked up. He'd received no visitors this summer.

"I sent her the other way, towards Izmirean. She's probably still walking, poor thing."

"Attractive?" Impatiens asked.

"Not classically. She was very insistent. Told me she'd heard about our Lycaste from the usual source, those damned Players."

Impatiens tried to drink his tea, gasping at the temperature. "From which Province?"

"Sixth."

He pointed at Lycaste. "That reminds me—Lycaste says he's seen someone new about."

"I wasn't sure," muttered Lycaste. "I told you that."

Elcholtzia examined him again. "What did you see?"

"Like I said to Impatiens, it could have been one of us, just far away." The make-believe had endured for far too long. Lycaste didn't think he had the creativity to stand up to further questioning.

Elcholtzia frowned. "That would be the likely explanation."

"A person could hide in the Province and we'd never see them," suggested Impatiens. "Easily."

"So there might be someone around?" asked Lycaste cautiously, not meeting Elcholtzia's eye.

"Exactly what did you see?"

Lycaste had no choice but to own up. "I didn't actually *see* anything."

"You told me you saw someone," said Impatiens, exasperated.

"I felt stupid. It was more of a feeling. Like someone was watching me."

Impatiens threw his hands up in despair.

"I didn't ask you to mention it."

"Shush, Impatiens," said Elcholtzia softly. "People see things from time to time. Things they can't explain."

"Like who?"

"Musa claims he met a dwarf up Mount Gebiz. Abies saw it, too."

"A dwarf?" Impatiens smiled. "You mean a little person? It was probably only that bore Jotroffe."

"Well, I don't know about that. But Ipheon saw someone last year, too, or thought he did. A yellow gentleman, strolling in his garden. Nobody he knew. He went in to fetch his daughter, thinking they had company, but when he came out the man was gone."

"Do you believe in ghosts, Elcholtzia?" Lycaste asked, speaking before he'd had time to review his words.

"You're thinking of Pentas's stories?" Elcholtzia sighed. "Superstition. Ghosts are of no more danger to you than the smoke in my hearth."

"What if there was someone?" said Impatiens, blowing on the mist rising from his tea.

"Someone deliberately hiding from us? Why would they do that?"

"Any number of reasons. He could be a robber, a thief, someone out to snatch maidens."

Elcholtzia set his mouth. "We don't get those sorts of people down here." He directed a bony finger at Lycaste. "It's the boy's imagination."

"Indulge me."

"Hypothetically, then, the person may very well be lost. He or she might have come far, possibly en route from the port to Kipris or another island. It's possible they would be frightened of us, not knowing what we're like or how we'd be inclined to treat strangers." Elcholtzia finished his bowl of tea, pouring another from the pot without delay.

"But that's conjecture. The actors don't come back this way until Atu-minter, so we'll hear about visitors on the roads then."

"What if he didn't take the road?" Impatiens asked. "There are plenty of other ways through the Menyanthes."

"Everyone takes the road."

"Maybe they don't want to get in anyone's way or trouble us for hospitality," suggested Lycaste. Someone lost in the wilderness could survive indefinitely in any Province; travellers were just as likely to gain weight in the hot coastal lands, where food drooped from every branch.

"Then they're not lost, and we need not trouble ourselves."

"How about a sign?"

Elcholtzia's orange face turned to Lycaste.

"We put up a message somewhere."

"Saying what?" Impatiens asked, a smile forming.

"I don't know."

"There's nobody here, Lycaste." Elcholtzia stirred and got to his feet, all dangling, wasted nakedness beneath the wiry grey hair of his belly. He went to the pantry, clearly wishing an end to the debate.

"You'd have to write the message in every language," said Impatiens. "If there's a lost traveller roaming the forest and peeking in at us at night, he won't speak Tenth, or probably Ninth or Eighth, will he?"

Lycaste hadn't thought of that. When Pentas first arrived from the Seventh, far to the north-east, her muddled grasp of their language—in essence the twin of her own, featuring only minor alterations in grammar and spelling—had indicated once again how impossibly intricate the grand voice of the world was, that the smallest change might require years of extra practice. Eranthis's own Seventh-tinged accent still sounded faintly ridiculous, and she'd lived with them far longer. The moulding pressure of countless, unknown millennia had gifted Melius-kind a library of nearly three hundred precisely attenuated words for every noun or adjective. Writers of fiction could craft subtler images than any master painter, the range of tools at their disposal wider and finer. Lycaste, more briefly educated even than Pentas, knew only a fraction of his own immeasurably expressive tongue, and smaller still was his command of the ruling dialect, the language of the First, which his father had struggled for years to teach him in the hope that Lycaste would one day make something of himself. Though he spoke a global language, someone three Provinces away would have to work very hard to understand him, and First, the speech of power, sounded like lyrical drunken rambling in comparison.

"The sign would have to be enormous, or we'd need to make plenty next to each other," continued Impatiens. "Are you going to do that?"

"Forget I said anything." Lycaste was growing tired of the ridicule and wanted to leave. The light had slanted to a rich ellipse since they arrived, mellowing the reflected colour in the smoky room. He'd missed his afternoon nap.

Impatiens stretched to make sure Elcholtzia wasn't about to return to the withdrawing room. "Look here, do you think I should tell him about our little venture or not?"

Lycaste didn't care. As far as he was concerned, Elcholtzia could take his place on the boat. "Why are you asking me?"

"He might object."

"And if he does?"

"I suppose you're right. He's not my father, just as I am most certainly not your mother."

Lycaste shook his head, watching a butterfly that had alighted on the curved windowsill. It flexed its trembling wings in the afternoon sun, casting a sharp, translucent bow-tie shadow. With each fragile movement, patterns on the wings changed colour, like their own skins. The tips, green and dazzlingly leopard-spotted, flashed scintillating blue, while tawny strips of orange closer to the creature's body became sweeps of violet.

"If you're debating whether to tell me about the shark, you're wasting your time," came the old man's voice from the pantry, interspersed with the clink and clatter of dishes. "Eranthis visited me this morning and told me all about it."

Impatiens clenched his teeth, shaking his head. "And what do you think?"

Elcholtzia arrived carrying a jug and saucer, placed them next to the bowls with a sigh. He shook his head.

Impatiens waited. "That's it?"

Elcholtzia noticed the butterfly still sitting on the windowsill and looked sadly at it. "I never told you about poor Sabal, then?"

"Who was that?" asked Impatiens, his eyes suddenly widening. "The woman who was eaten?"

Elcholtzia looked down at his big gnarled hands, rubbing them together at last. "We were friends, she and I. At one point I was even intended for her—my great-aunt's wishes." He appeared to remember something and turned to Lycaste. "It was your Uncle Trollius who really loved her, though, Lycaste."

"Trollius?" said Lycaste, surprised. "I can't imagine him loving anybody."

"He never told her, but I think she knew."

They both fell silent.

"So what happened?" Impatiens asked eagerly.

Elcholtzia looked at him, irritation wrinkling his narrow face. "Well, one morning she went out swimming and simply never returned. A whole day had gone by before anyone noticed she was missing."

"How do you know she didn't drown?" Lycaste asked him.

Some time passed before the grizzled old man replied, glancing occasionally at the butterfly on the window ledge.

"We found her head, Lycaste. That's how. It washed up on the shore not far from your orchard."

The butterfly vanished in a glittering flash.

Lycaste could see it in his mind's eye, dark and small and far away, lying canted in the sand. You wouldn't have known what it was at first, not until you were almost upon it, the green tide slipping between your toes as you bent to see.

"You were friends with my uncle, weren't you?" he asked Elcholtzia, after a period of silence.

"Great friends."

"I can't imagine him falling in love."

"You mustn't have known him well. He was a hopeless romantic. After Sabal's death, Trollius never walked on his beach again, and it piled up with driftwood and flotsam. It's good to see you caring for such a beautiful place—I had feared, when I first met you, that it would be neglected."

Again he was a child, summoned, if not for a reprimand, then a lecture. "Thank the birds. They do all the work."

"Yes, they're a valuable commodity these days. I am surprised your mother didn't have them sent back to Kipris Isle. There was nothing in Trollius's wishes concerning them."

Lycaste had also received a copy of the wishes but never read them. He wondered now why Elcholtzia had, and what he might have received.

"He would be pleased with you, Lycaste," the old man continued. "Many of your rejected suitors come back this way and comment on the pleasant aspect of your house and land, even if the master's hosting skills leave something to be desired."

"I don't ask for people to visit," said Lycaste, affronted. "Why should they be disappointed when I turn them down? I just want some peace and quiet."

Elcholtzia snorted a laugh. "Don't worry, Lycaste. Your looks shall fade one day, as mine have, and they'll stop coming. Then you'll have your wish. In the meantime, spare a thought for those less fortunate than you."

"I don't see how you're less fortunate," mumbled Lycaste sulkily.

"Is it really loneliness you crave? You are free to have some of mine, could I but give it away."

Lycaste looked at the man, unable to think of what to say.

Elcholtzia leaned forwards, his voice soft. "This business with Pentas—it happens to all young men at some point. You are lucky to have such little experience in the matter. Think on that."

"Has she spoken to you?"

"Oh, yes. She's very shy, of course, but I know how to speak to her, make her feel at ease."

"She's told you everything?"

"Most of it. The unfortunate business with the Mediary that resulted in her coming here."

"She should have gone to a Plenipotentiary," Lycaste grumbled, "brought that man to justice."

"Sometimes it's not as simple as that, Lycaste. Justice is not so easy to come by these days."

"I would have protected her."

Elcholtzia smiled warmly at Lycaste for the first time. "I don't doubt that."

*

Lycaste walked back along the hill road they'd circumvented that morning, Impatiens as usual staying a while longer with Elcholtzia. Not for the first time, it crossed his mind that the old man, though only just beginning the third stage of his life, might be dying.

A solitary cloud drifted far out at sea, exactly obscuring the low sun so that its outline blazed. He watched it as he walked, not wanting to miss the moment when the corona reappeared. A tiny, unique eclipse, just for him. The thought made him look around again, lengthening his stride down the hill, but the scrubby, stunted palms on either side were empty.

The air was crisp, cooler than the previous night and carrying the musky perfumes of the orchard. His single cloud had long since gone when he reached his home, replaced by the slow kindling of a handful of weak stars in the dense blue. Lycaste saw the wavering light in his third tower; a fire must have been lit in the central grate of the round chamber. That was *his* place; the helper birds knew not to go up there. Tiredly climbing the spiral stairs while he composed a reprimand, Lycaste found he could smell her, lighter, sweeter, intermingled with the coarse veil of woodsmoke that hung to greet him.

Iro

Sotiris's feet lead him treacherously back to the port. A half-hour walk at least, but he's there in an instant, just in time to see the men disembark from the boat. One of them has a car waiting and gets in without waving goodbye. It moves quickly away from the curb into the empty midday street, carrying a scent of baked rubber. Sotiris lets his gaze follow the dwindling vehicle, a battered, antique solar Citroën that twinkles in the sun, wondering where it's going in such a hurry. He looks back to see his sister Iro taking the skipper's hand as she walks along the wobbly gangplank. He smiles, a broad grin that might just stretch his face in two, knowing that for some reason, in some long-lost where-and-when that eludes him, he has missed her very much. Perhaps he has been on the island a long time, but that doesn't feel quite like the truth.

Iro, wearing an elegant red summer dress from some London high-street label, sees him, her smile faltering as she glances back at the boat.

She has brought a guest. Sotiris continues to watch her, feeling as if he hasn't seen her in a lifetime. At last he looks to the boat. A tall, slightly stooped man is being helped from the ferry, one long leg steadying itself on the slimy stone. He is clothed in Amaranthine style but the drapery is opaque, dark swathes that the light never touches. Sotiris stares, not realising that the two had ever met.

Maneker smiles at him. His old friend looks as he always has, gaunt-cheeked and long-featured, handsome like a well-bred whippet. His skin is coppery, the sun gleaming from the tip of his nose. The traitor Amaranthine grabs him in an embrace, and Sotiris looks over Maneker's shoulder at his sister once more, pleased simply that she has found the time to visit. Something nags his mind, the memory of a presence he felt sure was on that boat. He looks back, but the boat is empty now, all the passengers departed.

He takes Maneker to his chapel. He's not sure why—it wouldn't be his first choice—but it's merely the place where he becomes aware. They both sit looking out at Kefalonia, hazy in the morning air, their legs dangling over the warm rock wall.

"I was sorry to hear about Iro."

Sotiris nods, sure for a moment that he has just seen her. He looks back to the view, the thousands of deaths registering from somewhere, some*when*. "They tell me she did not suffer."

"Still."

He looks briefly at Maneker's profile, then back at the large island in the distance. "Your timing was good."

"Was it?"

"Sending Stone to escort me out . . ."

Maneker lets the sentence hang there for a while. "Are you grateful?" he asks at last, swinging his long legs.

"Yes."

"Enough to wish to repay me in some way?"

Sotiris knows what Maneker wants. He feels his body stir somewhere beyond where they are, all around them, as if the sea and sky and islands are all contained within a racing molecule deep inside himself.

"You want my cooperation."

"Only what I'd ask from a friend."

He nods. "Then of course."

Maneker grins and drapes an arm around Sotiris's shoulders. "All is well, then." His smile falters. "As well as can be, anyway. You must go to your sister, mourn her."

"Yes."

"Then come and be with us in the First—what do you say?"

He watches the man waiting for the ferry, their farewells completed amid a small crowd of impassive island commuters. All of it is a construct of his mind, he has no doubt, but still Sotiris watches Maneker. The man who used to be his friend stands patiently, not talking to anyone, thin hands stuffed into unseen pockets. The ferry is a ponderous white smear churning the harbour water as it turns, ready to disgorge arriving Kefalonia traffic.

He wonders briefly what will happen once the ferry passes out of sight, if Maneker and all those people will simply fade, no longer needed in the canvas of his dreams. He looks at the islanders as he walks away. Their faces aren't clear. He searches out Maneker again, finding the man watching him, unsmiling.

When he returns to the house she is there, unpacking her suitcases. He looks at what little she has brought with her for a two-week stay on the island; they will make their way to the small supermarket later to buy supplies—bread, tomatoes and oil, halloumi cheese, rich red wine in plastic bottles. He remembers that they have one less now for dinner, but the name of the departed guest is suddenly a mystery to him.

They walk side by side to the supermarket along the narrow road between the white cuboid buildings. He knows she has something to tell him.

"What is it?" Sotiris asks, sure that she will say she is pregnant. Briefly, absurdly, he worries that she won't let him buy wine for their dinner.

"I have a guest coming to stay with us," Iro says, not looking at him. "I hope you don't mind."

He is about to say that she has just brought a guest, but that isn't true—she stepped off the boat alone. "Who have you invited?"

"A man. You've met him once before, in London." She glances at him shyly. "It's not what you think. His name is Aaron."

"Aaron?" He tries to recall the name, but he knows a few Aarons. "Did he come to your house in Holland Park?"

"Yes, just the once. He's holidaying in Venice and wrote to say he would try and catch the morning ferry. He should be here tomorrow evening."

Sotiris takes his mind back to the days he spent in West London, seeing the sights while Iro was at work, but it is difficult to recall the details. "He's a bit older than you—that Aaron? Some sort of . . . diplomat?"

"That's right. I said he could stay for the week—he was very excited to see Ithaka."

Sotiris looks at her. "All right. So he's to have his own room?"

"I told you, it's not like that."

He laughs. "Fine, I won't ask. Just don't get your heart broken—it would ruin my holiday."

They make their way back to the house with a shopping bag each, sweating as they climb the hill. He thinks about the man who will come to stay but can't remember his face. Iro hadn't had many boyfriends that he knew of, but the ones he had met were invariably older, sedentary professionals she'd met through her contacts at the newspaper.

Sotiris opens the fridge, taking a beer as he hears his sister turn on the rusty shower. He hopes the man she is inviting isn't easily bored, for there's little to do on the island that doesn't involve eating, sleeping or swimming.

He considers this *Aaron* as he steps out onto the veranda. He was English, his accent pure cut-glass, but something in his voice and mannerisms suggested that Aaron had been born abroad, perhaps on the Continent. Sotiris drains his beer and sits in one of the plastic chairs to look out at the port, wondering why the man's heritage should interest him. He thought at the time, when he met him in London, that Aaron had been leading his sister on. She had been falling in love with him even then. He hopes she knows what she's doing, inviting him here.

Someone strolling along the harbour-side catches his attention and he sits up, placing the empty bottle on the table. Sotiris narrows his eyes, feeling the world move again. The figure is far away, one of many walking or driving sputtering scooters along the quay where the yachts and fishing boats are moored, but he sees this one clearly enough. It is small, like a dwarf, its skin a brilliant white. It looks up at him, little pointed ears pricked, and waves.

Prism, he thinks, trying to find a place for that apparently familiar word. He wants to stand and shout, to warn the people walking past the creature that it is not safe. The tiny person—more primate than human—should not be here, on his little island.

Suddenly he remembers, as the breeze ruffles his collar with a sound like a sigh, that his sister is dead.

Threen

Corphuso thought he could see a star. The tiny point of light was almost too faint to notice, wavering as if glimpsed through a column of rising heat. It was the only source of light he could make out, enough to know that the trees didn't entirely obscure the deep valley where they had made their camp. As he watched it, another twinkle caught a nearby surface: the Threen sitting opposite him glancing up, the reflection of the starlight in its large round eyes. It had been watching him and now was looking to see what drew his attention. He'd thought perhaps it had gone back to the outskirts of the camp, having heard no sound around him for the last few minutes, but it had been there all along, inspecting him, close enough to reach out and touch.

Their night-sight was said to be better than any other Prism. It surely had to be in the dripping fungal rainforests that bordered the Light Line. There was no difference between day and night here in the foothills of the Hiobs, and all was silent but for the pattering of a gentle rain from the leaves. Long ago on the Old World, the ancestors of all the imported species here would have screeched and howled into the darkness; now they kept still—life in the black rainforest made its way in creeping, careful silence, or burrowed and hidden.

He watched the starlight glinting off the wetness of the thing's eye a second longer, and then it was gone. He listened, waiting until he thought he heard it move away before he let himself relax. The Threen were their guides here, it was true, called by ancient debts to the aid of their Amaranthine masters, but still he didn't like them. They spoke no Unified besides the most simple words, relying on a creole Zelioceti dialect with the Vulgar interpreter they had brought with them, and laughed glottal, high-pitched laughter if Voss—the Immortal who had accompanied him from the fortress at Nilmuth—ever tried to speak to them herself. There were originally eight Threen escorting the party of Vulgar over the Hiobs, though Corphuso suspected from the chatter whenever it was time to move again that more might have come through the forest to join the unseen group. Each day they climbed higher and higher into the mountains, the steepness of the ground the only suggestion that they might be ascending at all. He and the twenty Vulgar were connected by a rope tied around their left wrists to prevent someone from accidentally wandering off the forest trail. The Shell itself was secured inside a huge metal chest and dragged along behind them on a pallet.

Corphuso remembered watching it being packed away in the ruined fortress at Nilmuth, jealously directing the careful wrapping of the object, its twisted digestive tract of cast bronze sealed away for the delight of some new owner. The Amaranthine Voss had told him that the attack on Nilmuth was just the beginning. News of the import of his invention was already spreading across the Prism Investiture, attracting the attention of kingdoms that might do almost anything to secure the Shell for themselves. Corphuso's party were likely being followed through the black jungles of Port Obviado by any number of different hominid breeds, though the Threen scouts that brought up the rear were hazy in their details. He looked into the darkness, attempting to think rationally for a minute. They'd had a head start, setting off aboard a departing destroyer within a day of the failed attack on the fortress and breaking orbit near the cold equatorial port of Hrucho-Rash in a rusted Zelioceti Voidship. The Amaranthine herself had suggested they take the more well-travelled shipping lanes, slipping into the superluminal wake of a colossal bunk barge from Port Halstrom where they'd be almost impossible to spot.

The journey through the blackness was hard and tedious, but light was absolutely forbidden here. In his mind, Corphuso pictured their progress, guessing at the density of the forest by the feel of the trunks and the distant sound of the Threen ahead hacking through undergrowth. He called to mind the vague maps he had studied before landing here, tracing their zigzagging path through the foothills against what he could remember of the charts.

He'd first met the Threen at the hatch of the Voidship, the anaemic mint-greens of the forest illuminated briefly in the light from the hangar. Taller than their Prism second cousins the Vulgar, indeed almost as tall as an Amaranthine, the Threen looked like skinny, undernourished children. They had covered their wide, pale eyes with strips of cloth to protect them from the hangar lights and their mottled cream skin looked glossy, as if it would be slick to the touch. Corphuso had only found out later—after hearing their unsettling slurping sounds through the night—that they used their own saliva to bathe, licking themselves clean with long pink tongues. During the short introductions as the Shell was unloaded from the hold, Corphuso had time to notice that at least one of the Threen was quite obviously unwell, its skin jaundiced and blotchy. Certain races of Prism could become ill, unlike the Amaranthine or the Melius; overenthusiastic inbreeding had made pedigrees and mongrels of them, like the dogs of the Old World. Such misfortunes rarely affected the more civilised of the Vulgar, who could live well into their fifth century if the serendipity of wealth and title placed them safely above the grind of their society. But still disease scared him, especially in this dank, lightless place.

Corphuso closed his eyes, noticing no difference in sensation, and thought about sleeping. They would be moving again in less than three hours. The camp was dug into the side of a small earthen rise in the forest, damp tree-roots extending like buttresses to trip anyone who did not feel ahead. The smell of the makeshift latrines wafted across the camp with the light forest wind, and even now he could hear one of his Vulgar guards bumping into things as he made his way towards one of the holes.

Port Obviado had once been an Amaranthine world, a moon cowering almost permanently in the shadow of its parent planet in the former Solar Satrapy of Kapteyn's Star, many thousands of years ago. It was now held, like much of the system, by the Threen and their slave Prism, a dark place where no eyes could penetrate. The air here, thick with scents of urine, moss and earth, was heavier and stronger than that of some of the Vulgar kingdoms or the Old World, and Corphuso remembered as he sank into sleep some snippet of his education and the great mystery that had confronted the pre-Amaranthine conquest of the Firmament.

Since the exploration of the first extrasolar worlds twelve thousand years before, it had been noted that around twenty-five per cent of the totally lifeless planets and moons discovered already possessed atmospheres that were perfectly agreeable to human habitation. No forms of animal, plant or microbial life existed on them and yet the air beneath their topmost clouds was harshly breathable, often with a higher concentration of oxygen than that of the Old World. After much of the Firmament was colonised by the proto-governments and kingdoms that would make up the Immortal Amaranthine, it was speculated by some that the specific concentrations of gases in many of the newly discovered realms were all roughly equivalent to that of the Old World's early atmosphere, many millions of years before. In essence, the smell of Port Obviado—or perhaps more accurately the *stench*—would be perfectly recognisable to a beast of the ancient past such as the early mammalian progenitors of Amaranthine and Prism alike, perhaps even to a dinosaur. Why such facts felt important to him now was suddenly beyond him, and yet as his mind finally dissolved into sleep, Corphuso wondered what would happen if he just stopped breathing the rich, prehistoric air, what they would do with him and his fabulous machine. Its operation, though not exactly simple, could perhaps be understood through trial and error, even though many would surely perish in the process. There were others—some still locked in oubliettes on Drolgins and Filgurbirund—who had worked with him on various stages of the Shell's design, but Corphuso knew that whoever eventually came for him would prefer the machine's architect alive and functional. With a bitter irony he reflected that the Soul Engine (as his technicians had referred to it before the more popular name was chosen), would keep him alive only so long. Corphuso had other plans, of course, other ideas and inventions, but none so grandiose or life-changing as the machine they were currently dragging through the darkness. If he could only remain under the Immortals' wing—unfailingly cruel and selfish though they might be—he might yet live to see them through.

The Hiob Ranges, stretching like a pocked, serrated belt around Port Obviado's black waist, were positioned directly between the moon's two warring Threen Principalities. It was impossible to cross the Light Line—whether in sub-orbit or higher—from the northern to the southern hemisphere due to Lacaille corsairs, battleships and privateer fleets patrolling the shipping lanes, and since Port Obviado and its parent planet Port Cys represented the invisible border between the outer Prism Investiture and its inner regions, the only practical and efficient way around was to traverse the Hiobs. A motorized convoy in or above the blackness of the jungle was an instant and slow-moving target, and so it had been deemed necessary to land in one Principality and transport the Shell on foot through the rainforest into the next, one hundred and thirty miles south.

If all went to plan, a squadron of Vulgar cutters would be waiting in the capital port to take them further into the Firmament and out of the Lacailles' reach. The Vulgar were occasionally loyal and useful allies to the Amaranthine, always on call if enough influence and capital could be thrown their way. A brief end to the Vulgar's dispute with the Lacaille—their close cousins in all but name—was theoretically possible if enough territory could be awarded to both sides, but it was a process those among the Amaranthine who oversaw such things considered one step closer to giving over the Firmament entirely. The Prism as a whole—a loosely related amalgam of eleven hominid races populating more than a thousand individual kingdom-states—represented an encroaching and eventually terminal illness to the Firmament, a system of tumours gradually strangling the Amaranthine until there would be nothing left of them and their worlds. It was only through careful management of allies and influence that the Amaranthine still held any real power at all. But time was running out, and whenever one species was strengthened to repel another, the Firmament suffered.

Corphuso knew that the Threen—known Amaranthine-killers— had been punished most. Their holdings were among the poorest and most dangerous places in the Investiture. Despite their resentment of the Amaranthine, they were being offered a comprehensive pardon now—on the condition that they assisted Voss and Corphuso's safe passage across the Hiobs—as well as new lands elsewhere around Kapteyn's Star and a lifting of many of the crippling sanctions the Immortals had imposed on them over the centuries. Corphuso knew other Prism species would be taking note of the Amaranthines' diminishing ability to honour their promises, and yet still he doubted the Immortals' word.

He was awoken by the feeling of someone being retied to his wrist, and together they were guided further into the camp so they could be attached to another of the still-sleeping Vulgar. When all were accounted for, he felt the rope stiffening and the sounds of the camp being packed up.

"Corphuso?" It was Voss he'd been tied to.

"Good morning, Amaranthine," he squeaked as they trudged in darkness again, the rain pattering harder through the leaves. "Did you manage any sleep?"

"Very little, Architect." She sighed. "I expect I shall get less and less as we near the Light Line."

"Correct me if I'm wrong," he said, wary of sounding overconfident in his knowledge of their ways, "but is it not the case that Amaranthine need less sleep than us mortal creatures?"

The quality of Voss's voice changed, as if she had turned to face him in the dark. "Perennials, perhaps, but I am not so old as you appear to think, Corphuso."

He hesitated, embarrassed. "I did not mean—"

"Quiet," she whispered.

He felt her nudge his shoulder. The Threen were talking among themselves with an apparent urgency, and he heard one dash by them up the forest path to the front of the line, its feet slapping in the mud. He strained to listen. Something had happened.

"What are they saying to each other?" she asked.

Corphuso dropped his head as they walked, listening intently to the commotion up ahead. His understanding of Threen was imperfect—it did not share many similarities with Vulgar—but he could make out enough.

"They are worried, Amaranthine. The one close by says . . ." He paused to listen again. "He is saying it is possible that we are being hunted. What should we do?"

Voss stopped and Corphuso reluctantly slowed, feeling the rope tighten around his wrist. He listened to the sounds of the rain in the lightless forest. Eventually the rope around his wrist was tugged, softly at first and then harder. He waited, hearing a Threen mutter and turn back to them, the pattering of its feet growing louder.

Before it could reach them, its sounds ceased as if it had stopped abruptly in the path ahead. Corphuso held his breath. Suddenly it screamed shrilly, the rope yanking him and the Amaranthine to the ground. Sounds of a scuffle and more of the Threen running back down the path came out of the darkness as he was dragged along by the rope, the Vulgar behind falling and cursing one after another. They were pulled across the mud, bumping into trees and stones, the Vulgar men at his rear screaming now, too. The rope became warm and wet, thick chunks of hot material sliding into his hands, and a spray of damp droplets spattered his face. He tasted the iron in them.

"Pull!" Voss shouted, "pull backwards!"

Corphuso rammed his boot into the earth until it gripped. More Vulgar piled into their backs. Whatever was yanking on the rope stopped and snarled, and Corphuso found himself trying to remember the names of all the evolved Old World animals that had come to live here as he leaned backwards with all his paltry weight. The thing would come for him first—being at the head of the line—maybe sparing the Vulgar behind who were pulling the Shell, and that was perhaps just as well, but for a moment he hated the idea of sacrificing his life for them. He steeled himself, staring into the darkness, hoping Voss might have one or two of the Amaranthines' fabled tricks up her sleeve.

Something, most likely the leading Threen's corpse, crunched in the animal's jaws. Blood splattered Corphuso's feet with a sickening spurt as some organ inside its body burst, and then the rope went slack. He heard the thing move away, still eating, the smell of blood and shit and bile strong in his nostrils.

The sickly Threen had attracted the predator, their interpreter said in the darkness as one of the guides spoke, the corrupted stench of whatever disease had ailed it likely fragrant in the jungle air for miles around. They would be safe now in this territory with the hunter so recently sated, and could move on. Voss said she wasn't sure if she could believe what the Vulgar was saying to her, but in the blackness of the forest path they recounted and retied the ropes, fastening the Shell's heavy chest back onto to its pallet and resuming the long slog up into the mountains. The rope in Corphuso's hands was still wet but the warmth had leached out of it, and over the course of several silent hours he felt the clotted blood drying, stiffening the weave. His hands, he had no doubt, would be almost totally brown with the creature's blood.

By the evening of the fourth day he could hear a distant rumbling. At first it had presented itself as nothing but a nagging vibration through the soles of his feet, but when they stopped he thought he could make out sound, too. They were many miles from the nearest front, one of four chaotic Maginot Lines that had sprung up during the course of the small conflict, and the majority of artillery-based conflict was taking place in the moon's troposphere between the Threens' allies, the Zelioceti, and rival Lacaille fleets. It dawned on Corphuso as they approached the source of the sound that it couldn't possibly be the clamour of fighting but rather some natural phenomenon—a landslide, perhaps, though more likely a waterfall. He thought back to the maps he had seen before leaving the Voidship, remembering the concentric red lines of altitude as the foothills rose into the mountains, but could recall no sign of a waterfall on their proposed route. Either the maps had ignored large features, which struck him as unlikely since he had seen individual holy trees marked, or the Threen they travelled with were taking them an alternate way.

When the sound had become a roar, he knew the guides had taken another path. The Vulgar behind were growing anxious, registering at last the dampness in the air, possibly on the very lip of the thundering cascade. Corphuso could feel a mist of spray entering his nostrils as he breathed, everything else drowned out now by the falls. The rope in his hands suddenly became slack.

"What—" Voss began, the fury evident in her voice.

A presence stepped forwards, jostling Corphuso. The Amaranthine's scream as she was shoved from the edge of the falls was like nothing he'd ever heard, a shriek of rage and fear that brought him out in a tingling chill. Corphuso realised through nothing but sensation that he was standing alone, cut from the rest of the rope line.

A sudden flare of light forced his eyes shut. Through narrowed slits he looking down with difficulty to see the rope around his wrist had indeed been cut. The Amaranthine's screams had faded into the bellowing waterfall, visible at last. The forest loomed over him, the light reflecting from dozens of nocturnal pupils. Around him the Threen stood, their goggled eyes gleaming blackly.

"Lacaille say you, and only you," burbled the closest Threen in Unified. So they could speak it all along. He glanced behind him, knowing before he did so that the rest of his party would be gone. The huge metal case still sat on its pallet, mud caking the sides where it had been pulled, sled-like, through days' worth of undergrowth.

"What Lacaille?" he asked, wrapping his arms around himself and glancing between the tall, strange creatures.

"We take you to him now," the Threen said, its long, glistening tongue snaking from its mouth as it smiled. It hoisted the simple lantern and turned a knob, extinguishing the light.

Bloodfruit

They rounded the caves, aiming for a mottled swathe of darker green where the sea became deeper. Beneath them the sandbanks sank away into gloom, the depths hard to judge. The water was much cooler out here, and when Lycaste looked over the side of the boat he couldn't see any fish at all.

Drimys and Impatiens sat between a stack of baskets filled with the stinking sap of Lycaste's overripe bloodfruits. Drimys lifted a lid and peered inside. Lycaste thought he was going to say something but the man simply nodded, replacing the lid and looking off out to sea. None of them was feeling particularly talkative. Spots of crimson from the basket dappled the floor of the boat, their colour softening as they faded and mixed with salt water that had slopped over the edge.

"Leave it alone," Impatiens said softly, not looking at Drimys. He turned his frowning gaze out to sea, deep-set eyes lost in strong shadow. The two had argued that morning over preparations, Impatiens accusing his friend of not making enough netting for the trip. Now they were barely on speaking terms.

Lycaste carefully stretched a leg over the baking rim of the boat, lost in daydreams. A hot wind buffeted his face and he closed his eyes, secretly delighted that for once he and not Drimys was Impatiens's favourite. He relaxed into memory, letting the gentle swells that rocked the boat take him there. The crazed pink glow of the sun behind his lids was the firelight from last night; the breeze on his stubble the brush of a soft, uncertain mouth.

"Lycaste, wake up. We ought to go over it again. Drimys, are you listening?"

"Yes, Captain," Drimys sighed, bundling the nets and spitting overboard.

"You find something amusing, Lycaste?" Impatiens asked, ignoring Drimys. Lycaste sat up and shook his head, composing himself. Impatiens clapped his hands together briskly. "You both know your jobs. Once we sight it, I get within range. Drimys has the nets ready, Lycaste is at the harpoon."

Lycaste looked over at the weapon, a crude assembly of metal tubes welded together and bolted to the side of the boat on a long armature. Iron chains pooled on the floor, connected to a pile of barbed projectiles, their heavy edges still rough from the lathe.

"Lycaste aims for the head, or maybe the fin, if it comes close." Impatiens made a stabbing motion with his finger to illustrate for Lycaste's benefit. "If you can't take the shot you call to me and I do it."

Lycaste nodded, running his thumb along the edge of a barb. He knew Impatiens thought him perfectly incapable of aiming and shooting at things, but he would show him.

"Then Drimys casts the net and we reel it in. Simple. Because he hasn't made enough netting there's no second try, so we have to get it right first time."

Drimys squeezed the ropes in his fist. Impatiens stared impassively at him, waiting for an outburst. When none came, he pointed to the baskets and nodded. "Very well—drop the bait." He lifted a spear from the stack, pounded the twisted tip weightily on the floor of the boat and handed it to Lycaste. "Here."

Lycaste took it and examined the deck where Impatiens had struck it, but there was no mark. He positioned the spear and slid it into the contraption, wincing at the squeal of metal. Drimys stood and tipped one of the baskets, releasing the clotting bloodfruit into the sea. It bubbled and stained the water dark, clouding it up to a few yards down. They all looked over the side. When it had begun to dissipate, Impatiens steered them further out, turning so that the blood sap would settle in a wide ring. Drimys repeated the process, tipping another of the heavy baskets clumsily over the edge and almost losing it. He sat back, breathing hard. They both looked at Impatiens, who nodded, relaxing a little into his corner of the boat but keeping his eyes on the water.

Lycaste wiped some of the salt from his eyes, rearranging his leg and rolling his calf so that it touched as little of the scorching bow as possible. The other two men talked somewhere in the distance, his reverie already dimming their voices. He looked up at the flawless vault of gassy blue above and shut his eyes, relishing the slow sting of salt water in his lashes. It might be some time before they saw anything, if anything came at all, and he was feeling peculiarly calm. Calmer than he would ever have imagined he could be in such circumstances. He heard their low voices again, at the stern, perhaps looking back to shore. The baking wind toyed with his salt-stiff hair and his silent smile broadened.

He'd wanted to say so much to her, but some sense of occasion and romance had held his tongue. You weren't supposed to talk—he'd seen that in plays and books when he was a child and had never forgotten the rule. Pentas had stretched her neck and kissed him for the first time, so delicately and tentatively that their lips only brushed, connecting for a few brief seconds. It had reminded him of a wild animal eating out of someone's hand, trembling, unsure.

A tickle spread slowly across the sole of Lycaste's foot. He dismissed it dreamily, feeling it build until something firm and wet scraped the edge of his toe. Then he remembered—his foot was dangling over the side of the boat.

He sat up, jerking his leg away. The other two stopped talking and stared at him. Lycaste ignored them and slowly poked his head over the bow.

At first he couldn't work out what he was looking at; it was as if the pale, mottled sandbank below them was moving. Its alabaster surface was tinged with colour, like a rough pearl. For a few seconds more there was no form, then with a nacreous glimmer it writhed far beneath the boat. He fell away from the side in revulsion, staring at the deck.

Impatiens and Drimys rolled to the stern, tipping the boat a little, but they could see nothing. The water was too deep even for the gauzy shafts of sunlight that sank beneath the surface.

Lycaste's stomach clenched, suddenly feeling something like vertigo at the immensity of the abyss below them. He'd never seen one so clearly before.

"Is it beneath us?" asked Impatiens, sweeping the hair out of his eyes as he searched the depths.

"It was. I don't know where it is now. The water's so deep."

"You saw it?" Drimys looked up at him.

Lycaste nodded, replaying in his mind that briefest of glimpses, when the thing had finally taken shape.

Impatiens sat back, thinking. "Drimys," he said, touching the nervous-looking man's leg, "get your net ready. I'll take us in towards the shore. Lycaste, the harpoon."

Drimys stood up, his crimson skin—the reddest of all of them— oiled with gleaming sweat. He heaved a pile of netting onto his shoulder. Lycaste crawled to a crouch behind the harpoon and slid a barb into its second tube, a whining scrape of metal followed by the clunk of a latch closing over the projectile. He swung it with a rusty screech until it pointed out to sea.

The cove was still, tiny peaked waves glittering. They looked at each other, Impatiens risking a sly smile as he reached for the edge of the boat to steer it inland.

Drimys whispered something Lycaste didn't hear, muscles in his legs visibly tensing. They both looked at him curiously. Then they felt it: a sudden swell beneath the hull.

With a roaring slap the craft lifted from the water, spinning like a thrown saucer. Lycaste grabbed the harpoon as both Drimys and the baskets were hurled from the vessel. The pile of harpoon projectiles bounced and flew, one of them striking Lycaste across the shoulder, the rest tumbling past him, ringing as they slammed into things. His head struck Impatiens's, who had crumpled in one corner, holding viciously on to the side as the boat still twirled, raising white crests of surf over the bow. Lycaste felt nauseous as he was pelted with salty water, the spinning only beginning to slow, the tiny boat jerking this way and that with their applied weight. He looked briefly over at the hull where he guessed they had been hit and saw a wide, flattened section where the material had lost its curve. Then they heard Drimys's shouts. He was somewhere in the water. With an effort, they both crawled to the side, clinging to the bow of the boat as it still eddied confusedly under the impact, its mechanism now asymmetrical from the dent and unable to function properly.

He was not far away, but they had to keep turning their heads to keep him in sight as the craft swung. When Drimys saw them, he struck out with a powerful stroke, shouting as he swam. Lycaste couldn't hear what he was saying—the water that parted around his mouth was making him splutter and cough.

As the man neared the boat, a ghostly, faded tint appeared in the sea behind him. Impatiens moaned beside Lycaste, gripping the painted edge so tightly that his knuckles yellowed. At first Lycaste could only see the colour of the thing as it ascended, a paler shade of turquoise pursuing a small, struggling drop of red. Drimys stopped shouting and suddenly went still, stunned, treading water. He looked wordlessly down into the glittering sea, trying to see what was coming for him. Lycaste lunged forwards, stretching to reach him, but Drimys was still just out of reach and the boat turned lazily away. He hammered his fist on the side, but the tilt did nothing; they would have to press out the bulge in the hull.

Then they all saw it, the ugly white face gaining clarity as it followed them in the murk. Its huge, deep-set eyes were curious, the mouth studded with splintered teeth. Lycaste recoiled as he watched it; the face looked almost benignly human under the distorted light, an air of bewildered humour dancing in those warped eyes as it closed the distance, as if all it wanted to do was play.

Drimys wailed, suddenly realising how sickeningly close it was to his outstretched feet, and launched himself sideways against the length of the boat, a hand reaching for the edge. Impatiens cried out hoarsely and grabbed Drimys's arm just as the huge face, now devoid of charm, broke the surface in a storm of spray.

Lycaste squeezed his eyes shut and covered his ears, the screams still finding their way in. The boat lurched and he was thrown back against the inside of the hull, rolling over the blister and popping it flat. They accelerated away, stored-up force smashing a fan of water into the air. He gasped and opened his eyes to see the sea thrumming past as the craft spiralled. Impatiens had hold of something and was fighting not to let go, his elbow leaning on the stern, inadvertently steering the boat. Lycaste crawled and grabbed at the other hand that had appeared over the side, and together they dragged what little was left of Drimys aboard.

He spared the man only a glance, grabbing for the harpoon. It was still bolted to the side, and Lycaste swivelled it around to face the bow, where the huge creature clattered against the paintwork somewhere beneath the edge, pushing the boat through the water. The craft's design prevented it from capsizing, he knew, but they could still be knocked out of it. The harpoon wouldn't point low enough to be of any use, and he had to crouch again to stay upright on the tilted deck. Twin waves of bright foam appeared on either side of the bow as the small boat was pushed ever faster, and Lycaste glanced over his shoulder for the shore. It was closer than he expected, the cove and orchards hazily visible over the spray. He let go of the harpoon, slamming the armature awkwardly against the side in frustration, and fell forward to Drimys. The man's blood had clotted as soon as he hit the floor of the boat, but Lycaste was astounded at how little was left of him. Drimys was literally half-missing, his ragged torso crimped and severed from a bite that ran the length of his body. He was even missing one ear. Impatiens held Drimys's head, the eyes closed, peaceful, his chest rising and falling gently. A crimson saline soup pooled where the injured man lay, slapping between their knees as the boat was nudged roughly towards the shore. Lycaste stumbled numbly and fell in the bloody water. They could feel the vast head rasping along the underside of the boat, attempting to tip it. Occasionally it slammed upwards, spattering their bodies with the rusty brine. It was the hunger he could feel in those movements that scared him the most, the intent that resonated in each frustrated lurch.

The bulge in the hull had popped back out so he kicked at it twice, flattening it with a slam. The boat tipped and parted the crimson blot surrounding them, flying into cleaner sea. Drimys's mouth opened and he gave a tattered groan. Impatiens crouched over him, smoothing the man's soaked hair over his forehead.

Lycaste wanted to look back, fearing most that the creature would suddenly loom beneath them, just beneath the surface. Instead he focused his attention on the sunlit caves and twin strips of emerald and brown: home.

The tiny craft picked up even more speed, skimming its air pocket in a white trench of roaring surf. Every bounce and judder shook Drimys more than the others, his weight being so much less. With each spray of surf, Lycaste was convinced they would be overtaken; he closed his eyes and leaned back, summoning all his weight in a bid to go faster. When he opened them again, Impatiens was shouting ferociously, and he saw the beach rushing towards them. With a crack of hurled pebbles, the boat buried itself, shovelling a sloppy pile of sand towards them. Lycaste's face slammed into the brown pile, something crunching in his nose as they all careered into each other.

Without waiting to look behind him, he leapt from the boat, tumbling onto the stones under the weight of his dizziness. He tasted fresh, thick blood swamping his face and throat, waking him up. He scrambled to his feet, trembling, too afraid to turn, and ran up the beach. It was only after he remembered Drimys a few seconds later that he dared look back.

The boat was alone, wedged bodily into the freshly dug sand. The calm sea beyond appeared to be empty, bright green and calm again. Lycaste ran towards the boat, shuddering, wiping his face roughly with the sandy back of his forearm. It stung enormously, snapping him conscious again, and when he brought the arm away it was swabbed with clotted scarlet sand. He mounted the small hill of displaced pebbles and saw Impatiens giddily look up at him. Drimys was panting, eyes still tight shut, his chest rising and falling rapidly.

Without a word, Impatiens heaved the tattered man over his shoulder and stood up, swaying to the point where Lycaste was convinced he would fall. But he regained his balance and climbed from the hull with Drimys dangling from his back like some heavy, ragged clothing. Lycaste looked up the beach to his house, his mind bolting forward, trying to think of what to do. He heard the scrape and clatter of pebbles from the direction of the caves and saw people sprinting down the beach towards them.

Without waiting for them to reach him, he ran for the house, hot stones skittering from under his feet and stubbing his toes, skinning his ankles. He felt her hand on his, the warm salt tears between their fingers, remembered how she'd said they were alone out here, totally alone.

Lycaste staggered into the closest tower, sweeping cutlery from the long table with both of his arms and the last of his breath. He stood panting for a second in the shaded quiet of the afternoon, the haunting chant of the flowers making him tremble, his manic heart adding a moist, fearful beat to the chorus. A final bowl finished its clattering roll on the floor as he spun hopelessly, nothing in his wasted twenty-five-year education having prepared him for such things.

As he left the bedroom, where Drimys lay tucked safely and securely in a thick wad of blankets, Lycaste noticed with exhausted resignation the faint but hysterical red footprints scattered across the floors. His dull mind tried to sort them by size, to see which belonged to whom. Behind some lay trails of tiny droplets. Blood was a rare sight, their bodies hardly produced it; today he had seen more than he could bear, and he knelt with a clean cloth to wipe it up, meaning to follow the trail back. It came away easily, still wet. As he bent, another bright spot dripped from his broken nose and he realised. Drimys's wounds had clotted and sealed back on the boat. This thinner stuff was all his own.

Postcards

Sotiris looks around him. He is on the steps that thread down from Penelope Street to the harbour-side. Dates lie scattered on the stone, fallen from the palms that grow along the wall, and pink flowers brush his face. His feet are hot so he trots quickly to the Plateia, where he knows a little café that overlooks the water. He passes a restaurant where a couple are eating calamari, the girl laying her fork down to check something, perhaps a phone. He glances again to see what the device looks like, but when he turns back it is gone, along with the couple. He rounds a corner while he thinks about this, walking under closed, peeling blue shutters and into a bar of shade. The burble of a few dozen people in the café interrupts the cry of swallows overhead, Sotiris noticing as he walks that Iro and her visitor are in the postcard shop across the street.

He watches the man who is with his sister as he approaches. Aaron, that is his name. His surname is something English and uncomplicated, eminently forgettable.

"Here he is," she says to her guest, smiling at Sotiris with just a hint of apprehension. He looks into her eyes as he takes her hand and then turns his gaze on the man. Aaron has selected a few postcards from the rack, so extends his other hand. Something about his expression tells Sotiris that the man doesn't want to be touched and nods a greeting instead, smiling as best he can. Perhaps he's a germ freak—all too common after a century of international pandemics and biotic-resistant illnesses. His face is benignly kind and slightly chubby, pale as if he's wearing rather too much sunscreen. He looks like every Englishman Sotiris has ever seen.

"I believe we've met before," says Sotiris in his best English, "back in London?"

"We have," Aaron replies in a soft voice, "just for a moment. You were leaving the house."

Sotiris glances again at the postcards in the man's hand, noticing the photographs on their glossy faces. "Yes, I remember now." He remembers nothing but a blurred face at the gate, a brief hello, his sister's eyes wet with tears that night when he returned.

They walk across the street to the café for a late lunch, the blue harbour water slopping against painted plastic buoys and rusted chains. Her guest is tall, but not too tall, and dressed in a pale cotton shirt just a size too large, dark trousers and polished brown brogues that must be sweltering in the heat. It is as if almost everything about him is contrived to look ordinary, unremarkable.

Aaron settles in the chair across from him and glances at the menu, leafing through it quickly.

"How was Venice?" Sotiris asks to break the silence, seeing the man come to the end of the menu and close it.

"Venice?" Aaron thinks for a moment. "More beautiful than I remembered."

They settle on olives, bread and tzatziki to begin with, followed by plates of souvlaki, grilled sardines and pastitsio to share.

He watches Aaron eat, fascinated. The man uses his cutlery carefully at first, as if he's only seen it done by others and wishes to copy the action as faithfully as he can. Wrapped in a paper bag by his plate are the three postcards from the shop, all of them displaying the same view of the island. Sotiris watches Aaron's eyes as they flick to Iro while she talks, realising with unease that he cannot quite work out what colour they are.

Iro is asking him about the overnight ferry, and Aaron lays down his knife and fork to explain, pushing the plate away. The food on it is merely rearranged, hardly eaten. It reminds Sotiris of something he might do, in another life far away from here. The thought makes him pause, wondering why he would think such a thing.

"And Sotiris," asks Aaron, turning his queerly colourless gaze on him, "I hear you're an up-and-coming politician? Iro says you are running for Custodien of Athens."

"It's between me and one other," he says, trying to remember the name of the other candidate.

"Come now." Aaron leans back, indistinct eyes flashing. "I don't expect you'll have a problem beating Callinicos."

He stares, surprised. "You've been following the race in England?"

"Oh yes, there's very little interesting politics left over there. It's all too stable, too . . ." He smiles widely. "Too predictable."

Sotiris notices that, besides the lines around his eyes, Aaron doesn't have a single blemish. The man is surely fifty—he must spend no time in the sun or have access to the best treatments money can buy. Far too old for Iro, he decides again.

"Well, let's hope you're right. It would be a disaster for the country if that old conservative won."

Aaron puts down the glass, playing with the straw in his fingers. His hands are long and slim, as white as his face. "Greece will choose the right man."

His sister appears to take that as a cue to excuse herself and grabs her handbag. He wonders if she's going to put on make-up. They stand and watch her leave.

"I can see I am going to enjoy talking to you, Sotiris," Aaron says, sitting back down.

He nods absently, tracing a circle of spilled salt with his finger on the table. "Just what are your intentions regarding my sister, Aaron?" He looks up at him. "I won't see her hurt again."

Aaron laughs long and hard, juddering the plates and cutlery on the table. Sotiris waits for him to finish, insulted. Finally the man composes himself and stares at him. "I'm afraid she's not the one I'm interested in, Sotiris."

Once again the wind moans, a hollow sound that keens through the harbour, harried from a far-away place across deep, cold seas. With a jolt of fresh new pain the memory forms. He looks to the table, but there are only two chairs, two plates. She was never there.

Ghaldezuel

Corphuso's eyes followed the greenish haze of Port Obviado's horizon all the way to where the Light Line ended, the view distorted through the thick plastic of the porthole and his own stretchy suit helmet, clouded and milky from use. Made from a reinforced rubber, it was an almost perfect fit but smelled sour inside, like someone had vomited in it not all that long ago. He tried to breathe through his mouth and focus on the view, the hard acceleration of the Lacaille capsule sinking his stomach to his knees. The blackness above the horizon was empty, starless in contrast to the crisp brightness of the moon's edge, and a hard point of light high above was undoubtedly the Lacaille *Colossus* battleship they were heading for. He tilted his head in the helmet to look down, back into the darkness he had come from, remembering the Vulgar people who had died that day, and the Amaranthine.

The Three had taken him through the foothills for another hour, speaking freely in the darkness. From what he had gathered, still tied and blind, they were delivering him—and his precious cargo—to someone named Ghaldezuel.

Ghaldezuel. Corphuso recognised the poetry of a Lacaille name when he heard one. The Three had betrayed the Amaranthine and her Vulgar charges, as Voss had no doubt feared they would. He was sorry she had died, after all they had been through together. Though he knew the Amaranthine had never warmed to him or any of the Vulgar she had been sent to protect, Corphuso hoped it had been quick.

Ghaldezuel himself had met them at the walls of a submerged keep, materialising from the darkness in the wan light of a candle lantern. His brilliant white vacuum suit, pure as snow on a mountain top, had reflected the lantern light around the cowering Three as he introduced himself in Vulgar. Helmet hinged back, he did indeed look very similar to Corphuso: pale porcelain skin, pointed ears with rounded lobes dangling almost to his chin. His skull was a little longer than would have been considered attractive in a Vulgar person and his eyes perhaps a little smaller, but it was clear that the two Prism races had come from a similar mould. Corphuso had seen no point in behaving poorly to the Lacaille and had shaken his hand in the Amaranthine manner, glad just to be heading away from the darkness of Port Obviado at last. Whatever they had planned for him and his Shell, it would surely be more pleasant than any future he might expect should he resist. He thought of his family, dowried off here and there across the Investiture, and decided they would not miss him for the time being.

Now, as they ascended to join the safety of the enemy fleet that hung in the moon's mesosphere, he glanced over at the Lacaille sitting quietly beside him in the capsule. His suit was not entirely of one material, Corphuso noted, watching reflections of the moon's bright side slip across its polished faceplate, but lined with gnarled seams of silver and beads of gold that framed the small eyeholes. The gold was lustrous enough to be pure Old World metal, and Corphuso wondered with a small smile whether he might be sitting next to an Op-Zlan-Lacaille: one of the Lacaille Knights of the Stars.

Ghaldezuel sensed Corphuso watching him and looked over. Their eyes met through the haze of smoke drifting weightlessly from their suit generators.

"The Soul Engine is larger than I thought it would be," the Lacaille said, companionably enough, in his accented voice.

Corphuso glanced back to the Shell in its case. It filled the entire storage space of the capsule behind them, massive and looming like a block of granite. Some part of him was at least gratified to hear the Lacaille employing the machine's official title. Orange canvas straps hooked to the capsule's metal walls kept it stowed in place, while a single thick, padlocked leash secured the Shell's harness to the hardened breastplate of Corphuso's Voidsuit. The arrangement, though certainly dangerous, comforted Corphuso slightly.

"May I ask something, Ghaldezuel?" Corphuso asked, his squeaky voice amplified comically in the small space.

"Ask away," the Lacaille replied.

"Why kill the Amaranthine? She was not Perennial, she had few of the powers their elders have." He shrugged with difficulty inside his thick, rubbery suit. "Why waste a fine ransom?"

Ghaldezuel stared silently at him for a moment, his blue eyes moving to the Shell secured in its canvas straps. "One less Amaranthine in the Investiture, no bad thing. You would have preferred that she lived?"

Corphuso looked out of the porthole, then back at the Lacaille. "You risked more than you needed to. The Immortals do not forget."

Ghaldezuel chuckled, a sound like porridge being poured from a bowl. "They forget their own names, given time."

Corphuso turned again to the window as he thought of a retort, the small capsule juddering as it hit a pocket of turbulence in the high atmosphere. He watched as they passed through a bank of dark cloud, wondering at how high it lay. The Voidcraft they sailed in was almost at the emptiness—there should be no clouds up where they were.

A glittering red object suddenly passed beneath them through the black cloud and into darkness, soon followed by a few more, the light winking from them just long enough to leave an afterglow in Corphuso's vision.

"What was that?" He turned to Ghaldezuel, seeing as he did so that the Lacaille was busily unbuckling his harness. Without a word he reached over and disengaged Corphuso's. The Vulgar stared down at his belt floating free, feeling himself rising from his seat in the weak gravity. As he clutched the armrests, Ghaldezuel waved his hands away from them irritably.

"Zelioceti," the Lacaille said, reaching under his seat and producing an antique lumen pistol, also white, and slotting it into a holster at his hip. Ghaldezuel stood, forced to crouch in the tiny capsule, and pushed himself off towards the cockpit, a separate detachable module arranged above them like a periscope. Corphuso watched Ghaldezuel rap his knuckles on the back of the pilot's seat and mutter something to him in Lacaille.

Looking back out of the window, he saw that they had passed through the cloud—a fog, he suspected now, not cloud at all—and were much closer to the battleship, perhaps three miles or so from one of the gaping hangars they would dock at. Corphuso couldn't help but be impressed; its functional asymmetry bristled with rusted white turrets and towers, a small city held high in orbit. Belches of dark smoke poured from beneath its exhausts into the green atmosphere like ink dropped into water, curling down inside their own massive weather systems. Flocks of tiny black shapes curved and raced about it, the standing squadrons of Lacaille Voidjets, some breaking off and pursuing even tinier vehicles that caught the sun in brilliant flashes. The capsule passed through another pool of darkness, Corphuso now understanding it was the smoke from a ruined vessel, and into sunlight again.

He stood, thinking of trying to unbuckle himself from the great metal case, when a roar of rushing air pinned him back into the seat. The capsule banked, the view curving, loose equipment rising and bouncing off the ceiling and into his suit. Ghaldezuel, swimming back down towards the end of the capsule, grabbed Corphuso by the arms and hoisted him up, the leash attaching him to the Shell's chest pulling taut. The Lacaille clipped himself to the Vulgar's cuirass, their helmets butting and cracking together in the rattling capsule's ascent. Corphuso glanced once more out of the porthole to see something strafe the capsule just as the window blew out and the riveted walls peeled away, air rushing around him in a roaring flurry.

He and the case were thrown up and out, spinning with a rush of twinkling pieces of the capsule, Ghaldezuel disappearing somewhere behind or below on the stretched leash. The view spun, tipping from the darkness of the moon to the green horizon and back to blackness again. Jagged shrapnel whirled like a blizzard between him and the tumbling remains of the capsule, which suddenly broke apart and scattered in a blinding flash.

He was falling now, thrown back towards the moon's topmost clouds, his breathing loud and hectic in the claustrophobic suit helmet. Somewhere the Lacaille knight was shouting into his helmet, but the voice was too quiet and riddled with static to hear. The battleship became briefly visible and then disappeared again in the spin as Corphuso tried desperately to think of what he could do. He threw up into his faceplate, misting the thick plastic, his tumbling descent slopping most of it back into his face until he vomited again, squeezing his eyes shut against the acid stench.

When he opened them again, he could see Ghaldezuel falling parallel and struggling with the line that was still clipped to the hook on

Corphuso's cuirass. The Lacaille was trying to stabilise their fall with rocket attachments on his suit, which flared repeatedly, bouncing Ghaldezuel's small body up and away from the line, straining until the weight of Corphuso and the Shell yanked him down again.

A seven-winged, lividly red Zelioceti aircraft screamed past like a meteor, climbing and turning to pursue them as they fell. Ghaldezuel controlled his struggling rockets just long enough to aim and fire at the vehicle, missing as the leash wrapped around him once more and pulled him down towards Corphuso. Together they fell, swinging madly in a circle like spokes in a wheel. The aircraft skimmed past again in a red flash, this time close enough for Corphuso to see a blurred impression of one of the pilots clambering onto the outside of the vehicle, then the jet banked and hove towards them, the sound of the wind whipping around the suit's external speakers, obscuring its roar until it came close. As he spun, Corphuso caught a glimpse of the Zelioceti climbing along the wing, a thick harness and crampons keeping it attached and upright, the rushing wind billowing its fur cape. The lumpen armour it wore underneath was a bright red like the aircraft, spattered here and there with silver insignia. It wore no helmet, just goggles and a pointed, fur-lined cowl, and Corphuso spotted the long proboscis snout bobbing as it traversed the fuselage.

Ghaldezuel flared his rockets as he took aim again, the aircraft unexpectedly tipping a wing in their direction and scooping him out of the way. The line snapped, wrapping around the wing, and both Corphuso and the chest spiralled into the hot, thrumming side of the plane, lodging between two of the pectoral wings with a bang. The line attaching him to the Shell caught fast on a panel of raised rivets, fortunately bearing a weight that would have easily ripped Corphuso in half. The Zelioceti glanced down at him, unsteadied by the jet's sudden movement and throwing its arms out like a tightrope walker. The feral, unpleasant race were the Threen's allies on this world, but for some reason they, too, had been betrayed by the nocturnal beasts. There was nothing Corphuso could do but watch as the Prism uncoupled another set of leashes, advancing towards him through the rushing wind. He could hear its wheedling, slippery speech filtering into his local soundfeed, piped into the helmet through a transmitter inside the jet. The architect's rusty grasp of Zeliospeak was enough to understand that the thing was communicating not with him but with the jet pilot, explaining how he was going to snare the huge chest now dangling from the plane's wing. Corphuso realised as he listened that he was ancillary to the Zelioceti's plan and was going to be cut free once the creature was done. He swung his head, looking for Ghaldezuel, appalled that he should be in such a position and wishing desperately that his enemy would come to vanquish his supposed ally.

The Zelioceti was upon him, the jet tipping to take them away from the battlesphere and into safer skies. It slammed a spiked crampon against the lip of the nearest wing, dimpling the metal, and leaned over Corphuso with a harness clutched in one gloved hand. He looked into its strange eyes, shaded inside their goggles, and prepared to flail his one free arm if it came too close.

At that moment, the burn of Ghaldezuel's rockets roared into his helmet channel, the suit cutting the sound briefly as its simple auditory channels overloaded. He saw the Lacaille knight land on the wing, stumbling and throwing himself towards the surprised Zelioceti. It pulled a long, curved dagger from its belt and thrust it at Ghaldezuel, who blocked with the plating of his white suit's vambrace. The ringing clang reached Corphuso's ears through the suit as he watched them parry again, the Zelioceti once more swinging its blade at the Lacaille with a silver flash. Ghaldezuel, despite his short stature, was a more muscular foe than the Zelioceti was used to, and after deflecting another blow with his gauntlet he pushed towards it, grabbing the blade with a screech of protesting metal and gripping it. They struggled, the Zelioceti kicking out with a thin leg, its fur cloak wrapping around the Lacaille's feet in the screaming wind and almost toppling him. Ghaldezuel regained his balance just in time to pull the dagger free, cracking the Zelioceti in the face with its ornamental hilt and unsheathing his pistol. The stunned Prism, still clutching its face, ripped itself free of the leash that held it to the wing and jumped, disappearing in a snapping flourish of the fur cloak. Ghaldezuel watched it fall for a moment, then turned his attention to the jet pilot, who had been gazing at him through the rear cockpit. The Lacaille lowered his head and marched against the wind towards the cockpit, but before he could reach it, the pilot popped his ejector and disappeared, too, the plastic canopy shattering into a hundred pieces and blowing backwards into the atmosphere. Corphuso watched Ghaldezuel shrug as he turned to him and holstered his pistol, bracing himself against the rushing air.

"Are you secure?" the Lacaille's static-choppy voice said over Corphuso's helmet channel.

"I . . . I think so," he replied, testing the cords tentatively. They supported his weight perfectly. Without a pilot, the jet's nose began to sink, the engine thrumming as it considered stalling.

"Hold on, then," Ghaldezuel said, swinging into the open cockpit and snapping the oversized buckles around himself, "I'll take us in."

Corphuso looked down into the darkness as the engine's rhythm changed, the Voidjet tipping towards the distant white speck of the battleship, and leaned his vomit-filled helmet against the fuselage. Far below, through towering thunderclouds, pale lightning played across the deep, black jungles.

Pentas

Pentas watched the fire as it crackled on the sand, a small smile on her face. Lycaste had difficulty reading subtle expressions, often concerned that he might be the butt of a joke everyone else was in on, but with Pentas he didn't worry. There was no cruelty to her humour, no interest in making fun of him.

"Impatiens blames himself," he said, to break the silence.

"He shouldn't," said Pentas quietly.

Lycaste was not so certain but didn't contradict her. Impatiens's courage had returned briefly that evening to mention something only half-audible about revenge, before sinking back to a numb, debilitated silence.

She looked at him, and in the firelight she could almost have been her sister Eranthis. They weren't identical, you could tell them apart, but the eye had to see past a blur of shared features first. Pentas was half Lycaste's age—startlingly young to have left home, let alone be considering a partner. It was her first trip away from the Seventh, a new beginning. She had rare white eyes, seemingly all pupil unlike her older sister's mango-coloured irises. They both possessed the smaller features and yellowish tint of those from Provinces further inland, closer to the centre, although the colouration was stronger in Eranthis. He wondered occasionally if things would have been the same had he been one of a pair of brothers. His parents had made no great secret of wishing for another son, a wittier, less awkward boy they could proudly present to Kipris society as their own, while the handsome cretin stayed indoors. Lycaste looked back at the lights of his towers, no doubt in his mind that, had their wish been granted, he'd have found himself a good deal less fortunate.

He met Pentas's eye. She was sitting an arm's length away from him across the sand, and Lycaste began to worry that the silence would stretch out again, unbroken.

"I wonder how long it'll take this bruise to heal," he said, angling his shoulder so that she could see. It was cheating, they had already discussed the injury, but at least the silence was over.

"A few days," she said, reaching tentatively over and dabbing it with her finger.

Lycaste smiled, looking out between the stacked and burning lengths of driftwood to the dark sea, hardly visible through the glare of the flames. Absurdly, the place he really wanted to be was back home, sitting at his prince's palace, paintbrush in hand. There were renovations to be done, and the figures he'd selected to be repainted a few days before still lay untouched. So many unwelcome things had taken up his attention. If he let that sort of thing happen again, the palace would never be finished.

But then he imagined the walk back to his house, alone, and his eagerness vanished, the half-forgotten worry resurfacing. Did his watcher know what had happened, seeing the scene play out, unable—perhaps unwilling—to help? The yellow gentleman walking in Ipheon's garden, the dwarf on Mount Gebiz. He suddenly felt exposed to the night, cold despite the fire.

Pentas must have seen him shiver and dropped another couple of slim branches onto the fire. He thanked her and moved closer to its edge, eventually placing an aching arm around her shoulders. He had thought about colouring to cover the bruise but eventually decided he liked it, choosing a similar mottled tone that was the closest to a pattern his body could achieve.

Like most of the people he knew, Lycaste had spent his distended childhood insistently wearing a favourite shade, not dissimilar to the one he now wore: modest, earthen, unlikely to draw attention. Other boys and girls had chosen silver and gold, or the combination of intense primary colours, until they discovered the fashions of adolescence. Lycaste hadn't decided on his signature grey-purple for aesthetics or even originality, as some assumed before they came to know him, but out of simple fear, a desperation to remain unnoticed. Elcholtzia, walking down from the hills earlier that day to see what had become of Drimys, had noticed the fair timing of Lycaste's colour-wear, likening it to that of thunderclouds. The deepening humidity of the days implied a storm was on its way, he said, ready to burst the stagnant weather. No one believed him, not even the sorrowful, frequently drunk Impatiens. If such storms really did exist, as Elcholtzia claimed, you wouldn't see more than one in a lifetime.

The fire popped and spat, both of them flinching from the floating gulch of sparks. Pentas glanced up at him again as they moved back a little.

"Your nose looks better." She stuck a twig into the fire, cautious in case of any more explosions, and left it there, absently waiting for the tip to catch. "Back to your old beautiful self, I see."

He smiled shyly and pulled the small stick out, holding its flaming tip in the air and watching the flicker sink to a dull glow, smoke curling from its end, thinking about trying to write his name. His nose had healed quickly in the day since the hunt but still looked swollen. In quieter moments, Lycaste had stopped to inspect his new face, studying his profile in the mirror, quickly checking that nobody was watching. His large green eyes, artfully framed by sharp, expressive brows, carried a few more lines than he remembered and the flesh around his wide jaw felt noticeably looser. It would be many years before any grey appeared in his wild chestnut hair, but he was ageing nevertheless.

"So many people envy you," Pentas said suddenly, though not unkindly.

He looked at her, surprised. "Really? Who?"

"Most of the performers, for a start. They said they wanted you to join them because of your fame, but I think a few of them had other things in mind."

"They liked you more, I'm sure," he said, hesitatantly, wondering nervously if she would try to kiss him again. "Moringa always did, I could tell."

"Moringa was the one who wanted you to travel with them. He and Cardamine were the first to tell me about this incredibly beautiful man of the Tenth, the one who would attract everyone to their shows—if only they could persuade him to join the company."

"Maybe Moringa wanted me because he knew you'd come, too, instead of staying here with your sister."

Pentas shrugged sadly. "I wasn't asked to join. I'm only a painter."

"You're more than that," he said, careful not to appear too forward. "I have all the watercolours you painted for me—I wouldn't part with them for the world."

Her paintings were some of his most treasured possessions, not only because they were something she had made for him and no other, but also because they really were exceptionally good—the work of an extraordinarily talented hand. He had no idea how much they might be worth—not that he'd ever think of selling them—but had simply never seen any of a higher standard. To paint someone and actually make it look like them, now there was a skill he'd like to have. But it wasn't enough for the Players, who toured with their animals and games; it was a selfish skill, not dependent on the immediate entertainment of others for its value, and therefore something Lycaste greatly admired.

The Players had asked him formally last year while they lodged with Impatiens, dropping off the quiet and shaken Pentas to be with her sister. Moringa, small and fat with a voice Lycaste would even spend money to hear, had offered him a new life the day before they were due to leave for the Fifth Province, to start their tour all over again. *You won't see home for two years*, he'd told Lycaste as he packed their three wheelhouses with gifts and supplies. *You'll get to know hundreds, thousands of people and be adored for what you are. Why waste what you have living on the edge of the world?* Lycaste had waited politely while the little man spoke atop his ladder, stuffing bundles into wooden cabinets and chests. He liked Moringa and his Players adequately enough, but they clearly didn't know him as well as they thought they did. He'd never offered them rooms in his large and almost empty house; never stayed up particularly late with any of them, and never, ever expressed

an interest in joining the company. They were a group of the most talented people in the world—though of course the odd rival company that
came through every now and then would beg to differ—what on earth
would they want with him? He could not sing, dance or act. He never
remembered jokes or stories eruditely enough for repetition, only disappointing people when he tried. Lycaste could see but one last role
for himself—to be paraded in front of foreign crowds like Impatiens's
decaying shark: behold the Great Beauty of the Tenth Province. It was
the theme of so many of his nightmares.

Nobody appeared to understand the trouble Lycaste's looks caused
him. Since he was a boy, well before he finished childhood, his face had
brought him unwanted attention, usually from older ladies of Kipris
during his youth there who had mistaken his reticence for snobbery.
But they had intimidated him, those bawdy, hungry women, laughing together and saying things to make him blush. By the time Lycaste
escaped across the sea to claim his uncle's land, he was known as the
island's Beautiful Idiot, a waste of a man who didn't care for girls or
laughter or fun, deficient in every way but the single talent in which he
excelled by chance. He knew it shamed his family and that they would
try to forget him once he'd gone, but he missed nothing he'd left behind.
Everything here, in his cove, was the way he wanted it, a controlled
environment. Everything here was his.

Drimys was healing. His mangled body had induced itself into a coma
while it set to work repairing the colossal damage, diverting what nutri-
tion it could to the process. The torn skin had swelled where the shark
had severed it, flooding the wounds and sealing them in order to regrow,
the ballooned flesh humped like a landscape of hills beneath Lycaste's
sheets. Eranthis had been the one to inspect him, peeling the stuck blankets away while Drimys slept, crystalline secretions ripping and oozing.
The body was only the sum of its parts, she explained to them carefully.
If the creature had rushed him from a slightly different angle, too much
might have been taken. But there was just enough functioning apparatus
still within him, and he would live. In a year there would be no sign; in
fact, she said, smiling as best she could, his limbs and stomach would be
newer, perhaps more efficient than before. This was some vague comfort
to the grieving Impatiens, who had grabbed the man's hand just in time.

Lycaste considered this as he worked on some furniture for the palace that night, humming as he painted the legs of a tiny chair with varnish. The same could perhaps be said of his model: how much did you have to take away before it ceased to be a house any more? The roof? One entire wall? He sat back and looked at it all, taking in the groups of figures, the tapestries that he'd sewn specially with a tiny needle, the open, vacant chambers closer to the top. What was Drimys now, if so much of him had been removed?

He turned the chair in his fingers, applying the brush-tip to the next leg, lost in thought. He'd finally found time to work but was doing everything clumsily, rushing things to make up for all the distractions. It wasn't proving as relaxing as he'd hoped it would be.

"Where will that go?" asked Pentas. She was determined to help in some way, even though she was making mistakes that he would have to fix later. Lycaste knew she didn't really find his project interesting—might even have considered such pursuits childish if they were being undertaken by anyone she thought less of—and that she was only helping out so they could spend time together. He supposed he should be grateful but would rather have been left in peace. He didn't need help. It wouldn't be his any more if people helped.

He pointed at the top floor without turning around. "With the table I'm making." He glanced at her briefly; there had been no further kisses since the night in his tower and he was beginning to worry that the longer they left it before the next, the harder such things would be for him to repeat. He wasn't even sure he could remember how to do it.

She met his gaze, smiling uncertainly. "What?"

He steeled himself, trying to think of something to say beforehand, but nothing came. He leaned forward, placing his brush down with a trembling hand.

Pentas looked away quickly before his lips could touch her. She pushed her chair back a little, returning her attention to the palace as if it was the most fascinating thing in the world.

"Lycaste," she began, white eyes straying to the floor, "I . . . I'm sorry. I didn't mean to, before." She looked at him at last. "I was frightened I'd lose you."

He picked up his brush quickly, as if preparing to go back to work. Anything to cover his embarrassment. "Lose me?"

Her gaze went back to the palace. "You're my dearest friend here. I shouldn't have given you hope—Eranthis was right."

"You pretended to love me," he said, touching the tip of the brush to the chair leg again.

Pentas dropped her head with a shrug. "I love you as a friend."

Lycaste looked into her white eyes as they lifted again. "A friend."

When she had gone, he glanced to the door as if searching for any last trace of her that would imply he wasn't totally alone, not yet. The birds, often still awake at this time of night, had until recently lived in small rooms in the towers, their childish possessions cluttering the stairways and landings. When summer came around, they moved below ground where it was cooler, staying in the grander quarters he seldom visited. The tower was his again, silent and empty.

Memories Returned

The café is only moderately crowded, an evening festival in the hills occupying most of the locals. The crowd he walks through is full of tourists for the most part, rich Athenians, sunburned German families. Sotiris takes a seat at an empty table, checking around him carefully, not quite sure what he's looking for.

He studies the drinks menu, sun-bleached photographs of bottles on laminated card, thinking of ordering wine. As he waits, he looks out to the water, calm as the pink evening descends, and searches for his distant chapel on its hill. The year is not what it appears, Sotiris knows that much, other memories returning languidly with each breath of wind across the port. He remembers, piece by piece: a dream within a dream.

Somewhere beyond where he sits, as if just behind the sky or hidden within the light on the water, the year is 14,647 AD. Humankind has changed, fractured, *Prismed* into a dozen breeds of fairy-tale grotesques, the chaos of expansion, war and ruin flinging humanity like bouncing sparks around the blackness of space. Man has been resculpted in a hundred different places, and the world as he knew it—*this* world—is gone for ever.

Sotiris takes a sip of his crisp wine, instantly feeling its effect.

When people—humans, good old-fashioned *Homo sapiens*—left the world as conquistadors, adventurers, slavers, industrialists and a thousand other things, they found the one thing they weren't expecting. They found nothing. Apparently only one fixed constant, one unbreakable physical law, would saturate the riot of interstellar history: the law of sterility. The heavens, so promising to earlier eyes, were empty of life. And not simply of anyone to talk to, or play a game of I-Spy with—no microbe, particle or strand of anything microscopically self-replicating was ever found that had not been carelessly trudged in on the soles of filthy boots. The phenomenon of life, as far as anyone could tell, was unique, a one-off, beginning and ending on the Old World.

One last tease of a hiccup in this law came during the tedious project of cataloguing Saturn's rings in the thirtieth century, when a school of mining rigs chanced upon the wrecked hulk of an unknown and impossibly strange craft, embedded and deep-frozen within one of the trillions of rocks that made up the grain of the spectacular rings. Analysis revealed a wonder, however disappointingly tied to Earth it might originally have been. Entombed in permanent shadow within the flamboyant structure were two occupants, their shocked faces frozen in a death that had occurred approximately seventy-nine million years before. They were theropods, more specifically a subspecies cross-breed of *Caudipteryx* and *Dromaeosaur*, starkly plumed in hues of blue-tinged silver and ebony, elegant white machine suits of staggering complexity encasing their shrivelled, eerie bodies. Of course it was exciting that members of a race of *dinosaur*—long and quite famously extinct—had apparently been clever enough to escape the tug of Earth, but they still weren't what everyone was hoping for: something truly from another world.

Denial was replaced, reasonably enough, by extraordinary vanity, followed by the triumphant rekindling of religious dependence. Theology became a science once again and God was searched for with a hunger that humankind, in all its earlier childish fervour, had never known. But there was no trace of him, her, it or them, either, and by then humanity was unrecognisable. Only the precious few Immortals—the Amaranthine—had not regressed into barbarism, though their enemies waited, circling, for the ever-dimming lights to go out.

*

Dusk has fallen, a sumptuous half-light shrouding the harbour. One or two stars have found their way through the depths of sky. He glances up at them, remembering again that they aren't real, that the world he sees around him is sealed like a bubble of air in an amber nugget. Sotiris looks down at himself in the gloom, peering at his reflection in the wine glass. He is perhaps in his mid-twenties, suggesting it is somewhere around 2180.

Someone is making him dream this.

The petrol engine of a scooter growls to a stop. Aaron, his hair wet, sits astride. He nods a greeting and kicks out the stand, leaning the scooter carefully as if he'd never parked one before. Lights are just starting to come on in the harbour, the window of the gelati shop across the street flickering.

"You've remembered now," says Aaron matter-of-factly, taking a seat at the table.

"Yes, I think I have." He drains his glass. "Iro's gone, isn't she?"

"For the time being."

Sotiris looks at him, noting again the kindness in the man's eerily forgettable face. "What does that mean?"

Aaron picks up the bottle and pours himself a glass, inspecting it in the twilight. "We'll talk about that later. For now, it's just us two."

Sotiris nods, aware that the dream will end soon enough. "All right."

The man across from him studies his face for a while, spinning the glass deftly in his hand. It makes a sighing noise. "I have a proposition for you, Sotiris Gianakos."

Sotiris smiles, safe in the knowledge that he is conversing with an element of himself, some schizophrenic by-product of living so long. "You are Maneker's hopeful new king, aren't you? The one everyone's so afraid of."

Aaron scowls for a moment, the glass pausing in his hands. "You think me a trick of your mind."

"Of course."

He breathes out, the glass resuming its spin. Sotiris looks away to the dark water, hearing something slosh beneath the surface near the buoys. Suddenly he feels cold, a shudder passing through him. He looks back.

The putrefying corpse of some kind of animal sits where Aaron had been, staring at him with milky eyes peeled wide. Its body is bloated and yellow-black with decay, some kind of larvae wriggling in a hole around its torn nostril.

It bursts.

Sotiris woke screaming.

Thunder

They were dreams of extreme pressure, compressing and constricting Lycaste's skull without any sensation of pain, as if something huge had suddenly caught hold of him. In his dream, that danger had always been there, flitting at the edge of his vision, until without warning it had struck. He lay remembering the feeling as it dissipated, trying to stick the experience down before it left him entirely. Something other than the dream had woken him, but he had no idea what. He turned in the bed, recalling the shock of realising he'd seen the shapeless underwater monster in that colourful, sensory-laden nightmare so many times before without understanding what it was, and by then it had been too late.

Lycaste mulled over the night before, discarding the dream for the necessary space to think. Pentas was long gone, her scent taken with her so that only the sharp smell of his model paint remained in the room. He couldn't believe what she'd told him; couldn't believe that she was capable of such cruelty or that it was even true. She loved him, he was certain. It would simply take her time to admit it.

He stood and stretched in the main tower's spare bedchamber, watching through the open circular window as waves smoothed the pebbles down on the beach. There it was again, the knocking sound that had brought him from that horrible dream. He had a visitor.

Most of the local Province had already come to see Drimys in the last week, the headline news of the man's terrible injuries filtering faster than most local gossip. As Lycaste made his way down the tower steps, he wondered who might be so remote as to have only just heard. He reached the hallway, smoothing his hair quickly, and opened the door.

"Lycaste Cruenta Melius, good morning. Did I wake you?"

He blinked and looked down at the wizened, freakish form of Jotroffe on his doorstep. Only very strange people indeed bothered to use full names. He wondered how the hermit knew his. The shrunken little man—looking particularly unusual in the morning light—laid his crook against the wall and pointed to a covered basket on the front step. "For Drimys. I hear he did himself a mischief."

Lycaste wasn't sure that what they'd been through could constitute a *mischief,* but he was at least glad the man had chosen a current topic of conversation for once. "That's very kind of you, Jotroffe. I shall see he gets it."

Jotroffe cackled, exposing tiny square teeth in a small mouth nothing like Lycaste's own, and retrieved his stick. He pointed it vaguely to the sky, his small head turning this way and that as if in search of clouds. "I think the barometric pressure will be of interest today, worth keeping a record of." He leaned on his stick, suddenly looking at Lycaste with great interest. "Do you own a barometer?"

Lycaste took the basket on the step, making sure to swing the door shut behind him in case the old bore made a dash for his kitchen. "I don't think so, Jotroffe." He pointed at the basket. "Thank you, again, for the gift."

Jotroffe nodded with a smile, regarding the basket briefly and then returning his attention to the sky. "It is possible to construct a fully functional barometer using a bottle, a hollow reed and a rubber balloon, among other things—the resulting readings are often quite fascinating. One of these days I must pop round and show you. In fact . . ." He began to rummage in the small, colourfully woven bag he wore over his shoulder, voice trailing off. "I believe I might have some of the necessary equipment about my person—"

"I'll have to consult my diary," said Lycaste quickly, pushing the door open again to step back into his hallway. He kept his hand on the latch. "Do come again."

Jotroffe lifted his cane, leaning its tip carefully against the door to prevent it from closing. Lycaste looked down, astounded.

They stared at each other.

"Be careful, Lycaste," the strange man said. "Remember to be careful."

"I . . . shall," he stammered, watching as Jotroffe's stick came away from his door. The man smiled.

"Farewell, then," Lycaste said, "and . . . thank you for the advice." He closed the door slowly, waving, until the heavy latch *snicked* shut. When he was sure the old man had gone, he dumped the basket on the table and sat down, abruptly convinced that he had just been threatened in some way. He pulled the basket towards him and peered carefully inside, half expecting to find something made from toenails or armpit hair, instead lifting out a fine-smelling cake. Stored in the bottom of the basket beneath the cake were two sealed amber jars of quince jam and a ring book. Lycaste examined the book briefly and sniffed the jams suspiciously, taking one jar for his larder and reconsidering the idea of growing some quinces for himself.

Balloons and straws, barometric pressure. What had the fool been talking about? Lycaste cut himself a small slice of the cake to try since he'd not yet had breakfast and took the rest over to the steps leading to his underground cellar. It was possible that Jotroffe had been referring to the approaching storm, though what those random objects had to do with it, he didn't know.

He remembered that some of the others had wanted to see the lightning Elcholtzia promised would occur and decided to go up to the east windows to see if he could catch a glimpse before he went back to work on his palace, the thought of a whole day's uninterrupted model-painting lifting his spirits at last.

He climbed the spiral stairs up to the servant birds' winter rooms, steadying himself tiredly a few times against the cool wall. The chamber was filled with Sonerila's possessions collected over the years, fascinating things he didn't understand, found strewn on the beach or in the cliffs. By far the most interesting were the chunks of stone with animals apparently trapped inside. He took one from the shelf and turned it this way and that, trying to see how it was made. It had blended to rock, leaving only an impression. Elcholtzia said the rock surrounding such things was a kind of vomit, that the specimens Sonerila had found must have puked up their mineral-rich innards and been stuck within them as they cooled to a block. It didn't sound nice to Lycaste, who worried every now and then that the same thing might happen to him. Impatiens agreed with Eranthis that perhaps it was something their ancestors had done deliberately, discounting the ridiculous notion of a deadly incontinence. If that were true, it looked like the cruellest of punishments.

Lycaste's favourites were the large spirals, like oversized snails. Other things scattered about the room were undoubtedly man-made but had no discernible purpose. There were spheres, coils, twists of metal and the edge of something very hard and very bright, not dulled like the others by salt and coral, its surface embossed with clean symbols unlike any he had seen before. They bore a vague similarity to the runes etched inside the walls of some of the caves. Drimys had thought he might able to break the code and decipher them but there weren't enough of the markings. Lycaste didn't want to know what they meant; they were from another time, when things mattered that didn't matter any more. Some of the objects in the chamber were obviously collected just because they were shiny or glossy, and there were a great many of those, along with recent ring books and toys. The toys were mostly puppets and dolls from when Sonerila was small, often on loan to Briza on the condition that he was gentle with them.

The servant wasn't there so Lycaste crossed the landing to the window, noticing the heavy storm clouds coming from the direction of the hills. He stopped to gaze at them, intrigued.

It was like a landscape in the sky, the clouds mountainous towers of roiling mist sinking between shredded black spears to steep-sided valleys. He listened. There it was—a choked boom followed by a rolling, broken series of beats, like pieces of the world being dropped from unimaginable heights and hitting things as they fell. It came from the depths of the cloud valleys, as if the storm was crumbling in on itself. He strained to listen to the last of it, still quiet and distant. The sound was power, vast and voluminous even from that distance.

He descended the tower and went outside. The air was still and lit with a yellowish tinge—it was like waking from a confused dream at an odd hour. He could see people beneath the foil tree at the edge of the orchard, all observing the clouds. The valleys of thunder filled the sky but were not quite overhead. Rolling cracks like a drumbeat from somewhere high and far broke across the hills.

When the sounds of the sky subsided to a crackling gurgle, Lycaste heard them: Eranthis appeared to be arguing, her voice clear then lost again under a fresh boom of crisp, galloping thunder. He saw Pentas and walked cautiously over to the tree beneath which they stood, stooping as he brushed its overhanging branches, and tiny slivers of metal fell twisting from his shoulders. Small wild birds nested in its twisted canopy, chirping anxiously as the thunder splintered the sky.

The woman she was arguing with was Pamianthe, Briza's mother. She and Drimys, though still married by law, had been living apart for years. Lycaste joined them wearily, having always been nervous around the woman.

"I should have summoned a Mediary before I left Odemiz," Pamianthe said tersely. "Briza would be in schooling by now and know twice as many words. The children in Izmirean can already write!"

"We all know what Mediaries are like," Eranthis replied, glowering at the woman.

Lycaste watched Pentas flinch, wanting to hold her in his arms.

"I'm taking him, Eranthis. His father can't look after him."

Impatiens knelt by the boy, who was looking thoroughly confused, and whispered in his ear. He stood up again, turning to Pamianthe. "Lycaste is going to take Briza to pick some flowers for Drimys. It's better we have this conversation without him here, don't you think, Pamianthe?" He looked at Lycaste.

Lycaste nodded, taking Briza's hand and exchanging glances with Pentas.

Pamianthe caught his arm. "Bring him back before the Quarter's out, Lycaste, we'll be leaving."

He took Briza out of the orchard, deep concern on the boy's round face, and into the grove of wild flowers at its edge. Beyond them, the curling darkness choked the sky and blew a moist, surprisingly fresh breeze their way. They climbed the bank where tall orchids rooted in the jungle paths and pink grasshoppers bounced madly away at their approach, palms above the bank swaying lethargically like seaweed under the tortured clouds, thunder rupturing around them. Briza laughed, his troubles forgotten, and ran squealing among the slowest of the grasshoppers, their tiny shapes leaping whenever a boom ripped through the sky. Lycaste began picking the most elegant light blue flowers while he tried to see what was going on beneath the foil tree.

Briza trotted up with some weeds and dumped them into Lycaste's arms. "Are these for Daddo?" asked the boy, casting about for more of the unattractive plants among the rippling grass.

Lycaste nodded and pointed to some tiny scarlet flowers. "These ones, Briza, pick some of these here."

Briza crouched down, deciding which ones to select, his tongue sticking out of his mouth. "The man in the caves likes flowers."

Lycaste frowned, genuinely thinking he'd misheard. His hand clenched around an orchid stem but didn't pull. "The man in the caves?"

Briza hummed and tore some red petals from a flower, throwing them into the increasing wind. "He gave me some."

"When did you see a man, Briza?" He shot his gaze towards the rocks, in plain view at the end of the beach.

"Today," said Briza in a sing-song voice. He spied a lone grasshopper and ran to chase it, his flowers forgotten.

The caves. From there anyone could see most of the house and gardens. He walked back to the orchard to get a better look, making sure Briza remained in view as he played in the grass. The others were still arguing beneath the tree.

He picked up a branch the length of his thigh from the woodpile and swung it tentatively, feeling its weight, then set off along the beach. The first spots of rain began to speckle his body and darken the pebbles, while out to sea something flashed, bright as lit magnesium against the grim sky. He stopped to look down at himself, wiping away the slickness on his skin. Lycaste had felt rain before, but not for some years and then only briefly. That which dropped on him now was heavier, thicker. It smelled different. Bass thunder rolled over the beach as he shook his head and marched more quickly towards the caves, gaping greyly in the thickening rain beyond his overturned boat. He swung the stick again, reassuringly heavy in his fist, his fingers still stained from the orchids.

Lycaste had no idea what he was going to do when he got there. He looked down at his rain-slicked body as he walked, his dainty ankles coated in rough wet sand, and slowed. His slender physique wouldn't even deter a child. He hoped the stick might be threatening enough—if it had to be. He swung it again.

"*Who are you?*" Lycaste said to the whispering rain and grinding clouds, practising lowering his voice and settling his shoulders to look threatening. It was absurd, but the best he could do. He stopped, looking back to the dark green slope of orchard and ahead to the caves. He was soaked. In a drawer somewhere lay the heirloom—a finely wrought old pistol ring that he had never tested. He should have thought of it sooner, should have gone and tried it before he'd started out. Stupid.

Almost there, he watched the caves closely as he approached, looking for any sign of movement among their crags. The darkening sea slammed against the furthest rocks, white spray showering the cave-mouth. He had to enter there or walk around next to the heaving water. Another flash came from somewhere behind him as he stepped gingerly up onto the first smooth, barnacled slab leading to the cave.

The tumbling surf grew quieter as he stepped in. A bed of smoother sand reached far inside, soft on his raw feet. He crept further, trying to separate the volume of the waves from any sounds inside. Heaped seaweed rotted against the stone, rank and sharp in his nostrils. It became darker, but his eyes adjusted quickly to the bleak light that filtered from outside; the forms of rock reared and tumbled about him, sometimes narrowing so much that a man could only just squeeze through. Every time he reached those places, he was convinced someone would leap out, catching him trapped. But he heard nothing, just the dwindling grumble and smash of the elements.

Lycaste leaned against a boulder, dry and cool in the dark, waiting. He gripped the branch tightly, absently working the loose bark from its surface with his fingers as he listened. There was no sign that anyone had been here at all. No prints in the sand, no traces of a fire. There was no smell of people here, either, but then he could smell nothing apart from the foetid seaweed.

He waited for what felt like a long time. There were no portable timepieces in the Province, and nothing exact at all. They weren't needed anyway, in this relaxed age when everything was done by Quarter. Lycaste was sure he had passed from second to third Quarter by now. His stomach grumbled in the dark and he looked around in panic in case he was heard.

Cautiously, Lycaste stepped further in, where the light increased as the punctured cave system opened again onto the shore beyond. The sand became dry and loose, dimpled with marks. He bent, unable to tell if any could be footprints. He placed his own foot experimentally in the sand but left no impression other than a trough the grains quickly refilled.

It was here in the caves that he and Impatiens had first found the ancient markings. They appeared to be so old that they showed none of the fresh, scratched rock beneath, merely indentations of the same colour, as though they had always been there. Lycaste looked for more and found some just below head height on the inside wall. They were small, but varied in size up to about the length of his hand. Patterns repeated in the markings, like the modern writing he was familiar with, so he was convinced it was language. Impatiens had suggested that the markings might be numbers. He reached out and touched them, running his fingers in and out of their chiselled forms, repeatedly checking around him as he did so.

Finally he sat down, listening instead to the wind and rain outside. There was nobody here, unless they had retreated much further into the cave system that pocked the cliff face. He decided to return with Impatiens and whoever else would come later on, perhaps tomorrow. They would push deeper into the cliff, checking everywhere. It wouldn't even take a whole day. If someone had been here, they would know.

PART II

Procyon

The clipper dropped, a sinuous, ichthyoid shape thrown into black silhouette by the vast brightness of the chilly, reflective planet beneath it, and plunged like a streamered bullet into the outer layers of the exosphere. At its prow, a finely wrought figurehead spread the parting air into twin crests of vapour, gradually glowing like a wake of fire. Horatio Crook barely spared the dome of thundering cloud-tops roaring up to meet them a second glance, resting his head back and looking at Florian Von Schiller. The other Perennial was staring out of a porthole, his eyes following the grey seas and dark shorelines that traced like oily scum around the cold continent towards which they were dropping at supersonic speeds. Their staterooms aboard the Decadence craft, whilst horribly small and cramped, had been appointed as luxuriously as possible during the nine-day flight, with hangings and tapestries decorating the remoulded, utilitarian interiors. Here, in the forward operations capsule, they sat on gilded ottomans draped with furs and rugs for warmth as they looked out of the portholes, a jug of poorly filtered water trembling upon a table between them. The rules of the clipper commanded that they wear specially made Amaranthine suits for the entire voyage in case of difficulties, inter-Satrapy travel remaining an imperfect and inexact science for any Prism species, even in an ancient, hand-me-down Amaranthine ship such as this. Both Crook and Von Schiller had refused as a matter of principle, fearing for the integrity of their fabulously expensive garments. Their enlarged, custom-made suits stood locked against the bulkhead at the ready, monstrous bulging red sacks barely humanoid in form, chests and shoulders covered with scaled armour.

Outer Procyon, the second of three now-uninhabited planets in the Seventeenth Solar Satrapy of Procyon, was one of the homes of His Most Venerable Self, the eldest of the Amaranthine and Firmamental Emperor of the twenty-three Solar Satrapies. He might have chosen to receive them on Outer Wolf, the second of his private planets, since it was far closer to Firmament centre (even if it was equally uninviting), but such considerations didn't appear to cross the Eldest's mind these days.

Outer Procyon was relatively unmeddled with, its centre being still intact, not scooped out like many of the other Firmamental planets had been to make the Vaulted Lands that most of the Amaranthine chose to live within. It was home to a handful of boring, imported Old World species hardy enough to weather the conditions and, for half of his time, the Most Venerable himself. Few ever visited him in his self-imposed exile, despite his unimpeachable status as ruler of the 1,300 light-year volume of the Firmament. It was said he lived in rags, wandering continually across the continents until he came back to where he'd started, then crossing to his other world and repeating the process. Nobody even knew if he had Melius acolytes staying with him—he could conceivably be down there alone. The penultimate Amaranthine to visit had met with him on Wolf twenty-one years before, and since then he had only been called upon by one other, Hugo Hassan Maneker, on behalf of the new Parliament of Gliese and the Pretender himself.

Maneker, a Perennial Amaranthine who had lived through the inception and popularisation of Immortality, had been a Firmamental Satrap during the two-hundred-year Wars of Decadence. The campaign—the end of which had seen the creation of the Prism Investiture and the resulting forty centuries of darkness—had raged far beyond the boundaries of the Firmament, cutting into virgin volumes of space that had never before been explored. The proto-Threen kingdoms the Amaranthine fought to subdue had eventually capitulated, lessening their vast power and bringing other Prism species under Amaranthine rule, notably the ever-obedient Pifoon, whose crude monarchy had benefitted immeasurably over the course of the two-century campaign as a result of huge injections of Firmamental Ducats and the gift of hundreds of ancient Amaranthine vessels stripped down almost to the bare bones. The increasingly useful Vulgar, too, as a reward for their loyalty, had been given their eighth moon, Port Olpoth, further humiliating the Lacaille, who were even now—despite the slow rebuilding of their navy—languishing in poverty.

For his efforts, Hugo Maneker had been considered for the newly created role of Firmamental Vice-Regent, to rule from the throne of Gliese in the event of the Most Venerable's absence. Crook himself had agreed with the idea, until it was suggested that Maneker's closest friend, the universally admired Sotiris Gianakos, might yet be a better choice for the post. To avoid embarrassing Maneker or Gianakos, the idea had been scrapped, though every century or so the notion would grow in popularity once more among Immortals displeased with the dusty order of Succession, only to fade again, all but forgotten.

By the time news—carried by Amaranthine journeymen and Prism pilgrims—of a claim against His Most Venerable Self had percolated from the Westerly Provinces of the Old World, Maneker had long since retired to a life of gentlemanly study and contemplation, tinkering with economic models and reforms that might assist the undeveloped empires of the Amaranthine's nobler Prism allies. He hadn't shown an interest in Amaranthine affairs in more than five hundred years, and some had even begun to suspect that he might have gone to a Utopia—a place for the mad—to live out the last of his days.

It was with great surprise, then, that he suddenly became a vocal supporter of the Devout, the Amaranthine sect that had embraced the Pretender's claims and taken up residence on the Old World. The scorn of twenty thousand Amaranthine had—until then—ensured that their cause remained an unfashionable one, but all that had changed when Maneker pledged his assistance. The Devout (an order made up mostly of younger Immortals) had immediately declared Maneker their figurehead, inviting him to be among them in the kingdom of the giant Melius to await the crowning of the new Firmamental Emperor.

A ban on all travel to the Old Satrapy was soon imposed by the Parliament of Gliese for anyone less than vocal in their support of the Devout and their cause, though most polite Amaranthine society found this less than worrying; the Old World was a fearsome, dangerous place and nobody ever went there anyway despite its sacred protection within the Firmament. The fact that Maneker now apparently went by the Melius name of *Caracal* was evidence enough of his burgeoning insanity—common in Perennials of advanced age—and many thought that perhaps he should just be left there to do as he wished. What had caused him to side so absolutely with a group of impressionable younger Immortals remained a mystery, as well as the true identity of this Pretender. Most of the Vaulted Lands thought it of little consequence, even if the Most Venerable appeared inclined to hear the man's claim. What harm could the Pretender do, especially when the Firmament had the weight of two Prism empires on its side? But these facts now appeared to matter little to whoever was pulling Maneker's strings; the destruction of Virginis had proved that.

The clipper burst through the thermosphere and into the mesosphere, sizzling like an iron skillet despite the turbulent wake of air billowing from its fins. Smashed icebergs and cracked plates of land had become distinguishable from the blue-grey contours, beaches of brown shale choked with discoloured ice circling forbidding inland seas. Though any Amaranthine of sufficiently advanced age could tap into the weak magnetic lines of force that joined each Solar Satrapy and journey along it in an instant, the Most Venerable forbade any Bilocation in his presence or on his planets for obscure reasons known only to him. Consequently, the two Amaranthine had been forced to pay a small fortune in Firmamental Ducats just to secure passage in these troubled times. They were tired, and knew when they landed at their destination somewhere in the Procyon-Baline Ranges that coldness and dampness would also be included on the list of their miseries.

Mountains clarified from the tributary patterns of rock and snow, rising to meet the falling ship, and it slowed its descent in retro-rocket fashion, bursts of sooty, tropical cyan filling the portholes on either side. Von Schiller returned to his ornamental seat, the vehicle's gyroscopes keeping them stable and upright no matter what acrobatic manoeuvres it was forced to enact, and tapped Crook on the shoulder.

"If he's not there and we're forced to wait, we've got three days until the ship returns."

"He'd better be there," Crook grunted, rearranging his fur blanket and buttoning his collar.

"I might be able to persuade them to stay with us for a few hours while we search, but they won't promise anything."

The blasted brown outcrops of the mountain range came into view, cornices of brilliant, pure snow passing just beneath. The graceful clipper, its verdigrised scales repatched with strips of tin stained carbon-black by the heat of its entry, fell between the mountain summits to the foothills of the highest peak, Mount Lawrence, opening dirty cream linen sails along its fins to catch the wind. It slowed, bleached sections of its undercarriage extending like pectoral fins tipped with rockets, and roared into the gravel and stone, scattering rock. Finally it settled with a thump, the landing steps swinging down.

They exited quickly, gathering their bags and shuddering as a blast of frigid air filled the cylindrical airlock hung beneath the Void-ship's tubular genitals. Crook stepped out into the weak white sunlight clad in full ornamental attire, jewelled collar and ruffs feeling ridiculous should they never find the man they were looking for. The biting wind stung his ears as he looked up at the mountain, about two-thirds the size of Everest on the Old World. He could see five of the planet's eighteen moons, faded in the sky above, while rocky moraine slipped between his velvet boots and clattered down the hillside to make empty echoes in the light wind. Below, the valley stretched to the base of the next mountain, its rock-strewn floor patterned with grey, slowly moving cloud-shadows.

Von Schiller joined him, rubbing his gloved hands together. Behind them, the small crew were carrying elegant rococo-style chairs down the steps, staggering under their weight. They watched the Prism deposit the furniture, visibly exhausted, and make their way back to the clipper. The ship's sails furled slowly away, its forlorn, Amaranthine-sculpted lion-face regarding them dolefully. Smoke coiled about the rocks as the thumping, poorly-maintained superluminal engines idled, waiting for the two Amaranthine to decide.

Over the rise they saw him approach, a hunched figure in a dirty robe. He waved jauntily, pointing to a slope of large boulders closer to the bottom of the hill. Von Schiller turned and gave the ship the sign and it roared into life, scattering gravel.

"No fire. That's my bet," said Crook.

Von Schiller shook his head. "He must have fire. I'm not sitting here three days without a fire."

"You'll see."

There was no fire. His Venerable Self welcomed them in his boulder-strewn camp and showed them where they could stow their luggage. It was too far for the two to have carried the chairs, so they'd simply left them on the mountainside.

James Fitzroy Sabran, the Most Venerable, was indeed wearing rags, as the two men had suspected from the far-off glimpse they'd had of him. They were stained and lined with water marks and clinging pieces of gravel and sand, water from a trek through the ice earlier that day still darkening the hem. The man's face, frozen at around the age of sixty owing to the late introduction of the suite of treatments that would develop into Immortality, was slender, sun-lined, the eyes rheumy and distracted. It was just as well that none of them ever needed to shave—those sorts of bodily changes were no longer an issue—for Sabran's beard would measure more than six thousand feet long by now, a serious impediment to his global walks.

After lengthy handshakes and bows, the two found a place to sit among the boulders. By law they were the next two Perennials in line for Venerability—Von Schiller was a few days older than Crook and therefore would be ruler when Sabran died—but they still practised extreme, almost godly reverence for the one who could supposedly remember the longest out of anyone alive.

Sabran offered them water for swilling, as was the Amaranthine custom (the one totally unexpected and uncomfortable side effect of Immortality was an eternally dry mouth), and put some ragged garments on a clothes-horse made from twigs to dry. How he lived out here, exposed to the elements, was a mystery.

"Do you not have any servants to support you?" ventured Von Schiller.

Sabran appeared to think long and hard about the question, the dry wind sighing above the boulders. He still hadn't said a word.

"What use would they be?" he asked at last. His voice had a whistling, lispy quality to it. Crook remembered it had sounded deeper last time they met, about a century previously. "I live among ghosts. They are of greater help on my travels than any living thing could be."

Von Schiller nodded sagely, though Crook refused to. Everyone knew the man was destined for a Utopia before he died, but nobody quite realised how deranged he had become.

"Do the ghosts keep you abreast of the happenings in the Firmament?" Crook asked.

Sabran shook his head. "They are the ghosts of the mountains, spirits not born of organic life. They have no use for prattle and stories."

"Then you are not aware of the attack on the Satrapy of Virginis? The deaths of thousands?"

Von Schiller glanced sharply at him; they had planned to lead into the subject slowly, for Sabran's benefit.

Sabran shook his head thoughtfully. "No, no they wouldn't have known about that. Though it sounds very interesting, I'm sure." He said it in the way someone enquiring after a child's schooling would feign fascination at the answer. Crook could see he didn't care a jot.

"Your favourite Perennial, Hugo Hassan Maneker, appears to be responsible. He and your chosen successor."

"My successor?" Sabran chuckled. "No, no, no. Not Aaron the Long-Life. He is an Amaranthine of peace."

Crook hesitated, unaware that Sabran had even known the Pretender's name, content only that the Law of Succession was being honoured. "Then you at least believe Maneker capable?" He could hear the unplanned note of interrogation in his voice.

"I hardly remember Maneker. I thought the Long-Life might have come alone. It feels . . ." His Venerable Self paused, looking off gloomily to the mountains. "It is as if he came to me in a *dream*."

"Dream or no," Crook continued carefully, "your edict alone has caused this, Sire."

"Edict?"

Crook sighed, preparing to elaborate, but Von Schiller cut in. "To allow investigation into Aaron's claim, crown him Emperor and award his prophet Maneker the title of Vice-Regent and the Solar Satrapy of Gliese upon the Succession."

"Succession. What a beautiful word." Sabran had begun plaiting something together between his fingers, making a loose crown. "My ghosts here, they play word games with me when it grows too dark to read. They are quite clever—their riddles are very challenging."

Von Schiller smiled. "It is good that you are not lonely, as we had feared."

Crook leaned forward, exasperated. "What is to be done with him? Maneker must be removed from his position, tried for murder. Tried for *genocide*."

Sabran pulled a face, placing the crown carefully on his white-blond hair. "What do you think?"

Crook stared at it. It was made from living dragonflies twisted together. They squirmed on Sabran's head as if a huge pale blue parasite had wrapped itself around his skull.

Crook glanced back to Von Schiller. "Florian and I believe something must be done. You must allow us to find and punish Maneker."

"Must, must, *must*," muttered Sabran, adjusting his crown.

"He is responsible for the most appalling atrocity since the Volirian Conflict. The Devout have made their statement clearly—oppose us or suffer. Already Satrapy Parliaments are rushing to appease them. What are you going to do about it? They think they are protected on the sacred Old World, but we have debts we might call in; Prism armies are ours to command, should we need them. The Melius Provinces will not dare harbour him when they see our strength."

Von Schiller looked nervously at the ground. "What Crook means is that we must be seen to do something. Our strength must be observed." His eyes remained lowered. "But also our clemency."

"*Clemency?*" repeated Crook, disbelieving.

"Well . . ." Florian glanced between the two men, though Sabran was apparently transfixed by the mountains behind them. "I only mean that the Firmament's last act of retribution following the Volirian Crisis did not have quite the desired consequences. Perhaps this time we should be more sensitive. This fellow, Aaron the Long-Life as you so charmingly call him, Most Venerable, could represent our hopes and aspirations for a new age. He must see our . . . quality."

Crook wanted to strike Von Schiller. They hadn't come all the way out here to discuss clemency, to start talking airily about new ages like idiots sitting on a mountainside. His Most Venerable Self was still apparently paying them no attention, his lips moving silently as if in response to some conversation only he could hear. The wind whispered across the rocks, the sound of cold, dead eternity.

"What of the suspicious Prism movements recorded all over the Firmament?" Crook insisted. "The rumours of some new weapon being devised on Drolgins by those revolting Vulgar? They are the ones who need to see our strength—and our malice." He leaned forwards, lightly touching Sabran's sleeve, knowing Von Schiller would not approve. "Give me this power, Most Venerable, and I shall safeguard our beloved Firmament against all evils. I shall make sure you cannot be supplanted until it is your rightful and just time. Make me Vice-Regent: you shall not regret it."

Sabran spoke quickly for once, snapping from his reverie. "Power? What power? You do not know the meaning of the word." He looked off towards the valley floor again, his lips moving, and then he grinned. "I know," he said, as if to someone just at his side. "Yes, he is, isn't he? He doesn't understand." The Most Venerable suddenly burst into laughter, waving a hand in front of his face. "Stop!" he cried, wiping his eyes. "Stop it! You're too harsh. He is young."

The silence that followed was total. Crook stared at the ruler of all the Firmament, then looked back to Von Schiller, who was staring at the rocky ground. He could see then, as the wind moaned and his hair swept lankly across his forehead, that all was lost.

The Eldest got to his feet. "I must go now. I wish to be at the far side of the valley before dusk."

"You're *leaving*?" wailed Crook.

Sabran didn't turn back to look at him, instead collecting his rags and twigs. "Must get some miles under my belt."

The two Amaranthine stood to watch him go, the wind tugging at their exuberant dress. Crook turned to Von Schiller. "Thank you, Florian."

"Even-handedness—"

"I don't care about *even-handedness*. Signal that ship, get it back here. I'm not finished with this."

Von Schiller looked gravely at him. "You're not thinking of undermining him, are you, Horatio? Undermining the Most Venerable? It can't be done." He took a step towards Crook. "I will not allow it."

Crook glared at him. "You won't *allow* it? You are first in line, heir apparent, and yet you appear to have allowed a charlatan who somehow invades the dreams of men to become king. You allowed thousands of our fellows—those of the Virginis Parliament who still saw sense—to die." He staggered, wiping a sleeve across his mouth. "You'll see, Florian, that there are limits even to your influence."

The Voidship reappeared half an hour later, its engines bellowing into the rubble. Florian Von Schiller climbed aboard, his fingers numb. The small captain, caped in ruffled velvet likely bought with the proceeds of the lucrative voyage, looked at him questioningly.

"Just me for the return journey, Captain," he said, dumping his bag and peering out of a porthole. "My friend has decided he'd like to stay. Indefinitely."

Guest

Lycaste walked back along the drying sand from the caves, the stick still in his hand. He'd not had any imaginary friends as a child—hadn't wanted any—though he supposed it wasn't unhealthy in a young boy like Briza, especially on such a lonely, unpopulated stretch of continent. The boy had only ever met a few children his own age, those who accompanied the Players. He hadn't really understood them, nor they him, so used was he to purely adult company, and the prospect of sharing toys had finally smashed any prospect of even a frail truce between them. It didn't matter—Briza was already developing into the sort of boy Lycaste never was, sure to be popular and loved.

He retraced his steps along the water's edge, thinking of the night he met Eranthis among the fruit trees. The sky had cleared miraculously, the breeze now clean and cool. All sorts of lumpish strands littered the beach, landed by the waves, and he picked his way among them looking for anything interesting, turning objects with the end of his stick. Gnarled pieces of bleached driftwood were everywhere, their sinewy arms coated in places with olive strands of drying seaweed. It was good firewood, worth collecting and storing. As he picked up armfuls, he passed the remains of Briza's sandcastle and stopped to look. It had been battered by the rain and smoothed to nothing but a hump in the sand.

He came to the orchard, noticing activity through the kitchen window of his third tower. So they were making themselves at home in his house now without even thinking to ask. He looked at the stick in his hand and felt faintly ridiculous, dropping it in the snake-infested woodpile at the edge of the trees along with the driftwood.

Lycaste opened his door, knocking as he entered in the hope that it would show up their rudeness, but nobody noticed. Pamianthe appeared to have chosen to stay after all and was busily pouring something from the pot into his best bowls and cups. She looked up, shocked for a moment.

"Lycaste! Is it all right to use these cups? Only . . . well, you'll see—go in."

"What?" he began to ask, taking stock of his finest crockery and ceramics laid out, ready for the dining room. The servants had begun to prepare for dinner, though it wasn't nearly late enough. He looked at her, still wary of outbursts.

"Just go into the other room, you'll see."

Lycaste shook his head and headed for the next chamber, expecting to find the old fool Jotroffe there, snuck in while he was away looking for strangers. If the crazy old fart was going to start talking about balloons again he'd just have to head for bed, shut the door and be done with it.

"Ah! *This* is Lycaste, the master of the estate." Eranthis stood up from her chair in the centre of the room. Lycaste took a step inside as his eyes adjusted, aware their number had swelled. Impatiens and Pentas sat together on some cushions, Briza at their feet playing with some of Lycaste's figures from the palace. Another man sat next to Eranthis, someone he'd never seen before. He smiled and stood, roughly Eranthis's height—rather short for a man, though still nowhere near as small as Jotroffe.

"Lycaste," Eranthis said, "meet Callistemon, Plenipotentiary of the Greater Second. Did I get that right?"

"Perfectly," said their guest, offering a delicate yellow hand. He had a pleasant, boyish face, with light, slightly curled hair dangling over his smooth forehead. "Very pleased to meet you, Lycaste."

Lycaste took the man's hand awkwardly, noticing how it was turned down, expecting supplication. As he did so, he coloured a formal cream, hoping he hadn't remembered too late. Callistemon smiled and his pink eyes flicked back to Eranthis. He let his hand drop to his side and sat down slowly, picking up a cup and turning to regard Lycaste once more.

"I must say, Lycaste," said the Plenipotentiary, "this is an extraordinarily beautiful place to live. You must feel very fortunate."

"I do," he replied, carefully arranging himself on a patterned settle. The room was hardly used these days and the cushions were dusty.

"He was the envy of the port for a while," said Impatiens. "I think a few people had hoped the place would be up for sale instead of handed down."

Callistemon took a sweet from a bowl Eranthis was offering around. "How long have you owned the property, if you don't mind me asking?"

"Twenty years or so," Lycaste said. "I've redecorated some of the chambers."

"You've done a fine job. It was your uncle's, I understand?"

Lycaste couldn't see the point of the man's questions. He half-suspected the first Plenipotentiary he'd ever met had come simply to offer him a sum for his house. "Yes. I can show you the papers—I have them somewhere."

Callistemon laughed, exposing long teeth. "That won't be necessary. I have records."

There was a brief silence in which Lycaste exchanged a bemused glance with Pentas. He wanted to be alone with her more than ever and hoped the Plenipotentiary's visit would be brief.

"Now you're all together," the young man said through a mouthful of syrupsnap, looking around, "I expect you're wondering why I'm here." He dusted his fingers against each other with a smile. Lycaste scowled, noting where the powdered sugar drifted so that he could have the birds clean later.

"Well, the Second—and therefore to some degree the First—has decreed that it's high time for a census of the outlying Provinces. I'm here, first and foremost, to count you all, but I am also expected to make notations on the state of affairs down here—deeds of land ownership, assets, holdings . . ." He looked suddenly apologetic. "I don't mean to pry, of course, though I'm afraid my questions will need to be answered to the best of your abilities." Lycaste could hear the youth in his voice, even if it did carry the Second's lilting slur.

Callistemon sat up in his seat, smoothing the fabric of a cushion. "I also hear there was an accident recently—a man was bitten by a fish of some kind? He remains unwell?"

"A shark, Plenipotentiary," said Impatiens, glancing at Lycaste. "The seas are dangerous here."

"Gracious," he said, nodding thoughtfully. "I'd heard there were wilder things in the south, but . . ." He looked at Impatiens uncertainly, finally shaking his head as if to clear it. "Getting back to this census—I have it written that there are two hundred and six in the Province, but the information is, regrettably, rather old. It has been some time since the First attempted to catalogue what goes on in the Nostrum Provinces." He reached down into a small satchel, producing an expensive-looking paper book and ink-pen.

"There are three hundred and fifteen now," said Eranthis, watching the Plenipotentiary testing his pen.

"I will need their names and locations," he said, scribbling something. "They all have to be visited at some stage."

"How long will you be staying?" Eranthis enquired.

"It all depends on the cooperation of the locals, I'm afraid. I hope Impatiens here won't find me a nuisance while I'm staying with him." He laughed before Impatiens could reply, flicking through the book. "Now," Callistemon said, sucking the end of the pen for a moment and glancing to a list at the back, many of the points underlined, "I have rather a . . . specific thing to ask of you. I hear there is an unusual person here going by the name of Jotroffe? Jatrofe?"

Lycaste stirred from his doze, sitting straighter. He wondered what the Plenipotentiary wanted with Jotroffe.

"Yes," said Impatiens. "He wasn't on your last census?"

"No, he wasn't." Callistemon looked hard at Impatiens. "There are some things I'd like clarified, if you don't mind." He turned the page, pen poised, looking around the semicircle. "Where did he come from, does anyone know?"

Impatiens shrugged. "Possibly out west." His eyes suddenly widened. "Is he wanted for something?"

Callistemon's pen remained at the ready. "Do you know him well?"

"Not really—we see him from time to time, if we're unlucky."

"Unlucky?"

"Meet him yourself, you'll see."

Callistemon put the pen down. "Where does he live?"

"Nowhere. He wanders—he's a hermit."

"It is as I thought." Callistemon appeared to think for a while as he stowed his notebook. "I would very much like to be taken to him, perhaps tomorrow?"

Impatiens puffed out his cheeks. "That might be difficult. He sort of . . . appears when he wants to."

"I see." The Plenipotentiary rummaged in the bowl and took another sweet. "Nevertheless, I'd be grateful if you'd try to find him for me. I'm supposed to follow up on any . . . *irregularities* I discover on my travels."

"Where else have you been?" asked Pentas excitedly, surprising them all.

Callistemon cocked his head. "That's a Seventh accent, if I'm not mistaken? A fellow traveller, I see."

Pentas smiled and nodded. "So is my sister, Eranthis."

"Oh, I can see you are sisters—you share your beauty."

Lycaste rolled his eyes, noticing with a hint of jealousy that both girls looked delighted at the comment.

"In answer to your question, I have visited all of the Provinces on my way here, coming down through the Eighth and Ninth with a company of Players and staying in one of their fascinating wheelhouses. Next stop is the Eleventh, though truth be told I'm rather worried about my grasp of the local dialect."

"A company of Players?" Impatiens exclaimed. "You must mean Moringa's?"

"That's right. Charming, all of them. I offered funds to pay for my journey but they wouldn't take a thing."

"Doesn't sound like Moringa to me."

Lycaste didn't like this toadying. He thought it might be time to retire soon. He was just wondering how he could best get them all out of his house while subtly suggesting to Pentas that she could stay when the tinkle of the dinner bell sounded from the formal dining room next door. He sighed inwardly, realising he had at least a Quarter more of politeness ahead of him.

*

The sun shone its last as Lycaste sat in the window of his topmost room, a voltaic orange disc dipping below the gilded outline of the rocks. It was at its clearest at this time of day, a lamp left on in the next world. He looked down into the orchard, alive with animal calls and chanting flowers. Pink light drenched the vibrant greens, electrifying the trees, deepening the shadows dividing their branches. A creeping chill turned his head to the east. On the far side of the sky the green moon had risen silently, a crenulated, faded mint in the blue.

It was bearable in some company to be treated like a child—it even had its advantages—pressure to perform among guests was loosened and, eventually, removed altogether. It had taken his father years to expect so little of Lycaste, but when the moment finally came it was as if a great freedom had been awarded to them both, easing their relationship while it deteriorated so that its evaporation was entirely painless on the quiet afternoon when he left Kipris for good. He could feel it happening now in the presence of someone new, someone everyone thought they ought to impress.

He stepped away from the window to the lone table. Among the models and ring books that cluttered its surface was a thin tube. He picked the telescope up and weighed it in his hands before lifting it experimentally to his eye. At first the view was dark and he put it down, thinking perhaps it had all been some game of Elcholtzia's to see if Lycaste really would try it out. But of course it was dark—the cap was on. He removed it and swung the device around to see the hills, but was again met with nothing but a colourless smudge. Exasperated, he looked up at the moon, which sprang upon him in shocking, vivid detail. Lycaste gasped as he stared, mouth open.

Telescopes weren't rare—he'd been made to stare into them occasionally during his schooling years, but all the moon had yielded was a fuzzy green blob, not much clearer than when you looked at it with your own eyes. This was different. He smiled as he took in the dense, milky soup of cloud, wondering why Elcholtzia had chosen to lend him such a fine and undoubtedly expensive thing. Scanning the distant world, he could see no sign of anything man-made, reflecting after a while that not even a miraculous thing like this would see through cloud. The people up there were said to be long-dead, anyway, ancient prisoners consigned to the forests of the Greenmoon for terrible crimes.

His smile withered. The toy was a pleasant but ineffectual distraction from the day's events, and he looked briefly back at the chamber door, against which he'd pushed the table. Dinner had been an unbearably long-winded event, with speeches and toasts as the evening dragged on. After his eventual escape, he'd come up here, spying Impatiens taking their new guest home with him across the beach, Eranthis and Pentas following closely behind.

Lycaste put the telescope on the ledge, where it was rolled lazily by a breeze from the darkening sea. It wasn't that Callistemon was unpleasant, or even impolite—the Plenipotentiary had thanked Lycaste profusely after the meal, apologising for the abrupt manner of his arrival and the imposition of serving so many with such little notice—but Lycaste still didn't like the man. His speech was sometimes hard to follow, large words pouring out of him as if he were being paid by the syllable, and his face was even harder to read than most. Lycaste, of course, found it difficult to trust even the friendliest of newcomers so decided not to pay his doubts any heed. He was tired, overwhelmed by so many gatherings and events, tragedies and dramas. A week of not answering the door to anyone was what he needed, and some proper time to finish his palace in peace.

High Second

Impatiens's garden was smaller than his own, wild and unkempt, littered with Briza's toys. It contained fewer fruit trees, though the plants and bushes that did grow were more than enough to feed everyone who lived there with plenty to spare. He knew of nobody in the Province who went without; starvation, drought and blight simply did not exist—they had few terms for such phenomena save for negative spaces still lingering in their vocabulary, the opposite of what they'd always known. Illness was a more visible extreme, though confined at nearly all times to animals, even the speaking ones—the Cursed People. Sonerila and the birds were no exception, having lost their eldest brother to something too horrible for Lycaste to describe. He'd buried Mertensia during his fourth year at the house, unable to give them any real reason for the bird's death but simple bad luck and a poor constitution.

Lycaste trod carefully through the garden to Impatiens's side. He had to look where he walked for Briza's multicoloured toys hid submerged everywhere in the wild grass, adding even more colour to the garden. Small wooden men and animals, brightly painted or dyed, peeped from the foliage like dwarfish explorers pushing through a dense jungle. Lying in wait for them were mythical monsters made from metal and plastic, though the plastic creatures were rare and usually gathered up at the end of each day. Very few trees produced the stuff; they could be cultivated, of course, but there seemed little point unless it was to be traded. More common were the metals that gave some forests further inland a shimmer that could be seen from Elcholtzia's top room. The tin, iron and silver that fell from those trees was almost worthless, there being no industry in the region to require it, and littered the jungle floor until collected by anyone who did not yet possess a complete set of cutlery. The metal, alchemically seeded by long-ago peoples to multiply in the rock, was initially soft enough to mould and carve in a person's hand, with only a dip in salt water necessary to begin the hardening process. Every few miles along the coastline towards Mersin there glinted heaped stalagmites of silver as tall as the caves, where sporadic growths of metal trees had met the sea and shed their fruit over the years to harden at the water's edge.

"Is he ready?" asked Lycaste, glancing over Impatiens's shoulder at the house, a similarly sprawling dome punctured by three eggshell-blue towers vaguely similar in design to his own. He was already beginning to wish he hadn't agreed to come along. He could see no reason why he was even needed at all—Impatiens and Eranthis knew more about the Province and were on much better terms with many of the people living in it than he was. He watched Callistemon appear from the middle tower, his body coloured the same jaundiced yellow, striding quickly down the gentle hummock to meet them.

"It appears so," said Impatiens, waving. He was silent for a moment. "You see that shade of yellow? That's his own. I told him he could make himself comfortable at breakfast and dispense with colours—but he never had any on."

Lycaste didn't know which he found harder to believe, that the people of the Second were all such a ghastly colour or that the Plenipotentiary had arrived naked at his house.

"Rather grand of him, to decide not to wear a colour, don't you think?"

"Perhaps they don't bother with it," said Impatiens. "I was too embarrassed to ask."

"I wonder what other strange things he does?"

"I do remember he was *very* reluctant for me to carry his bag up to his room for him," Impatiens replied. "Gracious to a fault—wouldn't let me lift a finger."

It was still early in the second Quarter as they set off up the hill, fresh before the heat of the encroaching day. Only Eranthis accompanied the three men, promising that Pentas would join them later in the evening when the worst of the heat wore off.

"She doesn't cope well in these temperatures?" asked Callistemon as they reached the top of the first rise, wiping sweat from his forehead with a dainty monogrammed napkin. "I sympathise."

"It's easy to burn out here at midday," said Eranthis, who had coloured herself a bright gold, presumably for the occasion. "You should wear a colour, something dark."

He looked at her. "It is a shame you cover yours—it's a beautiful blend."

Eranthis smiled and returned her attention to the grass, walking a while longer without saying anything.

"Perhaps I shall pay you another visit soon, Lycaste," Callistemon said, turning to him.

Lycaste, who had been thinking hard on the possibility that he had just witnessed the two of them flirting, of all things, looked up guiltily.

"Oh? I'm afraid I won't be of much interest."

"Nonsense," said the man as they reached the dirt road at the rise. "You contrive to be quite the most mysterious person I've encountered since I passed through the Fifth."

Lycaste looked at the others in confusion. "Really?"

Callistemon smiled. "Well, besides this Jotroffe fellow." He pointed accusingly at Impatiens. "Who I'm still determined to meet, Impatiens, so don't forget."

They crossed the road, rather needlessly looking both ways, and continued on the narrower path that led north-east towards the thick brown and green haze of the jungle.

"This road will take me to the edge of the Province?" the Plenipotentiary asked, apparently addressing all of them.

"Yes," said Impatiens at his side, "but you can't walk it. There's a donkey train that leaves from here every eight days."

"So you're stuck with me until then?" He grinned, glancing down the road. "So, who are we visiting first, Impatiens?"

"That would be my friend Elcholtzia; he lives at the end of this track. He's the oldest of us in the Tenth."

Callistemon turned and looked back to the view of the sea. "How old would that be?"

Impatiens smiled. "I'm not sure even he can remember. On his last birthday we decided he was one hundred and eighty-nine, but the preservation of his vanity might figure in that somewhere."

Callistemon shrugged. "Not so old—in the Sixth I met a lady of two hundred and fifty who was about to wed for the third time. Her groom was only ninety-four. Can you imagine it?"

Lycaste wondered again at Callistemon's own age as the other two made appreciative noises at his side, but thought his standing with the man still too fragile to ask. He took his chance to look at the Plenipotentiary more frequently, snatching glances as they walked, and guessed that their visitor might only be in his early thirties, if that.

People grew slowly, mentally as well as physically—twenty years could pass without noticeable change—but there were signs. Callistemon bore the depth of line beneath his eyes to suggest he was approaching his first century, but was betrayed by a braying, immature laugh and a set of twelve notably short fingers. Since one's fingers stopped growing at around fifty-five, Lycaste could only assume the man was younger than him. His own hands still ached some mornings after a night of stretching, knitting bones, and he'd be glad in a year or two to see the end of it.

He looked up from his fingers to see that they were passing the borders of Elcholtzia's plantation. The western garden gate and the roof of his house were just visible above some tall sunflowers that nodded in the coastal breeze. At the land's northern edge, the deep, dry jungle began, aromatic in the growing heat.

"It's an odd house, I must say," commented the Plenipotentiary, taking in the garden. "Does he live alone?"

"Yes. Well, there was another, but he left."

Callistemon twisted to look at Impatiens, intrigued. "Another *man*?"

"That's right."

The Plenipotentiary smiled and shook his head, as if bemused. "I see."

They discovered Elcholtzia among his flowers at the eastern gate of the walled garden. The old man was spreading compost with a heavy-looking iron garden fork, singing softly to himself. Impatiens went to him, taking the fork just as it looked as if Elcholtzia would lose his balance under the weight of the compost on the end of it, and pointed over to the visiting Plenipotentiary. Callistemon waved, standing with Lycaste and Eranthis at the edge of the garden, examining the bizarre house behind rather than the old man.

"Good morning," said Callistemon, noticing just as they all did the clear contempt in the old man's eyes. The Plenipotentiary paused.

Elcholtzia met Lycaste's gaze, something in his expression deeper and darker than anything Lycaste had noticed in the man before. He turned his head to one side and spat. Lycaste recoiled inwardly, astonished and a little frightened at such rudeness. Callistemon looked on in wonder, perhaps never having been treated in such a manner.

Without a word, Elcholtzia planted the fork in the ground and turned back to the house, slamming the gate behind him.

Impatiens and Eranthis exchanged uncertain glances.

"Ez?" Impatiens called after him, but the old man had already disappeared inside.

Lycaste looked to Callistemon, who was staring with perplexed amusement at the garden fork still wobbling in the earth, his mouth slack. Lycaste saw that the insides of his lips were paler in colour. His skin flushed a darker shade of yellow, mixing to blend across his features quickly. He muttered something glottal under his breath. It sounded a little like High Second to Lycaste, who'd been forced to learn snippets of the fantastically difficult speech, the elaborate cousin of the First's ruling language, as a boy.

"Well then," Callistemon stammered, composing himself and nodding to Impatiens. "On to the next one I suppose. I think I'd like to take the aspect from the top of the hill, perhaps look at the coastline." He turned to Eranthis, still at his side. "Shall we?"

Impatiens glanced at the others, unable to hide his dismay. "As you wish, Plenipotentiary. This way."

They followed Impatiens back up the hill. Lycaste glanced back at the house, trying to work out what he'd just witnessed, the fear slowly returning.

Battleship

Corphuso's skin smelled of the rubber from his suit, a fine powder still coating the minuscule hairs on his arms and torso. When the first trickles of water began to fall he moved forward, turning his face down against the light, avoiding the gaze of the other Prism in the vast chamber.

Someone stepped close to him as he rubbed the metallic-smelling water over his forearms and beneath his armpits. He looked up, backing quickly out of the stream to make way for a bloated Wulm, obviously newly arrived. It was engaged in removing the sodden material beneath its cuirass, popping buttons and dumping the pile on the iron floor. It turned its white face up to the water-stream and let it slap and patter across its closed eyes. Corphuso watched it for a moment more, noticing how the water ran down one of its dangling, rabbity ears in thin red runnels, bloody from a seeping wound.

Corphuso turned and looked back at the Lacaille guards sitting around the edges of the chamber. They were vague and ghostly pale in the light that fell past the hanging pipes far above, uninterested in the bathing prisoners. As Corphuso's gaze took in the dark funnel ceiling, he understood that he and the other captives were washing in the battleship's coolant reservoir; the water that channelled through the rusted and ancient pipes would certainly be irradiated and likely wriggling with worms. He spat, wiping at his mouth with the back of his hand, and glanced back into the huge space at the collection of Prism species that milled and splashed, all apparently docile for the chance of a wash. They were mercenaries from any number of Great Companies, soldiers, scouts, pilots, smiths; hired or press-ganged to fight a war in the atmosphere of a tiny moon that meant little to anyone—a black pebble on a mossy, forgotten beach. He cupped his elbows, the hairs on his arms rising as a breeze filtered down from the ceiling and some other part of the battleship, studying the protruding vertebrae and ribs of the Prism as they washed. Shadows drooped beneath the bones that stuck out of their bluish-white skin. They would be hungry, far hungrier than he was, and would need to be fed soon after their shower if the guards wanted to avoid any trouble. His eyes scanned the crowd, looking for any notably unpleasant breeds, but all looked amenable or groggy, most technically allied to the Vulgar kingdom of Filgurbirund and therefore on Corphuso's side.

"Vulgar?" a thick voice said at his side, in Corphuso's own tongue.

He turned, his heart leaping. An especially sallow creature of fairly indeterminate race had sidled up to him while he was watching the showering Prism.

"You new here," the Prism creature said. As Corphuso stared, he came to the conclusion that the thing speaking to him was a Ringum: a cross-breed.

"Yes?" he asked, moving a hand hesitantly to cover himself.

The Ringum coughed, its wasted stomach muscles contracting violently. "Vittles?"

Corphuso shook his head, indicating his nakedness. "Nothing. No food."

The Ringum's large nostrils flared as it shuffled closer to sniff at Corphuso's body. Apparently convinced, it reached out a clawed finger to touch him. Corphuso flinched, pushing the creature's cold, four-fingered hand away.

"No food, I said." His eyes went to the nearest guards across the haze of the chamber, but they were busy arguing with a Zelioceti prisoner.

"Where you come from?" the Ringum asked, its wide eyes searching Corphuso's face. The breath drifting from between its needle-teeth was particularly foul, momentarily masking the reek of bathing Prism and sewage.

"I have nothing," Corphuso reiterated, pushing past it to collect his underclothes, stacked next to the wall. He reached the place where he thought he'd left them and scanned the rusted floor. All around were piled holed and stinking undergarments, mostly wet from the water that was now slopping up to the base of the huge iron doors. Corphuso hadn't thought anyone would notice the value of his clothes, but apparently someone had. He looked up from the floor. A scabbed Vulgar youth, the pinkness of his skin betraying him as a subject of the lawless moon of Stole-Havish, was leaning casually near the doors, Corphuso's expensive underclothes tight on his bony hips. The Vulgar looked at Corphuso expressionlessly, lowering his gaze as a guard shuffled past.

Corphuso shook his head, muttering under his breath and sifting a toe through the piles of damp clothes on the floor. He was looking for something not so conspicuously lice-ridden that might fit him when the Lacaille guards nearest to the doors clapped their hands and heaved them open. Corphuso watched the Vulgar that had stolen his underpants flinch and scuttle away, shielding his eyes from the light of the opening doors. Chained prisoners, their long shadows preceding them, sloshed into the huge chamber dragging vats behind them. At the sight of the containers the washing Prism squealed and yammered, hobbling to the chained cooks and pushing them aside. Two Lacaille guards shoved their way through and tipped the vats, releasing a clotted wave of sickly leftovers that mixed with the water on the floor.

The Prism screamed, wrestling and biting each other for the first of the food. Corphuso saw the fat Wulm burying itself in the mound of sludge, angrily batting away smaller members of its own race that strayed too near. Corphuso crept closer, avoiding a couple of snarling Quetterel that were slipping and sliding as they fought over some juicy chunk of spinal column. The Wulm glanced up at him briefly, baring its yellow teeth, and Corphuso decided to wait until the larger prisoners had eaten their fill.

After some time, the frenzy slowed, with most of the prisoners taking what handfuls they could from the increasingly watery feast and retreating to the edges of the chamber. Corphuso approached the mess, reflecting as he glanced inside the first of the tipped vats that he might stand a chance of getting some food still uncontaminated by the water from the ceiling. He reached in and scooped up a palmful of sludge, sniffing it. Offal, probably, from the battleship's galleys. Lacaille prisoners were well treated in this respect. Other wars across the Investiture were not so kind to their captives.

Corphuso turned too late. The Ringum that had tried to talk to him earlier had crept close, its claws rasping on the metal sides of the vat. The creature hissed, tearing the food from his hand and spilling most of it on the wet floor. Corphuso clutched at his wrist as the Ringum dived for the offal, shovelling what it could into its mouth before scampering away.

"How does it feel to be at the bottom here, Architect?"

He turned. Ghaldezuel had come for him, as Corphuso had known he would.

"I suppose you'd like something better?" the Lacaille continued, stepping up to the vat and peering inside. Corphuso nodded, noticing most of the sated Prism in the chamber watching them.

Ghaldezuel straightened and turned to look coldly at his staring captives, some no doubt considering rushing him. Corphuso knew such a mistake might be the last they made. The Lacaille appeared to single out one of the prisoners, levelling a pale finger at it across the chamber. The Quetterel he was pointing at cowered and shuffled back, lost in the gloom.

"Where is my machine?" Corphuso asked, wiping some of the gruel from his torso.

Ghaldezuel swivelled back to him. "It's safe." He moved towards the doors, beckoning Corphuso to follow. "Come, we have a journey ahead of us."

Corphuso backed away, his gaze trained on the Prism watching them. Among them, the Ringum's pale eyes considered him. "Where?" he asked Ghaldezuel, still too afraid to take his eyes off them.

"The Amaranthine Firmament," Ghaldezuel said, taking in his prisoner's offal-splashed chest. "I advise you clean yourself up."

Beach

Of the thousands of pebbles on the beach, Callistemon appeared to find all the flattest ones.

Lycaste had been skimming stones since before the young man was born, he was certain, but somehow his adversary was winning. He crunched across the shore towards the Plenipotentiary, who was teaching Briza to skim, scanning the littered pebbles on his way for anything that might sway the game. Lycaste picked a few up and took a sidelong glance at Callistemon, who still had twenty out of his twenty-five, all scoring three bounces or more. Lycaste aimed carefully, knowing the man was watching his technique, and sent a stone plunging into a green wave.

Callistemon pointed at where the pebble had sunk, whispering something to Briza, and looked up at Lycaste. "Lycaste, watch how I do it next time."

Lycaste dropped his remaining stones and stormed off towards the women, who were shading themselves under a twisted tree that had taken root in the smaller bluish pebbles at the beach's edge. Of all Callistemon had told them of the Glorious, Civilised Second, the most pertinent detail appeared to be that it was nowhere near a sea of any description. Where had he got so much practice? Lycaste refused to give any thought to the notion that the Plenipotentiary might simply be naturally talented as he sat down heavily on the stones. He'd forgotten his linen towel.

Callistemon stayed standing at the water's edge, practising with the boy; Briza watched him throw, copying the Plenipotentiary's movements and quickly looking to see where the man's stone fell. They all saw a pebble strike the water at an angle, bouncing across the low tide three or four times. The boy jumped up and down on the rocks in delight.

"Briza likes him," said Eranthis to her sister.

"He's showing off," mumbled Lycaste.

Pentas sighed. "He's teaching him."

Eranthis smiled and waved as the two looked back. "And *so* good with children; such a rare quality in young men these days."

Lycaste looked up from his attempts to make a comfortable groove in the pebbles. "Aren't I good with him?"

"Sometimes, when you're not telling him off for touching your dolls."

"And you're not young like Callistemon," added Pentas.

"I'm only a few years older. We don't even know how old he is, anyway."

"He's twenty-six," Eranthis said. "He told me the other day."

They both looked at her. She smiled a secretive smile.

Lycaste turned his attention back to the Plenipotentiary and the boy. All of them were growing fond of the man, even if Lycaste had trouble stomaching it. He was interesting and new, and even Lycaste noticed himself listening carefully to whatever Callistemon said when they all sat down to increasingly grand suppers together.

The previous evening, their visitor had told them each their flower—the Latish genus after which they were named. Lycaste already knew his was an orchid, his smaller name being Cruenta, but had no idea what the species looked like. Callistemon described the dapper yellow plant and its cinnamon scent for him, explaining that *Lycaste cruenta* were cultivated in the First, along with every other seed in the world. Each one of the people present, he said, had their namesake growing in the great gardens there. Callistemon explained how, through people's names, a careful observer might understand much about the state of the world and its inhabitants, their movements and history. Particular names were tied firmly to their own geography until a strong enough wind blew, swirling them to coalesce here and there across new Provinces and take root like wild seeds, only to be cast again into the wind. He returned often to the idea that Eranthis and Pentas shared a common link with the Second, the First's noble cousin Province, going so far as to formally invite the two sisters to visit him at his family home sometime in the future, at the pleasure of their guardians back in the Seventh, of course, and handing them both a tasselled slip of paper—their formal introduction passports to the Second—should they wish to join him on his return journey. Impatiens and Lycaste had exchanged worried glances as the girls compared the papers excitedly.

The Plenipotentiary had visited every estate in the Tenth during the eight days since his arrival, apparently satisfied with his findings. Callistemon's record books came with him to most events, since he would often remember to ask something when a topic was brought up in conversation, jotting down notes as people explained things to him. His enquiries encompassed a range of subjects: lineage and locations of family members; personal dimensions, weight and diet (for which he relied on a complex table of variables in order to calculate his answers— the units of the Tenth differed greatly from those closer to the centre); mastery of complex grammar and a spectrum of aptitude tests, which were supplied on a set of reprintable metal sheets. His meagre luggage, stowed somewhere in Impatiens's house, might contain a personal diary or something similar, but the work he showed them was nearly always numerical tables or spreadsheets. Callistemon's last wish—to meet Jotroffe—remained unfulfilled, however. Impatiens had asked at all the hilltop houses and even the port with no success, and there was no pattern to the strange man's wanderings that anyone could make out.

The previous night, Lycaste had taken out his maps of the greater continent, bringing them to his rooms so that none of the helpers would see. Old and careworn and untrustworthy, their rubbed engravings tentatively charted the geometric edges of each Province as they whirled like a spiral stair from the capital, somewhere—though the map did not extend that far—high above the crown of the great Black Sea. Lycaste traced the distance with outstretched fingers, dabbing his prints on the polished bronze plates, trying to see for himself the journey Callistemon would have made eastwards across the continent towards the Nostrum Sea and the Tenth Province. A journey of at least eleven hundred miles. So very far, just to count them.

Callistemon wandered up to them with Briza at his side. "I didn't see Impatiens last night. Did he stay with the old man?"

"Yes," said Eranthis. "Elcholtzia gets lonely up there."

"I can imagine." He kicked at some pebbles with a foot, Briza copying, while Lycaste and the women looked up at him. "Are they a pair?" he asked eventually.

"A pair?"

"A *couple*."

Lycaste had expected the question would come soon enough. They'd all been subjected to the most intimate of enquiries in the printed tests, and any sections left blank were returned to the culprit—albeit apologetically—to be completed. Impatiens had lied to Callistemon at the time, straying past the margins of the sheet to invent a broken heart, an exceptionally beautiful woman and a fictional island, but the Plenipotentiary must have seen through it.

"Is that not done in the First?" Eranthis asked their guest, disappointment tingeing her voice.

Callistemon played idly with some pastel-blue pebbles he'd picked up, their surfaces swirled with paler tendrils of colour. "*That*? No, that is not done." He laughed, tapping the stones together in his hands, perhaps trying to find the foreign words. They chinked like porcelain.

"Men never fall in love with other men?" asked Pentas.

Callistemon looked almost bashful, sitting down among them. "Of course not."

Lycaste shifted his feet out of the shade and into the sun to make space while Eranthis shook her head, looking at her sister and then back at the Plenipotentiary. "Does it matter whom he loves?"

The man didn't reply at first, his eyes running over Briza at his side. The boy wasn't showing the slightest interest in what was being said, preferring to busy himself with a few ants that had ventured out of the sparse jungle behind them and onto the hot stones. They scurried nimbly towards his outstretched fingers and up his hand, but were shaken off each time before they could reach his elbow. Some of the insects fell onto Pentas's leg and she brushed at them irritably.

"I do not believe," he began at last, "that a man can love another man. It's a perversion, a vice attributed to love so that it may be excused by someone as . . . caring as yourself, Eranthis." He looked at her tenderly. "Do not be taken in by such fraud—you're too clever for that."

"Am I really?" she asked in an apparently carefree tone. "Well, it's nice of you to say."

Lycaste squirmed uncomfortably between them, thinking he might take Pentas for a walk and let them thrash it out. Before he could speak, the Plenipotentiary took Eranthis's hand.

"I'm sorry. Let's not talk of this any more, please?"

Eranthis shrugged, the hot sea breeze fluttering her hair across her face. "Impatiens isn't going to be punished?"

"I've not come here to enforce laws."

"So a law *has* been broken?" asked Pentas worriedly.

He shrugged, apparently embarrassed.

"Tell me, Callistemon," Eranthis asked, rising, "are your views shared by everyone in the First and Second?"

Callistemon rose, too, loosing sand onto Lycaste. He struggled for a few moments with his answer, finally clamping his mouth shut. "Come, let's not talk of this any more," he said at last, pointing at the outcrop of cliffs that bookended the cove. "I'd very much like to see the next bay, if you'd show me."

Eranthis collected her book from the pebbles and looped it around her wrist, clearly unsatisfied. The iron ring with its brace of engraved plates would have been untouchably hot had it not been lying in the shade of the tree. "It's much the same as this one," she said.

"The sand isn't so fine," murmured Lycaste, mildly affronted.

"How *are* the laws maintained?" Eranthis continued as they began to walk on ahead, her voice still tense with irritation. "Plenipotentiaries are the First's representatives, are they not? But they only visit every few years—during the intervening time we're stuck with Mediaries."

Pentas glanced at Eranthis sharply.

Callistemon appeared confused, though clearly relieved that their debate had moved on to a different subject. "You've had some experience petitioning a Plenipotentiary?"

Lycaste looked for Pentas and saw her walking away across the beach to stand in the shallows. Her head was tilted downwards, as if she was fascinated with the tide as it raced away between her toes.

"Yes, well . . ." Eranthis glanced about, finally following Lycaste's stare. Her voice dropped as she watched Pentas. "My sister has. We don't talk of it much."

"And someone came?"

"No, nobody ever came. The man who attacked her was an Intermediary."

"Attacked her?"

All three studied Pentas for a moment as she waded, her back to them.

Lycaste wanted to hold her hand again, as if holding any part of her would make her feel better, but since Callistemon had arrived there was never much of an opportunity. The Plenipotentiary was somehow always in the background, lingering at any gathering or wherever the two women were present. Few things mortified Lycaste more than public affection—conducting any sort of romance while there were people in the room was out of the question—and so he had decided to bide his time, growing ever more frustrated. He told himself that soon, once Callistemon had concluded his affairs, he would have her to himself again.

Excusing himself, he went to Pentas, standing stiffly at her side to watch the retreating waves.

She looked back, sloshing some water against her legs, removing the last of the dry sand still sticking to her calves. "She wants Callistemon to do it," she said quietly. "That's why she's flirting."

"Do what?"

"To go back to the Seventh and find the man."

"The man who . . . ?"

"Yes."

Lycaste looked at her. "Do you think he can?"

"I don't know."

They rejoined Eranthis and the Plenipotentiary as they walked towards the outcrop, Briza running behind. Callistemon reached down and picked the boy up, hoisting him squealing atop his shoulders.

Eranthis pointed at the risen moon beyond the cliffs. "What about up there?"

Callistemon looked, swinging the boy's legs. "The Greenmoon?"

"Do your laws apply up there?"

"Of course not," grumbled Lycaste.

Callistemon's gaze remain fixed on the faint body. "It is as Lycaste says—they do as they wish."

"So perhaps, up in the Greenmoon, all the men love other men," said Eranthis with a smile.

The relief was clear in his chuckle. "I am reliably informed that they do not."

"What kind of men are they, up there?" Pentas wondered aloud. "Are they really trapped, unable to come down?"

"They made that choice a long time ago," Callistemon said.

The four of them waded up to their knees in the jade water that met the crumbling edge of the cliff, skirting the wall of rock that sank steeply into the shallows. They had to tread carefully; the chunks of sunken stone were caked with spiny black urchins, their barbs long enough to breach the water in bristling clusters every few metres. Lycaste gripped tightly to the rock, not worried about the creatures near his sliding feet, his attention instead on the open bay beyond, soft swells bending his view of the sea floor.

"So it's bad to step on these?" called Callistemon as he clung to the rock. The next cove lay unseen across the dazzling water, obscured by the first of the cliffs.

"The spines would go right through your toe," said Eranthis, treading cautiously.

Callistemon lifted his foot clear of the water. "I'll swim, I think." He climbed up on the steep ledge to make his dive, checking carefully that his legs were clear of the black needles before looking down at them. "Am I swimming by myself?"

"I suppose it's only a few feet." Eranthis leaned away from the rock face to see Lycaste and Pentas. "What do you think?"

"You must be joking," Lycaste muttered, slipping in the water and quickly checking his feet.

Eranthis edged around the rock to Callistemon's side as he prepared to jump. "What are the people like up there, on the Greenmoon? I suppose they're very different?"

Callistemon stretched his arms out to dive. "A whole different *species*, Eranthis." He jumped, Eranthis diving after him.

Lycaste clung to the rock, watching the water anxiously until they surfaced, laughing and pushing the hair out of their eyes.

He saw Pentas studying them with a strange intensity, unable to think of anything to say to her. She jumped and disappeared beneath the waves, resurfacing and paddling to the others. The three trod water, splashing each other and spitting out mouthfuls as the waves slapped their faces. Lycaste took a big breath as his heart fluttered. The sea beneath them looked very dark and very deep, but he had to follow. He closed his eyes and let go.

The terror hit instantly as he plunged beneath the surface, a cool black mouth closing around his tightly shut eyes. He forced his eyes open and struggled upwards, gasping in the light as his head met air. He looked about, at first thinking he was in the sea on his own, but Callistemon and the girls had only swum a little further out. Lycaste watched them, casting quick glances down into the water. He couldn't do it. The fear was almost immobilising; even the rocks he'd jumped from looked too far away to swim back to. He spluttered and swam towards them, climbing free of the water with a shuddering whimper that he was glad none of them could hear.

After a while, Callistemon swam over, looking up patiently at Lycaste as he sat on the rock ledge waiting for them.

"Scary?"

Lycaste picked at a blister on his foot, pretending he hadn't noticed the man approach.

"You can go home if you want, Lycaste," Callistemon said, bobbing closer and dropping his voice. "I don't think anybody will miss you." The man was rubbing a reddish welt under one nostril that Lycaste didn't think he'd noticed before. Callistemon examined his hand when it came away, looking at some blood on his finger. "Go on," he said, smiling and wiping his nose with the back of his forearm, "run back to your doll's house."

He sat at home and waited. He'd tried reading, but he was a slow reader and needed all his wits about him to begin to concentrate on a passage. He sensed that working on his palace wouldn't make him feel any better, either, and besides he wanted to stay near the door in case Pentas returned. Occasionally his green eyes wandered gloomily over to her large painting, hanging on the kitchen wall above the long wooden dining table. The scene, of Lycaste's orchard, was expressive rather than strictly realistic, and he wasn't sure he liked it as much as her others. The trees were suggested with quick strokes against sweeps of glossy blue and green, their multicoloured fruit jangling vividly against the simple background. Elcholtzia had told him the painting complemented the white room beautifully, and Lycaste was proud to show it off whenever people came by. In the corner of the picture, so subtle that you had to tilt your head so the light caught it just right, was a fingerprint pressed into the paint while it had dried. Her signature.

A new Quarter came and went. Perhaps the next day had arrived already. He scrubbed the ancient bathtub that sat grandly in his cavernous steam-chamber, the gritty stains on its cracked marble surface refusing, as ever, to budge. Such an odious job deserved a drink, and he plucked a few fat berries from his kitchen wall, eating one, then two, then three more. He was halfway through his seventh berry when the bell at the door tinkled and he raced to the window on unsteady feet.

"You were away a long time," he said, closing the door behind her softly.

Pentas turned to him. "Are you drunk? You look flushed."

He pressed a hand to his face self-consciously as she went to sit at the table. Some food was still laid out, though Lycaste hadn't eaten a thing. Now she was here he thought perhaps he could.

She started tipping things onto one plate with the intention of clearing the table. Lycaste went and sat opposite, taking her hand.

"Can't we start again, from the beginning? Tonight?"

Pentas pushed at something sticky with a long knife, eventually separating it from the patterned ceramic. He could see that she thought it was the drink talking and wished he'd spent more time composing what he was going to say. She gave up on the plates and looked at him at last.

"I was hoping you'd be asleep."

"I could never have slept until I'd seen you properly," he said, wondering at the bravado of drunkenness.

She shrugged and looked into the darkness outside. "It would have made things easier."

Lycaste picked up the knife and chiselled at the edges of the caked-on substance non-committally.

"Don't go," he said suddenly. "Draw me. Please."

"*Now*?"

"Now. I was looking at your painting today—it's the most wonderful thing I own." He could hear his own voice slurring, the words taking their time to reach her, like someone attempting to walk on a swaying ship.

"It's late, Lycaste. You'll fall asleep while I'm drawing you."

"I won't, I promise." Lycaste didn't give her time to say any more. From the pantry he fetched square sheets of paper and some sticks of charcoal, placing them on the table and sitting down once more, expectantly.

Pentas looked at them suspiciously, rolling a sooty charcoal twig in her fingers. "Quickly."

"You won't stay the night? With me?"

"I'm tired, Lycaste." She concentrated on smoothing out the old yellow paper. "How shall I do it? Shall I draw you straight on?"

"Yes. I want to look at you."

Lycaste watched her draw. For the first time all day he had her full attention. Each flicker of eye contact as she studied his face should have made him nervous, but the numbing pulse of alcohol allowed him to forget himself. He liked her watching him, experiencing once again what he felt enviously sure was an everyday sensation in those who weren't so shy.

Pentas studied his eyebrows, her charcoal briefly raised from the paper. "You have such beautiful features, Lycaste. Manly, I mean, handsome, but also beautiful."

"I thought you didn't think so," he said softly.

She redrew a line that was already there. "You will always be beautiful."

"To you?"

"To everyone."

"It's just my manner that makes me ugly."

When she didn't answer, he raised his voice, hating the amplification of the slur. "Callistemon says things more sweetly, doesn't he? Does that make him more beautiful?"

"You're not making him feel welcome. You never talk to him."

He sat up a little. "If you'd heard the way he spoke to me today—"

"Well, I didn't," she replied, drawing harder. "He's been nothing but kind to us since he got here."

"He's up to something, Pentas."

"He's not *up to* anything!" Pentas pushed the paper roughly away and wiped the charcoal dust on her thighs. "Here." She threw it across the table at Lycaste. "Your beautiful face."

He glanced down at what Pentas had drawn. His features, bold and intense in crisp black line, had been smudged from ear to mouth with angry fingerprints, like a nasty scar. Lycaste placed the picture gently onto the chair beside him and looked back at her.

"I don't care if you won't make a Prince of the Second feel comfortable," she cried, standing, "but that doesn't mean *we* shouldn't try. You should stick with your dolls—at least they'll always be your friends."

When she had gone, Lycaste took up the page and looked at it again. The charcoal was too dense for his features, making him appear swarthier than he was in life, but it suited him nonetheless. Pentas had used the room's shadows to flatter him, carving out his finest parts for show: the plunging cheekbones, dimpled where they met his mouth; the lightless void that drooped beneath his long, flat nose, dividing his face with an elegant strength. Even his eyes, though almost without brow, were in total shadow. Lycaste liked that, but couldn't quite understand why. He slid the paper back onto the table and sat staring at it for a while, realising that his only hope was to sneak into Impatiens's house and get his hands on one of the few things Callistemon had never been eager to discuss. His luggage.

Light

Sotiris is back at the table, the morning bright and noisy with passing scooters and people. Inside the café a music channel plays something from the charts of the age, long-forgotten except in mad Amaranthines' dreams.

In front of him coffee has been set. Sotiris looks at it uncertainly, the bitter aroma reaching him, and picks up his spoon.

The man has been standing there all along. He grabs the back of Sotiris's chair and pulls it out, the coffee spilling over the table. Sotiris swears, staggering.

"We're going for a walk," Aaron says, watching him stand and reach for the napkins.

"What if I don't want to go for a walk?" Sotiris replies, dabbing at his wet shorts. Nobody in the café appears to have noticed the commotion.

But he has no choice, of course. They are suddenly at the chapel, his feet aching.

Aaron walks up to the edge of the little white wall that looks out over the strait, his nondescript clothes fluttering, and sits down. Sotiris stands and watches, noticing how the man's shadow appears to hesitate before following each movement, copying his actions just a moment too late each time.

"We were discussing my proposal, Sotiris."

He is still looking at the shadow. "What proposal would that be?"

Aaron smiles, beckoning him over to the wall much as Maneker had done. "You would gain much from it, I think."

He sits down hesitantly, keeping his distance. "What could you possibly give me that I don't have already?" He looks around him. "An end to these infernal dreams, perhaps?"

"I can think of one thing," Aaron says, pointing to a long, elegant boat with tall white sails sweeping by below. Iro stands aboard, leaning on a railing. She doesn't notice them as the boat passes, heading out to sea.

Sotiris's eyes follow it until it is a speck in the haze. "Nobody can offer that. Not even you." His voice is tired.

The man's hand reaches out to him before his shadow does. "Do you know what my name means? Why I chose it?"

He looks across at the outstretched hand with vague disdain, trying to remember. "*Light-bringer.*"

Aaron grins.

Sotiris nods, unsmiling. "Is that what you think you are? A bringer of light?"

"That and more, Sotiris."

Reunion

The palace was finished. At least until he decided the figures needed repainting, which they might in a year or two. Lycaste sat back, his chair creaking, savouring the view. He'd added two new wings and a rather romantic spire in the few days since he had seen Pentas, working late into the nights with a new determination. Everything was gaily painted, polished and shining, the fittings fitted and the furniture furnished. Crowds of guests milled in the ballrooms, attending the sort of glittering party Lycaste himself would have hated, drinks in their little hands. He reached in with trembling fingers and corrected a toppled cup and saucer. There.

The plan to locate Callistemon's luggage had evaporated, slowly at first, as he thought more about the problem and the implications of being caught. While he considered it he had worked on the palace, thinking that he would find a solution while he painted and cut and glued. But none had come. The birds, who knew quite well how introspective he could be, kept out of his way, leaving a tray at his door on the nights when he wasn't likely to come down. There had been no visitors aside from Pamianthe, come to see Briza's father with her son in tow. He hadn't gone down to meet her, hearing them leave through a different tower and settling back to work with a sigh of relief.

Some nights he sat in his old bedroom while Drimys still slept, rummaging through his drawers and cupboards or reading old books. Drimys, Lycaste knew, had never really liked him, but still he stayed, smoothing the sheets and listening to the man's slow breaths while he healed. In the mornings he often looked out of the window to see his old friends down on his beach, but could not bring himself to go to them. His house was not a fortress; it was keeping no one out. He was growing paranoid that Callistemon might have been saying things about him behind his back, nasty things that kept anyone from coming to trouble him any more. In some ways it was what he'd always wished for—a long, uninterrupted peace, where his house was his own once more. They would come eventually, and then he could set to work proving the rumours wrong, whatever they might be. He wondered when Callistemon would be leaving. The horrible Plenipotentiary must have other jobs abroad, or his was certainly an easy position to fill.

By the fifth day of solitude he came to the conclusion that the clear head responsible for such ideas was overrated and began to drink, taking bottles and berries to his study while he tinkered with small details on the palace, not caring how clumsy he was becoming. Finishing the palace had left a void in his life that other diversions around the house seemed unable to fill, and so he took to drinking with an abandon he seldom had before, even during his introverted final years living in the top room of his parents' house on Kipris Isle.

He awoke one evening, his left arm bruised from elbow to shoulder, his stomach swollen, head aching dully. The kitchen was scattered with dishes and jugs, some smashed on the floor and swept beneath the table. He could smell the acid whiff of vomit somewhere nearby, mingled with the musk that pervaded the large circular room.

Lycaste lay and stared at the ceiling and the little black specks of flies that had arranged themselves up there. They sometimes settled while investigating his meals and bit him, but he never tried to kill any, comprehending pitifully that they were his only companions. There were seventeen today. Up four from yesterday. He looked at them a while, attempting to discern a pattern in where they squatted. He wondered if some were friends, and if the friends always stayed together. This interested him, and he tried to spot the ones they had turned away, the ones like him. There were none, not a single fly was particularly distant from the others. Maybe they liked each other equally. Maybe they didn't give a shit.

A noise came from down below, in the caverns below the tower. His bedchamber. Was Pamianthe there? He supposed she might be, not wanting to wake him. He started, suddenly wondering if it might be Callistemon rummaging, doing to Lycaste exactly what Lycaste had wanted to do to him.

He turned, sitting up stiffly in his grimy makeshift bed and watching the door to the lower stairs as the sounds increased in volume: a single, regular pounding noise. It came closer, breaths of exertion finding their way through the wooden panels of the oval door. It opened tentatively, shoved by a weak, childlike arm. Drimys stood there, sweating with the exertion, bracing himself against the white wall.

"Lycaste." His voice was thin, pained with the effort of the climb.

Lycaste pulled the grimy blanket around his chest, wondering what to say in return. "Drimys," he began stupidly, taking in the half-formed man. "You're awake."

Drimys hopped to the cluttered table, only one leg able to reach the floor. His right side was barely regrown, nothing but infantile limbs, their fingers and toes tiny lumps not yet equipped with nails. Lycaste could not stop staring, having never seen someone so odd in his entire life. Even old Jotroffe looked relatively normal by comparison.

"What happened here?" the deformed man asked, still perspiring. "What's that smell?"

Lycaste sniffed the air, unused to the company, not sure where to begin. He finally found his manners. "How are you feeling?"

Drimys considered the question. "Fine, I think. How long have I been asleep?"

Lycaste counted in his head. "Sixteen days."

"*Sixteen*. Where is everyone?"

"I'm . . . not sure."

Drimys picked up an empty jar and inspected it hungrily. "Why's that? Could I have something to eat, Lycaste? I think it was hunger that woke me up."

Lycaste went to his bare pantry, not hopeful of finding much. "Pamianthe's here, staying with Impatiens—she's been bringing Briza to see you."

Drimys sat silently for a moment. "I see," he said, looking wary. "I suppose she's started talking about taking him away from me again."

Lycaste closed the cupboard door, arranging what he'd found on a small plate. He slid the modest meal in front of Drimys. "I don't know."

Drimys started pushing food into his mouth with his good hand, nodding. "Can you take me over there when I'm finished?"

He leaned against the dented mirror, his coppery reflection bent into a caricature. The hot water ran down his face from cupped hands and sloshed into the full basin, spattering his feet as it overflowed. Pentas would see the weight he'd gained—he could hardly miss it himself, despite the distortion of the mirror. They were sure to make some comment on his appearance, even if it was worry rather than ridicule. He didn't want to go.

Lycaste studied the blotchy skin around his eyes and flashed some colour across his face in bands. Cuttleyfishes, they did that. What a useless thing to know. He turned from the mirror and regarded the still, dark reflections in his full bath. The water that bubbled up from the unstoppered hole in its base was flecked with gold, drawn from the rock. Now as he looked into the marble depths he could see the golden silt had sunk to form a sparkling bed. He reached in and stirred with an outstretched finger, spinning a glinting vortex around his arm as wisps of rich light skated the interior of the chamber. A drink before he left would prepare him better for the ordeal to come. Looking back into the mirror again he noticed patches of his new beard were still dry and pushed his fingers through the stiff hair until it stuck out like a madman's. A few drinks.

They hadn't talked much on the walk over, Lycaste supporting Drimys as he hopped along the pathway towards Impatiens's house. The deformed man had glanced often at the green sea down below, whatever memories he retained of the day in the boat drawing his eyes back to the water again and again. He broke into a wobbling bounce when he saw the people dining, looking suddenly hideous and pathetic, something from an old foreign tale come to devour the women and children. Lycaste saw he could maintain his balance and let him go, keeping to a deliberately airy stroll, his heart thrashing as he noticed Pentas sitting next to Callistemon. He heard the cries of surprise and delight as they recognised the disfigured man, and wondered where he was going to sit. He saw Pentas turn and search him out, her expression too far away to read. Raw, terrified shyness overwhelmed him, pleading with his higher mind to turn back, to leave and come again another day. Impatiens saw him, shading his eyes with the flat of his hand then returning his gaze at once to Drimys, who had hold of his son in a fevered grip, the boy's mother looking on dispassionately.

"This doesn't mean I've changed my mind," she was saying shrilly to her husband as Lycaste arrived.

Drimys sat, Briza curled in his arm, his face already defeated. "Can I not have him until the end of the year? You could take him when he's ready to start schooling."

Her face set hard as she contemplated his ravaged limbs. "Look at you. I daren't allow myself to think of what could have happened if you'd decided to take him along with you on that boat."

"I'd never have done that."

She laughed meanly. "Oh yes? Well, there's not much point arguing. I've got an Intermediary coming down here in a few days, he'll sort the matter." She eyed Callistemon, sitting silently, watching. "I was planning on asking our Plenipotentiary here if he'd represent my cause."

"Legal issues are not my area of expertise," he said carefully, refilling their cups, "but I can make sure the Intermediary is fair."

Eranthis smiled at Lycaste encouragingly as he sat down beside her, sensitive enough not to draw attention to his arrival. Impatiens nodded at him, perhaps a little coldly, then engaged Pamianthe.

"Business has been slow this summer, Pamian, and I've covered all the work he's missed out on. If it's a financial matter, let me deal with it."

Pamianthe sniffed, thoughtful. "We'll arrange it when the Intermediary arrives."

Lycaste tried to meet Pentas's eye, but it didn't seem possible. He tousled Briza's hair awkwardly and excused himself.

*

He swayed while he pissed, the alcohol reaching him at last, not bothering to aim into the central drain. Most of the waste that left him had evaporated on contact with the warm air anyway; it was only a matter of sweeping the handful of leftover yellow salts into the grate, which he did at last after studying his reflection once more.

Their excited voices echoed into Impatiens's steam-chamber, muffled from the toy-strewn garden. Before he escaped, he'd witnessed the boy leaving his father's lap to sit upon Callistemon's knee. Lycaste didn't know what to think.

The sounds of their voices drifted steadily along the corridor. Some were nothing but whispers, the last snags of which crept breathily into the chamber; perhaps related to him. Lycaste paused at the sink, his hands in the water, leaving them to sit pale crimson under the surface. He could hear them all so clearly outside, he knew that anyone entering the tower would be quite loud. He pulled his hands quickly out of the bowl and stood there, peering through the arch at the quiet blue hallway where driftwood from the storm lay stacked against the wall in a tied bundle. There might never be another chance.

He stepped out into the passageway, thankfully clear of toys. Impatiens's large stride had crushed too many in the past, adding a growing list of obscenities to the boy's vocabulary.

Lycaste knew the rooms they all slept in, leaving two spare options for a guest on the floor above. At the top of the stairs, however, it was easy to spot the chamber Callistemon had claimed. The painted round door was open to reveal a small space containing a large hammock draped with tousled linen. Lycaste walked in, smelling a hint of some exotic foodstuff, spiced and foul. The one window arch opened onto the garden, and he ducked to make sure anyone glancing up wouldn't see him there, almost hitting his head on the handle of a tall wooden cupboard. The room looked empty enough, the sheets on the hammock thrown back casually, the small table bare. He began to think perhaps the man had brought no extra luggage at all.

Something was different. Sweat popped out on his brow; there were voices in the tower. He hadn't heard them for all his concentration. Two people talking softly. They were climbing the steps to his floor.

Lycaste jumped to his feet, knowing in the simple room that his only choice was the cupboard he'd almost hit his head on. He dashed inside, cramming his arms and legs sideways to fit between two widely spaced shelves and scrabbling to close the door, which had no inside handle. Cursing it under his breath, Lycaste reached a finger around the edge, swinging it closed just as the two voices arrived at the landing.

Darkness pocked with warm light. He held his breath.

"I knew he'd come back."

"Do you think he's still in love with you?" asked the second voice, Callistemon's.

"I expect so. What? Don't laugh, you'll see."

"Such modesty."

"Close the door."

Sounds in the room, like the gentle slop of a foot on wet sand. He had a slip of daylight to peer through, seeing nothing but blank wall. By her third word he'd known it was Pentas, not her sister, in the chamber. The hammock creaked as they sat down together, Callistemon's muffled pleasure exorcising any last slip of doubt as to what they might be doing. She giggled, sucking her lips away.

Steadying his palm against the splintered wooden side of the closet, Lycaste tried to see through the crack in the door. He felt sick, winded, trapped. A moist click of teeth connecting as she kissed him back, and, breaking from the suction, the hint of a breath, a longing pant. The worst sound of them all. He scraped his fingers delicately along the rough fissures in the wood, his ears trained to them, unable to stop hearing. He knew what hell was supposed to be, Pentas had explained the concept to him herself along with her theories on spirits; but that wasn't quite right. Hell was this.

Callistemon's voice, close in a whisper. "We ought to get back."

"All right. Just for a little while, I hope."

"Just for a little while."

"I think I'll wait—I'd rather not see him."

Lycaste squeezed his eyes shut.

"Here?"

"No, come up to my room when he's gone."

"What if he asks?"

"Why do you care so much all of a sudden? Make something up."

*

Lycaste sat on the hammock, looking at the cupboard he'd been in, only a few feet away. Inside he'd found a travelling case, nestled up behind where he'd been sitting. It lay now in his lap, hardly noticed.

Leaving quietly from the far side of the house, he walked quickly through a patch of wild sunflowers still bent from the storm and headed for the borders of the forest, the luggage clutched under his arm. He could barely think, seeing only what was in front of him as he sprinted through the deepening foliage and into the trees. Darkness fell swiftly, the twilight augmented in the shadowy world, and Lycaste knew his only real option was Elcholtzia. Bright flowers, soft spots of colour in the gloom, became his distance markers, the dark blue light a negative space in the wilderness.

It was not long before the chattering began around him. The whisperers were excited, he could hear them yammering, shouting, perhaps goading him. Quick galloping motion on either side, brighter forms in the woods strobing through the trees. At the junction between two angled black trunks, he thought he saw something, a small person, duck behind a tree, but it was gone when he turned back to look. Fear won outright and he ran faster, one arm thrust before him to shield his eyes while the other clutched the case. A clearing ahead allowed him to see where the palm trees blocked his path, and he wove through them and into its open space, stopping hopelessly in its tangled centre. The sky above was surprisingly bright, still glowing from a sun long gone; the colourless circle of trees teemed with sound, guttural words and exclamations, roiling inhuman laughs and screams.

Lycaste saw with wide eyes that staccato movement again as bodies lighter than the woods circled and peered into the clearing at him, their details indistinct, just colours in the dark. He held the case in front of him with both hands, muscles straining in his shaking arms, ready to swing it at anything that came.

The cries blended into a language woven with familiarity just beyond his understanding. Then with a fright he heard his name. It came from just one place, but soon it was being repeated in the voices to his left as well, then his right. Finally from behind he heard one of them say it, and understood; they weren't repeating at all, they were talking about him. *Lycaste*. It was even pronounced without accent, exactly as he would introduce himself. Perhaps they knew him better, far better, than he had imagined.

Something stood just inside the clearing. It could have been a dangling branch, but he knew it wasn't. Then it moved minutely, cavorting a few paces closer, and he shuddered, crying out wordlessly. The talking ceased. The creature stopped.

"Get away!" he shouted, trying to project his voice.

The voices whispered. The figure scampered closer, stopping every few paces. It became more distinct in the grass, but the darkness was almost complete.

"*Away!*"

It crept forward. He saw eyes illuminated in the starlight.

"Lycaste."

He started at the rasping voice. "Yes?"

The eyes searched his face. Lycaste could see the outline of its body now. Something mammalian, lithe and sinuous.

The creatures began to yell. Lycaste looked around, flinching at the moist touch of their ambassador as it softly took his hand.

The Fall

Lycaste awoke to the booming of the forge in the courtyard, yesterday's events slotting neatly back into his memory in a bitter instant, the empty peace of sleep over for another day. He wished he could sleep more, and struggled with the embroidered sheets, piling them on top of himself to bring the darkness back. But the blind warmth only magnified his memories until he was back in that cupboard again, forced to listen to Pentas's gentle panting, the sucking of their lips. He threw the sheets off and swung his legs out of bed to peer through the window and judge the Quarter. It was late again, almost cool, the sky tinged with colour.

They had taken him quickly along paths that only they knew, he and his guide scampering behind, his hand securely gripped. Once more Lycaste thought he saw the pale, manlike form walking with them, just to one side, disappearing when they reached the gate.

He'd told Elcholtzia everything, his hunched body flushing in waves of colour as he spoke. Lycaste had not expected support but it took little to persuade the old man to help him; he had his reasons, but whatever they were, he would not say.

At the window, he watched the black swallows flitting for a few moments more, then followed the sound down to a semi-submerged pit in the walled courtyard, like a small amphitheatre. Sparks flew and snagged on the early-evening wind as Elcholtzia beat at a chisel held against the case's lock. The tiny engravings glowed in angry orange blotches under the hammer blows, flashes rebounding from their edges, but did not dent.

The tracery on the surface of the lock was a jigsaw of segments, engraved to a standard neither of them could believe was man-made. Countless writhing figures made up a tall and long-limbed tree, its eaves drooping and coiling around a straight trunk to form a composition so complex as to be almost impossible for the eye to follow. Each unique leaf, of which there must have been thousands, looked expertly engraved, even those as small as a stitch of cloth. Snaking through the branches and around each figure was a strip of lettering in High Second, lettering that appeared to be names in a family tree. And, at the top of the tree: *Callistemon Pallidus Berenzargol, SecondPrince.*

The two had pondered the workings of the design the night before but had not been able to move any of the sections individually, either by force or through careful logic. Lycaste had been little help with the latter, his mind muddled and tired.

They had tried tongs and hammers, but the elaborate lock-seal wouldn't budge, its dull metal hardly marking even under the hardest blow, the tiny scrapes and nicks on its surface the only sign that anyone had even attempted to break it.

Lycaste sighed a long, breathy sigh as he entered the courtyard, sitting down on the steps.

"How did you know he wouldn't come after me last night?" he asked Elcholtzia, not looking at the old man.

"I have bars on the doors."

Lycaste was surprised, glancing up at him finally. "Why?"

Elcholtzia patted Lycaste's shoulder, helping him to his feet with a skinny arm. "I've had them as long as I can remember." He dropped the long hammer and stared up at the evening blue. "Anyway, the day's almost gone."

Lycaste watched the last of the swallows, their cries echoing from the walls, then glanced back to Elcholtzia. He looked all wasted sinew in the hot, open bowl, the hollows of his body a brighter red with reflected sweat.

"You'll want something to eat, I suppose?" the old man said.

"I can't eat," he said, returning his gaze to the glowing metal. His face was tight and hot from the forge's glare.

Elcholtzia nodded and sniffed, looking back at the glowing design on the case. "The lock won't open like this."

"No." Lycaste shrugged and picked up the hammer from the ash-soft floor. Elcholtzia stepped back.

He strained to lift the tool, realising at once the other man's wiry strength. The hammer wavered at the top of the swing, and he almost lost his grip before slamming it down on the chisel set in its vice. The blow jarred his wrists and he swore, the cooling red metal indifferent to a force that would certainly have killed a man.

"Have you tried melting it completely? Just throwing it in there?" Lycaste asked, rubbing his arms.

"While you were asleep. But I took it out again because I was worried about the contents."

Lycaste spun the hammer on the ground, head down, making soft, blown circles in the ash. He didn't like being awake. The state demanded too much anger and sadness from him. He had a mind to return to bed, despite the still unanswered questions.

"Elcholtzia?"

"Hmm?"

Lycaste released the hammer, the wooden handle bouncing on the ground, and sat again. He remembered how Elcholtzia had greeted the creatures like old friends as their long, disjointed hands stretched into the hall for their reward, illuminated only to the elbow, afraid of the light. "I saw someone, among the whisperers last night."

"Oh yes?"

"A man—or something that looked like one."

Elcholtzia licked his lips thoughtfully. "There are a few who stop and live among them, from time to time."

"*Live* with them?" Lycaste asked. "How?"

"The whisperers—" The old man shrugged, as if thinking of staying silent, before resuming. "The whisperers are our cousins, not too dissimilar from us. They welcome pilgrims from strange places, just as those in the eastern Menyanthes welcomed me when I was a boy."

Lycaste studied him, on the verge of asking more, when Elcholtzia straightened, breathing in deeply.

"If we can't get this thing open," he said with a sigh, "you'll have to return it."

Lycaste flinched as if struck. "Go back? I can't do that! I stole from him, from a Plenipotentiary! I can't go back there."

"He'll know before too long, Lycaste."

"I *stole*." He shook his head emphatically and glared at the embers. "I'm a thief now."

"It was brave thing to do."

Lycaste looked up sharply. "Brave? Why? What's going to happen to me?"

Thievery. So revolting an act that parents did not even discuss it with their children. Lycaste dropped his head into his hands.

Elcholtzia sat down beside him without a word.

"I can't go back there, Elcholtzia," he whispered between his steepled fingers. "Please don't make me go back."

The man took a long time in answering. "If he finds out—"

Lycaste nodded, peeping between thumb and forefinger at Elcholtzia. "What happens when he finds out?"

"I don't know."

He pushed his face between his fingers again, stretching the lattice across his brow. His heart pounded thickly and comfortingly inside him. It was safe in there, in its dark, sticky little hole. Lycaste wished he could swap places with it—just for a while—and hide somewhere in the deep recesses of himself, blind and deaf to everything that happened outside.

"Why wouldn't you speak to him? That day when we came to see you?" He did not look up, hearing Elcholtzia's breath beside him.

"That was not my first encounter with a Plenipotentiary," the old man said. "A representative of the Second came to us many years ago. His name was Solenostemon. Perhaps some relation."

"*Solenostemon*," Lycaste repeated, tasting the exotic name. "Why was he here, in the Tenth?"

"For the same reason—to count us." The man paused, thinking. "I shall never forget the day he arrived for as long as I live. That was when my parents were still alive."

Lycaste nodded absently, his head still cradled in his hands. Every few moments the thought of being wanted for thievery returned to him, sending shivers across his skin.

"All the Province came to see this strange yellow man," Elcholtzia continued. "In those days, there were few of us, living close together in the northern Menyanthes." He hesitated, as if deciding where to begin. "The party lasted days. I thought it would never end. He promised to teach me many things, this man Solenostemon—we went for walks together, played on the beaches. All the while, he grew closer to my mother, angering my father."

Lycaste looked up at the man briefly.

Elcholtzia shrugged. "Then one day my father disappeared. We didn't see him again." He glanced into the garden. "To this day—sometimes when I'm out walking—I feel like I can hear him calling my name, deep in the forest."

Lycaste studied Elcholtzia sadly for a moment, suddenly ashamed to have ever been afraid of him.

"Solenostemon grew steadily bored of our adventures together after that and I saw less of him. When he did take me out, it was usually for the purposes of instruction—on the ways of the wider world, the hierarchy of the Provinces and our lowly place in it down here in the Tenth. Sometimes he appeared disgusted with me; at other times he looked at me almost lovingly. He left for long periods, always neglecting to say goodbye, but never failed to return.

"But the last time he came back he was visibly unwell," Elcholtzia said, standing and beginning to tidy up the iron implements, stacking them neatly in the corner of the forge. "He said it was something he ate, but even then I didn't believe him."

He hefted the fallen hammer and leaned it against the wall, tipping a pail of water over the smouldering stones. "My mother and I looked after him during his final days, tending to him in what had once been my parents' bed. Sometimes he babbled, incoherent, sometimes he was cruelly lucid, his eyes hateful. He died in agony not long after, and I suppose I was glad of it."

Lycaste put his head back into his hands.

"When my mother gave birth to his son later that year, the baby boy was orange—bright as a hen's yolk." Elcholtzia sat down again beside Lycaste. "But he had inherited the same strange illness, a malaise of pain and these . . . strange, bloody sores. I comforted him as best I could, but it was no use. He did not last long." The old man paused, examining his hands. "My mother took no interest in the boy while he lived—she had become confined to her chambers herself, morose and feverish with shame, so I named the boy after my father, Lathyrus, and took him away."

"Where did you go?"

"I came here, to the coast. And it was here that I buried him."

Lycaste kept his hands over his eyes. "I never had any brothers or sisters." He listened to the drumming of his heart, thinking on all the pain Elcholtzia must have felt during his life.

A change in the rhythm forced him to open his eyes. It wasn't just his heart he'd been listening to. "What's that?"

It was knocking, at the courtyard door. Elcholtzia strained his neck around.

"Don't!" whispered Lycaste harshly, gripping him by the wrist.

"I shall have to." Elcholtzia frowned and pulled his wrist free. "*Stop that*. The door isn't locked."

"We can climb the wall!"

"*You* might be able to. Just wait here." Elcholtzia disappeared up the steps of the forge.

Lycaste looked across to the garden wall where it joined the house. It must have been the height of two men, but secured to it was a wooden flower trellis that might just take his weight.

"Lycaste!"

He turned. Impatiens was standing, arms crossed, watching him. He came over to where Lycaste was sitting, Elcholtzia following behind. "Am I beyond understanding you, even after all these years?" He noticed Callistemon's case sitting at Lycaste's feet, his eyes widening. "Is that—? What have you done?"

Lycaste looked to Elcholtzia, then back at Impatiens. "Does Callistemon know I'm here?"

"I shouldn't think so. What's going on?"

He picked up the case and handed it over. "I stole it, Impatiens. I brought it here. Elcholtzia had nothing to do with it."

Elcholtzia grabbed the bag. "Enough of that."

Impatiens studied the satchel in Elcholtzia's hands, taking the information in. He lowered his voice. "Why?" he asked. "Why now?"

"What do you mean?"

"If you were so suspicious, why wait all this time?"

"It was the first chance I had," Lycaste said.

Impatiens cleared his throat and studied the case some more. "I suppose it won't open?"

Elcholtzia shook his head.

"You've tried everything?" Impatiens asked, taking it from Elcholtzia.

"We're short on time—someone has to return it before he notices it's gone," the old man said.

"I'll go," muttered Lycaste as he looked at Elcholtzia, without leaving space for objections.

Someone was up there in the darkness. He hoped and dreaded that it might really be her waiting for him, knowing that he had to find out.

Passing his orchard, he'd seen the light in his tower, the beacon that had drawn him to her before. Lycaste took out a long knife from a drawer, resting it carefully on the table beside the Plenipotentiary's travel case as he searched his darkened kitchen. He finished packing a small bag and took the knife, pointing it ahead of him up the stairs as he went, the silence thickening in reaction to his own withheld breath. The unsteady light was coming from the study, where his model palace now took up almost the entire chamber. As he came closer, he realised the light was unsteady because it was produced by fire, the shadows flickering across the wall. He quickened his step.

Lycaste pushed the door fully open with the tip of the knife, noticing the sharp smell of burning plastic just as he saw the interior of his palace. Three of the figures were alight, their bodies bubbling and running beneath little plumes of black smoke. He ran to the model, searching for a rag or anything that would smother the flames in the boxes under the huge table that held the palace up.

Something hit him hard on the nape of his neck. Lycaste fell forwards, head slamming into the table leg, dropping the knife. His feet were pulled from under him.

"This is what happens, Lycaste," said Callistemon's voice behind him. "This is what happens when you insult a man of the Second." He grabbed Lycaste under the armpits and hauled him to the window while he was still stunned. Lycaste opened his eyes and stared at the flames engulfing his precious palace. Now two whole rooms were alight, the fire climbing from surface to surface, floor to floor.

"Look at me!" The slap was hard, jerking Lycaste's attention back to Callistemon. The Plenipotentiary pointed to the flames. "This will burn until you tell me where it is."

"Where what is?" he managed.

The second blow was less of a surprise and hurt more. Lycaste felt his freshly healed nose splinter again, by now familiar with the sensation. He breathed thickly through the blood and tried his hardest not to make a sound.

"It doesn't really matter. You can't open it." Callistemon's face became clearer as Lycaste's eyes adjusted. It looked freckled in the light, like a banana that had begun to turn.

He heaved his arm from the man's grip and struck pathetically, Callistemon intercepting it easily in the dark. The Plenipotentiary clamped his fingers around Lycaste's slender wrist and bent it back. He couldn't stop the whimper as it escaped.

A humourless smile appeared on Callistemon's lips. "Theft *and* striking a representative. There's a revolutionary in you after all."

Lycaste stole a glance at the fire, now tasting the roof of the palace. "All right!" he yelped. "I had it—I can get it back."

Callistemon leaned away to look at him, his face defined suddenly in the light of the fire. "Who has the case now?"

What Lycaste had taken to be dirt before was dried blood, caked and scabbed across the bridge of the man's nose. "I can get it for you," he said, his eyes flicking to the palace again, knowing it might earn him another blow. "Just put the fire out!"

Callistemon wiped his face and inspected his hand while he restrained Lycaste. "I knew there was something unusual about you, Lycaste, the instant I met you." He glanced to the fire, watching it spread to another room. "You have that shyness that afflicts young men who aren't brought up correctly. Maybe something else, too." He smiled as Lycaste struggled, watching in horror as more miniature rooms became engulfed. "A touch of the syndrome, I think?" He took Lycaste's face roughly in his hands and leaned closer, his soft voice and musty breath tickling Lycaste's nose. "If you thought your difficulties would absolve you of responsibility, though, you're wrong."

The fire was growing very hot now, precious years of his life expended only in heating a room. Lycaste watched the roof collapse in a flurry of sparks that threatened his tapestries and looked back at Callistemon, an ember of rage igniting inside him as if it had floated from the burning palace.

He roared in fury, the man's grip tightening in surprise. "You took her from me! The only person I ever loved!"

Callistemon's eyes widened as Lycaste yanked his hand free of the Plenipotentiary's grip and grabbed the man's neck, swinging him around and slamming his head against the wall. He was surprised for a moment at how light his attacker was, realising as he shoved Callistemon into the stone again that the Plenipotentiary was a good deal smaller than him. Callistemon forced himself away from the wall, swinging a fist. The two gripped each other, swaying and staggering back towards the open window. Callistemon raised his fist again, but not before Lycaste shoved him hard to one side.

The man disappeared as if the wall had suddenly dissolved. Lycaste steadied himself, confused for a moment, finally placing his hand on the lintel of the window that he'd forgotten was there to peer out.

Somewhere in the darkness the waves sighed over pebbles. He stared down into the black orchard, searching for any sign of Callistemon. A crackle from the fire brought his attention back to the palace and he ripped a hanging from the wall, staggering across to throw it over the fire. He pulled it off when he was sure the flames had been smothered, inspecting the remains of the palace uselessly in the now dark room.

The silence rushed back in, dampening his adrenalin. Lycaste returned to the window, looking down.

Surely he hadn't. At the bottom of the tower, perhaps thirty feet below, he could just make out Callistemon's prone form. He looked at the black remains of his model once more before carefully descending the stairs.

Lycaste knew that breath was an indicator of life, and bent his head down carefully to Callistemon's mouth when he came upon him, straining to listen. His own heartbeat drowned out anything he might have heard. He needed light, but the tower's hanging lanterns were not responding to the movement of his blood. The bastard must have done something to the kinetics.

Lycaste tried to remember where he might find the pulse—somewhere on the face, he supposed, that was where most of the body's blood went. Lycaste grimaced as his thumbs kneaded the man's motionless flesh, warm and unresponsive.

"You can't hide this." Elcholtzia looked even more drained than usual. "Someone's going to come looking for him, sooner or later."

Lycaste gazed at the flaking wall miserably.

"You're well known here," said Elcholtzia as he gazed out of his window into the pre-dawn blue. "Nobody's going to say anything, but that doesn't mean it'll go away."

Lycaste chanced a look at Elcholtzia, noticing he hadn't said *well liked*. "We could say anything—tell them a shark got him, just like Drimys."

Elcholtzia pursed his lips. "The people who will come for Callistemon will have tools, things to bring the truth out of you and anyone who cares enough about you to perpetuate a lie."

Lycaste cradled his battered head in his hands, distraught. "What would you have me do, then? What would *you* do?"

Elcholtzia rubbed his weathered face but did not answer. Lycaste was about to repeat himself when the old man said: "You haven't many options. Stay and face the consequences—whatever they may be, and however far in the future—or leave. They will never find you if you go. You can start again, you're young."

"But I'd lose everything!" Lycaste cried.

"Everyone loses everything, eventually."

Lycaste pressed his hand to his eyes, the knuckles sore. Believing that any of it was actually happening was still difficult. It was only in the moments between talking that his mind could take stock and understand what had gone on.

"What will they do to me if I stay?"

"Other Plenipotentiaries? I don't know. There was murder in the Seventh, once. There was a trial."

"And I've killed one of their own," he said, almost hoping Elcholtzia would contradict him, but he didn't. There was no choice at all, really, once that part was considered.

"Can I say my farewells?"

"That's not up to me, Lycaste."

He thought about it. To do anything more than disappear would be to put those he cared about at risk. He couldn't go back and say goodbye.

"I'll have to write a note," he admitted wretchedly, glancing out of the window at the ethereal early-morning gloom. "Like a coward."

Leaving Home

Lycaste tried to avoid losing sight of the coast for as long as he could, grimly walking the crescent of hills to the dirt path and its dusty crossroads. Some wild goats and a scrofulous-looking cockerel held court at the crossing, scattering at a trot as he arrived. He watched them make their way down the hill and turned north-east into the dawn forest, cutting into the trees from the ancient path long overgrown.

When at last he turned to look, the green sea was gone. His eyes stung and he hefted his pack, Callistemon's case tied to it and jostling painfully against his hip. Birds and animals in the trees whistled and sang as he recalled what he'd written in his farewell note, going through the tightly packed lines in his head to make sure they'd been right. There was no time to change them now.

Lycaste stared at his dirty feet as they took him away from home; each step harder to turn back from as time crawled on and the forest awoke. What he'd done no longer screamed in his mind, instead appearing to have been absorbed uniformly throughout: a dirty rain cloud under which he travelled. He could return; burn the note, perhaps even burn the body—it was still within his modest powers to change things for the better. His eyes wandered from his feet as they paused, attempting to picture how it could be done, seeing the rising light colouring the topmost branches of the date palms. But Elcholtzia was right. His crime was bound to catch up with him eventually, and by then others would pay the price, too.

He descended into the tangled crevices of the jungle, trying to keep the sun to his right. He knew enough not to get lost, and was glad. To stumble out like a simpleton back where he'd started would be an ignominious end to his already poor excuse for an escape plan.

Perfumes hung dense in the depths of this world, parting warmly around him; bulbous and dripping fruit dangled everywhere like baubles, the thud of their fall beating a quiet rhythm for miles around in the still morning. Pale honey and black syrup drizzled over his forehead in runnels; cream seeped and bleached frayed trunks. Lycaste spied clusters of every food from his garden hanging darkly in the canopies and brushing his shoulders: sowberries and even sowsage, bullberries, kidneypears, droplings and starchfruit. Bunches of wild eggs, green and yellow and blue, popped from flowered shrubs to confuse the birds. Lycaste had heard tales of them hatching, just as spiders were supposed to grow inside old potatoes (or so Impatiens said). The Menyanthes jungle could give him everything he needed. He could reach that rotten log ahead, sit down and live out the rest of his life not four miles from home. But that was no good. It would be like hiding in the garden—he'd be found in days. Beyond the forest were places where he could settle for a while and think properly about things, before perhaps moving on, though actual settlements were probably out of the question for some time.

Lycaste had not been out into the Menyanthes for more than a year, and even then only a handful of times before, but he was fairly sure that it was less than a full day's walk to the borders. The landscape that followed was meadow, he seemed to recall, gouged with valleys that he'd stood to admire but never ventured into. Beyond that, the blue haze. That was where he'd go.

A mosquito whined under his nose and he flinched, suddenly conscious of the possibility of being drained like a wrung washcloth if he didn't get out of the jungle before nightfall. Disturbed ebony dragonflies zipped about him curiously, a few peeling apart from gluey airborne embraces, but he knew those didn't bite. In the highest orchids, scintillating gold beetles lumbered from rubbery petals and split at the wings, hovering out of his path, and something splashed for cover in an unseen pool, the shadow-dappled world alive with things too fast for him to see.

Lycaste looked up at the canopies, brooding on something that had struck him just as he entered the forest. As far as he knew, he was the only Lycaste in the Tenth or the Ninth, but there was no way of knowing how far he'd be hunted. There were fictional names from books and plays that he could of course steal, but he would have to choose one that wasn't well known. He'd already played with the vague logic of going by *Callistemon*, figuring anyone on his trail wouldn't think to enquire after that name—it would be a kind of trophy; he'd won it in a fair fight against a villain who no longer needed it, after all. The whole idea carried a perverse sense of triumph that he wasn't used to, having never won anything before. But no, it would just make things worse. It was a Second name and would attract attention like a forest fire. Even if he was never found out and his life went on and on for as long as he might expect, Lycaste would have to live forever hearing that name and remembering what he'd done. He might as well carry the man's rotting head around with him in a bag.

He wondered if the body had been found yet, if the search for the murderer had begun. Lycaste guessed it was the middle of the day. He needed to be on the other side of the forest soon, if only to put some physical distance between himself and the site of his old life.

The Menyanthes was larger than he remembered, and harder going. The day trips he'd never really enjoyed had taken well-known routes, trackways that he'd lost by now, despite still going in roughly the right direction. A dark, tumbling stream crossed his path as the trees thinned, churning cream as it babbled over a chain of water-smoothed, flesh-coloured boulders. He waded into it up to his waist, watching carefully for any sign of the stringy red eels that he'd heard liked to swim up the rectums of unfortunate travellers. Once safely on the far bank, Lycaste dismissed them as another of Impatiens's exaggerations. What on earth would they be after up there? It was surely another rumour, nothing but Impatiens's own inexhaustible fascination with that area.

His stomach rumbled treacherously as his legs dripped, totally uninterested in Lycaste's circumstances as it demanded a return to normal life, so he found a clearing by the running water to pick food. While he ate, he stared vacantly out between the widely spaced trees on the slope, composing his plans. Ahead a valley split the land like a crease on a rumpled blanket, fading to a blurred line of distant blue. That was where he'd start again, perhaps buy a house, some land, hire servants. How difficult could it be? He already knew what he'd do first, once he was settled in. The model palace wouldn't be too difficult to rebuild; he'd make it larger, more impressive, with gardens and pipes for running water.

Eventually he picked his way down the hill on already toughened soles, following the gurgling water until it cascaded sharply in a staggered tumble of falls to a dark plunge pool. Plenty of food grew around its edges, with wood for a fire and pebbles to shore it. The only downside of making camp there would be the noise of the water, so he trekked a little further, finding a copse of palms that offered some protection and enough silence to hear if anyone was coming.

The pack had been packed swiftly by Elcholtzia while it was still dark, and Lycaste was touched at the startlingly unnecessary things the old man had thought to include. Lycaste began to wish he'd got to know him better, wondering if it was senility or genuine thoughtfulness that had led to the provision of a children's book, a small bottle of spirits and a hammer in the same pocket. In the cloth compartment next to them sat his telescope, hurriedly retrieved from the scene of the crime—Elcholtzia had been pleased to see it was one of the few things Lycaste had thought to take with him. Whether through the blind coincidence of their respective ages or the situations into which they had been forced together, Elcholtzia had in the short space of the last few Quarters become something of a father figure to the younger man. No matter how much he still disliked him, Lycaste wished Elcholtzia were with him now on his journey. Not so much for the company—Lycaste didn't think he'd ever really crave that—but something much baser, often denied him in his childhood. As he'd bidden the man farewell, Lycaste had wanted suddenly to embrace him, to share the unspoken regard he was sure they'd both developed for each other. The fact that such an impulse would have felt absurd only a few days before somehow strengthened it, and he caught himself hoping that one day, when he had atoned in whatever way he could for what he'd done, he would see Elcholtzia again.

By the light of a small fire, lit with a box of phosphorettes, he opened the bag and looked at the book, flicking through its thin metal tablets. Lycaste didn't try to read anything in order, instead dipping in here and there to look at the illustrations, finally gazing into the fire until he was almost sure he was blind, the brilliant panorama of stars washing out when eventually he looked away. There were no voices in the Menyanthes at night, and if he was watched at all he didn't sense it. He thought of his journey with the whisperers; that stunted figure in the woods hadn't looked like a normal man, and it was only then that Lycaste realised he knew who it was: old Jotroffe. Lycaste admired him, even if he was quite the dullest person he had ever met. He remembered Elcholtzia welcoming the whisperers to his home and wondered if the two strange old men were friends.

He tugged another branch onto the fire. So the ghost in the woods was real, and a real man was now a ghost. He peered into the darkness around him, imagining his own judgement already under way in whatever dark pockets of the world the dead might still confer. Perhaps Callistemon was there now, explaining his case to their own Plenipotentiaries, pleading that they punish the wretch who'd taken his life.

In the night he dreamed of nothing, sobbing softly against his arm as he curled into a tight ball, his huge frame that of a little boy again.

The next morning was supposed to be the first day of his new life, but it didn't feel like that. Everything was the same: the light, the trees, the pool of water. And he was still a murderer.

Lycaste sorted dejectedly through the food he would take with him on his next day's walk, breakfasting only on sugary things. The cleansing saliva they'd inherited from generations of presumably having to clean one's own teeth was lightly honeyed, especially strong on waking. Breakfast was sweet, whether you wanted it to be or not.

"Give way to your opponent; thus will you gain the crown of victory," he said aloud as he packed, startling himself. A scrap of verse memorised by heart, hammered into Lycaste's brain by his soliloquizing father during a lesson in classics. Who wrote that? Arkimid? Well, he certainly hadn't learned from it. Lycaste sighed as he packed. He'd thought that boorish man sophisticated once. Now he could see his father for what he was: a simpleton desperate for any scrap of so-called wisdom that came his way.

Ovid, that was the poet. Lycaste remembered another line but didn't speak it aloud, thinking it more significant than anything to do with crowns or victory.

How little is the promise of the child fulfilled in the man.

PART III

Yanenko's Land

"He couldn't simply be detained?"

"Detained? *Imprisoned* might be a better choice of word, Amaranthine."

The Melius Tussilago shifted the oar from one huge spindly hand to the other, dropping it back into the sluggish water. Droplets arced and spattered the long boat like slow-motion footage, easily intercepted and deflected. The water and sky were mingling grey-pink bands, the lower liquid moving only slightly faster than its vapour twin as they drifted to the castle on the shore.

Sotiris felt a kind of shame as he looked at the battlements rising in the grey like a damp watercolour stain. He had not been here in decades, and in truth hadn't considered returning for many more. It was only now Iro was gone that he thought of travelling to her, and the shame returned tenfold.

Yanenko's Land was not a place any fashionable Amaranthine spent time on any more. It had become a backward, overgrown landscape of forgotten things, everything half-off the ground in the weak gravity. The only people who ever came here now were travellers destined for the Old World, as he was.

It began to rain softly and Sotiris raised his face to the slow drops, searching for the crescent through the grey. The enormous man tutted and glanced up, too.

"Can you see the Old World, usually, when it's like this?" he asked the Melius.

Tussilago looked west, his shrewd eyes—big as tea-saucers—narrowing. "The hint of it, low at this time of day, usually. There." He pointed. Sotiris peered through the rain, but the mist looked all the same to him.

"Better vision than mine."

The giant turned back to his oar. "*Paranthropus Melius* does mean *better man*, after all, Amaranthine."

Sotiris searched the cloud, thinking at last that he could see the hint of a curve, a sickle of light. The Earth, his old home.

He returned to the subject. "So he has never been gone this long?"

"Never. I've been a servant since I was sixteen, over two hundred years. Sire Yanenko's never missed a solstice in all that time."

Sotiris had been watching the castle through the man's long legs. He looked up at Tussilago. "You think the same fate awaits me up there, on the Old World."

The Melius shrugged his wide shoulders. The servants here were kept on long leashes; their manners, unlike their perfectly accented Unified, subject to change. Sotiris found it refreshing.

"What Province did your family come from, Tussilago? I have never asked."

"The Eighteenth. Sire Yanenko took me there on one of his visits once, but I had no taste for the place."

"You prefer it here, where you were born?"

"Of course. Families are overrated, I think." As he spoke, his oar tarried a little in the slow water. "I was sorry to hear of your loss, however, Amaranthine."

"Thank you." Sotiris studied the giant. His baleful face, the face of millions of men for thousands of years, was not at all human, at least not as he understood the term. Tussilago's enormous topaz eyes, sunk into wide cheekbones, were almost a foot apart. Dividing the man's face, a long, graceful nose four times the size of Sotiris's own stretched down to a heavy, pointed jaw. It was a face he would have found horrifying were he not so used to dealing every day with his Melius servants on Cancri or their Firmamental counterparts abroad. Sotiris was quite sure what the Melius saw was equally out of place, a weakling child born without facial features or musculature, an infant claiming to be a God. A God who had little more mastery of his own fate than Tussilago did. The Melius were pets, in a sense, no different from the baser animals that had accompanied humankind through prehistory. In this case, however, the pets were his successors, left to colonise what had once been his home like bacteria in the bottom of a poorly washed glass.

He looked into the water, black as peat beneath the churning oar. It might be fashionable in the Firmament to treat these creatures with derision—even to their faces—but Sotiris was abruptly aware out here that they were both just flesh and blood, the long timber boat all that protected them from the gloopy sea and whatever horrors it might hold. He watched the castle draw nearer, its shore fringed with thick, dark oak trees that bent heavily over the waters, knowing he might die at any time, a fall or accident increasing in likelihood with every year he lived. It was called *playing the trip game* by some Amaranthine—the increasing propensity for accidents the longer one lived—the game claiming an ancient life every now and then. It was the way most of them expected to go out, an ignominious crumple to the ground over some forgotten step or stone or wonky chair. Sotiris, who had broken bones recently enough, didn't care to think about it even now, as his sister lay in state somewhere on that crescent above, her eternally youthful body unable to decompose.

Tussilago nodded grimly and glanced at the castle, very close now. His long oar crunched into silt as they reached the shallows, the raindrops pattering harder on the oak boards. "End of the road."

The bulk of the fortress appeared to grow out of the rocks on the shore, dripping brown stalactites of oxide running down its battlements. A path in the grey sand led away from the boat canted on the beach and under an arch into darkness. Sotiris climbed down, accepting his servant's hand and thanking him. Tussilago nodded, easily lifting his master down and taking a large lunch from a hamper at the stern. "I'll see you when you're back, then. Good luck, Amaranthine. And if you were thinking of visiting the Eighteenth, don't bother. Fuckin' awful place."

Sotiris laughed for the first time in many days. "All right. See you."

He strode under the arch, slow rain collecting on the stalactites and dripping down his neck. He wished he were clothed in thicker things. Sotiris looked up to the grim, rain-slick buttresses, still unsure whether he might have been followed from Gliese.

The muffled din of animals usually disturbed his thoughts at this point, but today there was nothing but the rustling of rain. Yanenko had taken his pets, too, apparently, or grown tired of them and thrown them to his servants to feast on. Sotiris came to the huge Melius-built door, barnacled with green scabs of copper, and knocked politely on its flaking crust before letting himself in.

The blackness inside startled him, his hands going for the wall at once, expecting to hear Maneker's familiar nasal whispering in his ear, discovered at last. They touched cool granite, fingernails scraping along until they found a cage and opened the lock. He spoke the words, the incantation that woke the light, and saw a tiny orange spark kindling inside the hanging metal box. It floated, flickering, out through the cage door and hovered over his head, dimming at his command. Sotiris took in the bare, almost monastic cloakroom, remembering which of the three doors he'd last gone through fifty-one years before and taking it. The cubic chambers became no larger as he passed through them, retaining the look of any number of storage cupboards that might litter an unromantic age such as this. Their shadowy recesses, briefly illuminated by his passing, were packed with artefacts and trinkets from donated collections and Prism conquests, heaped and piled and wedged into corners. As an old arachnophobe, such places had once made Sotiris profoundly nervous, but no spider had ever lasted long on this lonely moon.

A larger cell indicated the start of living quarters, or what passed for such things in the Firmament. Sotiris's spark was replaced by others waking in hanging cages and levitating silently to follow his progress, the original returning to its cloakroom. One darted ahead, fairylike, waiting for him to open a door then gliding forward. Sotiris smiled at the phenomenon, yet another example of the inching entropy only the Amaranthine could see—a household spark gone eccentric. Even wishfully thinking, it was a far cry from Perception, the perfect artificial intelligence built and dismantled in a single day over four thousand years ago just to prove it could be done, but it was nevertheless intriguing to see the equivalent of a vacuum cleaner come to life after many thousands of years of service. Almost every year he met these little oddities, quirks in the laws of the universe that nobody and nothing should have lived to see. It was like growing tall enough to reach the building blocks of reality and discovering they were chipped and shoddily painted, a crude message or drawing scrawled up there for good measure, nothing more.

One last door brought Sotiris to a long, comparatively well-lit chamber. His sparks, including the rogues, extinguished themselves, and he was left in the blue light from a hexagonal window that looked out over a wooded courtyard folded deep into the centre of the fortress. Viscous water still pounded the ancient glass, warping the light that smeared the room. A person sat before a glowing hearth at the chamber's end, smoke from the fire rolling luxuriantly through the weightless air to meet him. Sotiris advanced, noting that the silhouette was feminine, too small for a Melius.

"Late greetings," he said in the gloom.

The figure twitched. "Sotiris?"

He knew that voice. "Honsiger."

The woman sounded like she'd been asleep but Sotiris knew better. The Amaranthine liked to pretend they were still the people they were born as, but thirteen millennia could do a lot to alter a person. Honsiger had likely been staring at the hearth, just thinking slow thoughts, for days. Sotiris himself was guilty of similar, they all were. And as more time passed, it became harder to break the habit. Their minds were ossifying, taking on a sedentary sleepiness that prohibited quick thinking. It meant that talking to faster creatures like the Melius became difficult, requiring them to expend mental energy at the same rate as something with a different metabolism—he'd had to work hard to focus on everything Tussilago had said earlier, unable now to remember what exactly they had been talking about.

"Welcome back." Honsiger turned, unchanged in the decades since Sotiris had last seen her. She reached out to a small table at his side and pushed a triangle of paper like a folded napkin across its surface to Sotiris.

"What's that?"

"A note from our mutual friend."

He looked at Honsiger a little longer. Not quite ten thousand, she was one of the youngest of them. Natural absent-mindedness made the Amaranthine before him appear older, though Sotiris was in fact two thousand years her senior. Most of the Lady Amaranthine went senile before their time, though nobody really understood why. He took the letter. It was handwritten in a careful, apparently flawless calligraphy, the text arranged almost as a poem.

> *It has troubled me this past year, ever searching the volumes,*
> *For the man that pretends to be our rightful king.*
> *In my anguish I step back, looking for the patterns,*
> *And there he is, plain for all to see.*
>
> *Beware he of one face but many titles.*
> *Saviour, Pretender, Usurper. All mean nothing, just another name.*
> *He is a demon made real, no more Amaranthine than the pen in my hand.*

An ink-splash here marred the writing, as if Yanenko had slammed his pen down.

> *I do not know what he is. Not yet. But I shall find out.*
> *History is his board, the lives of men his pieces.*
> *I have seen it in the volumes. I have found him.*
>
> *Do not give in to him, however sweetly he might ask.*

Sotiris read the note once more and slid it back to Honsiger. "This is his writing?"

Honsiger nodded. "I would know it anywhere."

"Where did you find this?"

"In a storeroom marked *Suicide Notes*."

"Plain for anyone to find?"

"Not quite, but I was convinced he'd left us something. I read each note—there were thousands—until I came upon this one tucked randomly into the pile." As she spoke, the castle's single housekeeper appeared from a minuscule doorway tucked to one side of the hearth, dragging a fresh copper scuttle loaded with wood.

"That must have taken some time," Sotiris said, nodding to the housekeeper and pulling out a chair at the long dining table. He looked at the note, uncertain. Yanenko had been incoherent the last time the two had met, repeating himself often, confusing his words. This letter, however, gave the impression of an Amaranthine barely in command of his senses. He wondered how many other random letters might have been hidden about the castle, meant for imaginary eyes.

"I can't remember." Honsiger shrugged. "Probably. I had Grinling here help me."

Sotiris looked at the butler, remembering the creature's grandfather from his last visit. The Pifoon, one of the smallest species of Prism, were unquestionably the Amaranthine's most loyal servants, having been bred to the task over many hundreds of years. Grinling bowed to Sotiris, his beady yellow eyes taking in the new Immortal guest, and deposited his fresh scuttle by the side of the one already in use.

"Shall I make up the southern guest chambers, Madam Honsiger?" he enquired, his trained voice clear and crisp. A scrotal-pink wattle, like that of a turkey, dangled around his monkeyish face to his chin.

"Yes, go and do that," said Honsiger absently, barely glancing at the housekeeper. The Pifoon nodded solemnly and made his way back to the tiny door, his little furred paws slapping on the flagstones.

"I believe," continued Honsiger when the Prism had left, "that being discovered came second to delivering this message, hence the location of the letter. It was quite obviously to be found there but took time to uncover."

Sotiris was hardly listening. He was thinking again of the dream. "Perhaps," he said dubiously, rousing himself. "But what can have become of him?"

"He has left for the Old World," Honsiger said, with apparent certainty. "It is his way of telling us."

"You think so?"

"I have visited him here for a thousand years. You have been coming here for almost that long, on your way to visit your sister in the Utopia. Yanenko had long studied the records that have been here since this land was known by other names. I assumed he was collecting volumes for some thesis or other, a paper he might submit before the third renaissance of Gliese, perhaps. But when Maneker announced that his Pretender would try to take the throne of Gliese for himself, Yanenko retired to his work with a fervour I had not seen in him before."

"The demon made real," Sotiris repeated doubtfully, looking at the folded note.

"He has gone to face it."

It. Sotiris looked into the fire, unsure how to counter such certainty.

"I know Maneker, just as you do," Honsiger said into the silence. "His will is iron. I admit, I did not think him capable of such cruelty as that which you have just escaped—" She paused, looking at Sotiris. "But Yanenko must have realised that it would take nothing less than a Perennial of considerable power to stop him." She shook her head. "I should have seen it—as a fellow German, one ought to recognise these things. You remember the last time Maneker was here? Forcing his views on everyone as usual with that out-thrust finger of his. Poked Yanenko until I thought he was going to snap at last. It was a shame he didn't. And that Melius servant he humiliated because she was 'too hormonal.' Doorknobs are too hormonal compared with most of us dried-out old things." She frowned, considering something. "They think it was the Jurlumticular Throng, did you know that?"

"What?" Sotiris glanced up from the table.

"The Prism responsible for bombing Virginis."

"Those that also started the Volirian Conflict?"

"The very same."

Sotiris frowned, idly picking up the letter again. The Jurlumticular Throng were supposedly extinct, eradicated in retribution for horrific crimes against the Amaranthine sixty years before. The Volirian Conflict, named after the furthest star in the Prism Investiture around which the resulting swift war was fought, had started after the Jurlumticular Throng had taken it upon themselves—for reasons that remained obscure—to invade the interior of a Vaulted Land at the very centre of the Firmament. Inner Epsilon India, an influential Solar Satrapy only one away from the capital of the entire Firmament, Gliese, was porous, meaning that it contained many holes to the surface, and it was through one of these gigantic orifices that the Jurlumticular had landed their ground troops. In just one day they had secured an entire continent, slaughtering hundreds of Amaranthine—who, out of decadence and total lack of industry, no longer maintained any inter-solar ships, standing armies or even Voidsuits of their own—and imprisoning their Melius acolytes before the rest of the Firmament had even discovered their treachery. Immortals are not easily slain, and many thousands of the Jurlumticular—a tall, slender Prism race more closely related to the giant Old World Melius than any other—had perished during the battles inside Epsilon India. Their forces had, however, prevailed due to the fact that almost their entire military, including privateer forces and militia, had been drafted for the invasion, a total of nearly seventy thousand individuals and a fleet of twenty-five thousand cobbled-together vessels. It had been unclear, upon the arrival of Vulgar and Pifoon squadrons from Gliese and Inner Cygnis, exactly why the Jurlumticular had chosen to invest so much of their population into what appeared to be a pointless and foolishly impossible task. Three days later, after fighting largely to the death, the Jurlumticular were defeated inside Epsilon India and their remainder executed after trials that lasted only a week. The Amaranthine, at the edict of the Most Venerable and every Satrapy Parliament, had decreed that an example must be made of the Jurlumticulars' entire race, and so the battle was taken to their vastly reduced colonies around the hopelessly distant and remote Volirian star. All found there were slaughtered, with purchased armies of Lacaille fighting alongside their sworn enemies the Vulgar, as well as Pifoon, Wulm and Zelioceti fleets swelling the attacking force to that of an unprecedented armada. Never had the Amaranthine spent so much on a conglomerated Prism army, reducing their speculated wealth by as much as a seventh and awarding their client Prism as yet unheard-of powers and territory. The results of the genocide, however, were supposed to have secured the Amaranthines' reputation and supremacy for the next thousand years, reminding any Prism that grew too greedy of the consequences of taking what was not theirs by immortal right.

All of that had remained true, until now.

Sotiris stared back along the dark length of the room, the rheumy light now subsiding. "How could they have returned?" he asked, running his fingers along the grain of the table. "And how could they have penetrated Virginis with such ease? Aren't there defences against that sort of thing now?"

Honsiger nodded, looking into the fire. "There are. It's a little known fact that the Firmament contains more Prism than Amaranthine. After Volirian, we gave them territories inside our Satrapies for the first time in an effort to quell any surprise attacks. There are Vulgar and

Pifoon sentinel colonies on the surface of every Vaulted Land, barring Gliese itself."

Sotiris looked at her. Honsiger had been an active parliamentarian during her tenure on Gliese and knew much that was kept largely secret. Sotiris thought of his home Satrapy. "Even Cancri?"

The Lady Immortal snorted a laugh. "Cancri more than any. It is the wealthiest and most exposed, lying as it does at the edge of the Firmament. We reward the Prism stationed on the Vaulted Lands with almost every comfort we ourselves enjoy. It keeps them radiantly faithful, we have found."

Sotiris considered this, surprised and a little upset that this had been generally allowed and known about all this time. Despite his carefully cultivated egalitarianism, he still found himself now mildly revolted that he had lived in such blissful ease with Prism cavorting just above him.

"So how did it happen?" he asked, after taking enough time to digest what Honsiger had told him. "How did they do this to us?"

"The Prism were told to," Honsiger said quietly. "By Maneker, acting on behalf of our would-be Emperor."

"But what could he possibly give them in return?"

Honsiger picked up an ornate iron poker and pushed one of the logs further into the fire. "Gliese, of course."

Virginis had not been cleanly destroyed. Its outer form still remained, but the Prism scouts that had first ventured inside after the furnace—which could be seen all the way from Aquarii, the nearest Satrapy—had found nothing but grey, perfectly scoured rock and a uniform inch of ash covering the entire inner surface. Whole mountain ranges had been ground away in an instant, seas boiled to nothing. Every single living thing inside the Vaulted Land had been vaporised, blown to a powdered storm that had thundered around inside the world. The outside, subject to weak gravity but otherwise perfectly habitable and bucolic, remained relatively untouched, with only those living near the orifices of the planet killed by the firestorms that had erupted from them.

Sotiris hadn't been able to look at Honsiger much as they discussed what had happened to Virginis. Not through any sense of guilt that he'd lived and others hadn't, but because truthfully he felt almost nothing and was afraid his eyes would betray him. Hearing the news on the Pifoon cutter as it made its way into the Inner Firmament had left him thoughtlessly numb, almost pleasantly free of emotion. It was a different form of grieving, Sotiris knew that—shock, perhaps, but also a certain lack of imagination. His sister had drowned, and so her body still lay shrouded, guarded, in the Utopia back on the Old World. Those others—Hytner, everyone who'd died instantly—were now just a com- pacted, footprint-smudged ash of their component atoms. He simply couldn't grieve, though he had tried, for atoms. It didn't appear to be in his nature.

An ugly part of him that had always slightly disliked Hytner spoke up inside him. They'd made their choice, all those who had derided Maneker's Pretender and wanted to be seen to do it. Virginis had served its purpose; the Firmament and all who lived beyond its limits had been warned.

The galvanizing effect of such large-scale destruction meant that the Vulgar Loyalists—fully a quarter of all the Vulgar in the Investiture— had now signalled their allegiance to Maneker. In turn, the Lacaille duke- doms closest to the Firmament had requested that sanctions be lifted by the neutral Amaranthine Satrapies in an effort to even out the influence in the region, reigniting the conflict uncomfortably close to the borders and forcing many Immortals still undecided in their loyalty to hurriedly declare for Maneker, his would-be Emperor and the Devout. Three cowardly Solar Satrapies had immediately pledged their support to the Pretender's cause within a day, and more were now following. On his journey from Gliese, Sotiris had to hire a Pifoon ship of his own to take him to Yanenko's Land. Everywhere the Firmament was changing, an invisible front eleven light-years long, pressed and defended, bent and reforged by abstract hopes, fear, jealousy and hatred.

The Pifoon remained, however, in the hands of sensible Amaranthine, still the majority for the time being, and so it was pos- sible to negotiate the eight-day journey without any course adjust- ments and in the relative luxury an Amaranthine could still expect. The morning Sotiris left for Yanenko's Land, the odious De Rivarol had formally invited him to head the new Amaranthine Parliament that would form upon the Pretender's succession. It was not the first offer he had received in his lifetime. New Parliaments were always being formed and disbanded whenever the Most Venerable's mental faculties were dwindling—there had been one hundred and seventeen rulers since the Amaranthine Firmament officially came into existence—but he had always declined; it was on this basis, once again blamed on his long record of unimpeachable neutrality, that De Rivarol had allowed him to leave for the Old World, making it clear, however, that Maneker would be extremely disappointed if Sotiris did not change his mind.

"Did you know him?" asked Honsiger, her voice sharp against the falling stillness.

Sotiris stirred. It was full dark outside and Grinling must have come and awoken the sparks. The chamber was now warmly lit and comfortable, the fire freshly refuelled, with jewelled goblets of water for swilling set upon the table. Above the table the sparks hung like twinkling stars, rising and falling gently in the smoky air. He had been staring into the hearth for a long time, his eyes dry and raw.

"I'm sorry?"

Honsiger looked sleepy, but wiped at her face and sat up. "Did you know the Pretender?"

Sotiris was shocked for a moment, thinking his dreams had somehow been discovered. "What do you mean? Why should I know him?"

"You haven't heard? You don't hear much. It is part of what makes his claim so compelling—and Yanenko's note so timely." Honsiger cleared her throat, sitting straighter in her chair. "Many have come forward—sensible Amaranthine, not supporters of Maneker—and remembered that they . . . recalled, even *knew* this man in their lives." She was silent for a minute, as if deciding whether or not to tell Sotiris something. "I knew him, too. Briefly. He lived for a time in the city where I was born."

"In Germany?"

"Yes. Stuttgart. I believed the man was German, but it appears I was wrong."

They blinked at each other. "Who was he?" Sotiris asked.

"A diplomat friend of my father's. Very influential, I was told. We never spoke, but I remember him visiting the house, and I was expected to be on my best behaviour whenever he came to see my father." Honsiger paused. "Herr Kaltenbrunner. That was how I knew him and how I was told to address him, though now of course they say he changed names."

Grinling came and refreshed their goblets, tipping the used water into a gleaming silver pot. He glanced irritably to the antique clock and left the jug on the table. Evidently it was his bedtime. Honsiger ignored him as he bade them goodnight.

"Others knew him by many names," she continued. "He must have circled the Old World ten thousand times or more but has never left it, as far as anyone I have spoken to can discern." She paused again, taking up her goblet. "There are some who say they remember him from their childhood, like I do. Some of *them* are almost as old as the Inception itself."

Sotiris took a swill, too, but the water suddenly tasted bitter. He knew now he would not tell Honsiger about the dreams, feeling instinctively that it was something he should keep to himself. "Your point?"

"My point? That he is not Amaranthine at all, like the letter says. He is something older, someone who might have . . ." She shrugged, a helpless look in her eyes. "Always been there."

Sotiris shook his head, twirling his cup in his hands. "But why reveal himself now?" he asked. "Why wait all this time to stake his claim?"

Honsiger cleared her throat gently. "I have a private theory."

"Oh yes?"

"He is the Assassin."

Sotiris laughed out loud, banging his cup down and wiping his mouth with his sleeve. "The Assassin? The one who haunts those who break the laws?"

Honsiger folded her arms defensively, shifting in her chair. "Perennials who oppose Maneker have begun to disappear."

"*Who*?"

"Crook, among others."

"Crook is old. They will find him in a Vaulted Land somewhere talking to himself."

"They are being reduced, thinned. It is documented. Maybe there *was* no edict to allow the succession of this Amaranthine—" She held up a finger for Sotiris to let her finish. "What if His Venerable Self knows nothing of this and it is all a ruse. He might even have been killed."

Sotiris stood, inspecting the water on his sleeve, and leaned against the hearth, smoke curling into his nostrils. "I have to say I'm a little disappointed in you, Hanne. You must calm yourself. The Assassin is a bedtime story. A joke." He shook his head, unable to think of more he could say and wondering whether it might be time to take his leave. The Assassin—Jatropha, he was called by the Firmament Melius in their Old World tongue—was the closest the Amaranthine got to extra-religious superstition, a scapegoat for any ills still present in their ancient society. Sotiris had blamed a fart on the poor fellow once, before even that talent had left him for good. Supposedly one of the oldest Perennials, perhaps older than His Venerable Self, the man had allegedly stayed on the Old World, living hundreds of lives under hundreds of guises. The legend of an immortal wizard who exacted his own justice still suffused some parts of Melius culture, if only to scare their ungainly children into housework. Provided his age was consistent with legend, the Assassin would be capable of nearly anything under the laws of their hierarchy. Only the very eldest of them—a rapidly declining number—could claim seniority and possibly remain protected.

"And if there's anyone who might be next on the list, it's you, Sotiris."

"I've had enough of this," he said firmly, stepping away from the fireplace and trying to remember where the guest chambers were.

"That's the only reason Maneker's left you alone this long," continued Honsiger quietly. "Once you arrive—perhaps not immediately, since he'll want to honour your sister—you *shall* be asked for. Any delay in answering, no matter how momentary, will be seen as a threat, a sign of schemes being hatched against him."

Sotiris scrunched the letter in despair and threw it into the fire. He was remembering Aaron's words, and his proposition. They watched it curl and float.

"When I have mourned my sister, I intend to return home to Cancri, nothing more. It is safe there." He looked at the woman, his anger softening. "You should come with me, Hanne, leave this awful moon for good, hand the castle over to Tussilago."

Honsiger shook her head. "You can't see it. Cancri will fall just like the rest of the Satrapies. It may take longer, but it will happen." She looked up at Sotiris. "Your private wealth cannot save you,

Sotiris. You Cancriites may breathe what air you need through a pomaded bag of emeralds, but that air will run out, and sooner than you think."

Sotiris clawed at his face, exasperated. "Florian Von Schiller, who lives in Cancri, is next in line for the throne of Gliese. He would not risk his home and comfort for the mystical ramblings of an impressionable few, most of whom are barely Pre-Perennial, and some megalomaniacal Amaranthine craving glory before his time."

"Von Schiller is conspicuously late in declaring his sympathies."

"And when he does he shall see sense, even when it has so spectacularly departed the Amaranthine." Sotiris became aware that he had begun to raise his voice and stopped, his old heart labouring gently into life. Honsiger wasn't looking at him, but at the floor.

The woman sighed into her hands, a shallow breath like the flicker of a candle. "You were there—"

"Yes. And they spared me," said Sotiris, remembering seeing Hytner walking away across the meadow.

"But not the others."

"No."

"And you won't help us."

Later, when Honsiger had chosen to sleep, he dragged some larger logs across the charred flagstones, heaving the wood—too heavy to lift on the Old World—onto the flames and damping some of them to smoke. The younger Amaranthine might sleep a week or more and Sotiris had already decided he wouldn't wake her before he left. Sotiris had no bodily functions that could disturb his contemplation, and he fed the fire until dawn, stirring it absently with a great rusted sword he'd found leaned up against the hearth. Since the dreams had begun he preferred not to sleep—he could probably go a month or so without it—and by then things might not matter so much any more, if they mattered at all.

In the morning, after looking in on Honsiger in her grand and dusty bedchamber and finding her still fast asleep, Sotiris went up to the castle battlements. The grey clouds were thinning despite the drizzle that chilled his skin, a dark green forest glimpsed on distant hillsides. Quickened terraforming, poorly done, had made the moon a dank place, but sometimes the weather lifted; the calm fjord behind the castle had already begun to shimmer silver where the light found it. He saw Tussilago in his boat and waved but the distant Melius didn't notice. Sotiris turned north, to the blue crescent just visible through the soupy cloud, splaying his hands firmly on the damp eroded stone of the parapet. For centuries Amaranthine had come to this spot, on the battlements at the moon's northern pole, to tap into the magnetism of certain Firmamental currents and travel the two hundred thousand miles to the Old World. The castle had once been a bustling, sociable place, teeming with Immortal and Melius, its emptiness now reflecting the sorry state of the Firmament and the broken Amaranthine worlds.

He slowed his breathing as he felt for the currents, closing his eyes and crumbling some loose mortar between his fingers. Slowly the colours came, flashing through his mind as his ears popped, then all sound died away. For the briefest moment he inhabited two places in the solar system at once, Bilocated like a saint of old, and then he was gone.

Bonneville

Reginald Bonneville, junior honorific of the Devout Amaranthine Under One Satrapy—more commonly known simply as the Devout—watched the Melius go about her work, her enormous hands kneading and soothing his feet with glistening oils. The chapel was so quiet that each gentle slop of the mixture echoed to the far-away ceiling, and her soft breaths, intensifying as she ran her fingers up towards his ankle, were loud as footfalls in the huge hollow space. He sat back a little in the wooden cathedra, his fingers gripping the enormous armrests as her strength shifted his whole leg, his slowing mind trying to concentrate on the extraordinary images above him.

The woman—or rather *female*, considering she was of a different species—pushed hard with her massive thumbs at some sensitive spot, finally making him wince for the first time. She smiled encouragingly, at last having found a place that was not yet totally numb to anything but temperature, and Bonneville suddenly felt a fierce urge to lash out at her, to clout that smile off her monstrous face. It subsided almost as soon as it had arrived, and he turned his slow thoughts elsewhere, back towards the far-away ceiling.

The painted chapel he sat in was a marvel of the Old World, a place of such unique beauty that Amaranthine—and sometimes even the wealthiest of the Honoured Prism—journeyed from all across the Firmament to look upon its grandeur. The fact that the chapel had been built and painted by the hideous giant Melius was often conveniently forgotten as wealthy travellers crept beneath it, muttering their awe in hushed voices. It had even been speculated that the beauty of the chapel almost single-handedly kept the First Province in power; during their pilgrimages, the Immortal were often guests of First aristocracy, bringing with them such quantities of Old money that each visit surely paid for itself hundreds of times over. Bonneville held the figures some-where locked in his head—he had been appointed temporary treasurer, after all—and they were huge sums indeed. How neat, he thought, how elegant, that a work of art situated at the highest pinnacle of the tallest tower of the greatest city on the Old World should be the very engine of the Province's continued dominance.

He closed his eyes dreamily, opening them again quickly to try and perceive an impression of the ceiling as a whole before allowing his eyes to focus on the parts that interested him. The scene far above was that of the hierarchy of the heavens, at least as far as the twisted minds of the people of the First saw it. One might expect a Melius hand to be crude, aboriginal in its simplicity, but the paintings were startling in their realism and power. Only the colour schemes—miraculous to the eye but painful when stared at for too long—betrayed the painter as being a touch unusual, the mind of a species other than his own.

He tipped his head back. At the north end of the ceiling, almost directly above the throne Bonneville sat in, was the origin of the Melius: *Homo sapiens*, as the remains of the Amaranthine had once been known, a gilded crown upon his five-metre-wide, expertly painted head. The Immortal was plain and white-skinned, his huge expres-sion one of stony ambivalence. He wore a robe of fantastical colours that draped the entire scene, hanging like curtains across the towers of his realm, the Firmament, its blue skies alive with extraordinary crea-tures and golden stars. Flocks of metal birds, intricately painted but hopelessly inaccurate, wheeled and soared among the golden points of light; a generous Amaranthine had obviously tried to explain the appearance of Prism Voidships to the clueless painter, who had then let his imagination run wild.

Bonneville let his eyes travel downwards slowly, soaking in the view of the four-hundred-year-old scene. From beneath the jewelled folds of the robe peered hideous and demonic faces—those of the Prism, as the Melius painter had imagined them. Some had long noses or large ears, bat-like faces and forked tongues. All were naked, like a Melius. They were examples of actual species, Bonneville knew, though simply reimagined by a painter who had never seen them, and they capered and cavorted between the curtains across a triptych of coloured worlds whose atmospheres blazed with fire and warfare. If one looked close enough (most Immortals brought spyglasses and telescopes with them especially for the occasion), the true horrors of the Prism moons could be glimpsed. Bonneville, though he couldn't make it out with his own eyes, had seen reproductions of what was going on upon the surface of the worlds up there; torture, scenes of sodomy and degradation, slaughter of children and animals on a colossal scale. Each of the hundreds of figures in the horrifying triptych was about three feet tall— coincidentally the real height of some Prism races—but the sheer size of the chapel meant they were mere specks teeming above him.

As his eyes wandered further down, the proportions increased again. The undersides of the hellish worlds were silver crescents of light, moons glowing over a magnificent map that dominated the rest of the ceiling: the Old World. Needle-sharp, stylized mountains pointed like peaks of meringue towards the heavens, the continents they grew from arranged in a dodecahedron around the First, with lettered scrolls unfurling wherever a fortress or city sprouted from the mountainsides.

Beneath the mountains, arranged below the tangled bowers of a beautifully painted forest of palms, the Melius held court. Their huge forms were the most realistic of all the painted figures, dominating the ceiling in a vortex of colours. Here the artist had clearly worked from life and some of the figures were breathtakingly painted. Their elephantine heads glared down at the distant floor, massive jaws clenched in that peculiar Melius way, enacting some scene from history the importance of which Bonneville had quite forgotten.

Occasionally, just as the trance of the scene's beauty was wearing thin, he remembered that the chapel's ceiling and perhaps everything it depicted could one day be his.

He stared at the top of the woman's huge head where it almost touched his knees, her hair scraped back into some sort of artful decoration apparently for his pleasure. She had moved to his other foot now and was obviously trying to locate the same sore spot. Bonneville, unlike other Immortals he knew, was glad he no longer felt things as keenly as he once did. He counted the many millions of days of his life so far as a time of trials, all of them building to the moment when he could be released from crude animal lusts and processes. To be older than ten thousand years was to achieve enlightenment, many of the Amaranthine agreed, for it left the mind nothing but time to contemplate the things that really mattered. He looked at his hands as they gripped the throne's huge armrests, trying to clear his mind.

Hugo Maneker, the Devout's great prophet and leader, had disappeared. Those who knew what was good for them did not trouble the loftier Perennials of the order with questions; those who did quickly vanished, too. Zacharia Stone, a taciturn Perennial fanatic, had been awarded stewardship of the Devout upon his return from Gliese. The volatile, boyish-looking Perennial presided over his peers with obvious relish, threatening members with imprisonment or exile from the Old World for any small transgression in decorum. But it wasn't Stone who frightened him. Stone was scared, too, Bonneville knew it. The Perennial expressed nothing but overwhelming adulation whenever Aaron the Long-Life was mentioned, but Bonneville could see it in him, just like all the others.

The man who claimed to be the oldest living Immortal was an enigma, a spectre-like figure somehow able to appear without warning especially when his name was mentioned. It was said among the Devout that Aaron the Long-Life had come from the Westerly Provinces, already known to the Melius there and ruling in all but name as a Provincial king. It was not unusual for Amaranthine to spend time among the peoples of the Old World—the myth of Jatropha, said to be the most powerful of any Amaranthine, was a fine example. There were even postulations from the younger, more overzealous Devout that Aaron himself *was* Jatropha, awoken at last from a slumber of lifetimes to claim his rightful seat on the Firmamental Throne. Whoever Aaron was, the man appeared in the flesh as he did in the dreams that some of the elder Perennials experienced, portly and kindly faced, his feet appearing to make no sound when they brushed the floors of his chapel. Bonneville had so far only seen him from a distance, a slip of grey in a procession of red and white—the colours of the Devout—as the Amaranthine had triumphantly entered the Sarine Palace and the protection of the Melius Lyonothamnine monarchy of the First. He'd tried to keep his head above the crowd to catch another glimpse, but it had been useless in a caparisoned procession of multicoloured giants almost twice his height, and assumed that the time for his presentation to their new master was still to come.

Bonneville had done almost nothing so far but wait, occupied only occasionally in his study—a hastily cleared guest chamber in one of the Sarine's outer spires—with the business of the Devout and their absolute rule over the newest Satrapy of the Firmament, the First Province. In the bleakness of the Old World nights his thoughts slowed to a crawl, gnawing at the possibilities of his actions, the threat of discovery, the glories of success. The business with the Satrapy of Inner Virginis, mercilessly expunging the opposition concentrated in that beautiful Vaulted Land—that was not something one took lightly, even when the perpetrators were on your side. And there would be more to come. Sometimes the impulse to run and never look back was so strong that Bonneville found himself glancing at the door of whatever room he was in, considering his chances. He had never heard any of the other Devout voice doubts, but then he had never expressed any of his own, either. For all he knew, each and every member of the sect had plans to leave and he'd be left all alone at the final hour. There had to be some way of finding out before it was too late, some subtle method of testing the water without Stone discovering his treachery.

He knew exactly where he'd go if he had to run, a place beyond even the Amaranthines' reach. He returned his gaze to the distant swarm of violence above him, taking in the painted scenes of the Prism Investiture in all its vile glory. The Vulgar were not quite the barbarians they were made out to be, though their fleets leapt between the fringes of the Firmament like fleas on a hound, and they had made a promise to harbour him should he be their champion during the coming chaos, whatever form it took. An Amaranthine, even just one, would certainly give the Vulgar an edge if things turned sour, and in turn Bonneville would be revered as something close to a God.

He had a good deal to think about.

The enormous hands at his feet paused as he heard the sound of the Perennials entering from the nave. Bonneville sat up, pulling his bare feet out of the woman's grasp and standing quickly.

"It's Reginald," said one of them in an echoing voice, still too far away for him to see clearly. It looked like Christophe De Rivarol, a cadaverously thin, unpleasant Amaranthine he had never liked, and the short, umber-skinned Trang Hui Neng, third in line to the Firmamental Throne.

He watched them walk across the bronze-plated floor towards the five cathedras, their boots ringing through the chapel.

"Testing the thrones, were we?" asked Hui Neng as they approached. The Melius bowed and hurried out. Bonneville stared at the metal floor, mortified, and said nothing.

"Count yourself lucky *he* wasn't with us," continued Hui Neng, glancing up at the distant ceiling.

"Haven't you somewhere else to be, Reginald?" asked De Rivarol, eyes narrowing. Bonneville opened his mouth, thinking of what to say.

"*Let him stay*," said a sonorous, perfectly enunciated voice in the chapel that appeared to come from everywhere. The Perennials glanced around, their expressions suddenly furtive. The voice of the master. Bonneville looked past them to the huge Melius cathedra where he'd been sitting.

A man stepped slowly out from behind the backrest, as if he'd been there all along. He was dressed in the most recent of Amaranthine fashions, a loose, pale blue cape trimmed with auburn Old World furs fastened at his neck. Upon his head he wore a slanted cap of dark material that framed his sallow, full cheeks, not a single hair spilling from the sides. The ensemble was almost without ornamentation, bland and unjewelled. They all stared at him, the Elders remembering at last to

sink to their knees. Bonneville watched them stupidly and then hurriedly did the same, wondering just how long he might have been sharing the chapel with the fabled Pretender.

Aaron the Long-Life looked at them briefly, then at the painted
ceiling. Bonneville flicked his eyes up to watch the man pass them,
studying his benevolent, upturned face, remembering the rumours. It
was the face of a thousand men he might have known, long ago.

"Amaranthine come from far and wide to see this ceiling, Most
Venerable," said De Rivarol, still on his knees. Bonneville was always
shocked to hear the title used on another while the Emperor Sabran
remained among the living.

Aaron said nothing, continuing to stare upwards. De Rivarol
shifted on his knees. Bonneville knew that he could not speak out of turn
or leave before he was bidden. He didn't like to think how long he would
have to kneel, staring at the crusty green bronze of the chapel floor.

Aaron turned back to them, walking around the group of kneeling
men. Bonneville made sure he kept his eyes down.

"I have found three men in my house," he said, still circling them,
the soft pads of his pointed boots making no sound at all, as the others
had said. When he came to Bonneville he stopped, a presence beside
him. "All are faithful servants."

They hesitated, all still looking at the floor. "Yes, Most Venerable,"
said Hui Neng. Bonneville stuttered and quickly repeated the words,
followed by De Rivarol.

Aaron arrived once more at the central cathedra and swept back
his cloak to sit facing into the circle. Bonneville found himself staring at
that eerily vague, middle-aged face, then cast his eyes down again.

"What do my servants want of me, I wonder?" he said, staring
brightly at them.

There was a pause as Hui Neng and De Rivarol looked at each
other, then at Bonneville.

"It would be desirable, Most Venerable," said Hui Neng, "if we
kept our conversation among Perennials."

Aaron turned his head minutely to Bonneville. "This one." Bonneville could feel the man's eyes on him, taking in every detail, peering
effortlessly through the layers of cloth and flesh to settle on his pitiful
soul. "Send him out, then."

"Thank you, Most Venerable," muttered Bonneville, rising to his feet before either of the others could scold him. He walked stiffly away towards the far doors. With every step he felt the weight of Aaron's gaze on his back. At the huge doors he stopped and looked round once. Hui Neng was speaking, but the Most Venerable's head was still turned towards the doors. Bonneville slipped between them, catching his sleeve on the massive latch and struggling to release it. Finally he made it through, closing them as softly as he could behind him.

He moved to the wall and pressed his back against it, closing his eyes while his old heart fluttered.

"Flesh and blood," he said to himself. "Just flesh and blood." He opened his eyes and looked to a high window, the wind rattling the rusted frame. He would go soon, this day or the next. It would be done.

Plateau

From his wild camp, Lycaste had a view of the valley floor, wide and flowered and flat, stippled for a few miles with elegantly spaced poplars winding into the shadows of the hills.

He stood and surveyed the spectacle, his route no longer dictated, his freedom absolute. He could climb the nearest summit, which would take him across the valley's high crest, or march for mile after mile through the shadowed interior, where the hint of a long blue lake slithered among thickening trees. Height would be better, he reasoned, pushing a hand through his sweaty hair, if only to get one's bearings more often. If there were any disadvantages he couldn't see them, and that was good enough for him. There was no danger of running short of food and firewood looked plentiful in both directions, eliminating the need to wade through the sunken forests in the valley floor where it would be easier to get lost.

Lycaste waited a little longer, finishing his morning routines and covering them with dirt. It was likely, possibly inevitable, that the lands ahead would be more dangerous than the Tenth. The Menyanthes had been the last barrier between his little world and the unknown stuff of his maps. He knew that Pentas had lived to the east, occasionally telling him things about the greater continent that had made him glad to spend his days in a remote and sheltered cove. Gardens had walls to keep things and people out, she'd said, doors had locks. That didn't sound like somewhere he wanted to go.

He backtracked slightly to rip a branch from a silver tree, stripping twigs from its length until he was satisfied that it tapered to a decent tip.

Lycaste regained some small confidence as he strode north through waist-high orange flowers; anyone pursuing him would have more to fear than he—he was a killer now, armed and ready for trouble. They'd best watch out.

After each day's hike he slept deeply, curling up like an exhausted animal, sometimes not even bothering to light a fire. On the third day out of the forest it occurred to him, thoughtfully rubbing the engraved patterns of the lock on Callistemon's case, that it might have been a mistake to bring the thing with him. Whoever came to collect the body would naturally enquire after the man's luggage. He considered abandoning it, throwing it as far as he could into the trees where it might lie for eternity and never be found. But he'd brought it this far, it was his now. The thought was enough to quicken his march, and by the sixth day Lycaste felt a stab of delight every time he climbed to look back at his progress. Behind him the Menyanthes had dwindled to nothing, rolling on a long line of hills nearly to the edges of the horizon, where it broke up into green and gold diagonal stripes. He knew the sea was just beyond, that if it weren't for those hills he might be able to actually see the tiny bitemark in the coast that was once his own. He was glad the hills were there; leaving home would have been that much harder if it was always visible whenever he turned around.

The floor of the valley proved wilder than it had looked from afar, and along its side ran a series of eroded clefts wide enough to have once held a path, which he climbed instead. Ancient trees with roots bulging in the rock above bent tiredly over it, draping fronds of twinkling metal. Lycaste occasionally found flat chunks of rock on the path, different in its grain from growthstone but quite obviously manufactured. The route had the look of somewhere not travelled in hundreds of years or more.

For half a day he'd watched a sinuous worm of smoke rising from some trees in the valley floor, and drawing level with it, Lycaste spotted a tall chimney, though whatever house it was attached to was concealed in the jungle below. He scanned the forest, keeping his silhouette tight against the edges of the rock face, but saw nobody. At night there was no light, and by the next day the smoke was far behind him.

The path eventually chose Lycaste's destination for him, appearing to tire of his indecision and rising smoothly to the summit of the hill, where it wore away to nothing and he found himself wading through wild flowers all over again. He looked back to the meadows he'd crossed, understanding that he was about to reach a blind spot hidden from view by the topography of the land, knowing that if he kept going forward he would lose sight of everything he'd known.

Pentas, so often banished from his mind through simple exhaustion, was the last thing he thought of before he turned from the view. She'd seen more of his real self than any other, knew him better than even Impatiens did. Lycaste wondered with genuine irresolution whether she missed him or hated him, what she might be doing at each moment when his mind turned to her. In the cool mornings, while his back still ached from the hard ground, he allowed himself to speculate on when her relationship with Callistemon began, spooling through the memories to find anything amiss. But she had either been too crafty or he hadn't noticed; for all that time he'd assumed Eranthis was Callistemon's target, the pretence had been so well maintained. Would she have told him eventually? He didn't expect so. He'd have been forced to discover it the hard way, which of course he had. Lycaste's disloyal heart rejoiced again with a circumspect delight at what he'd achieved, having destroyed the very thing she'd betrayed him for.

The ground fell away to either side of the widening meadows and stumpy, wind-tortured olive trees. It was the view to the north, directly in his path, that troubled him. He lingered at his new vantage point for half the day as he had with the rising smoke, the Quarters rolling by as he watched the sun arc overhead, contemplating the land before him. At last he fumbled in his pack for the telescope.

The meadows descended and were cut off by a stone wall that traced along the land and curved away. There was no gate that he could see, although from this distance it was impossible to be certain.

His telescope was too powerful, of no use to him unless he planned to study the grain in the wall's blocks. He brought it out nonetheless and squinted into the eyepiece, uselessly casting his magnified gaze around. Running into the hot expanse beyond the wall grew acres of some regimented purple shrub, blocks of violet only visible once you'd reached the top of the valley. Further north he thought he could see a structure, but it grew too hot to be sure as everything dissolved in the thrumming heat. Lycaste ate and drank, surveying the scene in the distance with narrowed eyes, waiting for some sign of people in the obviously artificial landscape. When none appeared and his meal was finished, he set out towards the wall, loosening his stick. Coming upon the head-high barricade, Lycaste saw that its large, pale blocks were made of a heavier-duty kind of rough, thickened growthstone. Springing as high as he could afforded him brief glimpses of the crammed purple rows of plants. He landed back in the dusty borders of the meadow and looked in both directions: he'd seen no obvious way around that was within another half-day's walk.

It was the hottest Quarter, mercilessly free of shade and breeze. In the high flowers and grasses around him there was no sign of anything edible. He cursed himself for eating everything before he'd reached the wall, hoping he wouldn't find the land ahead barren and need to backtrack. He scowled and flashed mahogany, his first colour since leaving home, trying hard to think of what he had in his bag that might get him over the top of the wall.

At last he looked the stick up and down, thinking he could maybe use it as a pole vault, something he'd not tried since childhood. He couldn't even remember how to do it properly, planting its base experimentally in the soil and rushing towards the wall, both hands at its splintered tip. He slammed side-on into the unforgiving surface. The second attempt was more successful, ending with a graceless scrabble at the parapet. He heaved a long brown leg over the edge and sat straddling the crest, grinning with satisfaction, his skin leaching back to crimson. Hoisting his weight to the other side, he dropped carefully into the high grove of violet plants, bending and snapping stalks with his weight. There was shade here under some of the more sprawling leaves that had begun to defy their boundaries. The paths between them were too straight to have been long-neglected, and he flushed a politely neutral grey in wary anticipation of company, setting out among the rustling lines of plants.

Lycaste hoped he wouldn't see anyone. The longer he shunned social contact, the harder he knew it would be to take up again, finding he forgot how to talk to people entirely after periods of solitude. Grey was a formal introductory colour in the Tenth, the sort of shade he supposed you wore when straying onto someone else's land. It suited him and implied a degree of modesty that gold—the other acceptable colour for strangers in someone's home—could not. They were the rules he'd been taught, and he adhered to them purely out of ignorance regarding any other fashion, hoping that if he had to meet someone, he might achieve safe passage with little more than an awkward *how do you do* and a respectful nod.

There was little to be seen ahead but purple. At a possibly imagined deviation in the path about a mile away, Lycaste thought he could make out the domed roof of the building he'd noticed before he climbed the wall. It was only the apparent ruler-straightness of the pathways that convinced him he was still heading north as he hopped experimentally through borders and into the next clear avenue. The tall plants gave off a sappy, sour aroma, and he vowed not to eat anything until he reached the other side, practising what he would say should he be discovered. He was a traveller, off the boat from Kipris Isle. He wished to head into the Central Provinces where he had family. People might well leave him alone if they heard he had connections in the Second. He would need a better chart, too. Consulting the map before he reached the wall had told Lycaste nothing. He was certain he was not far into the next Province, either the Ninth or Eighth (confusing due to the spiral nature of where one Province ended and another began) but the valleys and groves did not appear in the basic metal plates he'd inherited from his uncle. Instead, the spaces were filled by tracts of blank land spotted with engravings of spear-tipped trees all the way to the northern shores of the inland sea, where a monster's portly Melius face reared from the triangular waves, spouting fountains of water from its nostrils. He'd studied its crude, laughing face by the light of the last evening fire, thinking it wasn't all that different from the creatures that swam in his cove.

A sudden echoing boom froze him in his tracks, and birds that he hadn't known were there bolted from the surrounding purple groves in multicoloured flocks. Lycaste had no idea where the sound had come from, immediately crouching among the stalks. He rose slowly until his eyes were level with the tops of the plants. A head, outlined against the blue, stared suddenly in his direction.

He ducked too late. Clattering footfalls bounded in his direction. He swung his neck out of the grove and into the path, catching a glimpse of the woman dashing towards him, her body strung with hammered green plates of what looked like copper armour. Lycaste sprinted to his right, crashing through each lane in an attempt to slow the woman's progress, hoping the suit was as cumbersome as it looked. The metallic clanking behind him grew louder, as did the grunts as she pushed her way through the plants after him.

He veered into another avenue, soil leaping from his feet, and chanced a look behind him at the grove he'd just left. The whinnying of donkeys, or maybe even zeltabras, drifted over the nearest hedge. A stable. Taking his hammer from the pack, Lycaste slowed to a stop in the dust. He thought of running and mounting an animal, but he hadn't ridden since the Kipris fair and now wasn't the time to relearn. He breathed heavily, waiting.

The woman leapt from a clump of stalks ten feet closer than he'd expected, almost tripping as her breastplate swung away from her waist. She aimed a couple of ringed fingers before he had time to duck, firing a burst of light and smoke at the gravel just in front of him. He swore and sprinted into the next row, grazed shins bleeding from the ricocheted stones. He was going to die, at last, after everything he'd been through. Jumping that damn wall was the worst idea he'd had since murdering a Plenipotentiary. Lycaste raced from path to path, pushing head first through each line of purple plants, his heart feeling like it was going to explode. Strong-smelling sap began to coat his body, startling him with an idea he should have had much, much earlier.

Twisting north again, he snapped his skin the same colour as the groves, bending his legs and sandwiching himself between two high shrubs. The jostling of his pulse was enough to make the leaves shake about him as he waited. A minute went by before he could make out the clattering of the woman's approach. She'd tired, he could have made it if he'd carried on running. Now Lycaste had to focus on remaining still.

He turned his face away from the line, hoping to present as much blank purple flesh as he could.

She came closer, panting and clanking. He peered from his stoop at her as she neared, curious despite his hammering heart. She was red-skinned like him, with a peculiarly attractive face and tousled dark hair. She came closer; it was as if she'd painted her features on, somehow complementing the length and darkness of her eyelashes with thick black outlines. His cautious gaze slipped to her armour. It was carefully made but basic, with notches and grooves where other pieces could be added. She wore an oversized cuirass that she had to keep tugging towards her throat as it sagged and a couple of shin guards. The metal was indeed worn, greenly oxidized copper, not the grown stuff that never turned bad. The weapon on her fingers, two conjoined rings gnarled with inelegant knobs and spokes, flashed in the sun. He wondered if it used light, like the heirloom he'd gone and forgotten to bring with him, having seen no projectiles in the blur of the attack. She approached his hiding place, muttering something unintelligible under her breath, exquisite eyes probing the groves to either side. In a couple of seconds she'd look directly at him. Cold sweat pricked Lycaste's face.

Her gaze found him, dark brown eyes, almost black, searching, and moved on. She walked past.

Lycaste exhaled softly and shakily, metering out his breath. He studied her from behind, seeing pink lines tracing her neck where the breastplate's old cloth ties had chafed. The woman's body was slightly too thin for that painted face, the muscles of her lower back and calves scrawny and wasted, though there was no way she could be older than forty. Still being schooled, perhaps. He tried to think of some explanation for her condition as she disappeared up the path, her head still twitching this way and that, alert. Shuddering, Lycaste squatted in the foliage to relieve himself, trying to imagine how he might have disarmed her. He still had to escape this walled trap, and that weapon would have made a persuasive bargaining tool. When he'd finished, he inched his head from the grove and into the avenue, peering at the distant figure.

Far ahead, he saw the corner of a structure. Its low dome was strung with paper flags and weathervanes. There was no alternative, he'd have to retrace his disorientated steps to the meadow wall and go around. It would be madness to try to sneak past the house.

Without much thought, he tugged a couple of leaves from one of the purple plants and chewed on them, considering his next move. They tasted better than they smelled, so he pulled down a handful, stuffing the wild things into his mouth and crawling away through the stalks from the subliming puddle he'd made. He'd need to pop his head up again to find the wall, deciding to leave it a little while. Working his way slowly through the foliage, he saw large brown spiders dash into holes in the ground, one of them rearing meaty forelegs at his approach. He went around it, watching carefully where he put his feet, back aching as he ducked his long neck. The spider shuffled to face him in a tight semi-circle, blank little eyes following him as it waved its feelers.

"I'm not going to hurt you," Lycaste whispered at it in a soothing voice, feeling distinctly odd. He pointed feebly. "Just going this way."

He looked ahead. The violet plants were a close, shifting pattern in his face, their shadows and stalks bafflingly complex and beautiful. It worried him faintly that he couldn't focus on detail, his eyes unable to find their own range. He didn't think you had to do that consciously. He carried on pushing through the leaves, not caring about the spiders. Somehow he knew they wouldn't hurt him.

A breeze in the warmth altered the flamboyant patterns and he sat down to watch them move. Creamy, sumptuous purple. It looked delicious. What was wrong with him? He shouldn't stop—she might come back. But so what? More like a girl, so young. She really was very attractive. They'd fall in love. He could live here with her, she'd hide him if he asked her, everything would be fine.

"I think I love you," he whispered, giggling to himself. "Beautiful painted eyes. Beautiful."

It was so warm and comfortable in the girl's garden, and the wall would keep them out, all those people who would surely come after him. They'd never find him here.

The sky above him was flushed, late. Lycaste remembered running and running, faster than he thought he could, his legs feeling longer than they should be. He remembered glimpsing things as he sprinted—faces in the purple drifts—and hearing far-off thunder. He'd seen so many curious things that it was hard to recall them all. He'd sung and laughed and screamed and bellowed. His throat felt scrubbed raw. He sat up in the plants. Something skittered over his arm in a flash of mottled brown. So the spiders had been real, at least.

He was badly frightened. He was in a strange place far from home and something terrible and quite ungraspable had happened to him. The evening groves looked peaceful enough, so he stood up.

He was near the house. Churning smoke, fuchsia in the setting sun, curled thickly from one window in a fat column that drifted eastwards across the field. The surrounding plants had been charred to stubble, their sour reek far stronger than the burning wood from the building, which smelled almost pleasant by comparison.

Lycaste crept onto the closest dirt path, keeping his head low. The smoke was diminishing slowly above the field, golden sky peeping through it. Whatever had happened appeared to have stopped happening now; Lycaste remembered the faces from his trance—there were more people around somewhere. His feet met the warm, stinking ash of the ruined bushes and he crunched, still crouching, past the house. Only the far wall mattered.

Something multicoloured poked out of the plant ash, catching his attention as he passed a window. It was a melted child's toy, plastic. There were more, all deformed by the heat. He stooped, resting his hand on the hot wall. That a child, or maybe even a family, lived here had never crossed his mind. He heard something smash and clatter distantly inside, as if from a basement or chamber below. Then an angry voice berating a softer one. Lycaste stayed leaning on the wall, his ear not quite pressed to it as the heat radiated out.

He had no business trying to help anyone; he didn't even know what had happened. He had been lucky, extraordinarily lucky, and if he weren't careful that particular ration would run out. Besides, the woman had tried to kill him, why should he help her? Small children were not his problem. Lycaste walked slowly away, keeping the west-facing wall of the house to his back, worried that he might be seen from the northern side. He would curve around through the groves and hit the edge of the field, wherever it might be. He cursed quietly under his breath—the stick was missing. He'd have to find some other way of getting over. Soon he saw the large gate, hope bursting inside him.

Before it lay a crumpled figure face-up in the path, light glinting off green armour. It was the woman, one of her knees bent as if she were resting, staring straight at him. He froze, looking into her painted face. She was dead, he was quite sure, but the angle from which he approached meant that he locked eyes with her. A few more steps and he could make out the wound at her throat, the lifeless distraction in those dazzling eyes. Lycaste had now seen two dead bodies in a week, the previous tenants of both having tried to harm him. There was something feral in her face that he'd not seen in Callistemon's, an animal look; he supposed it was the bared teeth, dry in their gaping mouth.

Lycaste stepped around her, noticing the ring lying closer to the gate. He went and picked it up, examining it briefly and looking back towards the smoking house. The grizzly spokes of the weapon were sharp, their power almost tangible. Now that it was his he could do whatever he liked. He ran for the gate, Callistemon's case swinging against his hip with repetitive insistence, a poking finger pointing out that there was something he could do, one little thing that might just perhaps be of use to someone in trouble.

"You bastard, Callistemon," he muttered breathlessly. He shook his head and walked towards the house.

Melilotis

Lycaste checked the ring again and slipped it on as he came to the dim entrance of the ruined building, hoping it wasn't out of charge or whatever powered it. He'd fired one once, at the same fair when he'd ridden the zeltabra, the man who'd owned it telling him that such weapons relied only on the magnetism of a person's body. Lycaste couldn't test it now without alerting whoever was inside. His heirloom—handed down with a brace of ancient keys that appeared to fit no locks—had always looked too old and dangerous to experiment with, and he'd kept it shut away.

He stood in the black remnants of the ground floor, looking up into the crumbled hulk of a twisting staircase. The whole place was a cinder, there was nobody here. He squinted into the smoke, remembering the sounds had appeared to come from deep in the house, and began to search among the ruined furniture. The entrance to the basement was in the corner of the room, much like each of his own towers. Small steps led through a smashed trapdoor and down into cool hollows under the ground, and he knelt in the ashes, eyeing them with suspicion and contemplating the staircase above him, hoping it wouldn't fall in. More distant shouts and curses some way along the tunnel. Lycaste climbed clumsily down, trying to keep his ringed fingers raised. He crept along the smooth, tubular corridor. The walls were panelled with carved scenes, somehow untouched by the fire, only the pleasant smell of charred wood giving away any sense of the destruction above. Dim light pulsed with his heart, quickening as he noticed it might give him away. Kinetic lanterns—ever the perfect method of lighting for generations unremembered—must have ruined a fair few games of hide-and-seek. Ahead he could see a series of corridors branching off at different angles from a central circular landing and shuffled forwards, regretting his impulse not to run for the gate. By now he could have been back in the valley again, heading east towards the inland sea.

He hugged the wall as he heard speech, stopping nervously then moving closer. Though quite foreign, the intelligible accent was also slightly familiar.

"We'll find it eventually, Chaemerion."

Another voice, softer: "I *told* you—they come and get it, once a month. How many times do I have to say the same thing before you'll believe me? There's nothing here but stock."

A third, nasal: "You have nothing left now, no family, no future—why not just tell us the truth?"

"What have you done with them?" Chaemerion's tone was suddenly livid. "Tell me where—"

"Your pretty little lady?" replied the first voice, silencing him. "Your little—"

"You can look!" Chaemerion interjected. "There's nothing here!"

"We're sick of people like you, Chaemerion—the time has come to cut you down to size."

There was a snap and a scream. Lycaste shuddered, his limbs tingling.

"Leo!" The first voice cried. "Have you . . . ? *Now* what?"

"That was nothing! All I did was bend it."

"We're going to have to look for ourselves now! I don't want to see that, roll him over."

Something clattered to the floor, objects being moved. Lycaste still couldn't see around the bend in the tunnel. He moved another two inches and a yellowish elbow became visible.

"What about the man we saw in the field?"

"He'd gone when I went back up. Why? You think he's still here?"

"He might still be in the bushes somewhere. We should have taken him when we saw him on the hill."

"Messenger?"

"Maybe. Go up now and find him."

"It's getting dark."

The first voice was silent for a moment. "Then go *now*, Leo."

They were talking about him. Lycaste shivered at the thought of being followed all that way.

Footsteps, heading towards the corridor, halting briefly.

"And be quick."

Lycaste flung himself into the room, ringed fingers poised, yelling as loudly and incoherently as he could. Someone lay face down on a huge, ornate table between two startled young men. The one closest reached quickly for something out of Lycaste's view, so he thrust out his arm and fired the weapon, bursting open the man's stomach with a mighty roar and slopping the room with bright streaks of red. The other cringed and ducked as his friend fell thrashing to the floor, the scream of the ring echoing through the other chambers and tunnels. Lycaste swung his hand at him, trembling and blinking at the blood in his eyes, the disembowelled man convulsing below them in a stink of shredded guts.

Finally he lay still. The survivor stared wide-eyed at his companion, then at his own blood-splattered body, before throwing himself to the ground in front of Lycaste.

"Take everything!" he grovelled. "Take it all! I don't care!"

Lycaste tried to work out which of the voices he'd heard had belonged to this man.

"I know where the money is, you can have it!"

He'd killed the nasal one. The young man peeked at him through blood-sticky fingers. He had beady, slightly bulging eyes set in a thin, intense face the colour of a ripe pumpkin. Lycaste kept his shuddering fingers pointed at him, glancing about the panelled chamber. The man-shaped heap on the table was trussed and very still; he couldn't see the face. Straining wooden shelves loaded with elegant bottles and vials lined the curved walls, all labelled and stuffed with purple plant cuttings. The man he'd shot was a collapsed heap beneath the legs of the table, one eye staring sightlessly upwards. Through another passageway he could see a row of oil-shiny devices, like huge measuring scales.

"Money?" asked Lycaste with an uneven voice.

The young man took one hand away from his face and looked up at Lycaste, then at his fingers. "Money, yes! It's yours, just let me live!"

Lycaste glanced over at the dead man on the table. "You killed him to take his money?"

"No! Not me!" He shook his head viciously. "My brother did it. I didn't want him to die!"

"This one was your brother?" Lycaste pointed at the ruined corpse at his feet.

"Yes. Leonotis. Don't take another son from our old father, I beg of you!"

"You killed a man just for his money?" Lycaste edged away from the body, his feet sticky where they stepped in everything that had come from the brother's stomach.

"*I* didn't! I told you—it was my brother! He wasn't supposed to hurt Chaemerion, just frighten him!"

"That's this man's name? Chaemerion?" he asked, thoroughly confused.

The man nodded.

"You killed the woman outside, too?"

His bright eyes darted about the room. "She was . . ." He shook his head and gulped. "You don't understand."

"What about the children? Are they dead, too?" Lycaste asked, beginning to gag at the stink. He hoped, shamefully, that they might be. Then he could leave.

The young man returned his gaze. "Children?"

"I saw toys and things."

His eyes widened and he sat up slowly to a crouch, his large hands thrust out in front of him; he had one more finger than he should have,

Lycaste noticed. "We didn't see any children, they might have run away—Chaemerion was a cruel man. That's why we came—he kept money that wasn't his, kept slaves who were far from their homes. He had to be brought to justice."

"How much money?" Lycaste had some in a cabinet at home, but it meant so little to him that he'd forgotten to get it before he left.

The crouching man took his orange, blood-splattered arms down slowly, watching Lycaste intently, new hope in his face. "Enough to last a lifetime! A dozen lifetimes! Much more than *they* needed. You're a good man. We can share it, what do you say? I take my half, you take yours, we go on our way. What do you think?"

Money. He barely thought of it, though it was true that the thin strips of coloured silk could be cut and exchanged for most things: an equivalent amount of plastic, metals or food, livestock and pets, even services. His father had explained to him how it worked, carefully bringing out the family's collection of ribbons as a demonstration one day, but Lycaste had hardly listened, already guaranteed to inherit land, possessions and property. The land gave you food and raw elements for a lifetime, enough to trade should you want more than you had, and his land, he knew, was particularly beautiful. But that had all changed now: now he was homeless, and that money might come in useful.

"So you know where it is?" Lycaste asked the man carefully.

He raised his eyebrows, an urgent look on his expressive face. "How do I know you'll let me go, eh? You might kill me like my brother!"

That was why he sounded familiar. He had a Seventh accent, just like Pentas and her sister. "You called me a good man, that's why," said Lycaste, attempting to smile. "What's your name?"

His captive hesitated. "Melilotis. And you?"

"It doesn't matter. Just call me Good Man." He considered Melilotis. "So—why do you think he might have been . . . lying about the money?"

Melilotis smiled, his eyes fixed on the ring. "It's here," he said, spreading his hands like he'd explained some mystical secret only he could understand. "I don't know exactly where, but it's here—don't you worry. You could put that down first, *Good Man.* Then we can look."

Lycaste sucked his lips, thinking. Perhaps there wasn't any money at all and they'd come here for some other reason. He knew he couldn't kill this Melilotis, that he'd hit his quota for the day already, but what else was there to do with him? The intense, unnerving man was quite clearly saying what he thought Lycaste wanted to hear. It wouldn't be safe to just leave him here; he'd follow Lycaste, cut his throat or something while he slept in the wilds.

He peered into the next chamber with his fingers still trained on Melilotis, looking at the lines of weighing machinery. The other adjacent room, to his left, was a soaking area or something, full of big vats of steaming water. Through a small door, standing ajar, was a comfortable-looking solar, its ottomans piled with embroidered cushions.

"I'd like it if you went into the other room," he said through a mouth thickened with saliva, gesturing carefully with his fingertips and allowing Melilotis to stand. "We're going to start looking."

"Anything you say, Good Man," Melilotis said. He shuffled towards the weighing scales, their eyes locking until Lycaste followed. He was short, his body atrophied and malnourished like the armoured woman's. Lycaste saw that he had extra toes, as well.

"*I* look, is that it? While you point that thing at me? Not very nice, Good Man."

Lycaste said nothing, searching for a place where he could sit with the man in sight. Whatever those leaves were, they'd made him feel extraordinarily ill.

Melilotis turned to him impatiently. "So? Where shall I start? Chaemerion didn't tell us anything useful, but we know he keeps all the money here."

"How do you know that?" Lycaste felt weak, suddenly very thirsty, only half-concentrating on what Melilotis was saying. He needed food and drink.

"He never leaves, not even when his servants go out. And he keeps that wolf chained to the house."

"*Wolf*?"

"Leon killed it while it was looking for you." He trailed off and laughed slyly. "That's right. We saw you, Good Man. Did you enjoy yourself in the field? Eh?"

Lycaste remembered how it had affected him. "What is that stuff?" He looked again at the glinting rows of bottles in the room they'd left, their poisonous contents floating in thick, piss-coloured oil.

"That stuff's why Chaemerion's *rich*, that's why we're all here, Good Man."

"That's not why I'm here," said Lycaste, collapsing onto a chair.

Melilotis's eyes narrowed. When he spoke, his voice was louder, more confident. "Why *are* you here, then? That's what I'm wondering, while my poor brother is dead in the next room because of you. Why is this man, this *good* man, here at all?"

Lycaste tried to look uninterested, even bored by the question, despite the sweat running down his face. He waved his fingers gently. "I have this, and that's all you need to know."

"All I need to know," mumbled Melilotis, smirking. Behind his head, Lycaste saw a gleam of metal. It was a chart, mounted and framed. "Go and get that map off the wall."

Melilotis looked to see where Lycaste was pointing and dutifully brought it down, handing it over. He watched Lycaste glance at it. "I think I understand you now, Good Man."

"Oh? Why's that?"

Melilotis beamed, a tiny trail of tears, barely more than a glint, rolling down his cheek. "You're lost," he said, shaking his head at the absurdity and wiping his eyes. "You don't know where you are."

"I'm not lost, Melilotis."

"You are. You don't even know what you're doing, do you?"

Lycaste knew it was only respect for the weapon that kept them talking at all. He spotted a fold of material that looked like it might tear lengthways and went to it, keeping a straight line of sight between him and Melilotis.

"Turn around."

After he'd tied Melilotis, Lycaste went in search of food. They had a lot of it, including some things he'd never seen before. Ornately wrought sugar sculptures and sweet pastries wrapped in waxed paper, all boxed in casks in the four larders that he found. Perhaps this Chaemerion really was as wealthy as the robbers had suspected.

He went up into the light breeze of the rustling plantation. Curls of smoke still whispered from the ruin, bright lime night descending as he stood there, the vivid moon almost full. It felt good just being away from the man. He scanned the black stubble for what was left of the wolf, but even that might have been a lie. Nothing prevented him from just leaving, blocking the cellar door, perhaps taking the food and condemning the trapped man to starve. A horrible end. The first things he'd eat would be those plants, then maybe the cushions in the sitting room as he quickly went insane, cursing Lycaste for eternity. *Cursing the Good Man.* He mulled the possibilities over in earnest, knowing that he might have to shoot Melilotis after all.

Melilotis sat back, observing him with a wary silence in the dim, cushion-piled sitting room. "You promise? You give me your *word*, Good Man?"

"I promise. Show me exactly where we are and tell me everything I ask about the maps. Then you can go, with your share of the money, and we never have to see one another again."

The trussed man leaned his head against the shelf behind, closing his eyes.

Lycaste went and squatted beside him. "Do we have a deal?"

"Give that here," Melilotis said, opening his eyes and looking at the charts spread between them.

Lycaste pushed the map over and Melilotis studied it briefly, locating where they were on the engraved border between the Ninth and the Eighth. He shifted his bound ankles and pointed a toe delicately at part of the chart. "This is the valley, Uzunpinar."

Lycaste leaned over cautiously, keeping his ringed fingers pointed in the man's general direction. "I know that, what's up . . . here?" He indicated an engraved line leading eastwards towards the inland sea. "What's that?"

"An Artery."

He waited for more. "What is it, a road?"

Melilotis nodded, his curious, beady eyes wandering to the ring. "If you take it north, you go all the way past Erbaa." He raised his head quickly, pointing into the air with his nose. "All the way out past the sea."

Lycaste looked at it, tracing its progress. "But it goes *through* the Black Sea—it can't be a road."

Melilotis sighed. "It's a . . . route. Sometimes a road, sometimes you take a ship or whatever to cross the Karadeniz, the Black Sea."

"A ship? You've been on this route?"

The man scratched his cheek with difficulty on the bony edge of his shoulder. "Maybe." He gestured at Lycaste's lap with his nose. "Give me some of that food there first."

Lycaste didn't see the point. He threw him something—a last meal—nonetheless, surprised when Melilotis snapped it up expertly, like a hound tossed a piece of meat. "Tell me something, Good Man," he said, slavering.

"What?"

"Tell me something I'll like, to make this all less boring. I look at you, that face of yours—you must get a lot of butterfly, eh?"

"Butterfly?"

"*Women.* I can see it—man like you, they love that, eh?"

"Perhaps."

"Perhaps? Only perhaps? Come on, tell me. What do you do with them?"

"What's this here?" Lycaste pointed to a common symbol he didn't understand.

"No no no. You tell me first. You tell me about all your tasty butterflies."

"We're going to talk about the map." He frowned and scrutinised some broken islands, mouthing the name of their sea under his breath. *Aegeanite.*

"Like that, is it? Don't be so boring, Good Man."

Lycaste was beginning to tire of his new name. He looked up. "There's not much to tell."

Melilotis laughed suddenly. "Maybe the butterflies don't like you. They can see how boring you are. Have you ever even been with one?"

"I have."

"No you haven't. I can see it in your face. Look, you're blushing! It makes you prettier, you know." Melilotis giggled again. "That's it! You don't like the butterflies at all, do you?" He sat up. "You like good *men*, don't you Good Man?"

"I like butterf— I like women. Good women. And I have been with one."

"I don't believe you, Pretty Man. That's what I'm going to call you from now on. Pretty Man."

"I don't care what you call me."

"Yeah, I bet you'd like being called Pretty Man, eh?" he sat back, smiling. "You wanted my advice, well, I've got some for you: don't go north—they don't like pretty men there."

"I wasn't planning on it."

"No? Where are you going?"

"None of your business."

"I don't think you know," said Melilotis casually. "You don't know where you are and you don't know where you're going. You need someone like me, Pretty Man."

Lycaste ignored him, tapping the metal plates. "The sooner you tell me what I need to know, the sooner you can go."

Melilotis looked back at the map. Extending further in all directions than anything Lycaste had seen before, the never-ending continent filled the plate. He traced his own journey, a pitiful afternoon stroll across gentle slopes. After a long silence his captive resumed.

Melilotis began to build a picture of the land beyond the plantation's gate. He suggested that the Artery branched in tributaries like a broken vein, although when Lycaste pressed for detail the man was less certain, citing a poor memory, and under scrutiny the ships became vague apparitions. Lycaste's new charts themselves, while displaying interesting topographical detail—as well as listing the names of landowners, his Uncle Trollius included—and frequent engravings of plants that varied by region, still only gave a hint of what might lurk in each new Province. At the main map's northern edge they found the Second Province, described in islands and fjords that became less detailed the further out they went. To the west, a new continent began in the shape of a dangling, deformed leg with a clawed heel. It didn't look right to Lycaste, like something made-up. He asked what it was, but Melilotis, despite trying to answer the question as if he himself had been there, quite clearly had no idea. He was repeating himself more and more, burning away his stock of answers until Lycaste found he could predict the man's responses in order. The places and settlements Melilotis claimed to know well were glossed over with the dismissive wave of a hand; names were thrown around with little explanation, people who'd wronged his family, liars, thieves, men who were once great and had dwindled to obscurity. The places he didn't know were systematically denounced as dangerous, not to be visited. Often the monologue would arc back to Melilotis himself, his prospects, his future as the eldest son of a fine family. Lycaste rubbed his eyes in the late night, dropping the black he'd forgotten he was wearing, thinking he'd go and look for the money one last time before he tried to get some sort of sleep.

Melilotis's thin face beheld his red nakedness for a while without expression, then he chuckled, as if at an old joke. "Hey, Pretty Man, you're looking sleepy."

"I'm going to look around some more. Maybe you should try to get some sleep yourself."

"Oh no, I don't need to sleep."

He glanced at Melilotis's bonds once more and walked through to the weighing chamber, wiping a finger along the oily surfaces of the metal scales. Where would he have hidden the money himself? Lycaste liked hiding things but couldn't think of anywhere he hadn't already looked. He stooped, the headache from his plant hangover flaring again lightly, and looked under each of the scales. The rinsing chamber was much the same, the water in the vats relatively clear, no good for concealing anything. He reached a hand into the cold water anyway, probing the sludge of leaves in the bottom.

"I don't think we'll find this money, you know—" Lycaste began as he arrived at the sitting room once more. He stopped, glancing about and snapping the rings back onto his index and second fingers. The cords that had tied Melilotis lay ripped and cut, the door to the sitting room swinging. Lycaste dashed through the corridor and up the steps, retracing his path more cautiously until he reached the entrance to the underground chambers they'd been searching. Melilotis was trying to wedge the door shut. Lycaste fired at it, shattering the hinge in a spray of splinters, and climbed the stairs after Melilotis, reaching the garden in time to see the man's slim form scuttle into a grove of swaying purple. By the glow of the bloated moon he saw Melilotis scaling the gate, his head swivelling to glance back at Lycaste as he reached the top, then dropping over.

The ring's spokes sighed and whined upon his fingers, little flashes arcing between them. He slid the weapon off and gripped it in his fist while he looked into the night. Briefly turning back to the house, Lycaste glimpsed strange black shapes in the green light of the moon. Against the north-facing wall, from the highest windows on the first floor, hung three small figures. He stared. The children were arranged by height with a tiny body, a baby, dangling at the end.

Contract

Bonneville instructed the Melius closest to him to light their lamps as his striped zeltabra trotted to the stream's edge. He remained in the saddle, his cloaks warm around him in the northern dawn light, waiting for an answering glow somewhere in the cloud. He had ridden five miles from the Sarine Palace along a road that wound through vast sculpted gardens and coloured topiary alive with strange creatures, the pleasure lands of sympathetic noble families. Bonneville had made sure to outbid any possible reward for their treachery, but remained on edge. He was required at Psalms to the Long-Life back in the painted vaults beneath the chapel in two hours; they'd better be on time.

A dim glow surrounded a bank of grey cloud to the south, solidifying as the vapour parted. He whispered to his Melius servant and the giant placed his hand across the lantern three times in quick succession. The light in the clouds responded in kind, lowering slowly towards them.

So the clipper relay had worked, taking his message beyond the Old World without anyone noticing. Or so he hoped. He remained seated on the skittish zeltabra, watching as the grey mists bulged and parted around the ichthyoid silhouette of the Vulgar ship—the privateer *Wilemo Maril*—its yellow-and-blue-plated hull screaming and shuddering like an injured sow as it fought the strain of gravity. The last of the cloud strands hugging its body burned away as it fired growling bursts of pale green flame from its aft superluminal exhausts, a crackle of thunder adding to the noise as it fell. The appalling wailing of the Voidship's descent began to frighten the mount, and as Bonneville fought to regain control of it he worried that even out here they might be discovered. He yanked on the leather reins and leaned back in the gale of leaves to observe the chaotic landing.

The privateer dropped, issuing gusts of superheated air and steam from orifices set into its great rusted belly, yellow sodium lights flickering to life along its flanks. Its militarised design reminded Bonneville vaguely of an enlarged Threene-Wunse bomber, the kind that had laid siege to the outlying worlds of the Firmament during the Wars of Decadence, but adapted now for the absurd speeds and hardships of space—what the Prism called Voidfaring. Such adjustments were not so difficult for the Prism as they seemed: along with the discovery of superluminal travel was the revelation that, mechanically at least, the construction of an engine that could exceed the speed of light was an exceptionally simple endeavour. Indeed, a child in possession of no more than a bucketful of inexpensive equipment could make one in less than an hour. The Prism—lawless, greedy beyond words and now foolishly awarded such knowledge, travelled where they wished, pilfering and slaughtering to their hearts' content.

He watched as a tile of hull plating sheared off and spun into the grass. The ship had likely passed through the hands of many Prism races since its construction, each owner adding and subtracting at their leisure. Its scraped and dented nose, buried among a bristling collection of forward cannon of various lengths like whiskered jowls, appeared to house the flight deck and was decorated with painted black symbols of conquest: Bonneville could just make out Quetterel and Lacaille ship names and numbers in the tally, with crude paintings of the species' skulls daubed beneath. The hull, stretching streamlined behind the dozen heavy guns, had been replated in hundreds of places with coloured strips of salvaged metal like an ancient trawler, producing a patchwork-blanket effect of tropical yellows and blues stained crimson where rust had spread between the welding.

Bonneville glanced along to the broadside guns as the privateer completed its descent, taking in the three fins that angled up from its flattened body. A fourth had apparently graced the stern until not long ago, its remains patched over with bright silver plating like the smooth stump of an amputee. He saw the Voidship turn as he gripped the reins, feeling more than a little dismayed knowing that he had entrusted his contract, and a trip of many trillions of miles, to this contraption and its crew.

Blistered gun turrets on the fins swivelled with a groan to settle on him, while a second pair in the nose angled outwards to scan for any danger from above while it landed. As he watched, a section of the craft's curved belly opened above the neat lawns to disgorge a stepped rectangular platform bathed in yellow light, some rogue piping falling from the hull. Inside he could see a glowing hangar strung with fluorescent tubing. A few tiny silhouettes came to the edge of the platform, waving it down until the scarred metal ripped into a rectangular hedge with a shudder, then stepped aside to let three bull-sized tanks and a convoy of troops trundle onto the grass through the steam.

A whining alert switched off, as did most of the lights, and a large hatch in the rump of the vessel hinged open. All of the little figures glanced upwards, waiting. A hot-air balloon attached to a chain rose out of the hatch, ascending quickly on a burst of flame and dragging the chain with it. Bonneville could just see a figure with a long scoped rifle leaning from the basket and looking out over the labyrinthine garden, the early-morning wind tugging at the flame. He smiled, enjoying the Vulgars' pompous sense of security, and waited for the captain to approach. The small tanks bellowed into life, their engines idling, while more Vulgar and equipment issued from the settling hull of the ship, some climbing into turrets on the sides of the tanks. Two soldiers went to the amputated back fin and busied themselves with unscrewing a heavy metal cap. They stepped aside as the hole spluttered and began to pour out waste and sewage onto the lawns.

The Vulgar captain stamped up to Bonneville's zeltabra, escort at his side, and stood waiting for the Amaranthine to dismount. Instead, Bonneville covered his nose delicately and remained in his saddle, making sure the tiny people knew their place.

"You have my contract, Captain Maril?"

The waist-high gnome nodded briskly, taking a rolled paper from his belt. He looked cautiously up at the Melius, almost three times his size, and handed it to Bonneville with a grunt. The Amaranthine unrolled the paper, delighted to notice the elaborate wax seal dangling from its end that completely failed to serve a purpose. He began reading, very slowly.

The Melius growled at the Vulgar captain until he stepped briskly away from the zeltabra's side, which looked down dubiously at him before finding some grass to crop. Maril was of no importance within the jumbled ranks of the Vulgar, just another opportunist privateer captain, the first to have a ship ready when word of a large commission reached the ports of Drolgins. His pinched face was that of an elf from a fairy tale, white as the skin on Bonneville's scalp. The orange Voidsuit he wore was patched and resewn, in just as much disrepair as his ship. The pointed helmet in his hand squeaked to him and he replaced it to listen carefully. The radar operator was no doubt informing him of the location of enemy privateer ships over the hemispheres of the Old World, though Bonneville didn't expect any this close to the Amaranthine-protected First.

Bonneville finished reading, noting that the contract was in fact a warrant for his own death, should he betray the Vulgar. He took a pen and scratched his full name at the bottom, then smiled at the captain and handed it over, noticing work was being done to the privateer as the light improved.

"I want you to be away as soon as I leave, Maril, so stop your men tinkering."

"Yes, Amaranthine," the captain said in a helium voice, tapping his helmet and speaking into it. Vulgar with huge plastic water barrels were making their way down to the river and filling them, passing a group just returned from the garden's maze towing a protesting hedgehog in a net.

"They can't do that on the viscount's land!" grumbled a Melius in Bonneville's retinue. "Amaranthine, please, send these goblins on their way!"

Bonneville sighed and put a hand to his eyes. "Maril, we're going now. It's time you did, too."

More of the Prism passed with a saw, some cords of wood and piles of salvaged metal hacked from the sculpted foil trees. They heaped it all on the back of a tank and drove it into the belly of the ship, leaving one of their member behind to pick up pieces that had fallen off. He strayed too close. The Melius closest snarled and jumped from his heavy mount, lashing out to grab the little man and shaking him. The Vulgar squealed, helmeted head swinging and clattering against his armoured collar. Captain Maril turned, reaching for his pistol but not unclipping it from its holster.

Bonneville had begun to climb down from the zeltabra when the Melius ripped the struggling Prism in half, roaring and hurling both pieces in opposite directions. The small men in the garden stopped, their weapons raised. The giant looked apologetically back at Bonneville, ears flattening.

"I'm sorry, Sire—" he began, a rifle crack from the balloon severing his head from his shoulders before he could finish his sentence. Bonneville watched the bloodied body slump, its head rolling away across the lawn. The other Melius struggled to control their whinnying mounts, some bolting with a thunder of hooves back down the path.

Bonneville watched them go, finally dismounting from the zeltabra and walking up to the Vulgar captain, wondering if his missing Melius servant would be his undoing. Perhaps he would have to dispose of the others, too, when they got him back.

"Bring your sniper down," he commanded.

Maril spoke into his headset uncertainly and they waited for the balloon to descend. The small sharpshooter, armoured in a coat of painted mail, came trudging to meet them, not looking at the dead Melius. He began to remove his helmet until Bonneville held up a hand for him to stop. He stared at the armoured soldier, everyone in the garden watching.

At first, nothing happened. The Vulgar stood looking at him, bowing delicately. Then smoke began to rise from the sniper's cuirass, coiling and wafting across the grass. Bonneville continued to stare, casual as a man reading a newspaper. The sniper hopped from foot to foot, staggering into the captain. He tried desperately to get his helmet off but the metal had fused, and black smoke was now pouring from the binocular eyeholes. The smell of overcooked flesh filled the garden and the sniper crunched to his knees, gauntlets at his helmet, red-hot metal hissing and popping. Captain Maril withdrew slightly, shielding his little face as the armour around his sniper melted, crumpling inwards into a small, screaming ball. The jagged metal sphere became white-hot, burning the neatly cropped lawn around it, then was still.

The captain and his men watched wide-eyed as Bonneville walked to the glowing ball and picked it up.

"Remember your loyalty, Maril, as shall I." The Amaranthine turned and threw the sphere into the stream, where it splashed with an angry cloud of steam. "Now get out of here."

Wilemo Maril

The Vulgar privateer *Wilemo Maril* departed the Old World after two days spent submerged deep within a jungle of the Thirteenth Province, its pumps recirculating fresh water from a gushing river while much-needed repairs were carried out for the long voyage ahead. Large, strange-looking fish were caught, gutted, chopped and frozen, small mammals skinned and salted. On the second day it tested its motors, expelling a burp of thick, noxious smoke over the running waters, and heaved into the sky, exhausts roaring like a monstrous animal in pain. As it climbed through driving rain, it tested its communications and radar, listening hard for enemy traffic and finding none within the three-hundred-mile range of its terrestrial antennas. The rain grew softer; the Old World's horizon became curved, indistinct, blotched with geography and the haze of encircling atmosphere. Portholes froze over, the foot-thick plastic useless as it escaped the fog of particles and headed for the void in which it belonged.

After a couple of minutes, the Greenmoon—a place the Amaranthine masters of the Old Satrapy still called *Yanenko's Land*—passed by below to starboard, a coloured, far-off dot sweeping below the demisted portholes. The privateer's course was plotted in the red-lit tunnels deep inside the Voidship, tiny Vulgar bent over sheaves of thick, unrolled maps. Their route would take them—as usual—on a trajectory that avoided most of the Solar Satrapies, minimising contact with both Amaranthine influence and the interest of other, less civilised peoples.

The superluminal filaments were running at just over two thousand miles a second as Mars-Gaol, a blasted, orange speck of no-man's-land, passed by high and far to port, the routine of the privateer settling into its long journey, finally switching on its wave antennas to listen for anything within a twenty-seven-thousand-mile volume around it. The tiny Voidship whizzed far from Jupiter's Amaranthine-inhabited moons and flicked under Saturn-Regis, correcting its course through the hail of asteroids that flew past in the crackle of its radar. They were burning at just over seven million, five hundred thousand miles an hour when they passed Neptune—the electromagnetic vibrations of its rings tinkling like a bell—climbing up to the edges of interstellar space until they were outside the heliosheath of the sun altogether and bolting at one hundred and eighty million miles a day towards the next Solar Satrapy in the Firmament, the starlight beginning to blend together into a silver glow that sparkled through the portholes. Had the septuplet engines not increased rapidly in efficiency with almost every mile, the journey just to the fringes of the Solar Satrapy would have taken them over sixty days, and they could not reasonably have expected to enter the next for another three hundred and eighty years. But as it stood they were due to pass Proximo, the nearest Satrapy to that of the Old World's star Sol, in just under fifteen days' time.

The ship arced, curving away from the Satrapy of Proximo—its Vaulted Lands heavily occupied and guarded by great shoals of Prism Voidcraft loyal to the Amaranthine—and roaring through the empty gulf in the direction of the Fourth Solar Satrapy of Port Elsbet, once named Barnard's Star.

Maril studied the thick pile of maps in the dim emergency light, the continual cries of radar operators verifying accurate distance and wave-signal checks piped into the small operations capsule. Port Elsbet was a chain of five planets, only one of them Vaulted, modestly populated. Their unusual route dictated that they would have to stop there before resuming their journey out of the Firmament, despite the increased Prism activity of late. Any of the dozen other hominid breeds could obstruct his mission, even supposed allies of the Vulgar, and all were to be avoided. The Prism usually lurked around the borders of the Firmament, feeding on the scraps from the Amaranthines' table, squabbling, warring, creeping into the light only to steal, but sometimes they swam closer in, just to see what there was to be seen.

He wondered exactly what might be happening—certainly something unprecedented in his thirty-six years as a privateer captain. The usually sedate Amaranthine were now Bilocating between their realms more often, their trailing gaggle of subservient Prism droning behind, transporting them where necessary. With Virginis scoured and dead, any Prism who weren't so loyal (the majority, Maril found) had seen in the Immortals' appalled silence how the Firmament might be wrested from its owners' hands, how the Ancients might be overwhelmed. Losing his sniper to that greedy Immortal had been the tip of some kind of unspeakable iceberg on the Old World, he knew it. There was something in the Old Satrapy, something terrible, and from its mouth blew the first chill winds of a new age.

Utopia

Lycaste suspected the broken finger hadn't healed properly. He flexed it, watching the many-jointed knuckles slide around beneath his skin, but it wouldn't stretch any more. There was no pain, but the realisation was enough to distract him from what the tiny bird had said. He looked up and scratched his wiry beard, trying to concentrate on the creature as it perched on the branch of a slim, red-skinned sapling.

"Did you wish to attend?" it squeaked. "The speech is at midday."

Lycaste tried to recall what they had been talking about. The drowning of the Immortal.

"Ah, yes. Yes, I'd like to come," he said in careful Third. It was the only language spoken in the Amaranthine Utopia that he could understand perfectly, being the closest to his own.

"It's very sad. Some of us knew her for a long time," sang the bird, no bigger than the final joint of his thumb. It was a wonder, he thought, that the animal could think and speak at all, its brain must have been the size of a peppercorn. Its body was a feathered white ball surrounded by iridescent red fronds. Twig-like legs poked from beneath to grasp the tree, and a set of beady black eyes studied him as it warbled. The bird's tongue flicked to lick the end of its stubby beak after each word, leaving thoughtful pauses.

"How old was she?" he asked it.

"Old enough to qualify as Perennial, I think. My Great Mothers knew her well, but she would've been here long before that, of course." The bird cocked its head suddenly and whistled shrilly as another flitted and landed in a nearby tree. "Excuse me," it gasped, springing nimbly into the air. Lycaste watched it go. "Midday on the lake," it called back, surprisingly loudly.

Lycaste sat cross-legged on the red grass and gazed out through the coppices of cultured trees at the perfectly circular lakes beyond. In the haze of blue and pink he could barely see the furthest ones, their muddy beaches crammed with a multicoloured, babbling throng of socialising birdlife.

There were dozens of lakes—how would he know which to go to? He'd have to ask, though he wouldn't get a decent answer out of any of the Amaranthine. He bet that not one of them knew, or cared.

From the cycles of the Greenmoon, Lycaste worked out that tonight would be his eleventh night in the Utopia—one of three great gardens that encircled the Black Sea—and many more since he had last seen Melilotis disappearing into the darkness. He hadn't counted the days at first, only deciding he ought to once they began to slip by unnoticed. He could imagine only too well how easy it could be to forget the passing of time while living among Immortals. He might drop dead like a dayfly while they went about their demented business, and only then would they give him more than a moment's thought, probably forgetting he'd ever existed within the Quarter. This sacred Utopia, or *Paradise* as the Glorious Bird referred to it, was like that: a sump for the forgotten, ruled over by a power higher than he'd ever known existed.

The gardens were, he thought, a bit like a carnivorous plant he'd once kept in his bedchamber on Kipris: a long, tubular throat of a thing that preyed on any flies unlucky enough to fall into the pond of corrosive juices that filled its gullet. One day he'd looked in uninterestedly to find the insides of the plant crawling with beetles, their hooked feet clamped to the sides of the tube while they fed on the dead flies, happily munching away and unaware of any danger below. The Amaranthine were those beetles, cheerfully inhabiting a world where others must appear to perish in an instant and disappear from sight, day trippers they needn't bother to get to know.

He stood, pins and needles fizzing in one leg, and hobbled across the flat lawns to the closest pillar. It towered eighty feet above him, its black, shining bulk inlaid with seams of gold. Hundreds more stretched roofless into the shrieking distance, their excrement-streaked columns studded with woven nests. At the top of each column a naked statue crouched, its outstretched arms obviously designed to hold whatever the pillars once supported. No two figures were alike—he'd spent days with an aching neck looking at them all. Some were quite explicit, their legs stuck at glistening angles into the bird-flecked sky. Others frowned sulkily at whoever walked beneath. Across the lawn, another set of mirroring pillars ran, their figures peering down at him. Hundreds of the columns near the shores of the Utopia were pocked with holes and gashes and cracks that Lycaste often ran his fingers along, scars from a violent life nobody remembered.

He strolled up to an enclosed nest, a pocket of flowers and stems with a small hole for an entrance that hung from one of the pillars, and tapped on its side. There didn't appear to be anyone home so he went to the next one, a larger, more complicated structure with single petals sewn into its walls like scales.

"Hello?" the minuscule voice inside asked sleepily.

"Er, hello—do you know anything about a eulogy? Where it might be held?" Lycaste leaned his face into the musky depths of the hole. He flinched as a long magenta beak jutted out like a dagger.

"How should I know?" The creature cawed. "Ask him."

Lycaste glanced around to see one of the Amaranthine mincing by, eyeing them with a jolly smile. The short man's pale skin was lividly sunburned, but he didn't appear to be in any pain. He wore a cape of bright feathers around his shoulders that trailed along the grass, picking up debris and the occasional squeaking baby bird that had fallen from a nest. Lycaste didn't like trying to talk to them; it was akin to conversing with someone who didn't wholly believe you existed, or that if you did you would soon cease to. They were such a strange disappointment to Lycaste, despite the fact that up until the last few days he'd had no idea of their existence. The person in front of him had lived for at least eleven thousand years—probably more—before falling victim to the madness that had seen him sent here. Lycaste looked down at him, unable to understand how such a thing could live for so long. Snot hung limply from the man's nostrils as he tittered, waving his short, burned fingers in greeting. Within a minute of meeting one he'd noticed the resemblance to old Jotroffe: five fingers on each hand, small puffy face and tiny glinting eyes. It was beyond doubt that an Amaranthine had been living among them in the Tenth, but by choice rather than being consigned there.

Lycaste stepped into his path, for it was the only tactic he'd found that worked, and gripped the man's shoulder.

"Old friend," he said, in the custom of the Utopia, "where is the memorial service? On which beach?" Lycaste didn't expect much of an answer, suspecting he'd spoken too quickly for the little man.

The Amaranthine furrowed his brow and looked back towards the lakes in the distance, uncertain. He stared with bewilderment up at Lycaste. "You . . . you are very big today! They get bigger every day, don't they?" His breathy voice was nothing more than a whisper at first, as if slowly arriving from somewhere very far away.

Lycaste nodded. "I'm big, you're small."

The man grinned and cackled, his head swinging up and down, the snot loosening and flailing. "Much smaller than you! Haha!"

Lycaste laughed despite himself. The Immortal abruptly rushed forward without a word and hugged him tightly, warm moisture from his nose running down Lycaste's stomach. "And they will get bigger." He nodded, looking up. "But I'll always stay the same."

Lycaste pulled away, watching his new friend cackle and totter on. This one could speak Third well, unlike many of the others. He'd try to find him again and ask more questions. He began walking towards the closest lake, occasionally meeting the mad men and women trotting by in twos and threes, some accompanied by their curious pets—various species that looked content enough talking among themselves.

He'd never known the dead woman, now at rest for over two months but unable to decay. Apparently birds used to settle on her head and shoulders as she sat and whispered in the yellow mud of the beaches, understanding her every word. They said she told stories of when the world was different, but none of them would deign to tell Lycaste what they were. He hoped that at her eulogy some of those tales might be recounted.

The tribute was held on the island in the centre of the next lake, and Lycaste reached it just after the Glorious Bird had begun to speak. He'd had to swim through the murky yellow water the Immortal had drowned in, terrified of feeling a hand grab his ankle and tug him down. Of course, such fears were nonsense, though: the body itself lay under a shawl of brightly dyed blankets on the island. The coloured shawl, one of the many rituals the birds observed, was supposed to attract the attention of a forgetful Creator in the event he'd lost track of the Immortal's spirit, left for so long to wander the world.

The miniature beach swarmed with jostling colour and fluttering feathers as he stepped ashore, the Glorious Bird politely waiting for him to sit comfortably in the silt before resuming. Slippery, slug-like fish somehow able to breathe air flopped across to the water as he sat, the shallow holes they had been scooping in the mud abandoned, and a few brightly plumed heads strained and twitched to see him, chattering in a musical chorus of greeting.

"She was one of us," the bird continued from its roost in the small island's single splendid tree, hung with egg-shaped nests that swayed when he shifted his small weight from claw to claw. "A loved and cherished resident of the Paradise, given to us to look after." He paused, gazing around, a comfortable orator. Beneath the finger of branch he perched on hung his long golden tail feathers, their tips glinting in the ruffle of a warm breeze.

"Everyone here has a legend about her, her kindness, her gift with language, even on the days when she was not, admittedly, at her very best."

Some of them nodded in a shuffle of colour and plumage, and Lycaste looked over at the only other person sitting among them on the beach, a small man who had not been there when he sat down. The man was partially hidden by birds that perched casually on his shoulders and thighs, but Lycaste could see enough. His squat, miniaturised frame, finely boned head and small, dark eyes betrayed him as undoubtedly Amaranthine (now that Lycaste knew what to look for), and yet something indefinably peculiar set him apart. He looked *fresher*, somehow unweathered by all those thousands of years, a daisy as yet unpressed between the pages of a book. As Lycaste watched, a tear slid falteringly down the man's olive skin to the fold of his mouth, where it rested, shining in the sunlight.

"And so we say a joyous farewell to another of our charges. Our friend, our mother, our daughter, the builder of our lands and the architect of our minds."

Without a prompt discernible to Lycaste, a flock of garish parrots began to sing. There were no words in the high lament, but it brought a tingle to Lycaste's still-drying skin. Behind the birds' splayed crimson feathers, the nests twisted like all the small bodies he had seen hanging as he'd walked the Artery north towards the Black Sea. The song reached higher, and he saw again the branches bending under the weight of three or four children at a time, some upside down, their faces slack and flyblown.

Every two days' walk on the empty, darkly forested road he'd come upon them, some ripped and desiccated by animals and heat, some fresh, as if it had happened that day. In death they'd lost their favourite colours, every one of them a shade of rotting red.

The money was far from Lycaste's mind as he'd started firing, first at the barrels of water and then at the ottoman in the sitting room near where Melilotis had been tied. The elegant lounge erupted, scattering wreckage and cushions, their gaudy stuffing spilling across the floor. Lycaste had aimed his fingers again before he understood what he'd found.

Ribbons of dyed silk of various lengths, more than he could count, had been packed into every cushion and soft surface, the wealth of a modest estate of the Second squirrelled away in a single room. He ransacked the rest of the house ripping holes in things, finding more and more. The ribbons he collected in his arms and stacked in piles in the centre of the room could buy him everything he had lost. He counted them, repeatedly having to start over; it was more than everything he'd lost—he could have anything he wanted.

While he'd been questioning Melilotis, the partially burned house had felt like as good a place as any to stay for a while longer. Now that his captive was on the loose, that option was less attractive. In the morning, cautiously watching for any sign of the man, Lycaste left for the closest intersection with the Artery. Into his pack he'd thrown pastries from the larder and a sample of the leaf in a finger-sized vial, as well as the ring and some new maps. The tight coils of money—less than a tenth of what he'd ended up burying—packed the cloth sack until it was quite heavy, and shielded his shoulder blades from the sharp metal edges of the charts he'd decided to bring along. He'd taken

Callistemon's case and stared at it for some time, eventually throwing it into the purple field.

Lycaste passed the hanging forms of the three children without looking back, though they haunted him from the corner of his eye with the eerie whine of feasting flies. That buzzing, he knew now—*that* was the sound ghosts made.

Steerilden's Land

The privateer successfully set down on Steerilden's Land, the fourth planet in the Solar Satrapy of Port Elsbet. After almost exactly one Old World month, their supplies were depleted enough for bones and broths to have become a staple of every meal on board, all solid food long gone. The compartments within the hull of the *Wilemo Maril* were fitted to accommodate sixty Vulgar mercenaries, engineers and navigators in relative comfort, each little person requiring a volume of space no bigger than an old-style suitcase. Captain Maril, knowing the danger of the journey ahead, had filled his ship with more than a hundred men, their triple bunks squeezed between engine components, water pipes and even the layers of woolly insulation that packed the tin hollows of the hull. One especially small gunner was made to sleep full time in the scarred forward turret blister above the ship's nose, the long guns draped with a moth-eaten blanket.

The small craft had heard no echoes of other Prism activity during its thirty-six-trillion-mile dash from the Old World, the six-light-year void between supply stops apparently empty and silent, nothing pursuing them even if they had been spotted.

Maril and his engineers sifted the wad of sun charts, consulting the carefully plotted constellation lines of their route as the Fourth Solar Satrapy grew in boldness ahead, a black disk in a silver field of blended stars. Locked in a vault in the captain's quarters was the pile of Firmamental Ducats—the inviolable currency of the Firmament—given to Maril by the Amaranthine Bonneville: half up front, half upon delivery of his signatures. Maril had been surprised; the Immortal could easily have paid the same sum in Old World silks, knowing full well that the currency meant little anywhere in the Vulgar Empire. *He wants this badly*, the captain thought to himself, looking up at Jospor, his master-at-arms, as he entered the forward operations capsule.

"Two points out, Captain," the master-at-arms said, patting the sun charts. The haunting electromagnetic reverberations from Steerilden's Land filled the chamber, moaning louder as the privateer approached. Mixed in with the howl was the musical tinkling from the Satrapy's four other planets, too distant for their own rich signatures to dominate. Most Prism used sound in this way to navigate the Firmament, their ears attuned like bats' as they fell between the unique voices of the worlds.

Maril nodded, listening for a moment to the timeless wail of the planet's ionosphere. "All gun crews to the forward battery," he said, collecting a chart from the stack.

Jospor hesitated. "You think there'll be trouble?"

The captain shrugged briskly. He hated having to explain himself. "The Treaty of Silp is over—we're at war again. There are plenty who use Steerilden's Land for resupply."

The master-at-arms continued to stare at him. "Should I signal Port Elsbet for permission to land?"

Maril grimaced, pulling on a vacuum-sealed chainmail glove and fastening it to his Voidsuit. "Absolutely not. We can drop in unspotted." He straightened, clapping and picking up his helmet. "To your station, then, Jospor."

Jospor returned the clapped Vulgar salute and left for the cockpit. Maril shook his head, looking into the eyes of the bulbous helmet for a moment as he cradled it in his arms. Like many who had spent time on Filgurbirund or Drolgins, Maril had heard his share of stories about the machine that would solve the Vulgar's problems. They called it the Shell, among other names, though exactly what it did only drunkards and cretinous beggars could say with any certainty. Foolishly entombing it in a fortress on Drolgins had only pricked the ears of every enemy of the Vulgar in the Prism Investiture. The subsequent Lacaille invasion had now smashed any chance of peace between the two empires, the very reason he was fastening his suit on now and readying the forward battery.

Maril smiled drily as he lowered the helmet over his head, locked the faceplate and fastened the collar cuffs, the weight of it paining his neck and making him slouch. That Amaranthine, Bonneville, he knew about the Shell, too. Maril couldn't have said how—the Amaranthine were not generally invited to the Imperial planet of Filgurbirund or its moon, Drolgins—but somehow the Immortal knew and had chosen to act now. What Bonneville thought he could achieve was beyond Maril, but the Amaranthine were crafty, their antique minds accustomed to a selfishness no mortal could comprehend.

Steerilden's Land was temperate, forested in places and home to a range of vaguely familiar Old World species they would be able to hunt during their brief stay. The predominant plant was a variety of poppy that had taken to the climate almost too well, large swathes of continent stained a pinkish-red when viewed from orbit, the forests like islands in the huge flower meadows.

Something had squealed on the privateer's radar as they thundered down through the landscape of clouds, the red fields vast and bold beneath. If it had been another Voidship, it was now on the far side of the planet, obscured from the view of their antennas. Maril had listened carefully to the equipment while they landed in a storm of thick smoke, their rockets roasting flowers and grasses and causing small fires, but heard nothing more.

The planet was about twice the mass of the Old World, its gravity strong and cumbersome. The forty per cent oxygen atmosphere was abrasive but energising, and consequently slightly counteracted the dragging weight the Vulgar crew felt as they disembarked into the poppy fields, heavy weapons raised. Maril ordered scouts ahead into the closest ring of forest half a mile away, tired already of lifting his legs to walk through the thick carpet of flowers. He knew the next planet in the chain held pestilence in its atmosphere and hoped no diseases were present now on Steerilden's Land. He hinged up the sharp steel nose of his faceplate and sniffed the rich air, watching the hunting crews departing through the poppies. A breed of enlarged hare was populous here, as well as a predatory, bearlike sea lion that had evolved stubby legs. One of those, spitted and roasted, might see them all the way back to Filgurbirund.

Despite what Maril had said to his master-at-arms, only two Prism races were likely to be present anywhere near the volume of Port Elsbet: the Lacaille and the Bult, both committed enemies of the Vulgar. The Lacaille, to whom the Vulgar were most closely related—physically, if not ideologically—could be found anywhere in the Firmament between Steerilden's Land and the Gulf of Cancri. Their monarch-state was technologically on a par with the Vulgar, composed of an organised network of ships and moons, though possessing no full planets of their own. They had long lusted over the Vulgars' single planet, Filgurbirund, attempting and failing many times to seize it by force, and it was for this reason that the Vulgar felt superior—if only by a hair's breadth.

The Bult, on the other hand, were very different. Slightly taller than the Vulgar and Lacaille, skinny-featured and dark-skinned, they were itinerant pirates loosely clustered in the vicinity of the Fourth, Fifth and Sixth Solar Satrapies. The Vulgar feared them because they were known to be cannibals, observing no distinction between animals and other Prism. Maril had spent his life keenly avoiding any sign of the Bult and had so far been successful, for they were few and reclusive.

He led the water team west to where they'd spotted the curve of a great, glittering river on their journey through the clouds, organising tanks equipped with snowplough noses to push through the dense flowers, their cargo of water barrels dragging behind. As they drove, his helmet buzzed and crackled—teams reporting in. The air was dense, perfumed, the light strange after so much time spent breathing recirculated gases in almost total darkness, and he saw no birds or wildlife of any kind, assuming they inhabited the woodlands that stuck out of the red like green oases.

Maril had lied to his crew, as he often did. Normally he told small lies, fibs that helped them believe in the job at hand, but this had been big by anyone's standards. It was Jospor's fault really; he'd assumed Maril had been to Steerilden's Land before, even though the captain had said no such thing to any of them. In truth, Maril had never been to the Fourth Solar Satrapy before. Everything he knew about Port Elsbet and its four planets he had gleaned from notes in the *Sun Compendium*, a series of fat volumes on his bookshelf given to him as a boy and now mostly outdated.

His helmet began to crackle again, high-pitched Vulgar whispers chattering to each other, then whined like a burst of tinnitus. He scowled and threw open the faceplate, pulling his helmet off a second later to inspect the earpieces inside. The radio operator sitting behind did the same, yammering into a microphone. Abruptly the earpiece in Maril's helmet awoke, his scouts gabbling, their voices repeated in the channels of the four senior officers sitting atop the tank.

"What was that?" he barked, looking around at the others.

"Presence in the forest, three miles west," the radio operator said, listening again. "Enemy. Voidship sighted homing in on the *Wilemo*'s position."

Maril ordered the tank convoy to stop, their turrets swinging up and out with hydraulic groans, searching the deep blue sky. He climbed down from the vehicle, tapping his helmet, and stared across the poppies to the forest.

Plumes of smoke, the sound of the explosions just reaching the convoy, were puffing above the topmost trees and drifting with the warm breeze. He crouched, his officers piling out and doing the same, unhitching his lumen rifle. He couldn't see the privateer, there were too many of the damned chin-high flowers in the way. He tried to call his ship, pressing a gloved hand to his ear to drown out the questions from the other men, but nobody was responding. He knew it—they'd defied his orders and gone out with the last hunting party, unwilling to stay cooped up in the smelly hulk for another month without air.

Maril waved to the soldiers sitting uncertainly on the other two tanks, calling them over, and headed back through the smoothed trench of bent flowers they'd made on their journey. Something screamed through the air above them, barely registering before the sonic boom that followed it. Maril dropped, crawling just out of the trench of poppies and squatting with his rifle poised, sighting on the glinting shape as it raced towards the forest but not firing. He had to get to the privateer. His tanks opened fire as he ran, crouched, half a dozen troops following him through the meadow while the rest manned the anti-air turrets on the vehicles' sides.

His multicoloured ship came into view. Snow white, fully vacuum-suited warriors were engaging what was left of his third hunting party around the edge of the burned clearing the rockets had made. *Lacaille*.

He almost laughed. At least it was Lacaille. They could even talk to each other in the same language while they fought if they wanted to. He opened his comms as he aimed, listening in. Some of them were doing so already, swearing at each other. Good for them.

Maril blew a hole in the closest trooper, alerting its squatting comrades and drawing their fire. He rolled and ran for the closest of the ship's ladders, ducking in the fizzing rain of Sparkers and claw bolts as he heard the screaming coming through the poppies. A company of his men staggered into the burned clearing through the wall of flowers, some dropping under concentrated fire from the Lacaille. Something large and red lolloped after them, springing and grabbing the closest Vulgar in its jaws. It shook the soldier and bellowed into the group of stunned little people, lowering its tufted ears and charging straight for the white Lacaille.

Maril stared at the bear-creature, feeling the sudden urge to laugh again. He shouldered his rifle and climbed the rungs of the ladder into the ship, leaning out once more to make sure some of his officers were following. When a few of them were inside, he made his way to the nose-turret, sweeping aside the festering blanket and flipping switches at the gear controls. His master-at-arms must have reached the cockpit because the clearing was filling with smoke, pumped from the still-recuperating engines. Gradually the fighting troops lost sight of each other, the beast still loping among them, its roars inaudible through the reinforced vacuum plastic of the nose-gun. Maril fired at random into the crowd of staggering, ghostly white shapes, deliberately avoiding the creature, and climbed back down into the cockpit, slamming himself into one of the seats.

A dial on the radar units clicked and chirruped, indicating something large and metallic was heading their way, fast. Maril stared down at the traded bolts of light and colour in the smoke-filled clearing and sealed the flanged outer doors. He glanced at Jospor and ignited the engines, almost certainly roasting anyone close enough to the rear and deafening everyone else in the clearing.

The *Wilemo Maril* climbed and swung away from the black crater of smoke, veering out towards the line of tanks glinting in the red haze. Captain Maril leaned forward in his seat, squinting at the twin blocks of red and blue that made up the horizon for any sign of the enemy ship that had screamed overhead but seeing nothing. They rose higher, the tanks suddenly opening fire beneath them, clouds of chaff bursting in the sky nearby as something whipped below the privateer's cockpit, radar twittering madly to itself. He stood in his seat and pointed, the two pilots sat in front bringing the privateer around and accelerating hard after the Voidship. He saw it clearly at last.

"It's a Lacaille Nomad Class," said Jospor, squinting through his antique telescope before handing it over.

Maril snorted a breath, taking in the sleek curves of the ship as they caught a flash of sun. It was fast, but not bristling with weapons. That was why it hadn't attacked as it made its pass over the tanks. The hardest part would be keeping up with it before it managed to broadcast their whereabouts.

The Nomad climbed, loosing distraction rounds. Maril held his fingers clear of the triggers, letting the shrapnel fall past them, and fired two or three narrow, well-aimed single shots into the fuselage of the long ship as it arced. A thin exhaust of smoke began to trail behind the Lacaille vessel as it flared its exhausts, bursting the sound barrier again and heading for the troposphere. It flung flying mines behind it, their stubby wings sending them in chaotic patterns across the sky, and the pilots of the *Wilemo Maril* went to work ducking and weaving through the falling machines. Maril sat down heavily, buckling himself into the seat. The privateer would never be able to catch up with a Nomad, merely try to shoot it down. He launched from the aft canisters most of their own supply of flapping torpedoes, hoping at least one would find their target before it pulled too far ahead, while at the same time trying his hand at some more carefully placed hull shots that might cause the enemy craft to disintegrate higher up in the clouds. A perfect end to the day would be a chance to get his hands on some of the engine components inside the Lacaille ship, but it looked like there was little possibility of shooting anything down from this height and finding it intact in the fields. The Nomad could probably make it out of the Firmament in less than two weeks, rather than the month it would take the *Wilemo Maril*. It was the sort of craft you gave up chasing even before it was out of range.

He fired a few more desultory shots wide of the dwindling ship and signalled his pilots to stand down. The flapping torpedoes were trails of white smoke disappearing in every direction, not even one straying close to their target.

Maril's ship swung back, sighting the battle in the distance and loosing three bombs into the forest as they passed over. The Lacaille troops in the scorched clearing fired up at the ship, but its three-foot-thick plating easily repelled everything they threw at it in a firework display of musical ricochets. Maril glanced down to the clearing, listening for any of his troops who might still be alive, but heard nothing. The privateer banked, dropping a salvo of bombs into the clearing, and headed back for the tanks, skimming past.

They circled once more, firing rockets along the trench of crushed flowers to ignite part of the meadow between them and the approaching soldiers before settling to collect the vehicles.

In other circumstances, Maril liked to think he would have stayed and fought, repelling what he could of the distant lines of Lacaille they'd spotted beyond the forest, but he had a reward—and a well-earned retirement—to claim. Half his men were scattered, lost, killed, but he had to leave.

The privateer rose and burned back up into the clouds, firing most of its largest munitions in the rough direction of the Lacaille legions chasing after it. Maril watched incendiary explosions blossom behind it in the poppy fields. The *Wilemo Maril* twisted, spinning, and charged straight up into the farthest reaches of the atmosphere. The plan had been to circle the globe and land somewhere near the pole for a half-day's supply grab. They wouldn't need anywhere near as much now, Maril reflected, as he paced the cockpit, listening to the reports of the handful of engineers as they called out distances and radar checks, searching for any sign they were being followed.

Half a day later, its larders brimming with hare and fresh water, the *Wilemo Maril* departed the Fourth Solar Satrapy of Port Elsbet, curving away into the vacuum for another month's silent run through the dark, dangerous sea of the Firmament.

Meeting

"Who was the Amaranthine on the beach?" Lycaste asked the Glorious Bird after the funeral, looking away from the jiggling nests crowded with squabbling colour, the faces of Chaemerion's dead family fresh in his mind. The Utopia had endured a restless and seemingly never-ending wooing season since Lycaste's arrival, ancient lineages intermingling in a jealous heave of pigmentation and noise. The crowd had dispersed from the beach in a burst of conversation, rivalries and passion reigniting almost at once, but the Immortal had left the rutted strand of beach without Lycaste noticing, the glossy imprint from his buttocks and feet all that remained in the dropping-caked silt.

"He is the dead woman's brother," said the bird, slicking back an electric feather beneath its wing. "Not from around here."

"He was crying."

"Yes." The Glorious Bird caught sight of a dowdy grey sparrow in the sky. He tilted his head to follow her flight before looking back at Lycaste.

"I didn't think they knew how to cry. He's not from the Utopia?"

A lilting screech from the pink trees on the shore distracted them both. Another bird.

"Who do you suppose that is?" asked the bird, eyes brightly searching the trees. "He's doing very well this year, too well. Do you think I could say those were my trees? I could, couldn't I?"

Lycaste shrugged. "If you want a fight."

"But I'm the *Most Glorious*. I should have all those trees over there."

Lycaste was barely listening. "You've got a whole island."

The Glorious Bird studied Lycaste, his pupils great black apertures. "I'm going to see who that is. *My* trees now." A few birds in the nests whistled as he launched himself from the branch.

"So beautiful!" crooned a voice from a circular hole in one of the nests. A ruffled brown head poked out and regarded Lycaste. "I wish he'd ask me. But he never does."

Lycaste watched him go for a while then trudged up the beach to the nest. "Did you see the Immortal?"

"Oh yes, he's very nice," said the brown bird.

"You know him?"

"Oh yes."

"Did he ever say where he's from?"

The little bird cocked her head. "He says a lot of things. You mustn't think too much about them."

He looked at the bird cautiously, by now used to the eccentricities of the Utopia but never beyond frustration. "What do you mean by that?"

"Well, I mean, his stories couldn't possibly be true, so there's no point thinking too much about them."

"Why couldn't they be true?"

"He's mad, my dear, like the rest of them." It looked up at him. "Why else would he be here?"

The feast was held beneath the pink, sculpted trees of the Glorious Bird's newly won territory, having seen off his rival from across the water. Lycaste followed the burbling conversation into the circular clearing to find the strange Amaranthine from the beach sitting cross-legged among the celebrations. On each of his shoulders perched two adoring birds, upon his head a large black owl with sharply pointed ears. The owl swivelled its head to follow Lycaste as he made his way into the clearing, its eyes like amber paperweights.

The man nodded to Lycaste in apparent recognition, a minute dip of the head. Perhaps twenty of the Amaranthine sat or squatted at the far edge of the circle while the birds feasted on a heaped banquet at the centre, hopping and diving and squabbling. The same rivalries that existed between the birds appeared to prevail among the Immortals, their group divided between the followers of two alpha males. Typically of the Amaranthine, these rivalries were forgotten every day, rotating the honour of leader almost fairly among the men. Since, for some reason unknown to Lycaste, women were more common in the Utopia, there was always a nebulously sexual suggestion to the groupings as the man chose his harem. The remnant of desire clearly puzzled them, for neither the gentleman nor his small-breasted ladies had any idea what to do with themselves once they'd accumulated such social status, usually spending the last few hours of the day sleeping. The spectacular feast was of no interest to them, the urge to eat gone completely as far as Lycaste could tell. Gone, too, was any other major bodily process; defecation appeared to alarm and shock them, and Lycaste always tried to go out of sight.

Lycaste made himself comfortable a respectful distance from the new addition, taking his established place within the group that had accepted him that day. They muttered agreeably as he sat down, patting him on the back and shoulders. Their talk among themselves was non-sense-speak, songs and imitation, grunts that started raspberry-blowing competitions and uncontrollable fits of giggles that could spread from group to group across the Utopia.

An Immortal jogged giddily forwards, gripped Lycaste by the arm and pulled him closer into the circle. It was the well-spoken man he'd met that morning.

"Big fellow, like I told you, brother!" He pointed at Lycaste with a cackle, thrusting him towards the man sitting among the birds.

"I noticed you at the speech today," the strange Amaranthine announced in a sighing voice. "Did you know my sister?"

It took Lycaste a moment to understand his own tongue, having been without it for so long. The man was speaking in a rather antiquated but nevertheless perfect version of Tenth, the sort his grandfather would have used.

"No, but it was sad all the same."

"Why do you say that?" enquired the Amaranthine after a moment, cocking his head.

He hesitated. "It is always sad when someone dies."

"I see."

Lycaste reddened; quite clearly he'd said the wrong thing.

"What is your name, Melius?" The man's penetrating stare forbade anything but the truth.

"Lycaste."

The Amaranthine nodded and glanced away indifferently. "Sotiris."

It was the first proper name he'd heard in the Utopia. The other Amaranthine smirked or scowled when asked, and the birds here appeared to have no need of nomenclature, never addressing Lycaste as anything but "you." Only the Glorious Bird possessed any title, as appointed overseer of the sanctuary.

He remembered his manners. "Well, I'm sorry for your loss, Sotiris."

Sotiris adjusted his feather scarf, the owl on his head watching his fingers as if they were scuttling mice. "And what's your story, Lycaste? What brings you to the Utopia?"

Something flew between them, aimed at a small man just arrived in the clearing. He staggered, wiping at his face and giggling shrilly.

More fruit was slung about the circle, the screams of laughter accompanied by hoots and whistles of encouragement from the birds, many of whom were making for the tree branches to avoid being hit themselves. Two women dashed into the centre to grab more food, scooping armfuls as the rest of the Immortals hurriedly chose sides. A chunk of something slapped Lycaste's new friend on the side of the head and he grinned, ducking, his black owl flapping away into the late afternoon light.

"Into the water!" cried someone excitedly, and more than half of them disappeared through the trees, the rest quickly following. Lycaste watched them chasing one another across the grass, heading for the nearest lake. He was glad they'd gone—they were like children tasked with a treasure hunt so the adults might have some peace—but was nervous at now being left alone with Sotiris and the few birds that had stayed to pick at the decimated feast.

Sotiris was gazing up at the sky. He looked up, too, seeing nothing but the deep, dirty orange-blue of twilight.

"Meteor shower," whispered the man, as if hunting something rare and timid. Lycaste looked again for longer, eventually seeing one, then another, dashing across the luminous sky. He looked back. The well-spoken man lay in the Amaranthine's lap, his eyes narrowed, apparently asleep. A cracked smile spread across his thin, wet lips as he saw Lycaste watching him.

"I heard him call you brother," said Lycaste.

Sotiris looked down at the man. "He was my sister's lover for a long time. Before they both forgot each other."

Lycaste glanced at Well-Spoken again. He'd asked him where the eulogy was to be held only that morning, and the man had looked at him without comprehension. He didn't even know she was dead.

"He wouldn't understand," said the Amaranthine. He looked off through the night-dark trees, eyebrows set hard. "They lived side by side for centuries without recognising each other." He leaned over to see if Well-Spoken was awake. "Hello" he said sweetly. The other Immortal giggled.

"Do they remember you?" Lycaste asked.

"They remember an idea, a scent . . ." He trailed off, smoothing the reddish hair on Well-Spoken's head. "Nevertheless, if I were to spend too much time away from them it'd be very hard to persuade even Garamond here that he knew me."

Lycaste considered this. "Why are you not . . . the same as all these people, Sotiris?"

The Amaranthine studied him again, as if he was meeting Lycaste for the first time. "I'll make you a deal," he said. "Tell me who you're running from and perhaps I'll tell you what you want to know."

Cherry

Lycaste had used the new maps to find his way to the Artery from Chaemerion's burned plantation, hoping that not everything Melilotis had told him would turn out to be pure invention. He found the strange causeway only by accident, noticing the hoof-prints of a donkey or zeltabra turning suddenly into the forest at the edge of the hills. There were no signposts or gates leading into the quiet line through the woodland, as if Chaemerion had wished to keep this branch of the road secret. Knowing what he knew now, Lycaste assumed he probably had.

The Artery's floor was emerald grass, growing in a thick, flawless carpet for as far as Lycaste could see and walled in on either side by silver-barked trees. He could find no evidence that another person had ever set foot on this road: no ash from a fire, no discarded food or litter, no footprints ahead in the springy grass. He pushed sideways into the forest on more than one occasion with the ring secure on his fingers, spokes glowing, sure that Melilotis would be hiding there waiting for him. Inside the forest, the cloisters of trees were regimented in mathematically exact rows until they dwindled into shadow, perfectly dark once afternoon turned to evening. He quickly learned that the only way to find the Artery again once he'd entered the woods was to keep a fire lit on the narrow road, and had done so only by accident, struggling blindly through claw-like branches until he'd noticed the spark of his camp in the distance. The only food that grew did so in narrow margins on both sides of the lane—lose the road and you'd starve.

Lycaste measured his progress by counting Artery exits, working out their symbols on the map from a key set into the back of one of the charts and scraping notches on the metal with some pronged cutlery he'd taken from the burned house. The Artery curved north-east with every step, threading across two hundred and fifty miles of forested countryside to the southern shores of the Black Sea, where it skirted the water for the same distance again until it met a port, Pirazuz. *Owned by Salix*, declared the map in fanciful lettering beneath a poorly engraved portrait of an unfortunate cross-eyed gentleman.

Connecting branches of the road wound off through the trees to join each Province, but Lycaste had decided at length to wait until he found the shore before choosing an alternate route. He had always lived near the water's edge, and if his new money could buy him anything in a distant land, it would go towards a nice little house by the sea, as accurate a copy as he could find of his last beloved home. Until then, the Artery seemed to provide a reasonably pleasant and apparently safe way to travel to his next life, however far away it might be.

But on the morning of his second day—and roughly every forty miles after that—Lycaste found them. He grew to dread each alternate day as he was forced to walk past the creaking, twisting shadows in the trees. First, two girls and a boy. Red-skinned, fresh. He'd forced himself to look briefly at their faces, still uncoated with flies. Underneath their small feet dangled a wooden sign, a mysterious demonstration quite wasted on the empty road. Scrawled in First, it read:

3/21
Done with pleasure in his name
If you love him do the same

Lycaste read it twice, mouthing the words to himself, then hurried on along the road making sure not to pass beneath them. With each new cluster of corpses he noticed one thing they had, or rather didn't have, in common, besides their colouration. Though they all bore the same simplistic poem, every sign he encountered was written in a different hand.

Sitting in front of his small fire just off the grassy road, Lycaste began to grimly suspect that it was simply what they did here, in the northern regions of the Sixth—which was where he guessed he must be by now. There was no point ignoring what he could see plainly; the children were all like him, crimson once they'd joined colourlessly with death. Melilotis and his brother had been different—finer, daintier, with a jaundiced complexion that was almost yellow. Rather like Callistemon, he supposed.

For all of his life, Lycaste had assumed that the thinly spread people of the world were rather like him; not in appearance, perhaps, but in spirit. He'd lived without wanting to travel, content in the knowledge that there was nothing but more of the same out there in the blue haze that he regarded as the border of his Province. Kipris Isle, his rugged birthplace, was cosmopolitan and much visited, yet he couldn't remember encountering a single person with yellow skin, let alone someone possessing the sort of murderous tendencies he'd become used to in the last few days.

The next morning, Lycaste decided to change his colour, blending an almost headache-inducing golden yellow. He wondered at the implications of appearing too well bred, for anyone who passed him would naturally assume he was of a Province a thousand miles from his own, but it struck him that the alternative might be worse. Only closer inspection of his long, narrow Southern face might tell him apart. It was misleading, really—the weight he'd gained had dissolved early in his exile, constant exercise easily counteracting his paltry appetite each night, and so Lycaste looked even more foreign than he actually was.

On the ninth day, he came upon the harsh eastward turn that he had started to think did not exist, his new map perhaps overcompensating for some error in the drawing. Once the Artery turned parallel with the inland sea he would be able to follow a tributary out to the coastline, free to choose any route he liked from then on. Lycaste began to walk faster, excited that he would soon be out of the eerie green lane and in sunlight again.

He rounded the corner. The people and animals saw him before he could duck into the woods. They were picking fruit from an orchard of wizened apple trees near the turning, birds and mammals in aprons and smocks, singing softly among themselves. In a small field by the road there was a picnic set out, presumably for their masters. There was no opportunity to hide or slip by, so Lycaste carried on walking, making sure to keep his face lowered and his stride assured.

With hushed whispers and pointing fingers they observed him, but at first made no effort to approach. Just as Lycaste thought he might get away with no more than a wave, a youngish boy caught up to him, crossing the Artery sheepishly.

"Master Plenipotentiary?"

He turned hesitantly to the slender boy, the strength of his disguise still dangerously untested. A round girl of perhaps sixteen joined the boy and took his hand.

"Would you like to share some of our lunch?" The boy indicated a pile of baskets stacked against one tree.

Lycaste tried to remember how Callistemon had sounded, recalling the dead man's voice in his head, but he had no talent for impressions. "No, thank you. I have plenty." He spoke his best First, hoping that because it wasn't their dialect either, they wouldn't notice his errors.

The girl frowned. At that moment, an older woman came walking quickly through the trees. She was tall but plain, her yellowish body looking as if it had birthed more than one child in its time. He noticed painted lines around her eyes, like the armoured woman.

"Sir?" she enquired. "How may we help?"

"I was just on my way." Lycaste nodded modestly, turned and began to continue up the Artery.

"Won't you join us?" she called after him. "We'd be most honoured."

"We've offered already, Mother," said the girl.

"Might we trouble you for news before you go?" the boy called after him.

Lycaste ignored the question, continuing to take long strides away from them. He heard quick footsteps in the grass and turned once more to find the boy at his heels.

"Please join us," the boy pleaded. "You must know something of the battles?"

Lycaste stared down at him, his disguise temporarily forgotten. "Battles?"

"We hear nothing but rumour out here," said the woman, taking her daughter's shoulders. "Here," she said, pulling back the cloth lid of a basket and distributing covered bowls and bottles on the grass. "Please, eat. I am Jasione, and this is my daughter, Silene." Silene's frown remained, but her attention had shifted to the steaming bowls. Hot food. Lycaste hated hot food.

The young boy offered his hand in the traditional way. "My name's Ulmus."

Lycaste took it gingerly. "Pleased to meet you all." He had a sense, as the girl and the boy looked at him excitedly, of what Callistemon must have felt meeting the people of the Tenth for the first time.

"You've come far?" asked the woman. Even the questions were the same.

"Yes," he said simply, sitting and peering into one of the bowls to sniff at the stew.

Ulmus didn't touch his bowl, his eyes bright with curiosity. "Have you been in the Fifth?"

"The Fifth? No."

"You haven't heard anything?" All eyes were on him.

"No. What should I have heard?"

"The last we knew was that Elatine had killed Zigadenus at Vana-dzor, and that the stronghold is theirs now."

"Oh." Lycaste didn't understand a word of what the boy was saying. It all sounded made-up.

"And that now he intends to march on Echmiadzin," the boy continued. "Do you think he will? Then he'd only be a few days away."

The girl, Silene, shook her head emphatically. "There's nothing worth taking at Echmiadzin. And anyway, those Jalan cowards wouldn't risk a fair fight by telling anyone where they're going."

"Stop interrogating our guest and let him eat something," chided Jasione gently, pouring Lycaste some hot wine. He took the conical cup uncertainly, passing it under his nose.

"Now you know our names, sir," said the woman, "would it be inappropriate to ask yours?"

"Onosma," Lycaste said uncertainly, blurting the first thing that came to mind. It was the name of his favourite strip serial, the story of a boy and his pet monkey, hopefully local only to the Lower Provinces and Kipris.

"Onosma." She nodded thoughtfully. "I hope you'll excuse me, but that doesn't sound much like a Second name."

"Neither does his accent," whispered Silene to herself, finishing her bowl.

"Well . . ." Lycaste looked off towards the edge of the orchard, where the animals were studiously eavesdropping. "In truth I'm not an *actual* Plenipotentiary . . . I'm a Plenipotentiary's assistant."

No one appeared to know what to say. Silene coughed into her second helping of stew.

"What happened to your master?" asked Ulmus, confused.

"He went missing. I was on my way home, to wait for him there." They continued to stare at him silently. "I became lost on the Artery," Lycaste added.

"Well," said Jasione, appearing to choose her words carefully, "we're honour-bound to put you up with us until your master comes for you."

"I'm sorry for the misunderstanding."

"Not at all," she said, glaring at Silene, who was barely stifling a giggle. "You're very well coloured for a mere equerry. Lots of people must have made the same mistake?"

"A few, yes."

Silene scowled, her giggle at last subsiding. "How did you manage to get lost on the *Artery*?"

"I don't know." He glanced back at Jasione. "You're very kind, but I can make my own way."

"I have to insist, Onosma. We are required to, by the law."

"And you might get lost again," added Silene with a sly smile. "Ulmus says there's dangerous Cherries about."

The boy glowered at her. "It's true."

She peered at Lycaste and whispered to Ulmus in a stage-aside, "Onosma looks a bit like a Cherry himself—do you think that's why he was spared?"

Lycaste looked at her, barely concealing his dislike. "What's a Cherry?"

"The *Melius*, downcountry," she explained, as if to a child. "Ulmus says they've started attacking people on the Artery, stealing from them."

The boy nodded vigorously. "They *have*! I saw some!"

"The cheek of it," scoffed Silene, running her piggy eyes over Lycaste. "They come this way now, if they're being sold." Her voice took on note of genteel disdain. "Some are more than passably handsome, I'll admit."

"You should tell your master about the robberies when he comes for you," said Ulmus.

"My master? Ah, yes, I'll do that. He would be most interested."

Jasione appeared to remember something. "A Plenipotentiary came through here last year, didn't he, Silene?"

"Last year, Mother," said Silene, quickly taking another bowl for herself before Jasione could put it away.

"*Yes*, that's what I said. Do you remember his name?" She turned back to Lycaste. "He didn't stay more than a day, his business was elsewhere." She considered him as she spoke. "But he had no . . . equerry, no one else with him."

She had a shrewd face, the mother. Lycaste didn't think he had any more energy for deceit. He'd been fiddling with the drawstring of his pack nervously while they stared at him and now reached and pulled it open. The ring would be more than enough to threaten them until he could get away. Nobody needed to get hurt. The bag leaned over under the weight of his rummaging hand, spilling an armful of silk. Ulmus and Silene gasped. Jasione's expression grew shrewder still.

"He's richer than Chaemerion!" exclaimed Ulmus, wide-eyed.

"He's richer than anyone," said Silene quietly.

Lycaste froze, looking at the bundle of colour. He pulled a shimmering strip of blue from it and handed it hesitantly to the woman. "For everyone I meet on the Artery." Their eyes widened further. He gave another, shorter ribbon of yellow to the girl, which she snatched with a shrill laugh.

"A gift from my master, for whom I'm afraid I must continue searching, despite your kind offer," he said, presenting another piece that was immediately torn out of his hand by Silene. Lycaste placed his hand over his bag, beginning to see for himself the changes money could make in people, still unsure what he was doing.

Jasione retrieved the ribbon unceremoniously from the girl. "You are too generous, Onosma." Silene whined for her taken piece. Jasione held the ribbon away from her. "Stop it! Or you won't have that first one, either!" She looked at Lycaste sharply. "I see you can pay for your stay—we're glad, but we don't need gifts." She glanced at the servants, who were scrupulously working away, and stuffed the money into one of her picnic hampers. "Silene, have the spare bedchamber aired."

*

He'd spent the first few days keeping mostly to his cramped room at the top of their house on the outward edge of the redoubt, awkwardly passing people on landings and in quiet rooms without any real idea what he was supposed to do next, effectively imprisoned by law. Approaching it from the Artery, the citadel of Koyulhizar—in which he was now an unwitting guest—had looked quite unassuming: a series of stout walls and keeps painted with huge, gaudy murals, overlooking the boundary between the Fifth and Seventh Provinces. Turrets on the outer walls climbed a storey here and there—houses or larders for the sixty or so people who lived inside the city—looking out over walled kitchen gardens and wooded hills. His own window opened down to a terrace of fan palms and the garden beyond, home to a russet marmoset with black ears that stared unblinking up at him from the leaves as it chewed. Leaning out of his window to peer north, he could just make out a line of iron grey—his first glimpse of the Black Sea, if it wasn't his imagination. The air was almost imperceptibly colder, thickening his skin just after he'd felt the tang in the wind. As long as his disguise succeeded it was a fine place to stop for a while, far more comfortable than the Artery. For a quarter of a ribbon a day, it ought to be.

Silene's father, Eremurus, was a thoughtful and softly spoken man who spent much of the day alone in his garden. He had accepted Lycaste with a warmth he hadn't felt in a long time—almost certainly kindled by the prospect of a rich tenant and any possible favour Lycaste's stay might generate with the Second—though he appeared to be a genuinely kind man, from what little Lycaste saw of him.

They called Lycaste for meals in the late afternoon, apparently eating only one a day, unless there were others he wasn't invited to. The supper always involved the sort of revoltingly hot cuisine he'd been subjected to at the picnic, and Lycaste learned not to arrive at the table with high hopes. Ulmus, he discovered, was not Silene's brother but the nephew of Koyulhizar's Patriarch, one Hamamelis, and so lived in the centre of the citadel with his large extended family. It left Lycaste with only the three of them—Jasione, Silene and Eremurus—sitting together in the long chamber, the conversation from Eremurus's side wilting before it could reach Lycaste's end of the polished table.

At his first dinner, Lycaste was offered more of the hot wine in a metal cup. The rich, fruity smell of the drink made his guts turn over, as did most of the slop served up by the head helper bird, Luma. She was more attentive than he could bear, smiling encouragingly while Lycaste tried to swallow whatever it was she'd given him in grimacing silence. There were twelve courses that first day, each less edible than the last, and he wasn't sure how much longer he could leave his planned escape, fearing that dramatic weight loss was almost a more pressing danger than being discovered as a fraud.

Talk at the table was mostly gossip about their friends and neighbours within the walls of the citadel and any local politics that might stray close enough to matter, though the greater *Troubles* outside the Province cropped up whenever Eremurus had drunk more than a cup or two of wine. He didn't share the Patriarch's optimism that the troubles would spare them and their extended families, nor that it would fizzle out before getting anywhere near the Inner Provinces, citing examples of the past and the strength of support for the opposition abroad. He scoffed at rumours mentioned by Silene of unusual people on the smaller roads and sightings of machines and spies, claiming them too babyish to discuss in company, but nevertheless dissected anything new she'd heard each mealtime with obvious interest. To Lycaste, such grand talk of politics and war sounded like little more than high-minded paranoia, a way of grumbling about the world without being thought petty and childish. The state of affairs, whatever they might really be, affected him only in the citadel's new tendency to bolt all of its gates at night and post hired guards on the ramparts—precautions which, even if he managed to leave the house at night, kept him totally imprisoned until he could devise a better escape.

The family attended a banquet with Patriarch Hamamelis once a week, though Lycaste had no intention of staying long enough to be invited. He hardly said a word unless asked a direct question, and even then avoided giving anything but the minimum of information, never elaborating beyond his own story of waiting patiently for his master. The news greatly concerned Eremurus, who had rubbed his smooth double chins and announced that it was very grave indeed, the idea of a Plenipotentiary being in possible danger on the road. He'd suggested forming a search party, offering to leave the very next morning and spread down the Artery to the Fourth. Jasione shook her head after a moment's thought, catching Lycaste's eye with a painted flash, saying that a search would only embarrass the Plenipotentiary, who should be left to find his own way out. Lycaste had swallowed with difficulty and agreed.

Silene avoided speaking to Lycaste directly, engaging her mother and father in conversation but stealing stealthy glances at him while she spoke. She was a precocious, outspoken girl, commanding the conversation at every opportunity. Lycaste disliked her enormously. He managed to see her only when they were supposed to eat together, even though their chambers were on the same floor. Regardless, he was forced to hear her at night, singing, humming and—once—doing something different entirely. Ulmus was not allowed to stay over, and Lycaste had to assume that whatever she was doing, she was doing it alone.

The family coloured only at the table, Silene—apparently without irony—often choosing a clean, pure white. Keeping the exact blend of yellow in tight reserve beneath his own skin required concentration since it dissipated overnight and needed to be remembered anew each morning. The girl was sharp, like her mother, and Lycaste felt her eyes inspecting him closely for any alteration in tone whenever they met.

Silene and Lycaste were finally forced together on the morning of the Patriarch's banquet, when Silene asked him begrudgingly as she stood in the sun-warmed hallway if she could bring him anything before they left, obviously a chore her mother had given her. Lycaste hadn't been invited and was glad of it. He thanked her but said there was nothing he needed, taking her hand quickly before she could withdraw and pushing a ribbon of silk into her palm. She looked at him with a startled gratitude, smiling shyly and dashing out of the door. He wasn't sure why he'd done it, really, but the power of money was new to him; he liked the way people changed whenever a length of it appeared in his hand and had begun to hope that his eventual escape would become a lot easier if she was even fractionally on his side.

That day was the only time he had the house to himself, so he used it to investigate the place as best he could, thinking there might be more to know before he went disappearing blindly off to foreign lands. There appeared no other immediate danger in their quiet, ramshackle house, the awful curried smell of cooked stuff all that ruined the pleasant surroundings. They were themselves clearly well off, perhaps in the employ of this Patriarch or whoever he was, and weren't at all concerned with leaving a wealthy man to his own devices in their home. This unearned trust appeared to be yet another unexpected benefit of having money. Lycaste fancied he could get quite used to it.

The helpers went with them and they had no pets to worry about, and so he was secure in the knowledge that he could go anywhere in the house without being watched. That word Silene had used, Cherry—it troubled him as he stalked about, investigating its rooms and cupboards, making sure he didn't move a single object or book from its place. He sifted through the indexes of obscure metal ring books belonging to Eremurus, examined the girl's toys and drawings of animals and yellow people, but he couldn't find the word or anything like it mentioned anywhere. Investigating the last remaining chamber, where Eremurus and Jasione slept, was especially difficult. Lycaste found himself tiptoeing despite the emptiness of the place, worried that his feet would leave marks on the boards or that he'd forget something crucial when placing ornaments in their old positions. The cool silence of the place appeared to judge him, marking with disdain every jug he lifted and peered into, every print and handwritten letter he examined. He backed out of the chamber, examining the layout critically with narrowed eyes, a painterly technique he'd learned from Pentas. For a moment, the thought of her quickened his pulse, an echo of a feeling. He closed the door softly behind him as he left.

The family returned when they said they would, discovering nothing amiss in their turned-over house. He'd waited in the dining room, hearing their creaking footsteps on the upper floors, watching the bowed beams above as he listened to determine which room each person was in, waiting for his intrusions to be discovered.

Jasione came down holding something wrapped in a cloth.

"Here," she said, handing it to him, "you're looking too thin, Onosma. From Hamamelis."

Lycaste took the parcel uncertainly. "From the man himself?"

"From his table, at least." She smiled. "It's cold. I know you don't really like warm food."

"No, I—"

She waved her hand impatiently. "Take it, please."

He opened the cloth and looked inside. Raw fruits in small bundles. Jasione looked at him a little longer. "Good night, then, Onosma."

"Good night," Lycaste replied, nodding for some reason, as if they'd just struck a deal.

The morning following his search of the house, Lycaste came down to find Silene in lessons. A few of the copper books he had seen lying around her room now lay on the table, their rings open at what looked like anatomy, a complex drawing of tubes and pipes and bloated organs.

He looked again. The organs were moving, *pulsating*, on the metal page. He went over, turning some pages unselfconsciously and watching body systems pump animated blood around the metal plate.

Silene watched him coolly. "Those are the hypogastric arteries."

He looked up sharply, turning back to the original page. Silene gave him one last puzzled glance and went back to her reading as Jasione entered the room.

"Did you enjoy the package?" she whispered.

"Very much, thank you." He indicated the open book. "Do you have a lot of these, the moving ones?"

"The books? They all move." She went and picked one up, opening it at random. An illustrated scene of men arguing passionately spilled out, though there was no sound. Words flowed out of their mouths and across the page.

"May I have a look at them?"

"Go ahead." She passed him several and he took them to a seat by the window, positioning himself so that the sunlight didn't hit the pages. Lycaste looked at the titles: *An Unabridged History of the Seventh Tropical Point*; *Azolla Japonica*; *The Foolish Prince*. He opened the *Unabridged History* and thumbed through several classical battles. He could feel the drawings moving beneath his fingers, some matt substance shifting on top of the metal. When he pushed against it, a piece of the painted image would fall behind and stream around his finger like sluggish liquid, parting and collecting in a dazzling vortex of screaming faces.

"Don't do that," said Silene, peering at him askance. "You'll damage it."

"Sorry." He took his finger away and the scene pooled back into place, revealing a small, armoured man astride a tiger, of all things.

Lycaste turned the pages. More battles between men in clothes that flicked through fashions and colours like he could change his skin: executions, skin peeled from living faces, silent pain. Lycaste turned back to a face so he could study it more closely. It was like nothing he'd ever seen, so coarse and animal.

"How old are these, Jasione?"

"I bought most of them for my son about thirty years ago. When he died, Silene got them. Why?"

He looked at her from across the room. Jasione smiled sadly back.

"How do the drawings show things that happened such a long time ago?" Lycaste heard the simpleton in his voice as Silene rolled her eyes.

"They're printed. You can copy a print as many times as you like. The original image could be as old as the hills."

"Printed?"

Jasione came over to him and opened a page in *Azolla Japonica*. An engraved couple walked hand in hand on the deck of some kind of barge. "Look." She pressed the metal page against the back of *The Foolish Prince* and waited a few seconds. The cloned people came away perfectly and un-mirrored, already moving.

"Oh, I see."

"Do you know these histories?"

He'd never heard any of it. "Partly. Who was the foolish prince?"

"You don't know very much for an equerry," muttered Silene somewhere behind him.

Jasione glanced at her but said nothing, turning back to the window and looking out at the garden. Lycaste studied the side of her face while she thought, beginning to admire the strength of her profile more than a little as he thought of her loss.

"He once ruled the whole world, or so the legend goes." She saw Eremurus and waved. "As long as he lived there was peace, and he could have lived for ever, if he'd wanted to."

"What happened to him?"

"He fell in love and stopped caring about anything else. So someone else took up his duties and the world fell to ruin." She peered into the blooming garden to judge the Quarter. It would soon be time to eat.

"They say he still lives, somewhere out in the world." Silene watched their exchange with doleful interest, rattling shut her ring books. She waited for Lycaste to hand her the last one and left the room without a word.

Over the next two or three days, Lycaste learned the rough history of the Provinces, sneaking books to bed with him at night and reading on his window ledge, a tiny candle for company. First had always been easier for him to read than speak, and he understood more than enough to be able to navigate the indexes whenever an unknown name or place appeared without warning.

He discovered a life he never knew existed, a life that would have remained invisible to him had he spun out his years by the sea. In a heavy and exceedingly boring-looking tome that he hadn't planned to read entitled *Geopolitical Landscapes of the Middle Anthropocene*, he found yet more. He found himself.

Paranthropus Melius. The Cherry. A race of bandits and thieves. Huge in stature and features, their culture simple and inherited, without any possibility of recovery.

In a map he found swathes of the Southern Provinces were dyed crimson, the blocks of colour leaching this way and that to show the distribution of his species over recent centuries. There were diagrams of anatomical differences, historical essays on the formation of a cultural divide. Helpfully included were illustrations of standard men in comparison, fine and upstanding specimens of the First ruling elite: *Homo Excultus*. Overbred to resemble girlish children, they made even Callistemon look like a lumpen country mule.

Lycaste flicked between histories and disagreements like a scholar of the age until he found the policies that had created such a carnival of monsters in the first place: sweeping reforms on a scattered population, something called Neonationalism and the glorification of one Province over all others, revolutions and dramatic coups. Attempts had been made every century for a thousand years at a well-worn word—*Standardisation*. Multiple-ethnicity was described as a flame that needed to be stamped out before it could spring up again. Provinces had merged, disbanded and fought all under one government, with legendary heroes either loved or reviled depending on the author of each volume.

It took four or five mentions of the same person's name for Lycaste to realise that his beautiful orchards by the sea had never really been his at all. He owned them about as much as a fish owned a reef. There was—or had been thirty years ago when Jasione acquired the book—a sovereign of the whole world. Lyonothamnus I. Lycaste looked at the picture beside the name, realising he'd seen it before. A reproduction of the same portrait hung not three feet away on the wall. Alongside it was a newer painting, the varnish that coated its surface still fresh and undamaged by the sun that streamed in each day. He squinted at it, seeing the familial resemblance. *Lyonothamnus II*. The new sovereign, their king, was just a boy.

"Do you remember the thunderstorm a while back?"

"Yes."

"I never saw one like that before."

He walked with Jasione in the garden, occasionally pulling things from trees whenever she pointed, but hardly listening.

"I'd forgotten what rain was like. I hadn't felt it in years and years." She sighed. "We need one or two of those." Jasione shook a branch and Lycaste reached to pluck the veined bulbs. He shouldered his basket again and scanned the crumbling garden wall, where a few hornets drifted in an afternoon daze.

"There's a hive in the wall somewhere," she said. "Eremurus says they're collecting food for their queen and her babies."

Lycaste remained silent. He didn't look at her. He was thinking about something he'd read, squirrelled away in the epilogue of a fat history book. Everything was different now, seen through new eyes. A side effect of his new-found knowledge was an almost total evaporation of guilt for what he'd done to Callistemon, an unexpected, bittersweet absolution after all his time in the wilderness. It was enough to set his mind onto thoughts of home and possibly returning to whatever consequences awaited him.

"I don't like them, though—they eat our bees," she said as they approached the nest somewhere in the old bricks.

"Why don't you do something about them, then?" Lycaste snapped.

Jasione fiddled with the tie on her sun hat, unused to his tone. "They've always been here. I suppose . . ." They locked eyes. "I suppose it's how the world works."

*

The food was cooked not by fire, as Lycaste would have expected, but steamed in a huge oven that could have swallowed three men whole. Why a small family like theirs needed such a thing was beyond him. Across its gaping mouth hung spits at varying heights, on which Silene and Lycaste threaded the food picked that day from the garden. The chamber was always a murk of steam and water, which hung in droplets from their hands as they worked. Lycaste was not hungry, having secretly taken as much as he could before bringing in the produce, but still felt a regret at the ruin of fine food. He hadn't wanted to help with the cooking that afternoon, wishing instead to be alone in his room, but it had been Jasione's request.

"Have you ever tried these raw?" he asked Silene after a particularly long silence, dangling an orange berry. It was changing him, living with them, but he wasn't sure if he liked the change. Exile had forced Lycaste to grow up, his shyness blunted on all the unforgiving surfaces it had encountered. He'd started to care less about things, particularly after everything he'd read and seen since coming here.

Silene eyed the fruit sceptically and took one. They were called *Winterbottom's pears* where he came from. She chewed it and grimaced, but not unkindly. "They're too crunchy. You prefer them like that?"

He nodded, taking a few. She smirked and reached past him to select a tough red fruit, brushing his sweating neck with her wet shoulder. "What about these?"

"Just as good."

"Eat one in front of me and I'll believe you."

He picked a fruit up by its stalk but Silene shook her head, pushing the one she held gently towards his mouth.

"Why do you sit with us in lessons?" she asked quietly, stroking the fruit against his mouth clumsily so that the stalk scratched his cheek. "You're grown already, you don't need to learn any more."

Her rosy eyes were predatory. He knew then that the gifts of money had been a mistake. He'd given too much, too fast.

Something woke Lycaste that night, the lights in his room glowing around him. Without twisting to look up he knew it was her, a silent presence considering him and his uncoloured body. He turned reluctantly, seeing her push the room's single chair against the door. They watched each other, her eyes moving over his red nakedness with a revolted fascination.

Tears welled in her eyes. Lycaste sat up, hunched, clutching his elbows. A thought occurred to him and he and pulled a knotted bunch of ribbons from his pack, counting them quickly. He went slowly to her and placed them in her trembling hand. She sniffed loudly, glancing at the ribbons.

"You're a sneak," she said tearfully. "You lied to us." She shook her head emphatically, shuffling back as he came closer. "You're not a man. You're a liar!"

"I *am* a man!" he hissed, pressing more money into her hand and finally pulling her to him as she wept, hating the sound and smell of her.

"Liar!"

"I'll leave tonight, I promise. Look—look how much you have."

She snorted and swallowed, wiping her eyes. "You didn't give me anything."

"What?"

"I never saw any money," she sneered. "You'd better hand it over, though."

Lycaste was stunned. He'd thought financial transactions were supposed to be sacred, despite having never really taken part in any until he'd met these people. "I gave you . . . !" He grabbed her wrist roughly, but she kept her fist tightly closed. He tried to prise open her fingers.

She pulled back her hand. "I'll scream! Hand over that money or you'll regret it, you nasty, lying, hideous *Cherry*!"

He slapped her. It felt superb. Silene gasped, pressing her hand to her reddening cheek.

Lycaste sat back on the bed, watching her warily. For a moment they both said nothing. Silene took her trembling hand away from her face and looked at it.

"If you don't do what I ask then I'll tell them all," she said, rubbing her cheek again. "I'll shout it from the highest window."

"Tell them what?"

She climbed and straddled him. "I'll tell them what you did to me, and tomorrow you'll find yourself swinging from Hamamelis's gallows."

"But I didn't do anything to you!"

She took his hands and placed them on her fat thighs. "You're going to *fuck* me, Cherry."

He hadn't heard the simple curse used in that way before; it shocked him like it would an old lady. He looked up at Silene's grim face. She kept her hands firmly clamped over his, squeezed now into the hefty meat of her hips. His body, whether from her weight on top of him or simple panic, began to betray him, stiffening under her. She felt it, grinning a wicked grin.

"Last chance. Do it."

And so she had her way. It was grim and fast and bloody, Silene's inexperience evident in her troubled, pain-stricken expression.

Afterwards she left, dropping the silk ribbons she'd kept coiled in her fist throughout as if they were suddenly useless to her. He heard her footsteps and a door squealing shut. After a while he reached under the sheets and pulled out the large ring book that had troubled him so much, leafing through to the end.

The broadening physical dissimilarities between noble First-ling families and their southerly relatives led to the spread of what was known as Shameplague, an incurable ague of the blood that regularly affected the aristocracy before its cause could be properly identified. Characterised by excessive sanguineous weeping and facial lesions, it was—in all docu-mented studies—the result of banned intercourse between Melius and Excultus, the symptoms appearing within a day of transmission of humours. Crucially, only the more refined Excultus blood was susceptible to the illness, the offending Melius constitution too coarse for it to penetrate and thrive. By 14,050, for reasons unknown, it had disappeared almost entirely from the Westerly Provinces, even among those known to have degraded themselves with slaves or soldiers. The moleculets responsible for this inevitably fatal dis-ease are now thought to be dangerous only to those of the high-est Firstling and Secondling lineage, perversely according a sense of pride among some at the knowledge that such things were once present in their family.

*

Silene refused to attend her lesson the next day, shutting herself in her chamber without explanation. Jasione looked relieved, glad at the prospect of a morning to herself. She took Lycaste into the garden once more, lending him her sun hat and basket.

She showed him a flower as they walked, stopping to admire it.

"What is it?" He bent to have a closer look.

"It's my flower—*Jasione laevis*."

"That's your smaller name? Laevis?"

Jasione nodded, flashing the colour of the spindly flower, a washed-out blue. Lycaste thought she looked more beautiful than ever.

She pushed a stray hair away from her face shyly. "Would you like one?"

"A *Jasione laevis*?"

"To take with you, when you decide to leave here."

He coloured a formal gratitude blend, over the yellow. "It would be a shame to leave."

She studied him carefully, hopefully. "Yes. We're getting very used to you—we like having you here very much, Onosma. You know . . ." Jasione's eyes looked faraway as she ordered her thoughts, finally opening her mouth again. "Silene is especially taken with you. Did you notice?"

"Not really."

She struggled more with her next words. "I'd be lying if I said that I, too, didn't *like* you. I like you very much indeed. And I want you to know that . . ." She cleared her throat. "That it doesn't matter, what you may or may not be. That doesn't matter to me at all, not one bit."

He was allowed only a glimpse of her hopeful smile as they were interrupted by a man peering over the garden wall at them.

"Hello there!" he called. He was a very thin, vulture-faced creature with shadowed hollows to either side of his mouth. "And who might you be?"

Jasione flinched, glancing between Lycaste and the man. "Hamamelis! Good morning. How are you?"

"As well as could be expected, thank you, Jasione." He looked saddened as he spoke, and yet the inquisitive gleam remained.

"Yes, of course. I think Eremurus is indoors if you'd like to see him."

"Attending to the garden, I see?" He cracked a smile and she laughed nervously back.

"Yes, fine morning for it."

"Indeed." He regarded Lycaste once more. "And who is this? I've not met you, sir."

"Oh . . ." Jasione paused, searching for an answer.

"You're a tall fellow!" Hamamelis hopped lithely over the wall, exposing his shrivelled yellow body.

Lycaste forced a smile, extending his hand.

Hamamelis ignored it and reached up to clap Lycaste on the shoulder, observing his full height with a look of wonder. "A handsome fellow, too! I heard about you from my little nephew, Ulmus. It was a great shame you couldn't come to my dinner. *Onosma*, isn't it?"

"Yes."

"And I hear you're a Second equerry, is that right?"

"Correct."

He glanced between Lycaste and Jasione. "Ulmus tells me you've lost your master."

"A few weeks ago."

Hamamelis tutted with polite concern. "Most irregular, and concerning." He looked at them both, bobbing his head, affirming the resemblance to a bird of prey. "Who is your Plenipotentiary? I might be familiar with him—I presented my sons to the Second a few years ago for consideration."

"Callistemon." The name was out of his mouth before he could think of another.

"*Callistemon*!" Hamamelis exclaimed with a leer. "I was sure it would be! He has dined here at Koyulhizar before. We stayed with his brother Xanthostemon at their estate when my boys were presented. And you say he's gone missing? Unthinkable!"

"That is why I'm here, to wait for him."

"Of course, of course. I hope they're looking after you here."

"They've been very kind."

He pointed at Lycaste's basket. "You're making him work for his keep, Jasione?"

She laughed. "Oh yes, he wasn't going to get a free stay with us."

Hamamelis frowned, his slim features lengthening almost to a beak. "I'm sure it is not my place to bring up such things, but my little spy mentioned that you have a great deal of money with you, Onosma. Did I hear correctly?"

Lycaste looked quickly at Jasione, but her face was expressionless. "I have some."

"I see." Hamamelis did not smile, looking suddenly rather bored with the conversation, as if there were places he'd rather be. He toyed with a branch, glancing back to them. "Well, then, where is Eremurus? I've come to sample this new wine of his." He cracked a smile at last. "You might well find me on the floor this afternoon!"

Jasione smiled. "We'll join you later—there's still a little more to do here."

"Very well!" The vulture stared Lycaste up and down again, scratching the back of his neck. "It's very good to meet you, Onosma. Any friend of these two is surely a friend of mine." He extended his hand at last and Lycaste took it. "I should very much like to help you find Callistemon. He is as fine a man as any I know."

"Thank you, he is."

Hamamelis grinned at them both and ambled off down the path.

They watched until he had entered the house.

"How did I do?" he asked Jasione.

She clamped her mouth shut, thinking, for what seemed to Lycaste like a very long time. "I— *we* heard only yesterday that his youngest son had been found dead." She stared at Lycaste. "His name was Leonotis."

Lycaste opened his mouth but she held her hand up. "I don't want to know anything. *Anything.* Leonotis was not a good man. I wasn't sorry to hear of what had happened to him."

Good man. Lycaste glanced over his shoulder and around the garden. "How did Hamamelis find out?"

Jasione shook her head, her eyes looking sore. Her words were almost inaudible. "You should not have let him go."

"Let who go?"

She rounded on him, bringing her face very close to his until he thought she would kiss him, as her daughter had. "Don't you *dare* pretend—not with me! Don't you dare!" Her voice choked and she turned away again, gazing restlessly out at the wooded slopes beyond the citadel walls. "Don't even *think* of trying to insult my intelligence." Jasione's hands gripped the wall, as if she meant to push herself up and over. "If he decides you are what you are . . . It isn't safe for you here. Didn't you notice that on the Artery? Or are you all as stupid as they say?"

Lycaste didn't reply. They heard the gate, both looking to see Eremurus coming up the path. He glanced gravely at Jasione.

"Did he say anything?"

"Not a lot. He didn't touch the wine I gave him."

"What shall we do?"

Lycaste had the feeling that any suggestions he made would not be well received. He put down his basket, spying Silene observing them from the top window. His room.

"He's definitely gone?"

"I waved farewell to him."

"You saw him leave, then."

Eremurus looked back. "I saw him walk down the lane."

"Go and check."

He nodded with a sigh and walked towards the house.

"You've got to fetch your things and go," she said to Lycaste coldly. "And we'll need more money before you leave."

Jasione waited until there was no sign of Eremurus among the droning shrubs and suddenly hugged Lycaste fiercely. He watched the top window over her shoulder, but Silene's round face was gone.

She looked up. "Did you hear what I said? You can't stay here any more."

"How much money do you want?"

She hesitated. "All of it. It's only fair."

He pulled away. "What?"

"We aren't safe any more, either. Hamamelis has the favour of the Second."

Lycaste strode for the tower, the peace of the garden at odds with his thoughts; he'd already made his plans the night before, following Silene's departure. He took the steps three at a time to his chamber, a feat he'd never have managed in his old life, and slammed the wooden door behind him, wobbling it on its hinges.

He hoisted the pack, sensing simultaneously its massively reduced weight and the muffled arrival of men in the garden below, Hamamelis's harsh voice among them. He didn't look out, instead feeling quickly inside the bag. All she'd left him was the children's book Elcholtzia had packed, his wandering hand rattling roughly past it.

"You brat!" he bellowed, hearing Silene piling things against her own chamber door along the hallway. Her swift footsteps pounded to the tower window.

"He's up here! Quick! In the top room!"

Lycaste beat furiously at the wall, knowing that he would be trapped before he made it to the bottom of the stair. Feet drummed on the first floor, three, maybe four men. He threw a final punch at the blue door, something in his hand snapping. The girl in the next room shrieked at his roar of pain as he dropped to the floor, the tears welling in his eyes. He looked up at the prism of hot daylight blurring from his window, seeing a flange of old metal guttering hanging down outside the ledge.

"He went past you? Don't look at him, answer me. He must have done."

"I don't know. I had my door tight shut in case he . . . I heard him in there until you came upstairs!"

"You heard him in his room?"

"Yes, screaming at me."

"Why? Why was he screaming at you?"

"I don't know. Because I'd taken his things."

"What things?"

"No, I mean . . . he *thought* I'd taken his things, that's what he thought. He's a brainless Cherry."

"So you don't have his possessions in here?"

"No."

"You wouldn't lie to me, would you, Silene? You know I don't like liars."

"No, no—never."

"Get her outside."

"He forced us! He said he'd kill us if we told."

"That's what he said?"

"He tried to do things to me!"

"Take her outside."

Silence then, in the room below. Lycaste laid his head on the tapering, wind-chiselled roof that was part of the shell of the tower above Silene's chamber and listened to her retreating cries, suddenly louder again as she was marched outside and into the front garden.

"Cladrastis, go back and help your brother check."

A grunt of assent.

"Well, Eremurus," Hamamelis's voice said after a pause, "here we are. It looks like he's got away, hasn't he?"

They must have all been down there, in the front garden. Lycaste wondered what had happened to the servants.

Hamamelis laughed caustically. "An *equerry*! How could you both be so easily taken in?"

There was no answer that Lycaste could hear, and he began to think that perhaps the man was talking to himself.

"Of all people—of all my friends . . ." He cleared his throat and spat, his last word echoing from the rampart. "Your daughter has accused the Cherry of some truly awful things," said the vulture, composing himself. "Were you aware?"

"What has she said?" growled Jasione.

"Tell them, Silene."

"He took advantage of me!" she cried shrilly. "He called me into his room and . . . I couldn't get away. That's why I didn't come to my lesson."

Hamamelis had a smile in his voice. "She says the Cherry forced you to shelter him."

Again his question was met with silence.

"There. She tried. Never mind, I wouldn't have believed you anyway. In fact, I don't believe any of it. We all know what type of girl Silene is. Perhaps the Cherry refused you? Eh, Silene? I wouldn't be surprised."

Lycaste tired from lifting his head clear of the roof's grainy white surface, seeing nothing but the far hills, and settled his cheek down again. He coloured his purest white, splaying flatter on the sweltering slab. From Silene's room came the sounds of swift, orderly rifling. Lycaste remembered the layout of her large, brightly painted chamber from his own searches of the house, the boxes of secret things and trinkets. He knew exactly where he would have hidden the money had it been his room: the stage.

The huge model was the most remarkable thing in the spoiled girl's toy-piled chamber; a thing that had made him stop and crouch during his explorations, tentatively reaching into it and tinkering. It was certainly better-made, if not so grand, as his dear, burned palace back at home. Inserted into its gaily painted wooden frame were two-dozen layers of scenery that slid in and out from long slots cut into the side. They formed a backdrop for the girl's set of expensive plastic actors: men, women and animals whose swivelling heads could turn—as he'd found out after a few minutes' experimentation—to display one of four skilfully drawn emotions. But he had soon lost interest in them, his attention turning to the wonderful scenery, beautifully rendered in thick paint across each of the twenty-four boards. Upon one, a landscape of tumultuous clouds frothed and piled like nothing he had seen since the storm, while the next was a glowing blue day dappled with evening stars. Further slats were partial interiors, confusing Lycaste until he found that he could overlay them with another to create yet more scenarios. Between the stored landscapes lay enough empty space to hide the wealth he'd brought with him, the interior gaps hidden from chance discovery by a broad wooden lid. Engrossed, he'd slid them all back to look at each in detail, noticing too late that the girl must not have played with her stage for a long time and his fat fingermarks in the dust were obvious for anyone to see.

He lay baking on the roof, hearing the search draw closer to the as-yet-unnoticed stage. The searcher began to rummage directly beneath where Lycaste was sprawled, his hesitation evident as he regarded the intricate toy. There was a thump and Cladrastis entered the room.

"Look at this."

"What is it?"

"One of her toys. A theatre. Look, she has all the actors."

Cladrastis's silence was unimpressed. "There are fingerprints. Check inside those holes."

"These? Ah."

There was nothing. She hadn't hidden the money there. He should have known from the dust—Silene would never have thought of using it.

They moved on without replacing the slides. Lycaste wished he didn't know the admiring voice so well. The bed creaked and one of them uttered a gasp.

"That's more like it! *Look* at all that. Did you know Chaemerion had this much?" A pause as it was sifted through. "Is that the weapon he used?"

"That's the one," the new voice said.

"Good. Take half. We can come back for the rest later when Pap's gone to bed. Put it in that, the theatre."

As the footfalls thumped out of the room, Lycaste stretched, edging towards the parapet for a glimpse of the people in the front garden. Little by little he saw the tops of their heads, then their faces, their feet. Hamamelis was glancing at the house, ignoring his three neighbours, who sat dejectedly on the side of the path just outside the garden wall. Jasione glared sullenly at the dust while her daughter's shoulders heaved and bobbed. Cladrastis, less weedy and misshapen than his father, appeared from under the shadow of the tower, tossing Hamamelis the ring, followed by his brother.

Lycaste leaned, eyes trained on the back of the brother's head as he handed his father the money and turned to the people sitting in the road. Melilotis.

"Did you ever see such a wealthy Cherry?" exclaimed Hamamelis, holding up a fistful of ribbons. He waved the jaunty tassels in Eremurus's face. "Stolen!"

"That's his money," said Eremurus tiredly, his eyes on the path.

"*It's not his money!*" screamed Hamamelis in a sudden, shaking rage, striking the man. "That monster killed my Leonotis and you sheltered him, you looked after him! What did he promise you, Eremurus? Tell me that much—what did he promise you to hide him here?"

"We didn't know he was the one!" sobbed Jasione. "We believed him."

Hamamelis turned to the house and scanned the walls and gardens.

"What are you going to do with us?" asked Jasione.

Hamamelis stretched his arm behind his back, like a swimmer before a race. "I think you both know."

Tell Me

Lycaste flexed his finger again in demonstration, still tender from that day at Koyulhizar, but Sotiris didn't see. He was staring into the woodland where hanging lanterns glowed, as if he'd managed to fall asleep with his eyes open.

Lycaste took a breath, continuing uncertainly. "I climbed back in and waited until the evening, just before they closed the gates. When the brothers returned I managed to slip away, risking the north road forest."

He waited for the man to give some sign that he'd heard even one word of the tale.

Sotiris stirred, his shoulders rising. Lycaste could not see his eyes in the soft night lights. "Do you feel better?"

He thought about it. "A little."

The Amaranthine began tapping a finger at his mouth. "There is one part of your tale I would know more about."

"Yes?"

"This old man from the Tenth. *Jotroffe*. Tell me about him."

Nomad

The Nomad was a famous class of schooner, known throughout the Investiture as the pride of the Lacaille fleet, and yet Ghaldezuel had told him they possessed only three—the other two presently sitting in a hangar somewhere, too old and dangerous to take to the skies. Corphuso was granted chaperoned visits to the engine compartments to look at the tetraluminal filaments, the calibre of which he freely admitted his own empire did not possess, at least to his knowledge. The filaments, looming darkly in their housings like gigantic bundles of wound copper wire, were of course Amaranthine-made and fabulously old, a present from the Age of Decadence before the Immortal's relationship with the Lacaille had soured. They were cared for night and day by a separate crew, the Lacaille High Commission fully aware of their value. Corphuso understood well enough how to build a filament of his own, but also that achieving any speeds greater than the basic minimum was a feat the Amaranthine had taken with them into senility. Being given the chance to see such treasures firsthand was a rare honour, and he thanked them for it.

The encounter with the Vulgar privateer on Steerilden's Land had resulted in substantial losses, the captain of that ship—whoever he was—proving capable enough to evade and roast one of the legions that had escorted them from the battleship over the Threen moon of Port Obviado. The damage to the Nomad itself had proved debilitating enough to require an extra day's work, during which Corphuso had been permitted time to stretch his legs in the wild pink poppy fields. There was nowhere he could run to, and so he had apparently not been watched as he walked, exploring the small green islet's forests in wonder.

Dutifully returning to find the schooner in good health again, Ghaldezuel had announced to Corphuso that they would be increasing their speed towards Firmament centre. The Lacaille knight had handed him a heavy thrombosis suit made from capsules of a reeking yellow gel and watched as he put it on. The few suits aboard were given only to the highest-ranking Lacaille, and many unprotected troops died on high-speed journeys. Corphuso mumbled his gratitude, wondering briefly who might be going without so that he could be given such protection.

They sat together, upon finishing a large evening meal of Steerilden hare, in the aft hangar of the Nomad, its progress from the Satrapy of Port Elsbet measured in Lacaille code beeped via the intercom. Around them the vessel growled, the speed of their descent through the Firmament expanding the tin, steel and rubber fabric of the hull. Beyond them, the Shell, still encased in the giant metal chest, sat like a gunmetal block under the hangar's fluorescents.

Corphuso had ceased speaking Vulgar with Ghaldezuel, choosing instead to practise his Lacaille. It appeared from all angles as if his future now lay with the rival empire and their new, if inexplicable, loyalty to certain factions within the Amaranthine. It occurred to him that little had really changed—he was being transported in relative comfort and ease to the Vaulted Lands, and much faster than he might have been had his party of Vulgar not been betrayed. Honours and privileges could still await among the Amaranthine, and a chance to leave the Prism Investiture forever. He'd decided on his walk through the poppies that he should also begin his new life by brushing up on Unified, the Immortal language. It was a difficult tongue, filled with short, clipped words that shared a frustrating number of meanings, but it would stand him in good stead when the Nomad eventually reached its final—and as yet still undisclosed—destination.

He could see from the buckles on the huge metal case that the Shell had been inspected during his absence, perhaps even tested, but decided not to ask Ghaldezuel directly about such things. He knew that it worked perfectly, that they would not be disappointed should they find some poor fellow to test it on, but still the possibility of somehow failing them, after all they had done to secure him and his machine, unnerved him. The Soul Engine was unlike anything ever conceived of before, of that he was sure; it would be the start of a new age of daunting, unfathomable possibilities, perhaps even, he feared, levelling the power of the Firmament—a power held so long and so tightly—once and for all. Corphuso also knew, though, that whatever eventual peace it brought, whatever equality it ripped from the Immortals' indolent hands, his machine would still be an engine of death for generations to come, a plague against which there would be no defence. But change, he reflected, always began that way, destroying what was already there to make room for the new. He would do his best to warn those who finally took charge of the Shell, though he knew somewhere deep down that even they would not listen.

"We are at fourteen million miles per hour," said Ghaldezuel, taking a sip of water as he listened to the code from the intercom. He drank no ales or wines on principle and allowed Corphuso none, either. "I advise you not to do anything strenuous for the remainder of the journey as we increase velocity."

"I wasn't planning on it," replied Corphuso in Lacaille, the stink of the thrombosis gel reaching his nostrils again. He knew he would have to get used to it and was trying to breathe in as much as possible.

Ghaldezuel nodded, his Voidsuit replaced by a lighter though still preciously inlaid variant with superior inbuilt shock-absorption. "Your Lacaille improves already with practice. What other Prism-speak do you know?"

He shrugged. "I am fluent in Pifoon, and my Low Oxel is fairly good. I can speak limited but conversational Threen, Zelioceti One and Two, Wulmese Fifth Dialect and some rusty Unified, as well as a smattering of Quetterel." He thought for a moment. "I suppose I could also get by in First, should we crash-land in the Old Satrapy."

Ghaldezuel did not look at him as he wiped his mouth. "An excellent education."

Corphuso knew well the resentment in Ghaldezuel's voice. "My family traded with the Vaulted Land of Epsilon Eridani. It was profitable."

"I am sure," replied Ghaldezuel, looking off towards the stacked columns of rusted white half-tracks at the other end of the hangar. "Shall we take a look at your machine? I am eager to gain an appraisal of its abilities."

Corphuso glanced at the huge case. "You doubt the cargo?"

Ghaldezuel's sky-blue eyes looked into his. "Perhaps I doubt the inventor."

Sulthumo Leorgin had been a freeVulgar boot polisher working in the court of Count Andolp of Filgurbirund, a wealthy landowner and occasional financier of clever inventions. When Leorgin died after a short bout of breathworm—known by the Amaranthine as tuberculosis, and at that time a very common cause of death among the Vulgar scrape classes—he was inspected perfunctorily by one of the count's physicians and taken to be interred in the Serf Ponds.

What happened next astounded the various undertakers who carried his corpse, and would go on to capture the imagination of the whole Investiture. At first it appeared, after the body began violently shaking and wheezing, that Sulthumo was not dead at all and might begin to make a recovery. Only after he died a second time—being officially pronounced expired in the arms of the undertakers once more—did they resume moving him to the ponds to join his family plot. When Leorgin woke for a third time, his carriers decided they had little more patience for a body that could not make its mind up whether to live or die and called the physicians once more.

Leorgin died and came back to life again thirty-one times before they decided to shoot him, after which he apparently expired for good. As far as Corphuso could tell, the boot polisher was dead still, but developments would later make him question even that assumption.

Opening him up, Count Andolp's personal physician discovered that Sulthumo Leorgin's body contained certain abnormalities in Vulgar anatomy never before recorded; in his notes, carefully studied during the intervening years, the doctor wrote of channels in the brain and neck that were oddly formed, opening here and there into hollows where the spinal column should have grown vertebrae. It was a stroke of luck for the unfortunate Leorgin that he had never broken his feeble spine, although later discussion of the matter concluded that he would likely have returned to life even if he had. The channels and loops and caves of space, equivalent perhaps in size to a Vulgar digestive system, may have accounted for the "reflux of life," as the physician put it, that resulted in poor Sulthumo waking repeatedly after his own death, and casts were made of his exceptional interior in order to study it further.

Almost a year later, a young medical student discovered, through the accidental shining of an electric torch into the cast, that light behaved *unusually* within its confines, and apparently remained within its structure to glow long after the torch had been shut off. The news of such magic drew philosophers and alchemists from around the kingdom, and Count Andolp grew rich from the display of his ex-polisher's astounding innards. Before long, the news percolated beyond the Vulgar borders, attracting Prism travellers and magicians from all over the Investiture, and, eventually, Amaranthine.

Corphuso Trohilat, then a young architect engaged through family connections in designing a mausoleum for the prince of Drolgins, visited the Count's museum of oddities to view the casts, paying handsomely to see the exhibit alone. He understood, after taking careful measurements, that there might be further applications for the curiosity, known by now as Andolp's Astounding Light-Trap.

He appealed to his family and within a year had secured the funds to buy the Light-Trap from the count, who parted with it on the condition that he retained rights to a high percentage of all future profits made. Corphuso accepted willingly, knowing that such profits would be enough to buy Filgurbirund itself one day, and perhaps a good deal more.

Despite probable sabotage in which the original casts were destroyed, Corphuso's timely measurements assured he was able to build a larger-than-life-sized replica of the hollows and tubes, situating them within a surrounding case and experimenting over the years with different materials in the construction. It appeared that the geometry of the shapes had to be reproduced exactly—to within a fraction of an inch of the original measurements—for anything unusual to happen, such as light and even sound somehow remaining stuck for a time within the hollows, and Corphuso began to speculate at the incredible odds of finding such a freak of nature at all. When all was ready, he excitedly began the first phase of his experiments, purchasing Lacaille prisoners from jails and labour camps across Filgurbirund with the promise that, should the experiment succeed, they would be pardoned to a man for their crimes against the Vulgar and released.

One thousand and seventeen Lacaille prisoners climbed, one at a time, into the massive machine Corphuso had built, thin extension tubes connecting them to the coils and hollows within. Once inside, the hatch was sealed, suffocating them in a matter of minutes.

The same one thousand and seventeen Lacaille returned to their cells over the course of the trial, alive and fully functional, delighted with the prospect of their pardon.

The Soul Engine was a success. The year was 14,636 AD, Amaranthine Standard, and death had finally been conquered.

Corphuso studied the scratched metal surface of the table, glowing under the hangar lights, and the dead remains of the hare on its platter. Its buck-teeth were still visible, poking slightly from its splayed lips. The meat around its cheeks and eyes had been cut away. No one within the Prism Investiture, not least the Vulgar, appeared to be concerned by the implications of such a revelation. All they saw was a functional solution to a problem that plagued far too many in the kingdoms of the Investiture, as well as another way of gaining influence within the Amaranthine and punishing their Lacaille enemies further. Corphuso shook his head gently. His machine had found the *soul*, ensconced in its hiding place since the evolution of the ancient mammal phyla that had birthed the lines that would make the Amaranthine, Melius and Prism alike. His findings spoke not just of immortality—perhaps an even more perfect immortality than the sadistic decadents of the Firmament had ever dreamed of—but also the possibility that there was indeed something that came after, some world just beyond glimpsing. He had found the evidence of life after death. And it didn't even stop there. Corphuso's first fully formed emotion after realising his device worked was one of profound fear. It raised the implications that there might, after all, be a God.

He looked back at the hare, stretched and cold, its yellowish fur tinged with the blush of the vast Steerilden poppy fields, wondering where its animal soul had travelled to, and where it might reside now.

The Lacaille prisoners' pardons were later rescinded by the Vulgar kingdom, the high courts of Filgurbirund never really believing that such a thing would be possible and deeming the release of over a thousand prisoners an almost treasonously stupid act, and all were put to death again, this time without the help of the Shell.

By then, news of the life-conjuring engine was deliberately being hushed-up by Filgurbirund, the princes and dukelings deeming it a vital asset in the three-hundred-year Lacaille-Vulgar hostilities. Corphuso was arrested and forced to sign away his invention to the Principality of the moon of Drolgins, with all profits to be handed over immediately, and relocated to the fortress of Nilmuth to resume his work. There he remained a virtual prisoner, confined to his libraries and workshops with a force of technicians, most of whom had now either died in the siege or on Port Obviado, up until the day the Amaranthine had arrived.

"So," said Ghaldezuel, watching as the chest was unbuckled, "you were working to make it smaller."

Corphuso shrugged as the two Lacaille vacuum troopers swung open the chest at last and pulled away the gold-thread cloth, revealing the gleaming expanse of the machine. "It was hoped that we could make a wearable piece for each soldier, so that death would become nothing more than a minor irritation on the battlefield."

Ghaldezuel looked at him shrewdly. "But the device only succeeds if no part of the body is permanently damaged—I understand nothing messier than asphyxiation is viable."

Corphuso stepped up to the Shell, checking to make sure that it had not been damaged, beginning to feel possessive of it all over again. "A team of surgeons would accompany the armies—at least, that was the plan—to stitch them back together as quickly as possible. With the contraption on rapid circulation it would ensure continual healing and prevent brain death, even if our soldiers were shot through with bullets." He glanced at Ghaldezuel, who was standing with him at the edge of the machine. "In practical situations, I don't believe it was as simple as that. I was charged with ironing out the problems."

The Lacaille knight remained silent for a while, examining the shifting colours on the Shell's surface. "How far did you progress?" he asked at last, turning back to Corphuso.

The architect hesitated, having known for some time that this question would be put to him at some point. His only remaining power lay in what he had yet to publish to the Principality before his capture, information still locked away in his head. "I achieved little more than the early trials," he said, looking directly at the Lacaille. "The Soul Engine is not a machine for rejuvenation—that grail is still yet to be found, or"—he added thoughtfully—"remains in the possession of the Amaranthine alone. This device does one thing only, but does it well: it restores life energy to a corpse, capturing and, with my modifications, *returning* what we can only call its immortal soul. The state of the body within which this aura then finds itself is not a fault of the Soul Engine, but rather a fault of those who performed the killing."

Ghaldezuel sat again, taking up his plastic glass of recycled water. "Defensively put." He drained the water. "The Amaranthine will find its true potential now."

Corphuso went and sat at the table, too, the troops closing the case and returning to their positions at the huge doors of the hangar. A beep on the tannoy told them the Nomad was increasing its speed again, though it would be a couple more days before it passed the nearest Satrapy.

"Something has troubled me," he said to Ghaldezuel, maintaining eye contact. "Why would the Amaranthine begin the process of moving the Engine, the Shell, only to suddenly hire the Lacaille to do it, thereby sabotaging all they had just achieved? I mean no offence when I say that the Lacaille were never the trusted allies to them that the Vulgar have been."

Ghaldezuel snorted, perhaps at the obviousness of the statement. "My dear, innocent, Corphuso—as a scientist you make a dangerous assumption, assuming a constant that is no longer there."

"A constant?" He grasped the meaning only after he had spoken.

"Yes. The Amaranthine. They are broken at last."

"They are at war with one another? I had not heard this . . ."

Ghaldezuel shook his head, turning the cup over and placing it on the table. "They have crowned a new king. And this one pays whoever gets the job done fastest."

Message

"They say he's brought other Glorious Birds with him," tweeted the little white and red messenger bird. "They say they are at least as beautiful."

Lycaste didn't understand. "Why?"

The creature twitched. "There will be *such* jealousy."

Lycaste looked sidelong at it, wondering if he'd ever get a straight answer from anything in the Utopia. The Glorious Bird hadn't been seen in the garden for days, disappearing the same morning as the strange Amaranthine. Now the bird was returning to the fringes of the Utopia with a flock of his peers, Glorious Birds from other gardens around the Black Sea, and rumours were spreading. Mated pairs squabbled in the branches and around the lakes as the females preened to be wooed again, anxious that their plumage look as good even out of season.

Lycaste thanked the bird and nibbled on some breakfast, his appetite disappearing. He stepped over a crushed egg pushed from a conjoined blister of nests in a tall tree.

Their arrival was announced with growing volume, as if Lycaste's ears were being slowly unplugged. The background whistles and screeches increased as each successive mile of trees spotted the thin, bright line gliding over the Utopia. He looked up, shading his eyes. They were flying in formation, perfectly straight and very high. He couldn't see their colours. As they drew overhead, the foremost bird angled its wings and soared diagonally, looping beneath the others as they held their formation. It spiralled down until Lycaste recognised their Utopia's Glorious. A group of riotously coloured peacocks arranged themselves to meet the Glorious Birds on a lawn not far from where Lycaste stood with some of the Amaranthine, their senile muttering suddenly excited.

As he watched the display, a parakeet landed with a flutter on his shoulder, its talons puncturing his skin.

"How goes it, Lycaste?"

He stiffened, grimacing as the talons bit deeper, looking up into the creature's gimlet eyes.

"Who do you think they've come for?" it whispered.

"What?" He flinched and tried to sweep it away, feeling blood run from the punctures. The parakeet dodged and skipped to his other shoulder, clacking its black beak in a laugh. "Thought you got away with it, didn't you?"

Lycaste grabbed at it, bending in an attempt to shake the bird free.

"The Most Great and Glorious hears everything," it cackled, hopping to the back of his neck. "We've had your sort trying to hide in here before. Killing-men, despoilers, rapists. This garden is closed to you now."

The line of Glorious Birds above them dispersed, each plummeting towards him as the parakeet finally flapped away. Lycaste watched them javelin over the trees, trying to absorb what was happening. They knew, somehow. He turned to run, the crowd of birds and Immortals parting before him.

To Lycaste's side, a bird swooped low under the branches, aiming for his head. He ducked, striking out as he felt the breeze of its wings. Talons scraped and dug into his back. He tripped, the arm that was meant to break his fall held by something above and behind, and landed on his face in the shit-smeared grass beneath the tree. The Glorious Birds fell and covered him, prodding and scratching.

Lycaste heaved his shoulders and shook a screeching bird free, crushing its wing beneath his arm.

"His eyes!" screamed the Glorious.

A bird pounced on Lycaste's head and pecked frantically at his brow. He shouted incoherently and rolled again, digging his face into the grass.

"Stop!" he cried, his voice muffled. "*Stop!*"

"Roll him," said one of the birds. Lycaste turned himself, staying as limp as he could while trying to avert his face from their manic beaks.

The Utopia's own Glorious Bird landed weightily on his chest.

"Men who kill men are found out. They cannot hide, not even in here. The noble family of Callistemon Pallidus Berenzargol, Second-Prince," it said, looking around the lawn at the surrounding Amaranthine and birds, "expect you for trial."

There was only one nest large enough to serve as Lycaste's cage, that belonging to the Glorious Bird himself. After some deliberation he was forced within. He shoved aside objects and cloth, snapping shelves and pulling down hanging things until he was half-comfortable in the fishy-smelling hovel, his weight sagging the branches that held the nest up and drooping it almost to the ground. One of the colourful birds pushed the shutters closed and he was alone again.

Lycaste breathed in the odour and laid his head against the nest wall, his ear pressing painfully against a sharp piece of something woven into the structure. He began to cry, his convulsions jiggling the cage, part of him wondering how long it had been since he'd last wept. It was over, done. Imprisoned at last for some moment of thoughtlessness that he couldn't yet identify. He would have to accept what was coming to him.

He was awoken by a tapping on the shutter. It was perfectly dark, so dark that if he tried hard he could pretend he was confined to a full-sized room. A patch of grey appeared as the shutter opened.

"Sotiris?" he whispered.

The grey light chuckled. "Yes, yes. Sotiris is gone now. You are big and yet I am small."

He tried to remember Well-Spoken's real name, the one Sotiris had used. "Garamond?"

"Garamond," the voice replied. "Sebastian Saul Garamond. The good ship S. S. *Garamond*."

"You remember your name?"

"I am Sebastian. You are big, I am small. Here." He passed Lycaste a little bundle of wrapped linen, his supper. Lycaste hadn't realised how hungry he was until he saw it. He needed to piss, but somehow knew they wouldn't let him out to do it.

"And a message from Sotiris, yes," added the Amaranthine.

Lycaste paused, a berry in his mouth. "A message? From Sotiris?"

"Sotiris says be patient, you will see." Garamond chuckled again and closed the hatch.

Lycaste waited in the darkness, food forgotten, but apparently that was it. He wasn't sure what to make of it all. Was the message, brief as it was, something he could believe? He had been starting to consider, before Garamond's arrival, the terrible notion that Sotiris himself might have betrayed him to the Utopia's guardians. But that was impossible—why would he? Lycaste still knew nothing about the Immortal; a group of returning Amaranthine had interrupted their talk in the clearing and demanded that everyone dance. The next morning, Sotiris was gone.

He nestled his head into the side of the basket, knees drawn up to his chin. Perhaps it was just a hiccup in Garamond's mind, a replayed message meant for someone else centuries, even millennia ago. It meant nothing at all, really. He couldn't allow it to give him hope, not yet.

Song

The peculiar man plunged and sank, opening his eyes after a few moments of darkness. Far below his slim white legs the sand was eerily clean, like unbroken desert dunes. Not a single fish or crab sifted the rippled floor. He had swum in the coves of the Tenth Province for hundreds of years, returning almost every Midsummer to the cool green of the Nostrum sea where serpents slithered in the depths. He treated it like a holiday from his long exile on the Old World, staying at the finest guest houses on his way through, walking the near-endless fruit forests and listening to their whispers as night fell, the stars around which his fellows still lived twinkling in the cobalt evening skies.

The giant Southern Melius here were some of Jatropha's favourites—he knew them all by name, their daily lives, habits and desires. He loved them like his children, which, at a certain remove, he supposed they almost were. Of course they thought him odd, as prior generations had, but that was the price he had to pay. Jatropha liked to believe he had never been the self-conscious sort.

So, he thought, diving deeper. The war for the Old World progressed. Elatine, commander of the Jalan legions, was victorious and his regime now prevailed in the west, challenging the First's unbroken rule of these lands for the last six hundred years. Those who cared—and they were few—said FirstLord Protector Zigadenus's death was the most the Nostrum Melius could hope for, the greatest impetus to true change in the Provinces of the Old World. They said it wouldn't be long before Elatine took the Second and—he presumed—the massacres and segregation and all the rest of it began at last in the name of revolution. Jatropha shook his head underwater, enjoying the languid sweep of his hair across his view, enclosing him. He'd known both of them, the Asiatic warlord Elatine and his high-born Firstling nemesis Zigadenus, and they had known him, albeit in subtle shades of disguise.

The correct Melius had won, of that he had no doubt, but the reality was unjust. Zigadenus, blown to ash at the summit of a hill along with sixty-three mounted aristocracy, had always been the better of them: a wiser, kinder, more innately truthful creature than the ambitious Elatine. Zigadenus had been a friend.

Whatever the characters of the Melius involved, Elatine's forces were poised to mend the Provinces. Their legions stood for the time-honoured principles of distributed wealth and social equality—everything the First's dominion had denied to all but the elite within its lands. The warlord's personality, however disagreeable Jatropha might have found it when last they met, should matter no more than the grain of bread given to a starving man. It was the will of his armies and his home Provinces that propelled his advance, as well as a mysterious source of funds. Jatropha suspected there was Amaranthine coin—Firmamental Ducats—mixed in with the heaps of silk that filled Elatine's vaults, and more than a few crates of Prism materiel, too. What was important, he had to keep reminding himself when his ancient thoughts turned sour, was that Elatine appeared to hate the decadence of the age enough to be uncorrupted by it, publicly demanding as his first law of succession an end to almost six and a half centuries of tyranny, and the osmosis of all that accumulated power back to the freeMelius of the Nostrum Provinces. That was fair and right but—Jatropha knew—simplistic.

The Firmament, glorious as its ancient masters wished to portray it, was in essence an impossibly delicate, eleven-light-year-wide ecosystem; an ecosystem reliant on very exact balances of power and influence to survive. The Amaranthine (though he rarely felt any connection with them any more, having not visited the precious Satrapies for many lifetimes) held sway only through the ratio of butlers, gardeners, housekeepers and paying tenants to the riff-raff that inhabited the thin wilderness—the Prism Investiture—that surrounded their huge and desolate estate, the twenty-three Solar Satrapies. If a world within the Firmament fell into disorder—as had befallen Epsilon India before the Volirian Conflict, if he remembered correctly—someone had to make sure it wasn't swiftly colonised by undesirables like the Lacaille, the Vulgar, or any of the multitude of other savage primate races into which the fringes of humanity had twisted, some of which he'd been unfortunate enough to have had dealings with whenever they'd strayed onto the Old

World. It was the Old World, this murky globe of forgotten, monstrous life, that would fall apart should any of them gain a foothold, a rotten front tooth in a ruined smile. Not many of the Immortals cared all that much any more. Most were consigned to the Utopias in a dribbling stupor or swaddled in their fortresses within the Vaulted Lands, only the sharp mountains and deep forests for company. These relatively populous, cosmopolitan centres of the Firmament were where such dangers were supposed to be considered and discussed, but by the sounds of things the Amaranthine had already slipped into a coma from which there would be no waking. There were simply too few sane Immortals now to hold their protectorates, too many slowing, uninterested minds.

He rose a little in the water, watching mercurial light sliding under the surfaces of the waves; his ears keenly open to the thick sounds all around. Did it not make sense, then, to worry about who governed so much of a vital territory? To educate them, if one could, and warn them of powers that might wish to exploit them in the future? Elatine's success in the Inner Provinces would result in the joining of two very different continents under one regime, their giant inhabitants sharing so little in common; the Jalan Melius: almost fifteen feet tall at the shoulder, enlightened but passionate, brimming with testosterone; and their European counterparts: smaller, wilier, viciously supercilious.

But that was still to come, a hypochondriac's box of night-time fears. Right now there was nothing to report at all, his sources in the First, Second and lately Third having fallen silent. The silence troubled him more than any news could.

The Melius were a perceptive species with senses more attuned to the workings of the world than any other Prism (who were of course closer cousins to them than the Amaranthine, no matter what nonsense the First liked to propagate). They had long been sensible to the obscure motions of the Firmament beyond the sky, their history and culture filled with stories of peculiar creatures and flying galleons, magic that fell from the stars. They felt things even the Amaranthine could not feel, and as such Jatropha had listened earnestly to the generations of tales of a spirit that haunted the woods of the Westerly Provinces, a ghoul that took the form of a beast, sometimes a man, plump and vague and kindly in his appearance. On his many travels he had sought it out, intrigued by the origins of the enduring myth, but in the darkness of the forests he had felt nothing. Surely some as-yet-undocumented animal lived in the depths of those woods, something eerie enough to frighten the enormous Melius that had told him the tales, but he had not been able to find it.

But now he had a particular hobby to indulge, and another animal to find.

Jatropha extended an arm and swept it through the green gloom, meaning to swim deeper and investigate the dunes. There should be more fish about; at least two thousand individuals spiralling and flashing beneath his toes, but instead he counted only a dozen. A lionfish bristling with red barbs drifted amiably past, then changed its course and flitted away. He turned his head to watch it go. Something was coming.

Jatropha cupped his ears and dropped lower into the abyss. Since sounds moved much faster in liquid, he'd often thought the world beneath the sea was a more solid, real place than the world above, where beings dwelt in almost nothing by comparison: thin clearings of gas used as spaces to call home. At first he kept losing it, but soon the whispered song grew loud enough for him to turn away and close his eyes. The thing sounded almost human, more than whales or dolphins ever could. He'd heard those mammals speaking as spring turned to summer, warning one another of a recently arrived danger. Jatropha had called out to them tentatively, remembering that dolphins tended to shyness when they learned that men could speak their words. After enough careful pleasantries had been exchanged, they'd told him more about the creature than any of the Melius knew, even that poor Drimys. Now he wanted to meet it himself.

The Amaranthine took his hand away from his ear and opened his eyes. It was close now. Despite everything Jatropha knew, he was scared. It was coming for *him*, having undoubtedly felt his heartbeat before he'd heard a thing. But he still couldn't see it.

He began to mouth his own construction of the song, keeping it low at first while he practised, feeling only the vibrations in his throat. He spoke louder into the brine, having already had a few weeks' practice. The sounds around him stopped immediately. The Immortal waited, turning like a hanging body in the breeze. A child's body. At least *that* would end, unless they'd all been very wrong.

The huge face loomed to his right, appearing in the dappled shafts of light like a full moon through clouds, the opposite direction from where the songs had been coming. *Tried to trick me.*

It appeared to smile as it watched the Amaranthine, though he knew it couldn't, that it didn't know how. An accidental development producing meaning from the set of a predator's jaw. He floated, looking at it properly for the first time.

It was easy to see how some might guess the creature was related to white sharks, now reduced and rare in these waters, but this close it really didn't look much like them at all. Jatropha studied the lines of its ghostly body, the angles of its many fins—a greater number than any class of mackerel shark possessed—thinking the massive creature bore more of a resemblance to a huge, primordial sunfish than anything else. It waited, a white circle watching him in the empty green ocean.

The Immortal sang to it again, and this time the fish replied.

PART IV

Colour Blend

A bristle came loose from her brush as she ran it over the swab of blue, lodging just beneath a dry patch of white that she planned later to turn into the implication of a cloud. There weren't any clouds today, of course, but it would give the landscape some drama.

The bristle drooped in the thick blue and settled, some liquid collecting over it in a line of darker ultramarine. She looked at the hair critically, her hand poised, ready to flick it away with a nail. No, she would leave it, scrunching her eyes and twitching her head this way and that to see what others might see. The minute imperfection would give the future cloud an extra dab of accidental weight. She wouldn't tell her friends that, just to keep up the mystique. Half of each painting was finished by luck.

Pentas dipped the brush quickly in water as she glanced back at Impatiens, basking in the sun, and dropped it on the table next to Briza so that he might use it if he wanted to. She selected something small, wide and rectangular to block in his sagging, sleeping form, studying the brush for loose ends. She'd have to get some new materials from Sonerila; the birds had bought some beautiful things during their last outing to Mersin. Her watercolour set had come with her from the Seventh, containing blocks of mineral that never appeared to run low.

She wiped a line of water over the paper's crinkled surface and dabbed at it gently with a stained cloth. *Wrong colour.* Impatiens was pinker. She tickled some raw cadmium with the corner of the brush, rubbing it into the dirty mix on her palette, then adding white. Pentas knew the combination for her own skin without thinking, painting self-portraits in private that the others weren't allowed to see: sienna and rust, lots of white, finished with a touch of lemon. That extra yellow could be too much; it had to be applied very carefully. Sometimes, in a certain light, she didn't even think she could see it at all.

Pentas glanced for a little longer at the dozing man. He always sucked his tummy in. In sleep, the hidden extent of it rolled out, askew nipples and belly-button resembling a confused and idiotic face. Her hand moved about the scene, blocking and suggesting. It darted without thought to a space of blank paper just above the crown of the man's slumped head, swiftly implying a tower.

She stopped, looking again but painting nothing more. Lycaste's house was a wobbling haze in the thick heat beyond, its bougainvillea wailing across the distance. Several brightly coloured parrots hovered in the turbulence between the gardens; mating pairs, Eranthis said.

It was a lonely walk eastwards across the beach these days; she wouldn't go any more without someone to accompany her. The birds still lived there, pruning and harvesting the gardens, their haul of food too much for any of them to finish, but they found it lonely, too. It had been more than a month now since Lycaste had left, his crumpled note still making little sense. Elcholtzia wouldn't say much about the night Lycaste came to him, at first refusing to reveal anything at all. The stirrings of guilt were almost unnoticeable now as she looked at the towers, her crinkled work drying before her in the baking afternoon. Impatiens's dappled shade began to look more and more inviting.

She exhaled gently, seeing all the places where they had sat and strolled and talked. She'd fooled herself that his looks could mend what had never been there, feelings she simply didn't possess. He'd never have been satisfied. Life would have been unbearable for them both.

A shadow slipped across the painting, a cool, sharp drop of seawater on her shoulder. Callistemon bent to kiss her, ducking away when he saw he was dripping onto the paper.

"I like this one," he whispered, studying the painting. Briza hummed on the grass beside her, engrossed in his own drawings.

"How was your swim?" She was glad of the chance to stop. The work would remain an unfinished study.

"Drimys came with me at last. We trod water out by the Point until he could relax. Didn't see a thing."

She tilted her head to look up at him. "You look better today."

"You always say that."

He swam twice a day at her request. The salt appeared to do something for the lesions, drying them out so that they no longer wept so much. He smiled down at her with a halo of sun behind his head and she smiled back, taking one of his fingers in hers. Though she scrubbed Callistemon each evening until the rest of his light yellow skin was smooth and shiny, his face and arms grew ever worse.

He kissed her again and sat down cross-legged next to Briza, stroking the boy's curls as he painted. His mother had decided to extend her stay—the coastal climate congenial to her nerves—which had suited everyone. Pentas liked the way he and the boy were together, how instantly at ease in one another's company they could be without a word uttered between them. Often she would catch them just sitting, looking out at the sea together. But Callistemon was different now, anyway—quieter. Gone was the brash self-regard he'd first shown up with. He had even begun to accept Elcholtzia and Impatiens, though the old man hardly spoke to him.

Pentas watched them both. Callistemon had taken a brush from the table and begun his own small painting. His style was quick but accurate, more line than anything else; Lycaste's tower took shape in a succession of rapid, minimalist strokes. That look was in his eyes again, wary and far-off, as if Callistemon were witnessing something sinister moving slowly closer, something only he could see. Whatever that expression meant, it was his most private possession.

She'd often asked Callistemon about his family, whether they'd miss him now he was so far away. The subject distressed him, bringing to that serene surface more anger and sadness than Pentas had expected, sometimes even making her afraid. Yet she sensed his introspection hid more than that, carrying a greater weight behind it than simple homesickness. He'd run away from something, they all knew it—Callistemon's duties, whatever they were, would surely never have allowed him to stay on the Nostrum coast for so long. Pentas supposed she was glad he'd ignored his job. She loved him, and knew he loved her, too. They were both strangers in this land.

He'd been looking at her while she thought, observing her own glazed expression.

"I like Impatiens just sketched in." He smiled, pointing to the paper. "You shouldn't do any more to it."

She looked at it. "Good. I wasn't going to."

He glanced out at the parrots as they hovered in the thermals. "What were you thinking about?"

Pentas shrugged. "Lycaste."

Callistemon nodded. "What's going to happen with his house—did Pamianthe find out?"

"Nothing yet. His family still hadn't replied when she enquired in Mersin. She asked about the Players when she was there, too—apparently nobody's heard from them, either."

He was silent for a while. "Maybe they stopped off somewhere they liked."

"Maybe."

Callistemon cleaned his brush in the water jug, stirring it carefully without touching the sides. "I'm going in now—are you coming?"

"Soon."

He left for the house, his fingers trailing gently through her hair as he passed.

"Bye, Callistemon," Briza called after him, finishing Impatiens's balloon-like head with a satisfied click of his tongue.

Impatiens grunted gutturally, waving away a fly. That he and Eranthis missed Lycaste the most had been made explicit in the series of failed expeditions organised to find him and the dedicated study of his wandering, delirious message. Whatever Lycaste had done, it remained a mystery. His letter alluded to a crime without once explaining in the columns of tear-stained and spidery writing what it might be. The words of the Tenth were written with the flick of a hand, and if too much force was applied it changed the meaning entirely. Lycaste's panic that night had scoured his writing almost to nonsense, and they were still translating exactly what he'd intended to say. A segment addressed to Pentas began affectionately and ended with inarticulate rage. She'd torn that section out of the note, which they still kept at his old house should anyone wish to read it again, and wept as she burned it. Somehow he'd known. She thought at first that he'd hurt Callistemon, but the Plenipotentiary had insisted the wound on the side of his head and the bruises across his back were from a fall down some stairs, nothing more. Only Eranthis, proud and perhaps still jealous, blamed her for Lycaste's disappearance, refusing to accept her relationship with Callistemon.

Pentas took the paper by the edges and placed it on the grass so that she could stand, flexing her back and yawning after sitting in one position for so long, suddenly quite thirsty.

Wherever Lycaste was now, she hoped he was happy in whatever small way he could be. She hoped his travels might change him for the better, but also that, even if they did, he would ultimately decide not to return. It was an ugly, cruel thought, and she kept it deep inside herself. She was cured of her illness, her shame at what had been done to her lessened now, slowly admitting to herself with cultivated detachment that she had used Lycaste's friendship and trust to get there. Maybe in time she and Callistemon would move away, somewhere they could make new memories together, hopefully more. Before that, though, he would have to get better himself. If that meant her tending to him every hour of the day, then so be it.

Cargo

The Nomad's course had taken it in a wide curve beneath the belly of the Firmament, traversing a fifty-four-trillion-mile trajectory to its penultimate destination, an Amaranthine Satrapy eight light-years from the Old World.

Corphuso had spent the time playing *Zuo's Ruin*, a Lacaille crossbreed of Chess and Draughts, since there was nothing like a library on board. None of the Lacaille troops would deign to play against a Vulgar so he had grown accustomed to playing alone, swivelling the board in his quarters and studying each move carefully. Eventually, once Ghaldezuel had grown tired of questioning him, he began to eat in there, too, until there came a point when he barely left all day. The bare chamber they had given him was filled with a metal double bunk, the other bed mercifully unoccupied, and a washbowl/toilet combination that gave off a harsh chlorine smell whenever it was used. A black Lacaille bunk-mouse shared his tiny cell, nibbling the edges of his blanket when he slept and cuddling into his warmth as the schooner slipped through the silver light of passing stars.

After many days of listlessness, after the toilet had broken and even the mouse had found better things to do, there came a knock on his iron door. Corphuso dragged himself from the top bunk and waddled over to open it, a small bone still stuck in his mouth while he sucked out the marrow.

"Architect." It was Ghaldezuel, resuited in his blinding, gold-shod armour. "Get yourself ready, we change ships in an hour." He glanced into the small room, taking in the leaking toilet and litter-strewn floor, then back at Corphuso. "I do hope you've had a relaxing journey."

"Where are we?" he asked, ignoring the remark.

Ghaldezuel smiled coldly, closing the door.

He was permitted to stand on the flight deck, looking out among the cockpit controls to the glowing sphere they were diving towards. It shone across the windows, about twenty feet in diameter but growing larger every second. Corphuso knew enough about their rate of flight to understand that the Vaulted Land was considerably larger than Fil-gurbirund, perhaps more massive even than the Old World. He could hardly blink as he watched it loom towards them, the tortured cry of the world's reverberations echoing from the navigation equipment.

Its surface was a muddy, oxidized silver, the mineral-plated outer crust reflecting the light of its sun into the cockpit and dazzling their eyes. Where the silver continents—studded with twinkling black and blue dots like sapphires—broke apart, a great green and orange swirl, red where the silt formed beaches and strands of blown land, merged to blue and a sea that must have stretched over to the far side. Dappling the deep, hot blues of the ocean were speckled archipelagos of lighter, whirled currents and islands, spreading in their thousands towards each hemisphere like pale green algae. Not a single cloud marred the view of the stunning globe; the Amaranthine only appeared to care for weather when it could be beautiful, tolerating it on the insides of their worlds to improve the views. Ten golden orbs—Vaulted Moons—sparkled in various orbits; some were Tethered, bound to the world by delicate and impossibly long chains that glowed like fine links in a colossal necklace as the sun struck them, while others simply floated, naturally free.

Nothing in the Firmament, save perhaps the staggering interior continents and oceans of the Vaulted Lands, symbolised more the Immortals' power and their grip on all life between the stars. Even Ghaldezuel, silent beside him, appeared impressed. Corphuso had never seen this place before, but he thought he might have a good idea as to where they were.

Soon the blue dot they were heading for in the silver wall had swelled to a gaping cerulean mouth, not quite circular and branched with connecting tributaries. Corphuso knew those glinting channels were great rivers where sailing boats scudded their way around the outer surface, sometimes taking the other waterways to the great orifice seas and into the inner world below. This, however, was no ordinary Vaulted Land, and Corphuso was glad to be seeing it at last, even if he was a prisoner once more.

This was Gliese, the capital of the Firmament.

As they closed the distance, they were joined on either side by Pifoon temeraires, sinuous old Amaranthine ships still plated here and there with nacreous green scales and the remains of snarling beast faces, sent to escort them into the orifice sea.

"And you say this is all yours now?" asked Corphuso, barely able to suppress his smile. Ghaldezuel had not struck him before as the gullible sort.

"Not yet," the Lacaille said, turning to him. His helmet, bright with the world's reflection, was hinged closed at the mandible, his voice deep and synthesised. "I see your smile, architect. But the new Firmamental Emperor is desperate to have these pieces—the prize was offered to me before I had time even to consider my payment."

"Pieces?" He looked into the round, desolate eyeholes of Ghaldezuel's new suit helmet. "There is to be extra cargo, besides my device?"

The helmet nodded but said nothing, turning back to the pilots and the huge sphere. The blue orifice sea almost filled the view now, occasionally masked as one of the Pifoon temeraires overtook and glided silently ahead in the vacuum. Sun glinted from the sea's currents, losing itself in darker patches that were almost black.

"The sea bleeds down to the next world to make the oceans on the inner surface," said Ghaldezuel. "We are supposed to fly straight through it."

Corphuso stared ahead, nodding, the light in the cockpit turning a rich, tropical blue as the edges of the orifice disappeared and the view became completely one colour. "Have you ever been to a Vaulted Land before, Ghaldezuel?"

Ghaldezuel didn't look at him. "No," he said, inspecting a functional, many-dialled timepiece set into his gauntlet. "And I suppose you have? Accompanying rich old father?" The sneer in the voice was almost theatrical.

"Once," he admitted, ignoring the Lacaille's tone. "I went with my uncle on business to Epsilon India." He remembered running off before he was supposed to, gawping up at the world walls and vomiting before he'd had time to take the seasickness medicine his uncle had given him. "It's a fairly overwhelming sight when you first get inside."

Ghaldezuel adjusted some settings on the timepiece. "I'll bear that in mind," he said, without much interest. Suddenly the speaker channels in the cockpit opened with a loud hiss of static, making them flinch.

"*Voidship* Pride of the Sprittno," said a thickly accented and extremely squeaky Pifoon voice through the speakers, "*reduce your speed on mark to six below point.*"

"Six thousand below point," confirmed one of the pilots.

Corphuso looked at Ghaldezuel. "Sprittno? The fishing city?"

Ghaldezuel did not answer.

"*Mark*," said the Pifoon voice soon after. Abruptly, Corphuso heard the belching growl of the schooner's engines through the cockpit, realising they were travelling within atmosphere again for the first time since Steerilden's Land. The ruffled blue of the orifice sea looked very close, almost near enough for Corphuso to reach out and touch, like a curtain of tropical velvet stretched before the windows. A darker spot in the water—some kind of channel beneath the surface, Corphuso thought—swelled to meet them, growing until they could see that its strange marbled edges were moving. A rising mist steamed the windows for a moment before the outside wipers dragged across the plastic. Corphuso gasped, unable to contain himself.

The dark spot was a hole in the sea, perhaps a mile across; the ragged foaming of hundreds of waterfalls plunged into its black eye, their thundering mists swirling and twirling into the Nomad's path, the suspended water droplets glinting before they could hit the windows. The ship dropped past the edge of the hole, skimming a falling cliff of dark water, the fury of the engines deadened by the roar. Corphuso stared, open-mouthed, moving as close to the starboard window as his guard Vamzuel would allow. There were other boats and even Voidships inside the curved canyons of waterfalls. One strange sailed vessel spun past in the opposite direction and raised a fluttering yellow flag at them, a tornado of mist following the screaming rush of its engines.

"Quetterel Storm-Runner," one of the pilots said as it passed. "Showing off."

Corphuso smiled, warmed for a moment by the playfulness of the enemy Prism species. The superstitious Quetterel were known to flay the skins of those they caught defenceless in the Investiture, their infamy almost on a par with the fearsome Bult. Here, within a world of enforced neutrality where Gods ruled absolute, they capered like newborn lambs.

Beneath them, through a churn of suspended golden mist like upside-down cloud formations, a shimmering hint of sunlight sparkled, revealed here and there among the billowing spray that fell towards it. It enlarged to a dim orb, shadowed across its girth by the bands of some kind of apparatus. The Organ Sun, the internal lamp held aloft at the centre of a Vaulted Land, obscured by an atmosphere of churning steam.

The Nomad plunged towards the orb, a burnished gold glowing through the mist around them and twinkling from Ghaldezuel's suit and helmet. Corphuso felt like bracing himself on something as they fell, disorientated by the vertical drop towards thousands of miles of open, empty interior space. Gradually the light burned through the mists, the waterfalls dissolving into nothing and winding away to some kind of inner, upside-down lake.

They burst from the orifice, strange sunlight washing through the cockpit, and into a haze of water droplets. The schooner banked, allowing nothing but a glimpse of the staggering vastness now above and around them, its filaments bellowing as it slipped across the blue waters of what was indeed another inland ocean, raising a ribbon of coiling steam and mist behind it.

The hatches opened. Corphuso had removed his thrombosis suit and stowed it in a small plastic hand-held case that he'd found in his quarters. Water still dripped and ran from the smooth, riveted sides of the Nomad, darkening the wide square of blue lias flagstones on which it had settled.

He took a deep breath of air as he stepped out, studying his feet as he made his way down the steps. A hot wind snapped the simple travel cape, also from his room, about his shoulders, dragging it off to one side. At the bottom of the steps, once he was sure he was quite prepared, he looked up.

Ghaldezuel was doing the same, staggering occasionally as he tipped his head back to look all around the ungraspably enormous space within which they found themselves. He had hinged his helmet open, and Corphuso smiled briefly at the look of childlike wonder on his white face, imagining what he might have been like before age and cynicism had worn him down to the miserable creature he was now.

He returned his attention to the world, letting his eyes follow the twisting course of innumerable seas and mountains until they settled on the sun overhead, braced by a thousand colossal viaducts. The Nomad had landed on an outcrop on the foundations of one of the viaducts, and his gaze followed the structure down until he noticed the three figures standing at the lip of the square, watching them.

Ghaldezuel had covered his mouth, his face suddenly paler than Corphuso had ever seen it, and was staring at his boots. One of his soldiers tapped him on the shoulder, indicating the people staring at them. The Lacaille turned and glanced over, straightening and walking towards the three waiting figures. Corphuso shrank back behind the steps to the ship.

The figures at the edge of the square waited for him, standing between a long avenue of fat, fruit-laden palm trees. Behind them, fields of flowers and palms extended to the mountains, their wilderness broken every few miles by stepped castles disappearing into the haze. Corphuso peered from behind the ship's steps. Two of them, the men standing to either side of the shorter, skinnier Prism, were Amaranthine Perennials. Their exquisite clothes swept and fluttered around them as the wind picked up, jewels the size of Corphuso's eyes weighing the material down in places. He watched Ghaldezuel perform the Amaranthine handshake with both Perennials, then turn to the Prism between them. Corphuso recognised clearly the dark thing that had found its way into his library at Nilmuth, noticing the livid scar across most of its face where Voss's flame must have found it. Its genitalia were covered this time, perhaps at the insistence of the Immortals, but its gristly frame was still mostly naked, its long, black fingers toying with something Corphuso couldn't make out.

Behind them all, on a set of spoked wheels, a large golden container was being trundled up the small hill to the square, its sides painted with Unified and Lacaille lettering. It was a scientific word, Corphuso assumed, since he did not know it.

Ghaldezuel stopped to inspect the cargo, talking to the huge and colourful Melius acolyte pushing it. He opened a shutter in the side, standing on tiptoes for a few seconds to take a look, and appeared to find everything in order. Looking to the Amaranthine again, Corphuso caught the demon Prism's eye for a moment. The thing winked at him. He ducked back behind the steps, heart pounding.

A roar above their heads made them all look up. Another ancient, gifted Amaranthine vessel had appeared from behind the huge foundations of the viaduct and stationed itself above them, blocking out the sun. Its bloated body must have weighed five times more than the Pifoon ships that had escorted them into the Vaulted Land, its bow dominated by a gurning, demonic face, the toothy mouth yawning open even before it had settled upon the flagstones. Fins and barbs stuck out at angles from its irridescent blue body, many of them snapped or missing, replaced with riveted strips of glossy tin sheeting and patches of carbon black vulcanised rubber. The Pifoon were widely considered—due to the status they were accorded by the Amaranthine—to be the finest ship conservationists in the Investiture. Most of this particular vessel was likely over five thousand years old, forged during an age of magic no Prism history could remember. The great Voidship lowered to the stones, dust coiling around it, the palm trees billowing, and Corphuso understood at a glance that its unusual features had originally been designed for colossal speeds. It settled at last at the far end of the square, partially blocking Corphuso's view of Ghaldezuel and the people who had come to meet them.

Corphuso checked behind him, thinking that now might be his last and only chance of escape, and skipped around the landing strut, poking his head past it. Three Lacaille soldiers had made their way down the aft hangar steps and were eating lunch, two of them still unable to pull their eyes from the view around them. He waited, hoping the third would become distracted as well, and glanced back again at the ship that had descended into the square. Its enormous engine filaments screamed one last time and fell silent, the warble of strange birds filtering back into the square. Corphuso made his way to the edge of the steps again and saw that all three soldiers were now concentrating on their meal, spreading cheese onto hard bread and pouring out yellowish ale from a metal drum.

He pressed himself back against the steps, his suitcase held to his chest, seeing that off to one side the meadows ran into a dense forest of flowering trees.

"I thought I'd lost you then, Architect," said Ghaldezuel's familiar voice behind him.

Corphuso turned reluctantly, seeing the demon Prism trotting merrily past him up the steps of the Nomad with a group of nervous-looking Lacaille in expensive buttoned waistcoats. Ghaldezuel glanced across the square. The large golden case was already being loaded between the gaping jaws of the idling blue ship, followed closely by the chest that held the Shell.

Corphuso waited until the party had ascended the Nomad's steps and swung the outer hatch closed above him. "I see you have some questionable friends."

Ghaldezuel motioned for Corphuso to follow him out of the schooner's shadow. They walked across the square together towards the new ship, the hot breeze drumming in the Vulgar's ears.

"Come now, Corphuso, I thought you knew me better than that," the Lacaille said, smiling drily. "I have no friends."

"What deal could you possibly strike with one of *his* kind?"

"They want different things from most of us." He looked thoughtfully back at the Nomad, where the beginnings of some red-painted insignia—three vertical marks, splayed slightly like fingers—were already being painted across the silvery hull. "The trick is to show no fear."

Corphuso glanced at him as they approached the blue clipper. "He frightens you?"

Ghaldezuel reached the ornamented tongue ramp beneath the raised nose-plating, a wall of baking air shimmering from the surface of the ship. He motioned for Corphuso to enter first. "He particularly likes young Lacaille. Served raw."

The architect looked at him as the ramp closed behind them with a crunch, rubber flanges hissing as they sealed around it. There was a moment of absolute darkness before white light flickered on above them.

"You'll find your new quarters on the under-deck," Ghaldezuel told him, sweeping past. "Don't get too comfortable, we'll be there in six days."

Corphuso watched the Lacaille knight's back as he passed through the compartments, stooping where the Pifoon-installed hatchways were too low. "Six *days*? You still haven't told me where we're going!"

Ghaldezuel turned a corner and was gone without a word. Corphuso glanced at the sealed hatch behind him, which was already vibrating as the motors came to life, then back to the empty passageway, opening his suitcase with a sigh and taking out the stinking thrombosis suit.

Shadow

He stands, wrapped and warm, looking out at the flurry. Floating snow settles over his cloak and swirls around him in silent currents. Above him, trees like none he has ever seen droop, heavy with piled snow, their branches disappearing into the whiteness like the latticed veins in a slab of pale marble.

Sotiris sticks his tongue out, catching a few snowflakes. He grimaces, spitting. They don't taste as they ought to.

In the flurry around him he catches movement. Things as white as the snow are walking past. His eyes try to focus on them in the silent blizzard but are unable to make sense of their forms. Soon they are lost in the fog.

He hesitates, then follows.

The hanging branches brush at his face, strange fragrances briefly alive in the quiet air. The snow thickens, and he must shield his eyes as he walks. Soon he has caught up with the last of the walking creatures and follows it at a distance, to watch.

It is not an animal from his memories, he is sure, and nothing known to Prism or Melius, either. Its shape is hunched, secretive, the face hidden. Tendrils of albino material waft behind the thing, curling at the tips whenever a snowflake settles upon them, and just beneath something like a tail coils and flicks with its unusual step.

He steps into its small tracks in the deep snow, booted feet crumping them further down, and follows the strange figure along a narrow path through the woods. Above, the clouds join with the snow in a hanging pall of white shot through with darker swirls, the air damping all sound to nothing.

The trees thin out until he sees that he must cross a narrow stone bridge caked in snow. It has no handrails or anything to hold on to, and so he treads carefully, one foot in front of the other. The chasm that falls away beneath the bridge is misted, unguessably deep. The creature in front of him steps like a ballet dancer, gracefully negotiating the narrow bridge until it reaches the far side. Sotiris looks up into the blizzard, the day just beginning to turn dark, then back to the where the bridge meets the forest. There are lights ahead, wavering between the silent stands of white trees.

At the edge of the trees he stops. The creature is looking back at him through the snow and he begins to see its form. Long, slightly pot-bellied, the face nothing but a pair of dark holes for eyes. It turns away, heading into the trees towards the quivering sparks of light, and Sotiris follows.

In the trees there are others, creatures that skitter and scamper, but they are nothing more than patches of shadow in the whiteness. He feels no fear, only knowing that he must not lose the trail of whomever he is following. He sees it again as he pushes through the branches, more snow flicking and piling over the thrown-back hood of his cloak. The darkness is settling now upon the forest, making the journey difficult.

The trees part, and there in front of him he sees the light clearly. It is a doorway in the gloom, tall like an arrow-slit. The building it leads into is lost in the snow: there—but not there. The hunched creature ambles to the doorway, dwarfed by its monolithic height, and glances back once more. Sotiris jogs through the heavy snow after it.

Inside the light is warm, the air hot and dry. Some snow finds its way inside, turning to water in the entrance. He rubs his hands and glances around. The passage is finished with great tablets of carved, red-painted stone that rise to a high stepped ceiling. Shimmering metallic nodules like instruments of torture hang down into the passageway, equipment of some kind. He could reach out and touch them, they hang so low, but doesn't want to. Sotiris looks ahead, hearing the tapping of the thing's footsteps leading away, and follows a single line in the stone floor—perhaps some trackway for a narrow wheel—into a cathedral-like space larger than any he has ever entered, its true size lost in the gloom.

Only one distant light shines in the space and he walks slowly towards it, his feet disappearing in the greyness. He can see more of the creatures around the single light-source, and judges by their minute scale that the structure emitting the glow is over two storeys high. As he steps closer, the creatures become clear for a moment—one of them barefaced—and then indistinct again, bleached of form by the light emitted from the edifice they crowd around. Sotiris experiences a flash of recognition, knowing that he has seen the creature somewhere before, but then it is lost, extinguished in the gloom. He notices in the light that the walls of the place are like those of the passageway—a deep blood-red, carved with patterns too intricate for his eyes to understand. The form in the gloom, the edifice, is a warped diamond shape bristling with spikes and nodes. The spark of light glowing somewhere within its structure kindles for a moment, and in that light Sotiris notices the unmasked figure raising a large, cruel-looking hammer. It brings the tool down against the side of the edifice, the sound ringing through Sotiris's head, and the glow flickers.

He winces at the savage, deep-throated roar of pain and fury that rips into his mind. At the second blow of the hammer, it rises to become a scream.

*

"I awoke you from another dream. What was it?"

Sotiris rubs his eyes. There is coffee set out before him. It is early morning at the port. "What?"

Aaron continues to stare, taking a sip of his own. "What were you dreaming?"

"You don't see my other dreams?"

He hesitates, putting the cup down. "Not all of them. What did you see?"

Sotiris blinks and looks around to the still water. "Nothing much, it was just Iro again."

Aaron does not appear convinced. "You were distressed."

He folds his arms. "You find that unusual?"

"Mildly."

The waiter appears, carrying menus. Sotiris shrinks in his chair. It is a giant Melius of the Old World, patterned with churning colour. It looks down at them, massive head sombre, and slides the menus onto the table with a huge, gnarled hand. He recognises the Melius, but the giant shows no sign that he has noticed either of the men at the table.

"Lycaste," Sotiris says, rising slightly from his seat. The giant stares at him gloomily, then walks away.

Aaron watches the huge man as he leaves, his eyes narrowed. "You feel guilt."

Sotiris shakes his head and touches the coffee to his lips, sitting back down. "I don't want to talk about it." As he drinks, he looks over to the postcard shop. They are having a sale of inflatable dinosaur lilos.

Aaron sighs, leaning back in his chair. "Very well. You've had enough time now to consider my offer, Sotiris."

"What offer? That you can somehow bring her back?" He looks at the apparition bitterly. "You *insult* me, Aaron the Long-Life."

"You shall have your sister returned to you."

"In exchange for my loyalty, is that it?"

He pauses. "In exchange for taking up your rightful position as Firmamental Emperor, yes."

Sotiris coughs, setting his cup down. "Excuse me?"

Aaron looks at him contemptuously through half-lidded eyes. "I don't see it myself, but others do. The Amaranthine Firmament would support you, and only you, in any endeavour you care to suggest. I have rarely seen a more persuasive personality among men, and yet you are *wasteful* with your gifts." He shrugs, the early light momentarily glowing on the crescent of his vague iris. "I know you now, I *see* you for what you are, but still they idolise you."

"You want me . . ." Sotiris points at himself, aware of how ridiculous he must look. "You never wanted it—for yourself? The throne was never your goal?"

Aaron smiles. "I had hoped Hugo Maneker would prove equal to the task, but I was disappointed." He inspects his coffee cup, a hint of care creasing his kindly eyes. "If I'd known how disappointing the Amaranthine as a society would turn out to be, perhaps I'd have pursued other avenues. Never mind."

"I don't think I understand," continues Sotiris. "You would come this far, do all this—Virginis, everything, just to . . . *give it all away*?"

"I would give it all to *you*, Sotiris, to rule in my stead."

"And where will you go, once everything is mine?" Sotiris asks.

Aaron shakes his head with apparent wistfulness. "Somewhere that does not concern you, and never shall." He leans forwards. "But you will be *happy*, Sotiris, happy once more. You may reshape the Firmament to your design, do anything you wish—become a tyrant, the greatest humankind has ever seen, or seed the Firmament with the equality it craves. Banish the Prism primates, or nurture them. All choice will be yours." He shrugs again. "And, most importantly, you shall have *her* back." He steeples his long white fingers beneath his chin. "I ask for nothing but your ascent to the throne of Gliese. Is that so terrible a prospect?"

"You want more than that." Sotiris grimaces, looking away. "Of course you do. This cannot be all there is to it."

"What I want," interjects Aaron swiftly, his expression suddenly taking on a new intensity, "will never in your life affect you. You shall die contented and ancient, and I'll be far, *far* away." He drums his fingers, their shadows unable to correspond with their motions. "But you need not decide now. I have given you the choice, and your choice it shall remain."

"I cannot believe you, Aaron."

"Think on it. I will see you soon."

Mediary

Light burned a brilliant weave through the mesh of the nest walls just as the Intermediary arrived and opened the shutters. His visitor glanced in, wrinkling his nose.

"Good morning," the Intermediary said in a clear, officious tone. Low Second, Lycaste guessed, rubbing his itchy eyes in the golden sunlight. He didn't bother replying.

"My name is Rubus Hochstetterorum, Gentleson of Molotaran." The Mediary stepped away from the shutters. "Could you climb out of there now? I'd like to take a look at you."

The Glorious Bird landed on Rubus's shoulder, its blank eyes meeting Lycaste's.

Lycaste stretched and pushed one leg free, almost kicking the Intermediary, disappointed that he hadn't. His feet touched the grass unsteadily, cramped and stiff after so long in one position.

"Good," remarked Rubus encouragingly. He took another step back to observe Lycaste. "I suppose he is average-sized, a fair appraisal."

"My appraisal was *accurate*," murmured the bird.

Rubus took in Lycaste's face. "Extraordinarily handsome features, wouldn't you say? Stylised, quite the work of art. Drogoradz will be abuzz when we turn up."

The Glorious Bird produced its impression of a shrug. "If you say so."

The man looked at a loss for a second, then turned brightly back to Lycaste. "Well then, Lycaste, we'd better leave now if we're going to make it to the rail in time. Can you walk all right?"

"He can walk," spat the bird.

The Intermediary nodded and opened his hand. In his palm was a loop of red plastic or rubber. "Extend your wrists, please."

Lycaste extended his arm uncertainly, noting that if it was indeed rubber the Intermediary was twining around his arms, the Second was a far richer place than even the bragging Plenipotentiary had let on. The material was spectacularly rare; anyone lucky enough to have any in the Tenth certainly wouldn't be binding prisoners with it.

"There we are," Rubus was saying. "Now, don't get excited in these, they'll tighten and get very uncomfortable indeed. Best to follow me and try not to wriggle." He smiled again. "Good. All right, Glorious, we're ready to go."

The bird looked Lycaste up and down once more, his eyes void and uncaring. He gave a sharp shrug and flapped off across the water, a trail of mates climbing from the shore to meet him.

Lycaste stooped to whisper to the yellowish man once the bird had gone. "I have a very large sum of money buried where only I can find it," he said, having spent much of the night rehearsing his speech. "Release me and it's yours, all yours."

The Intermediary blinked and chuckled. "We have your possessions waiting at the tracks, Lycaste. I had that book as a child, though, and will happily take it off your hands."

"Yes! It's yours! Now unbind me."

"You're very kind, but I can't do that."

Lycaste stumbled along in dismay, sure that bribery would have worked this time, beginning to understand the weaknesses in money's sorcery over people. Silene had refused it out of passion, but with Rubus it was something else—perhaps fear.

"It's not far, then you can sit down," Rubus continued, noticing at the same time as Lycaste the Amaranthine arranged on the banks. They were kneeling in the mud and draping their rags in the water. Lycaste didn't think they ever did such things, but he'd never been up this early in the Utopia before.

Garamond was among them. He waved, carefully folding his feather cape on the grass, and dashed over to a wooden boat moored at the water's edge.

"Goodbye, Big! Have a lovely time!"

"Farewell, Garamond." Lycaste sighed, taking the madman's hand limply as he climbed onto the boat.

They pushed off from the bank, some Amaranthine waving as they washed in the early-morning sun. A little parasol stuck up from the middle of the bowl-shaped craft but did nothing to shade them from the almost horizontal morning light. Rubus steadied the hull and raised a hand to the Immortals, placing an oar into the water to push away.

"Now then." He stood, watching the waters trail by. "When we get to the train, you'll be given paper to make your written testament, all right?"

Lycaste saw Garamond return to the group of Amaranthine on the bank. Their shawls didn't look as if they were getting any cleaner in the muddy water. "What?"

"You have to describe your version of events. You may deny, of course, but you're supposed to write something. You are expected to write in First. Can you? Because I'll have to translate it if you can't, and I'd rather not."

"I can't, I'm not very good."

"But you speak Third?"

"Enough."

"The Glorious Bird informed me you were proficient."

"I'm not."

The Intermediary coasted the boat to the bank of silt and began to sweep back with his oar. "It'll delay the trial. Not a good thing for you."

"Why not?"

Rubus looked down. "In Drogoradz you'll be under what we call Familial Law. The relatives of the Plenipotentiary in question are obliged to keep you as their guest until the beginning of the hearing." He glanced at Lycaste and then back at the yellow silt until the boat came to rest with a sucking noise. "Callistemon's family may treat you as they please until that point. It is encouraged—for their satisfaction, you see."

The two men climbed awkwardly out, mud oozing around and up their legs. A trio of long-billed birds watched them with interest.

"While you're their guest you are at their mercy, I'm afraid. I have seen some people accused of crimes never make it to trial. It is an archaic law, and I must say I don't approve of it."

Lycaste concentrated on the mud, lifting first one leg free, then the other until they were crossing the grass with long yellow socks of cracking slime reaching almost to their knees. He presumed *archaic* meant something truly horrible. He watched the Intermediary's back, thinking him not altogether a bad man. If Sotiris came for him, he'd make sure Rubus wasn't punished.

Lycaste said nothing more, following sullenly behind until only half a Quarter later the grass thinned around a line of dull metal in the ground, its edges caked with ancient guano. They both looked at it.

Rubus pointed. "Not far now."

Up ahead, something gleamed in the quivering distance. It looked to Lycaste like a large open cylinder. "Is that it?"

"Ah, you've got good eyes. That'll take us all the way to Zielon."

"That's in the Second?"

"The border, yes. This line is slow but should take us well past the war. The Jalan armies have been pressing the front here for months, though, so don't count on getting any sleep. When I came through the bombardments were relentless, all night."

It was a tube, partially cut away so that front-on the contraption appeared C-shaped. The shaded interior was scattered with embroidered cushions and blankets, as well as some flat sections where jugs stood on metal trays. There was enough room inside the tube for both men to stretch out, but Rubus appeared to have other ideas. He stopped and examined a set of holes drilled into the ceiling of the tube, inserting a key. A cage of slender metal bars dropped and snicked into place, one side left open for Lycaste to enter.

"It's more comfortable than it looks," the Intermediary said as he climbed onto the blankets.

Lycaste thought he'd have more time. He stood by the train, looking around for any sign of Sotiris. But the grasses here were brown, strangely neglected. Weeds grew in the tracks. The sky had warmed to a dirty faded blue; somehow he knew Sotiris wasn't coming today.

"Climb on," Rubus encouraged, leaning on a plate at his end. The cylinder began to move very slowly and soundlessly, dragging Lycaste by the wrist where his ties were secured to the cage bars. He walked alongside, glancing back at the Utopia.

"You won't be able to do that for much longer—I suggest you get on now."

"Is there nothing I can do?" Lycaste asked plaintively, starting to jog as the train picked up speed.

"No. I'm afraid not, Lycaste. Come on, it's comfortable up here."

Lycaste climbed over the lip of the C and dangled his legs over the edge, through the bars. Rubus smiled at him briskly, clicking the end face of the cage closed. He shifted and sat cross-legged in the shade. "It's two days to Zielon, depending on connections, all right?"

Lycaste gazed out at the moving view, wondering what the man would say if he declared that no, it wasn't all right. Thin coppices of red and yellow trees rustled past in a blur of lawns as the tube sped up, the hairs on his legs trembling in the warm slip of air. In other circumstances the ride would be pleasant, even thrilling.

"If they . . ." Lycaste began, not sure how to phrase his question. "If it's decided that I'm guilty, that I did what they said I did, what happens then?"

Rubus rustled in some bags at his side without looking up. "I wouldn't worry about that just yet."

Lycaste stared at him. "What does that mean?"

The Intermediary pulled a sheaf of papers from one of the bags at last. They flapped in the wind, folding over one another until he rolled them into a tube. Lycaste remembered his telescope.

"You have plenty to worry about before that time, Lycaste. You must keep your wits about you and write your statement. Here." He passed Lycaste a blank piece and a small dipette pen.

Lycaste took them, gazing back at the passing world. The carriage was beginning to climb through a ravine of trees filled with chattering blue birds. Rubus waved at one until it took the hint and flew alongside. It grabbed the piece of paper scattered with dense writing that the Intermediary handed it and vanished above the train.

Lycaste watched the man write quickly and steadily with a series of sharp flicks of his wrist. He had no pen. A long nail on his smallest finger (another specimen with too many) did the writing, dipped after a minute into a lidded inkpot set into the side of an armrest. Rubus glanced at him and turned away slightly, like a boy nervous of someone copying his work.

Lycaste wrote nothing, unable and unwilling to express himself to those who already knew he was guilty of his crime, and lay down instead on the soft, rumpled fabric. There was food and drink in a basket near his head, but the smells made his stomach turn. Soon they left the ravine and were passing one of the lakes. He sat up, looking for the customary island in the middle, but he couldn't see it.

"It's the Black Sea, Rubus said. "Haven't you seen it before?"

"I didn't think we'd gone so far already."

Sloping below them was a huge strand of white, untouched beach. Puffs of creamy yellow cloud dotted the late-afternoon blue. Further along the sand he saw small figures strolling. There were large sailed boats anchored at the jetty.

"The Keeper lives across the shore. He's the one who sent for me."

"Are we stopping there?"

"No, there's no need. We can stop in the evening, though—I expect you'll need to stretch your legs."

Lycaste studied the Intermediary again while he watched the water pass by. He appeared to treat his task as what it was—work—but it was increasingly obvious there wouldn't be any reasoning with him. Looking back out to the silver-blue lines of the sea, Lycaste began to think of what Garamond had said to him, trying, despite his hopes, to understand why the Immortal had given him the message, wondering once more if it had really been from Sotiris at all. He felt a sudden fury at the idea, that the madman had given him hope, but it was hard to remain angry for long.

The Second

They needed to change tracks, Rubus explained quietly without his customary descriptive flair. The usually talkative man had grown increasingly taciturn as they neared the Second, falling silent after reading a selection of letters from the bottom of his satchel. Lycaste was permitted to stay on board while the Intermediary pushed the tube across two parallel rails, its flat underside hinging out on a bright metal fulcrum and popping into place on the slimmer track alongside.

Throughout the rushing night, Lycaste had heard distant thunder, faint pops and flashes like brief moonlight coming from the north-east. Sometimes the booms and rumbles stopped for a while; sometimes they cascaded like a dropped bag of boulders, piling on top of each other. The exchanges resembled an argument, growing in indignation and then silencing after one particularly cutting remark, each side retreating to ruminate on clever things they should have said, and to prepare new insults that might finally wither the opponent into submission.

At dawn they passed dwellings secreted in the misted forests, first one a Quarter and then more frequently, until the generous walled gardens reached right up to the track and yellow faces waited to stare. Lycaste hoped they weren't going to stop, but they did, slowing before a curious crowd that milled up to the edges of the train. He wanted to raise his hackles like a cornered animal, retreating as far as he could to the back of the train and covering himself partially with a blanket.

Rubus climbed out to say hellos, thawing to his old self before the crowd. Lycaste peeped out. They were all women, small and yellowed and shrewish, with childlike faces. A few caught sight of his eyes and giggled, whispering to their friends. The blanket was tugged away, Lycaste unable to keep hold of it, and the ladies gasped, some feigning a swoon, others cackling appreciatively. Foreign smells flooded the open train compartment and animals on leashes poked their faces in, cats and bears daubed in fantastical patterns and colours, snuffling and exclaiming in accented varieties of their mistress' tongue.

Rubus was kissed on both cheeks by each lady, though in almost every case their painted eyes strayed to Lycaste. Some appeared to want to talk to him, but Rubus held a hand up and explained it wasn't allowed. Third, rich and gabbling, was tossed around the crowd. The Intermediary was brought refreshments, even though they had plenty still in the basket, and politely sat on the edge of his seat to eat. Lycaste tucked his knees under his chin and stared at the floor of the carriage, blushing furiously as their eyes lingered over every surface of his body. The lunch appeared to last for ever. After finishing and thanking the ladies graciously, Rubus collected a thick sheaf of papers from his side and held them aloft. Birds swooped from window ledges and nearby trees to collect them. A vulture, its neck collared with silver rings, landed on the seat next to Lycaste and dropped more papers and a metal tablet with a clang, its matted feathers giving off the charnel reek of spoiled meat.

Lycaste looked away, up towards the pointed white turret of a house. There at its pinnacle sat a black owl with amber eyes. It looked down over its glossy tufts and met his gaze with haughty indifference. He couldn't be sure, but it resembled a bird from the feast in the clearing—Sotiris's owl.

But then they were moving again, Rubus collecting and stowing the vulture's packages of documents and waving farewell to the women walking beside the carriage. Lycaste held the owl's eye for as long as he could before it vanished out of sight along with the remaining ladies. Small children ran to keep up with the train, but quickly tired or grew bored as the walled gardens gave way to lush, dark green hillside.

Rubus took one of the new letters from where it lay beside him and flashed it at Lycaste.

"This is about you. From a certain Hamamelis and his sons—acquaintances of yours?" He studied the paper, holding it at a distance while his lips moved silently. "Intermediaries, like me. Coming to join the trial to give evidence against you. Seems you've upset a lot of people, Lycaste." He held his hand out to catch a few drops of rain that had begun to fall. "Do you have your statement ready?"

Lycaste handed over his crumpled, half-finished sheet, watching the rain himself. The Intermediary examined it briefly, appearing to notice that it was incomplete, but folded it carefully and stowed it nonetheless.

"They were impressed with you, those ladies, but you were rude to them. If you do that where we're going you shall find no sympathy, none at all."

The train climbed, leaning them back into their cushions, food in the basket rolling and almost toppling over the side. The rain thickened among the forests, fat drops running from the carriage's metal sides and wetting his beard as they blew in through the bars of the cage. Lycaste's skin had acclimatised so well to the rapidly cooling weather that in place of shivers all he felt was a numb weight about his body, thickened skin reacting to the cold. He would have no choice but to get used to it as they travelled along the fringes of the war and into the Second, knowing he would begin to gain weight if it became any colder. Behind them somewhere that owl was following. It had to be; why else pursue him this far? He hoped it didn't mind the rain.

Hope, warming in the numbness of the rain. All he needed was to see that owl again, just one more time.

Rubus's replacement did not introduce himself, climbing the steps at Gmina Second to confer with his predecessor as the carriage slid and clanked into place above a wide, blindingly white stone square. It was evident the two Intermediaries had hated each other dearly for some time, and after a series of shoves and pointed fingers Rubus dismounted, throwing some scattering papers into the fresh wind. The stout new Intermediary swore and scuttled off to fetch them while Lycaste, unacknowledged, watched Rubus descend the steps with his back to the train. Lycaste waited for him to turn and look up, to give perhaps some signal that their time together was at an end, but he disappeared without ceremony among the throng of bright yellow people setting out to meet the train.

The replacement reappeared, flushed and angry, a bundle of crumpled letters in each hand.

"Out," he commanded in Second, releasing the bars. It was the only time he ever spoke to Lycaste. There did not appear to be a choice, so Lycaste uncurled and allowed himself to be hauled across the platform towards the crowd ascending to meet them. The brightness of the stone hurt his eyes, so he looked up at what he thought were bulky, jagged clouds settled in the distance above a few of the strange scaly green roofs. He stared, uncertain for a moment.

They were mountains. Real mountains. He was suddenly aware of his mouth hanging open.

A cheer rose and he tore his gaze away. The Intermediary held up first his own arm and then Lycaste's, and they cheered again. Some of the people, patterned not with colour but monochrome tattoos, clapped their hands together. Lycaste had no idea what that was supposed to signify. The Intermediary didn't look at him as he began his speech.

"Here is the gift I promised the Second! And isn't he a beauty?"

Another cheer, louder than the others. Children sat on parents' shoulders and waved their arms, infected with the excitement. Lycaste willed himself to look back at the glorious, toothy mountains, sharp against the faded blue.

The Intermediary grabbed Lycaste and shoved him into a spin for the benefit of the crowd, the way Sonerila inspected produce before dinner. The people whooped and came closer. It was his face that they really wanted to see, he knew. He was turned back, confronting a host of small, pink-gold eyes.

"Look at him and remember," the Intermediary continued, obviously relishing his task, "that sometimes the most alluring things can be the most *deadly*."

He gripped Lycaste's mouth before he could pull away, spreading his lips in a pink snarl to dramatic gasps from the audience. A girl tried to touch Lycaste's chest and he shrank away as best he could in the Intermediary's firm grasp. His eyes searched the square for Sotiris's owl, but there were only bright figures and white stone, green-peaked towers and the far mountains of the Second—a wall of huge, bleached, encircling teeth.

Perennials

Bonneville knew by reputation all of the Perennials sitting in the rough semicircle looking at him. Only about half had ever openly supported the Devout until now; apparently the threat of further violence to the Vaulted Lands had persuaded the remainder to join the cause.

Florian Von Schiller, newly arrived from Procyon and now in possession of the still-absent Maneker's position as head of the Devout, had joined them and was questioning each of the younger Amaranthine in turn. Wearing a brocaded gown of gold that dripped with precious black stones at the sleeves, he sat forward in one of the huge Melius-carved chairs arranged in the chapel. Bonneville could feel his pulse quickening, nervous of such a senior Amaranthine in their midst. There had been no mention up until now that the next in line to the Firmamental Throne of Gliese was among their number. He wondered what else might have escaped him.

Drifting song, a choir of dozens of high-voiced Firstlings, rose from the vaults below as his eyes wandered to the bleached skull perched on the table between them. It was far too small and dainty to belong to a Melius, and too large for any Prism breed Bonneville knew of. It was almost certainly a person's skull, an Amaranthine skull.

"Stone informs me that you are not yet eleven," Von Schiller said, sucking on a long pipe and blowing sweet blue smoke into the space between them. To abbreviate millennia was a Perennial's privilege, often used among the youngest so they knew their place.

Bonneville hesitated, about to reply, but Von Schiller continued.

"What compelled you to travel here to the Old Satrapy? Surely you can't have had *the dream*?"

He'd had his answers prepared for some time, worked and redrafted as the fear of questioning drew nearer. "I was unblessed by the dream, Sire, naturally falling far too short in age to warrant it."

Von Schiller nodded approvingly, glancing around the semicircle.

"But I had heard of its portent," continued Bonneville, "that there had arisen an Amaranthine who could join with the sleeping mind and summon those who would support his claim. I knew then that this man was truly the Eldest—perhaps the legendary Jatropha himself—and the rightful heir to the throne of Gliese. I felt impelled to offer my assistance to my brothers here in the First . . . to *your* honourable cause."

"A noble impulse," agreed Von Schiller with just the hint of a smile. "Tell me, Reginald, do you remember the Long-Life? Did your paths ever cross?"

Again he was prepared. "No, Sire," he admitted—for it was the truth. Many of the Perennials, and some much younger, admitted to remembering the man they had now chosen to deify, but he was not among them. Any lie would prove dangerous, and yet the best lies, Bonneville knew, had mixed in with them a grain of truth. "It is possible that our paths have crossed, but I will not confess to knowing our new Most Venerable." He watched the Perennial's satisfaction as he said the last, and was pleased with himself.

"Yes, it is possible," agreed Von Schiller. "The Long-Life enjoys the pleasure of delayed recollection—he prefers to wait until we have cast about in our memories for his face without taking it upon himself to remind us." He sucked on the pipe, appearing to think carefully before speaking again. "He was . . . a colleague of mine. I had presumed him dead, long dead."

"And my tutor," muttered Scarsbrek, an Amaranthine who had just become Perennial and was still basking in his new-found status. "I had almost completely forgotten him."

"He was present for my knighthood," said another, Snow. "Standing by the side of King James the Eighth."

They fell silent, each Perennial in the chamber perhaps lost in memory. Bonneville hoped he wouldn't have to hear all of their stories before his interview could end.

"You are of a numerical background, are you not?" enquired Christophe De Rivarol suddenly. "What are your duties here?"

Bonneville glanced at him, then at Von Schiller. De Rivarol—sixteenth in line to the Firmamental Throne—was perfectly familiar with his background. "I trained at the Trieste Mathematical Institute, before the Sixth War. Here, I am master of the treasury, overseeing the vaults during our tenure in the First."

"And is it not the case that you have connections within the Prism?" De Rivarol asked, a wicked gleam in his eyes. "Through the Ducal College of Drolgins, if I am not mistaken."

Von Schiller blew smoke, suddenly regarding Bonneville with more interest. A number of other Amaranthine who had been talking quietly among themselves stopped to listen.

"I did once," admitted Bonneville in a mild state of shock, rapidly feeding a warp of truth into the canvas. "As visiting Firmamental scholar—a purely honorary position. I was replaced by a Vulgar contemporary after the Volirian Conflict." He smiled at De Rivarol, composed once more. "I do not believe my successor lasted long. These Prism may doll themselves up in neckerchiefs and tails, but one can't seriously trust them with anything more than tying their own shoes."

"*Hear, hear,*" harrumphed Vyazemsky, a Perennial who had somehow managed to remain considerably fat for thousands of years despite having no functioning digestive system. Some suspected he ate in his sleep. "We must be ever vigilant that the Prism aren't indulged too much, even in the form of knowledge." He glanced to Von Schiller, nodding wisely. "It would ruin them, I fear."

Von Schiller took the pipe from his mouth, inspecting the glowing bowl. A tangle of smoke fumed from his nostrils. "Though the Pifoon, among others, benefit from our instruction as best they can—I remain hopeful for them." He looked back at Vyazemsky. "Hugo Maneker, if I might name such a wasted hope, would have seen them stripped of their territories for some invented crime."

"And what has become of Maneker?" asked Vyazemsky, looking around at Stone, the silent chairman of the meeting. "I was told he would be here to welcome me."

"As was I," opined the thin, sour-faced Hui Neng, sitting to one side and swilling water from a goblet. "It is most irregular."

Zacharia Stone, dressed more magnificently than any of the others in a jewelled gable hood, held up a finger and inclined his head to Bonneville, speaking for the first time. "Very good, Reginald. I think you can ask your friend Holtby in next."

Bonneville stood from his massive chair, the seat of which had been made for a rear much larger than his, and collected his cane. Many of the Perennials were already deep in conversation, ignoring him totally. Once again he was being ushered out, too young to be of importance, too old to be allowed to eavesdrop. He hesitated before pointing at the skull, its gristly jaw jutting towards Stone. "Might I ask to whom this belonged, Perennial?"

Stone snorted. "That is a traitor's skull, Reginald, something to inspire our younger members. His name was Yanenko."

Bonneville stared at it a moment longer. The eye sockets looked charred, as if flame had licked from within them. He smiled and bowed lightly to the indifferent crowd, recalling that Yanenko had not just been some junior Devout but a Satrap, commanding among his estates the Old World's moon.

Walking to the doors he glanced briefly to either side, expecting their spectral master to appear all of a sudden, but there was no sign of Aaron this time. He was glad. Great pale Melius faces stared at him from the cloisters, Firstlings come to look upon the Amaranthine, but he paid them no heed.

Bonneville swung open the heavy metal doors and stalked out, passing Holtby sitting in another of the huge chairs.

"Your turn, Caleb."

The younger Amaranthine stirred, a look of concern crossing his face. "What sort of questions are they asking? Should I have prepared anything? Is *he* there?"

"Never fear," he said in passing, gathering his gown and descending a broad stairway to the balconies, "I'm sure the Long-Life shall judge your soul to be just and true."

Opening another set of massive doors, he found himself alone on a high turret, the thin air numbing his face. He pushed the doors closed behind him and went to the balcony, throwing down his cane and picking a berry from a potted tree. Bonneville rolled the red cube in his fingers, noticing the relief of insignia stamped across its skin, and watched his steaming breath in the cold air.

The First, like the Utopias to the south, had been cultivated to a degree that made other Provinces of the Old World look shabby and overgrown by comparison. Fruits, berries and individual leaves bore the crest of a flamboyant designer from some lost generation, the mark of an ancient, barely remembered dynasty still stamped upon any produce that left the Province. Where natural shapes had once been, geometry and right angles now prevailed: sculpted acres of gardens were stippled with cuboid trees and star-shaped bodies of water, the various beasts to be found skulking within also appearing slightly geometric in profile.

He leaned over the balcony and dropped the berry, watching it fall as he looked out over the pointed steeples of Sarine City, glorious capital of the First—some still pale with the morning's frost—and the sharp white peaks of distant mountains.

The palace, more than two thousand years old and certainly pre-dating the current, albeit reasonably long-lived monarchy, was another work from the prolific hand that had designed the flora of the First. Its towers and buttresses only appeared smooth and regular from a distance—their surfaces were criss-crossed and indented with almost vertical stairways and grand plazas, such block geometry appearing impossible, almost hallucinogenic if one paused to look too long. On the horizon across the bluish city lay some watery streaks of high cloud, the day already turning frosty again. Bonneville pulled the loose material of his frilled collar up from his undershirts, wondering if it was cold enough for snow. He extended his hand to catch a drop of frigid rain.

It was Bonneville's commission as treasurer to the First, which included arranging documentation for Amaranthine and Prism visitors and overseeing their travels under the protection of the Devout, that had alerted him to the new developments, and only just in time. He shuddered a little with a jolt of retrospective panic as he thought of his near-escape, how all had almost been lost.

Their new master the Long-Life, one pale hand already gripping the throne of Gliese, had during the early days of his glorious arrival among the highest echelons of Amaranthine society apparently taken it upon himself to alter certain shipping lanes in the inner reaches of the Prism Investiture, securing the passage of an inestimably valuable and little-known treasure and ruining the Vulgar-Lacaille Treaty of Silp in the process.

The treasure, formerly in the possession of the Vulgar at a fortress on the moon of Drolgins, was to be brought here now, to the Old World. What the Long-Life presumably did not know was that the gift he had awarded himself upon his succession had, at the time of its disappearance, already been en route to an estate in the Hollowed Satrapy of Epsilon India. An estate, should anyone be curious enough to check, belonging to one Reginald Bonneville.

The Vulgar machine had been known as the "Soul Engine" when Bonneville first arrived to see it, a title he rather preferred. His tenure at the Ducal College of Drolgins had permitted him little more than a glance into its shimmering loops and coils, but a few Firmamental Ducats here and there had soon loosened some tongues.

Immortality. *True* immortality—not the fermented, degrading joke the Amaranthine had subjected their bodies to—was what the machine promised. He had seen quickly that such a thing of wonder could not remain in the Investiture; it would be fought over and destroyed, an unrepeatable marvel the Firmament would never see the likes of again. And so he had made arrangements with the Vulgar that would see the Shell's potential preserved.

It had now, however, become clear to Bonneville that his underling, Voss, tasked with taking the Shell out of Drolgins to Epsilon India, was lost to him. Turned, perhaps, *dead* most likely, she had been nothing but a courier, a method of deniability once he had secured the Shell and arranged its eventual return to the Vulgar under the condition of joint ownership and a ruling post in the Filgurbirund Protectorates. On Drolgins, in the equatorial city of Moso, the Council of the Three Dukes had been gratefully readying Bonneville's ascendancy as Defender of the Kingdom and Prince of all the Vulgar; they would never have known that their new Amaranthine lord and master had himself arranged the Shell's theft, nor that its design had been faithfully copied and reproduced during its time away. Bonneville had almost believed he'd got away with it, too, watching the Vulgar privateer *Wilemo Maril* groaning into the sky, his terms safely aboard and signed with the flourish of a man contented.

And then the news had come.

The Vulgar country of Vrachtmunt in southern Drolgins, land of the ruined fortress that had held the Shell, reported that Voss had left with the machine and its architect, Corphuso Trohilat, for the Threen Principalities some months ago, and that their entire party had not been heard from since. The Vulgar-Lacaille war, now reignited and raging with a fury that few alive in the Investiture had experienced, had prevented Bonneville from learning of his loss until recently, the postal lanes naturally subsumed by whichever ruling empire held their volume.

He let the raindrops shiver from the tips of his fingers, breaking away in the breeze and falling. Somewhere in the wastes of the Ninth Prism Realm, Voss had simply disappeared. Up until the last few days, Bonneville had been waiting for confirmation that she had reached the outer Firmament with the machine and its designer safely in her retinue, at the same time expecting a Vulgar fast corsair to arrive with the acceptance of his terms. The privateer captain, Maril, was long out of range of any messages now, a goodly sack of Ducats in his possession; the expectant trio of greedy Vulgar Dukes were sure to demand Bonneville's head upon finding that he had somehow lost their miracle device.

He smiled. But he had not lost it, not *yet*.

The Long-Life was bringing it here, Bonneville had discovered, to this very Province, stolen from under the Vulgars' noses and now in the belly of a superior Lacaille schooner dashing across the Firmament. He grinned at the thought, not noticing the cold any more. The answer had not taken long to come to him.

Since recovering from the news of the Shell's sudden relocation (permitting himself no more than one afternoon of luxuriant fury and despair) Bonneville had started borrowing—lightly to begin with—from the First's vaults, careful to take only what would not be missed. The Jalan Regiments of the Asiatic Oyal-Threheng Counties, now pushing their battlefront to the ancient cities of the Inner Second, of course had no idea where their new allowance was coming from. Bonneville hoped their vain and dim-witted figurehead Elatine might one day appreciate the humour of the situation, though, perhaps on the day of his coronation. That the First's own wealth had funded its downfall might yet be absent from history if the warlord did not wish his own skill in warfare and strategy diminished.

But even that was a secondary concern. None of the Perennials, not even the meddling and vindictive De Rivarol, had any inkling that Bonneville knew of the Shell's existence, let alone its secrets. To them he was nothing more than a bean-counter, an expendable junior with a head for numbers and a strict devotion to the Firmamental Order of Succession. Before the treasure was even due to arrive, Elatine's newly supplied legions would already have swept aside the Second's meagre defences and be lapping at the Sarine Palace walls. The Vulgar, a fresh contract already on its way to Filgurbirund through some of Bonneville's new friends, knew now to look for a relatively defenceless Lacaille schooner making its way through the fastest shipping lanes towards the Inner Satrapies. A small fleet coming the other way would have little trouble intercepting the Voidship and boarding it, taking the Shell before it ever had a chance to touch the Old World's soil, while a separate squadron continued on to assist the Jalanbulon in the occupation of the First. By then, Bonneville fancied he'd be snugly asleep in his own stateroom aboard the Vulgar whip-corsair the *Balmund Flechless*, untraceable as the Voidship slalomed across the Satrapies and out into the Investiture.

He leaned carefully over the edge, finding himself looking straight down into a courtyard five hundred feet below. He pulled back, head swimming, hands gripping the wall. A phobia he'd never quite managed to eradicate. As a distraction, he went through the plan again, trying to find weaknesses, wishing there was some liquid state of thought one could fill its mental boundaries with and then just sit back, watching for leaks. But all seemed well.

The Long-Life was old, perhaps—as he claimed—older than any of them. But that would not save him. There would be little opportunity for any of the Perennials to Bilocate once Elatine came for them—it was almost impossible to jump from one Satrapy to another unless one was near a magnetic pole. Any attempts to do so from the First Province would likely end in failure and instant death; few had survived a failed Bilocation, with even the lucky ones seldom ending up where they had wished to be. Bonneville felt sure he was quite safe from any future retribution; the plot was untraceable, any escape impossible. And soon he would, quite simply, be unable to die.

He shivered quickly, pulling at his collar, and turned his mind to the possible rewards, something he rarely did out of an embryonic superstition of counting one's chickens before they'd hatched. But to hell with it, he deserved a treat.

He smiled again at the view across the city, feeling old, disused emotions flicker into life. The Vulgar Dukes, keen to see Drolgins become the glorious capital it once was, needed Bonneville and his guarantees enough to grant whatever he asked of them. One might indeed ask why an Amaranthine, a member of the most pampered and envied minority in all of human history, would sacrifice so much just to live out among the savages; why, after all, become a king in a desert? The simple answer was that soon there would be no choice. The Firmament was due to fall, and quickly. The Prism had grown too strong and too numerous—not even a change of Emperor would hold them back. Ever since the Jurlumticular Throng had returned, assisting the Long-Life in the ruin of Virginis, the Immortals had been living on borrowed time. Perhaps before the year's end the Amaranthine would begin to see their precious Vaulted Lands overrun, the Prism gaining confidence as each Satrapy fell, the Firmament filling with bristling warships as the odious creatures squabbled and wrestled over each new territory liberated from their Immortal masters. Never would there be a more perfect method of escape and at such fortuitous timing. Bonneville liked to console himself—on the days when he felt less than pure—that indeed only the most suicidal of them would have chosen otherwise when presented with the same opportunity.

He dropped his eyes from the view, lifting his bejewelled sleeve to inspect the emeralds on the cuff, suddenly thinking of the two mummified dinosaurs found in the rings of Saturn, now cut from their suits and on display in the Sea Halls of Gliese along with the remains of their vehicle. Sauronauts, they'd been named, the two female corpses affectionately known as Thelma and Louise by all those who'd studied them over the years, after some reprinted slide in the archives that Bonneville hadn't studied. The beautiful specimens officially belonged to the Most Venerable Sabran, but Bonneville supposed when it was all over he might ask whichever Prism species ended up taking Gliese if they would sell them to him. The two *Caudipteryx* alone were worth all the Ducats in a Vaulted Land, but nobody from the Investiture would know that. They would likely *give* the rotten monsters away, providing marauders hadn't eaten them first. Once he had the two *Caudipteryx* and their otherworldly vessel, he might begin to indulge his fascination (a hobby he had successfully hidden from all but a few of his fellow Amaranthine) with where the rest of the dinosaurs went to, where they were now.

Nothing but a thin scraping of fossils had ever been discovered in the rock strata of the Old World, no tools or metals or structures that might suggest civilisation buried with them, and nothing like the craft and its occupants had ever been found on any other world within the limits of the Firmament. Those things had fled from something and died in freezing, lonely circumstances that nobody could understand. Perhaps somewhere their descendants still lived, warped by millions of years of extra evolution, but Bonneville didn't really think so, despite his hopes. What they had discovered in the rings of Saturn-Regis was failure epitomised, a monument to the unhappy fate of a species. But there *had* to be an answer to the question of what happened to the rest of them; and if by some fluke of chance the creatures' successors endured, Bonneville was determined to find them. The riches an eighty-million-year-old civilisation might confer upon him were not something he was prepared to forget about once he had taken the Shell and its full potential for himself. With the *Caudipteryx*, wherever they were, was the prospect of godhood. A lasting immortality that he might use the Shell and all its wonders to find. An escape within an escape, a freedom only released when all the Firmament crumbled and toppled around him.

Bonneville counted to a hundred, breathing very slowly as his heart chugged within him, swelling timeworn capillaries with syrupy blood. He counted and waited, soothing himself, hushing his mind until he was able at last to leave the balcony and walk calmly down the many glittering steps.

The Last Harbour

Tau Ceti, known as *the last harbour*, had once been the Twenty-Fourth Solar Satrapy and the border of the Firmament. It was a huge system of fourteen planets: four of them hard little globes of stone pocked with mine-shafts; three completely liquid water-worlds like suspended raindrops; and a collection of sixty-nine moons shared between seven vast, multiply ringed and splendidly coloured gas giants towards the system's edges.

It had been lost, spectacularly, by the Amaranthine during the Age of Decadence, the Prism flooding in when they and their sympathisers had departed. It was now colonised by a handful of secretive hominid races known to be particularly unwelcoming to visitors.

Maril flipped through the stack of charts, sitting in his quarters in a large baroque chair, its arms painted with gold leaf. He'd stolen it in a raid some years ago on the ex-Amaranthine planet of Zeliomandranus, the second of Tau Ceti's rock worlds, and hoped they weren't still missing it. The chair was far too big for him, making him look like a particularly ugly child clothed and waiting for a fancy-dress party as he pored over the papers. He had already decided they were going to bypass the system; it was a dangerous route out of the Firmament—part of an enormous gateway along with a second system under the control of the Zelioceti, the predominant Prism influence in the volume. The Zelioceti Empire was loosely affiliated with the Vulgar, but schisms within it resulted in kingdoms that recognised no kinship with such a different race, and the particular breed that lived on Tau Ceti were cut off from the workings of the Prism Investiture entirely. Maril wanted to stay close by, however, until the minute they left the Firmament itself, just in case. A five-day detour over the systems could avoid the toll required to pass through them, but Maril had begun to suspect that, no matter how unlikely in such a vast region of emptiness, there could be traps lying in wait for him. Getting away from Port Elsbet unseen had taken every ounce of cunning; they'd been forced to continue to corkscrew and weave for another three days to make sure they weren't being followed. Once again, Maril reflected on the surprising numbers of Lacaille they'd encountered on Steerilden's Land, not to mention their battle-readiness and provisions. The white vacuum suits they'd been wearing were some of the finest Maril had ever seen, beautiful examples he should have tried to get his hands on, and the Nomad was an exceedingly rare class of schooner. That sort of armament was a step up for the Lacaille, usually a rag-tag bunch at best, and Maril had begun to feel the paranoia setting in.

He bent over the maps again, scribbling little notes. Taking a short cut anywhere near the outer gas giants or their moons in a bid to avoid the toll was incredibly unwise. Ships that strayed near those planets usually never returned, but it might be his only choice.

Receding behind them lay the Gulf of Cancri, the last light-year of empty Firmament forming a barrier between the Amaranthines' decadent existence and the sweep of grindingly poor worlds belonging to their Prism cousins. The *Wilemo Maril* was due to cross the barrier between the Firmament and the Prism Investiture in a matter of minutes. He looked at a glowing display in his pointed helmet, sitting next to the charts on his desk. Six minutes and twenty-eight seconds, to be precise. He got up from the seat, swinging his legs and jumping to the equally ornamental foot-rest and then to the floor, and made his way along the dark corridor to the operations capsule. He ran a stock check of the ship's ordnance in his head as he walked, nodding occasionally to an engineer as they passed; they had depleted about a third of their varied missile stocks on Steerilden's Land, one hundred and seventeen out of a thousand hollow hull-piercing rounds as they chased the Lacaille Voidship, and ninety-one out of one hundred incendiary bombs. As per his design, the *Wilemo Maril*'s cache of five hundred thousand micromines remained untouched, essential to the privateer's survival if things went wrong at the last minute.

He entered the crowded capsule, ducking through the circular opening and depositing the maps to a chorus of greetings and salutes.

"Readiness, please," he said calmly, watching them return to their listening posts and the throbbing scream of Tau Ceti's various worlds being relayed by the forward-wave antennas. He nodded, leaving the capsule and making his way up a series of ladders and along another corridor, past the huge battery compartment and forward superluminal engine chambers to the cockpit, taking his familiar seat among the gaggle of pilots talking quietly to one another.

Forty seconds. Still nothing. He sat buckled into his seat, watching Tau Ceti, a shadowy disc slowly brightening as the ship decelerated from superluminal speeds, ready to give the order. All was quiet, the radio link to the operations capsule grumbling with gentle static, the soft ticking of the antique odometer counting down to nothing. This time he hadn't kept his concerns from the men, and all knew to be on high alert once they crossed the border. Such caution in a huge, empty region of space was incredibly, vanishingly unusual, but these were unusual times. He had felt political and martial winds changing ever since the Lacaille-Vulgar Treaty of Silp had crumbled with the disastrous siege at Nilmuth, to the great shame of the perpetrators. Maril had believed in the treaty, as had many privateer and Grand Company captains. There was too much trade at stake for the war to go on, engulfing ever more territories and kingdoms. Those winds, mysterious and dangerous, were blowing slowly inwards now, away from the Vaulted

Lands and right to the epicentre of the Firmament, the Prism interest that had been following loosely behind now opening their sails to it. The Old World, or *the Dominion Meliose* as it was known to the Vulgar, would not remain sacred for long.

He held his breath, unblinking. A small dial on the polished brass odometer clacked and turned; they'd passed the border. The pilots waited another thirty seconds before turning in their seats to look at him, the master-at-arms unbuckling his harnesses and removing his helmet.

Maril looked at his second-in-command's gleaming, sweat-shiny white face and began to do the same.

"All right, Jospor," he began, readying his reluctant apology. They had wasted time; the Amaranthine Bonneville was sure to bleed his second sack of Ducats for every delay.

He had the helmet half off his face when the ship lurched and spun with a colossal, ringing bang, throwing the master-at-arms to the ceiling along with everything that wasn't bolted down as if a giant foot had kicked them violently from beneath. The cockpit radar awoke, screaming, as tinny Vulgar voices babbled over the communications. Maril swore, snapping his helmet back on while the privateer twisted viciously through space, the master-at-arms flung this way and that, little arms waving. The pilots corrected the course, immediately locating and swinging the craft towards Tau Ceti at his command, its light filling the cockpit.

Maril growled through gritted teeth, clicking back the trigger-guards on the weapons array in front of him and releasing fifty thousand of the micro-mines in a controlled sphere around the fleeing privateer, counting to eight and releasing another fifty thousand behind them. Calls from the engineers registered detonations, uncertain whether they were from contact with any pursuing craft or just impacting enemy ordnance. A metal shield groaned and thunked across the thick windows of the cockpit, obscuring the huge star they were diving towards just as they were pummelled again by a sustained barrage of ordnance that had made its way through the wall of mines. Maril released another hundred thousand as the pilots corkscrewed the ship, the master-at-arms still clawing at the equipment dangling from the ceiling of the cockpit, his little body suspended upside down.

"Rear battery chambers!" Maril yelled into his flimsy microphone. His voice sounded gasping and desperate inside his helmet. "Loose all vacuum-ordnance! Now!"

He leaned back in his seat, feeling the ship groaning and twisting around his tiny body, hoping the trail of motor mines, flash canisters and torpedoes would encounter anything that had made it through the concentric shells of mines to follow them, but knowing they'd only punch holes in the defence if there was nothing far enough in to absorb their fire.

The *Wilemo Maril* released shell after shell of blossoming, glittering mines as it dived through the brightening blackness towards Tau Ceti, whatever was following Maril's ship making it through each chandelier of expanding detonations. The privateer tipped and aimed straight for the star, screaming towards the light in the hope that anyone coming up behind would be blinded in their wake. By the time they reached it they were totally blind, operating solely on radar and wave as they whipped through the boiling volume close to the star, a bright comet trail following them like exhaust along with the thrown sparkle of exploding mines. They would have to lift soon or they'd vanish like an ice cube in a bonfire, but Maril wanted to see if his opponent could take the heat. He loosed a slim stream of mines and detection apparatus, listening to the shouted readings as they spun, only the red glow of the emergency lighting illuminating the cockpit.

His master-at-arms slid and rattled across the ceiling, eventually finding purchase and trying to drop his legs to the seat. Whatever was chasing them was more than twenty-five thousand miles out of range, their instruments blind to it. It had most likely lifted away from the sun, perhaps in an attempt to outpace the privateer, indicating arrogance, fantastic raw power or a terrible combination of both. Maril had to make a choice while they dashed across the sun's face, the structure of the ship warping and protesting.

He listened hard to the engineers, flicking switches so he could hear the read-outs for himself. They were changing, the pops and screams mingling with the shouting from Operations. He smacked the dented auditory node on his helmet, refusing to believe it was working properly. A warbling, pained squeal announced a storm of new information as the radar and wave signals bounced from incoming objects, wailing louder as more entered the scope of the sensors. There must have been over two thousand of the things, each roughly the size of the privateer, and they were converging on his position.

Illness

Impatiens reached the crest of the hill and stared down, breathing heavily. He wasn't interested in the view or the scudding clouds—though there were more than usual—but the slope of his stomach; it was definitely getting bigger. He scooped some overhanging flab and jiggled it, appalled at the motion, then breathed in sharply despite his exertions and straightened his back. Even like that it stuck out. He would have to do something about it.

He growled and sat, his breath still labouring to leave his body. He would wait a while longer before attempting the path to Elcholtzia's. Eranthis had been badgering him to cut down on the after-dinner wine, and now that fleshdoctor treating Callistemon had told him the same. A third opinion couldn't hurt.

It had been another bad morning. Callistemon couldn't have long left—even Eranthis concurred; his agony was changing pitch, the prescribed salt solutions weren't working any more. Callistemon had offered to move, with Pentas of course, but Impatiens wouldn't hear of it. They were now sleeping in the largest chamber in the house, the topmost landing given up entirely to them. They had their own back garden and necessarium, their own study and solar, though Briza spent most of his time in there with them, too. As far as Impatiens was concerned, it was their home as much as it was his. The Plenipotentiary—though Impatiens wondered if that word had any meaning anymore—was part of their strange, mongrel family now; even Pamianthe fussed over Callistemon as if he were her own son.

It was becoming painfully clear as they all noticed Pentas's growing bump that Callistemon's child would arrive just as his father left them, and Briza would soon have to content himself with a smaller copy of his new brother. The paralysis never lasted more than a Quarter, but Callistemon had still been confined to his bed when Impatiens left the house this morning. The boils and lesions were beneath the skin now, too, and the yellow man's face had taken on a misshapen, drunken leer. Eranthis, though she had her theories as always, freely admitted that the illness was beyond her understanding; it was beyond anyone's. The fleshdoctor they'd sent for from Manavgat was equally flummoxed, admitting wryly that his area of expertise lay chiefly in surface wounds rather than things nobody had ever heard of and which shouldn't exist. He had recommended a cheaper doctor in Mersin, but Impatiens hadn't bothered to make enquiries.

Impatiens laid a hand over his chest and felt his heart rate slowing. That was better. It would take more than some useless doctor pronouncing him *absurdly and shamefully fat* to make him feel unwell.

Despite Callistemon's illness, which troubled all of them for most of their waking hours, he appeared to have undergone a remarkable change since Lycaste's disappearance. Vanished was the pride with which he spoke of the First and Second, the subject of his parents and family—something that had usually generated unbearable anecdotes of their importance and good taste—now glossed over with something like shame by the man during dinner conversation. Something had happened to him internally besides the bizarre affliction; he'd become almost humble in recent weeks, and Impatiens had begun to realise with a startling, genuine pain that he had come to like Callistemon very much. The Vasar-day before last he'd taken Callistemon to Mersin to collect Lycaste's family, stopping at the port a week before they were due to arrive. The old couple had come to catalogue their missing son's possessions and put the house up for sale. As it would be a depressing business for everyone involved, Callistemon and Impatiens had quartered themselves with the jolliest man in town, Phalaris, self-proclaimed Master of Mersin. They'd spent the week thoroughly intoxicated, with Callistemon speaking nonsense Tenth to any new arrivals at the water-front until they hurried off to buy phrasebooks and maps, thinking they'd landed at the wrong port. Though he was still quite obviously unwell, Callistemon had made an effort with all the new people he met, and when at last it was time to meet their guests at the boat he was effervescent and courteous, helping Lycaste's mother and father from the wooden gangplank and carrying their belongings. He'd never once, to Impatiens's knowledge, mentioned his title among them, and they'd assumed he was just an unusual-looking but pleasant porter, down on his luck and forced to travel the Nostrum.

Impatiens caressed his foot, staring at the earth without observing a thing. He wondered what Lycaste would think if he could see them all now. He was certain somewhere inside himself that his old friend (though hopelessly naïve and delicate and perfectly unsuited to the Big Bad World) still lived, and was somewhere out there in the blue distance doing who knew what. Impatiens could only wait and hope for news someday—the small stipend from the sale of the house given to him by Lycaste's parents in gratitude for his friendship still lay unopened and ready for Lycaste, should he ever return wishing to build a new life back in the cove he'd loved.

Elcholtzia's period of grace, the seventy-five years or so of gradual decrepitude that capped three centuries of solid health, wasn't due for a long, long time. But something was wrong with him, all the same. Impatiens watched him busying himself in the kitchen, spilling cups of this and that. Age frightened Elcholtzia, Impatiens knew, more than most elderly people. Recently the old man had been coming up with breezy asides about Impatiens finding a younger suitor for himself, perhaps one of their friends in the western port of Izmirean. Comments like that didn't just hurt Impatiens, they *enraged* him—it wasn't innocent self-deprecation, it was pretended ignorance of their love. He would not let that love be ridiculed, not by anyone. If Elcholtzia was doing it to generate a reaction, he wouldn't receive one.

Impatiens went to pick up a dropped fork. He knew not to try and say anything when Elcholtzia was in one of his moods, just to do his best and keep out of the old man's way. He'd come for supper—a healthy supper to aid his waistline—but it was growing late. He wished Elcholtzia would keep servants.

Walking out into the garden, he saw Eranthis running up the path.

"It's Callistemon," she said, stopping to lean on the wall. "He needs you to come."

The birds had thought to bring trays, in the bizarre and unlikely event that someone might become suddenly peckish. Pentas tended to things at his side, but the Plenipotentiary did not look at her. Callistemon's face was puffed into a pale yellow half-smile, the result of the growths beneath his eyes. When he spoke it was with a mushy slur.

"Thank you for coming."

Drimys bowed his head to study his feet. Impatiens wasn't sure if he was accepting the thanks or unable to look at what had become of their friend. Pentas leaned over to kiss the man but he drew back and waved her away. Impatiens thought she looked hurt. He went and took her hand to bring her with him to the wall, but she refused, kneeling beside Callistemon once more.

The yellow man propped himself against a stack of cushions, the tide-marks of some stiffened discharge marring their whiteness. He didn't know how he knew it, but Impatiens realised then that Callistemon would not rise from his bed again.

"I didn't hear what the man who came had to say about me, but I can guess from the way I'm being treated." He tried to smile, closing one eye as his breathing laboured on. "There's no point in delaying this," he continued. "I have things to say, things that must be said, things you all must know. You won't wish to hear any more by the time I'm halfway through, but it's essential you listen to the end. Even if, after I'm done, you decide to leave."

Impatiens's forgotten belly filled with panicked butterflies. He was eager to hear the way someone can't look away as a disaster unfolds before their eyes, but didn't really want to. He considered leaving immediately, but the idea was nauseating. A dozen conjured-up explanations presented themselves in his head, dispersing as Callistemon resumed.

"I'm sure you're all wondering why I've stayed here so long. Before I tell you any more, I want to remind you that I stayed because I fell in love."

Pentas stared up at him but his eyes avoided her.

"My life here with all of you has been the happiest time I've known." He paused, one eye searching the blanket before him as he traced out his thoughts. "I also wish to tell you, before I explain myself fully, that I have renounced everything. All of it. Now, when I think of home and family and . . . duty, I feel nothing but shame."

There was expectant silence. Eranthis met Impatiens's eye. His stomach told him whatever was coming would not be pleasant.

Callistemon brought one arm weakly out from under his sheets and wiped carefully at his brow, navigating around clumps of pustules he knew by feel. One of his fingers must have pressed too hard, a trickle of blood running into his eye. Pentas leaned forward with a damp cloth but he pushed her away.

"No, please, I have to say this now or I never will." He looked at each of them in turn, as if meeting them for the first time and marking their faces in his mind. Later, Impatiens would reflect that it was the last time the man would ever see them as they were: neutral, concerned. His blooded eye settled at last on Pentas, and he stared at her for so long that Impatiens began to think the man had forgotten what he was about to say.

"My instructions were simple," he began, looking away from her. "I agreed to them because I loved the First more passionately than my own home, the ideals it embraced, and because I was in favour there—in line to become more than merely minor Second nobility if I did not stray beyond my brief. I was somebody. There, you Southerners are treated with derision, punished for no reason and expelled to other places. It has always been that way, or for as long as I can remember, anyway. You are treated, indeed classified, as a different species, though I now consider this a vicious untruth."

Eranthis looked over at Impatiens again, worry creasing her brow. Impatiens could do nothing but shrug.

"The First has recently resurrected a decree that the outlying Provinces must fall in line with something called Standardisation. My family had long been sympathetic with this ideal, and when they came back into favour I was chosen, among others, to begin the process of unifying the Provinces through . . . certain methods. I wish now my family were still in disgrace—a state I have considered myself in for some time." He covered his eyes.

"I was told to select women, possibly even children, suitable to bear me offspring in every community I found." He took a sharp breath. "My cousins would be doing the same in nearby Provinces." Callistemon rubbed his still-closed eyelids and resumed quickly. "Surveying and quantifying the lands for the purposes of future reclamation was a secondary task. Any strong, healthy citizens I encountered were to be recommended for work details and shipped out from the nearest port once my relief arrived. I did have an allowance to purchase servants in bulk, but it was preferred that I release them from their service in whatever cost-free way I saw fit."

Now Callistemon opened his eyes. "Any person below the age of fertility, anyone too young for strenuous work, was to be dispatched. Culled." He laid his head back on the cushions, staring at the ceiling. "These were my instructions."

The silence in the room lasted for some time. Pamianthe lifted a hand to her mouth. Drimys started forward, then rushed out of the room.

"Briza is safe," said Callistemon, almost to himself, looking at no one. "I could never have done it." He held his hand up as someone tried to speak.

"I have one last thing, the most important part, left to say. Others will come, and soon. I'm sure they're already looking—I was expected to send word from Izmirean almost two months ago."

Pentas got to her feet and left the room. Pamianthe followed immediately.

Callistemon watched them go, a tear cutting through the dried blood at the corner of his nose.

"There is a war," he muttered thickly, his throat clicking. "Larger men than us, true giants who oppose the ruling Provinces could well come this way from the east before the others—my relief—get here. I hope they do: you and all the Tenthlings will need them." His tears broke through the restraint, diminishing his voice to a strained, childish choke. "The Second must fall. I want it to. I really do. I don't expect you to believe me."

Eranthis shook her head, clasping her hair with her hands as if it would help her to process the information. Impatiens thought abstractly what a pointless and helpless gesture it was.

"I had things, weapons, that might have defended you, in a travel case in my room, but Lycaste took them. So I left word and money with the Master of Mersin while I was there, and he will soon be in receipt of some powerful ordnance. I have done the best I can to save you. It doesn't atone for my actions, I know that, but I hope it may one day begin to reverse them."

Impatiens shivered at the mention of Lycaste. He strode forwards, placing his hands on the bed-posts. "Enough talk. Did you kill him? Did you murder Lycaste? Tell us the truth."

Callistemon stared through teary eyes at Impatiens. "No, I promise you. We had a . . . he, he ran away. With any luck he's found himself further east by now and begun a new life."

"How can we believe you? Any of this?" Eranthis asked him. "You've lied to us for so long."

"There are papers—instructions—under the wooden base of the fourth drawer here that I've kept hidden until now, in anticipation of your questions. It proves everything I say. See for yourselves." He nodded his head painfully at the chest of drawers to the side of the bed.

Impatiens waited for Eranthis to get them but she remained by the wall, hugging her arms as if cold. He went and fished cautiously in the chest, pulling out a light parcel. Inside he found documents wrapped in metal leaf. Eranthis was the best at Second, and she had asked the question, so he shoved the parcel across the floor to her.

Pounding on the stair. The door flew open and Pentas burst in, screaming in a rage of agony Impatiens had to flinch away from. She leapt atop Callistemon and slapped at his face with the flats of her hands, the colours of her skin rushing through cycles of pain and hatred. Impatiens watched the beaten man first resist, then relax and lay his hands at his sides as the blows continued, jiggling the bed's supports. Neither Impatiens nor Eranthis was prepared to stop her; Impatiens wasn't sure if he wanted to, either. Drimys ran in and pulled her away, glaring the two of them as they watched, pressed to the wall.

Galleon

On the final leg of their journey to Zielon Second, he was permitted to look at the mountains as much as he liked. They loomed overhead, impossibly high and sharp, vertical sections of continent drafted to a scale he couldn't comprehend.

Lycaste's lips hurt. He told the man so, but his new companion didn't seem to hear as he chatted to birds that settled on the curved top of the train while it wove its way through the mountain passes, olive and elm making way for rougher sorts of tree that carpeted the steep-sided valleys.

Growing like fungus from the ragged peaks were houses and spires, distant white châteaux with high, smooth walls. Some were connected by narrow bridges and arches, themselves dotted with towers and windows; others had presumably grown downwards after they had seeded to join up with other dwellings. Lycaste imagined what they were like inside, endless flights of stairs and small, poky landings. Steam or smoke curled greyly from chimney-pots, joining ragged cloud that had sunk to cling to the mountainsides. Wild charcoal-coloured mountain goats scrambled out of the way of the track with an echoing clop of hooves, and a stiff wind blew around them and into the carriage, Lycaste only noticing it when one of the baskets fell and scattered down a mountain slope. He stretched his neck to see the last of the fruit disappear far below. The Intermediary cursed and secured the rest of the food, shooting Lycaste an ugly glare.

Eventually the carriage, having crossed a narrow bridge between two improbably vertical houses, dropped from the mountain pass, altering some state inside Lycaste's head with a pop of brief pain, like when he used to dive too far underwater. He looked over at the Intermediary, who was shaking his head and flexing his jaw, and decided that the other man must have felt it, too.

Lights were glowing higher in the shards of rock above; across the valley, a late sun had escaped the gloom and glittered redly off water that milled with huge black shapes: the galleons of the Inner Second. One was docked at the shore, a three-storey cup-shaped hull festooned with rippling sails and flags anchored to a jetty among the rocks. Lycaste saw people on the top deck beneath the billowing flags and rigging, perhaps looking out for the arriving train.

They passed through a tunnel carved into the mountainside and clattered down a stepped series of diagonal runs to the wooded hillside at the water's edge. The carriage bumped along the last of the trackway and came to rest at the jetty, red-tinged water slopping on either side.

The Intermediary unlocked Lycaste's cage and hauled him across the jetty to the ship's stern, where chains and ropes as thick as his wrist secured the vessel to wooden poles on the shore. He was taken up a winding stair that traced the circular edge of the ship's stern until he was aboard and standing on the top step of an amphitheatre sunk into the rear of the craft. The fluttering sails, pink in the setting sun, stretched high above. He looked over the side to see Secondlings releasing the ropes. At first the vessel appeared reluctant to move, its bulk rolling slightly as the gentle waves from the lake took hold of its hull, and then it began to pull away. The receding mountain valley was a striking twilight cave of lights, the dented blades of peaks looming above, cast scarlet in the fading glow.

A man, orange in the evening glare, skipped up the steps of the amphitheatre to greet them, taking the Intermediary's arm and turning him so that he didn't have to make eye contact with Lycaste. The Mediary spoke with the man in rapid High Second for a while, taking his hand gratefully when it was offered, and Lycaste found himself unshackled and free once more. Without any appreciable glances in his direction, the men moved away to a table that was being carefully laid at the bottom of the ring of polished red wooden steps. Lycaste's stomach gurgled as he smelled and watched the food arriving and being set down while the man and the Intermediary laughed together, wine already in hand, wondering what he was supposed to do now. He turned and contemplated the shore, looking to the water below. Long shapes coiled and writhed down there, and as he peered closer he saw that the object of their interest was a small Secondling girl kneeling and dropping handfuls of something from the deck of the ship. Lycaste glanced over the edge again; it was far to drop, although from his limited experience of cliff-diving most likely survivable. He glanced back at the two men, who had now sat down to eat, some lanterns around them being lit by a group of animals that Lycaste had never seen before.

He approached the girl cautiously, apparently free to wander the galleon. She looked up happily as he neared, dropping a handful into a frenzy of slippery mouths that struggled just above the water. Lycaste watched the long green fish competing for their meal, each of them keeping one greedy eye on the girl's hand once it was empty.

"Hello," she said, taking another fistful from a dish at her side. "Are you a friend of Daddy's?"

"Not really," he replied, looking out across to the edge of the mountains, wondering how far it might be to swim.

"Oh." The girl's hand emptied into a splash of glistening lips. "Do you want to feed them with me?"

Lycaste nodded absently, taking some of the gritty food and dispersing it. The fish changed course wildly and sought it out, a few of them almost breaching the water.

"Are they friendly?" he asked, pulling his hand away from one extra-large and impatient creature.

"Daddy says they'll eat me if I go in."

Lycaste guessed they were half his length; nothing but minnows compared with his own experiences. He looked at the dim line of shore.

"Viola," said a throaty, accented voice from the deck, "it's getting late."

He looked round. Sitting on a bench by the railings further down was a gigantic person, its huge legs stretched out onto a footstool that looked like it might snap at any time. Lycaste guessed the Asiatic Melius was female, but it was hard to be sure. Across her lap lay a blanket that would have easily covered Lycaste's bed.

"Be there in a moment!"

"No, you'll come inside now," the giant chided gently.

The girl sighed and tossed her handful of feed in a wide arc, confusing the ravenous feeders.

"Farewell, then," she said to Lycaste. "You can feed them the rest if you like."

He caught the eye of the huge, distorted woman. The expression on her long face looked benign enough. She watched the little girl go, bending slightly to receive a peck on the cheek, and went back to the book in her lap.

Lycaste took the bowl of feed, nibbling on some experimentally when he was sure the giant wasn't watching. They were delicious, so he tipped what was left into his mouth.

"They're popping seed."

He dropped the bowl, delighting the fish.

"Are you hungry?" she asked, putting down the book.

"A little," Lycaste replied shyly, keeping his distance, not quite able to rule out the possibility he was about to be eaten.

She pulled back the coverlet to reveal an apron underneath, then fished into one of the huge pockets and produced a peach. As he approached, he noticed her wide feet and branch-thick toes, large enough to crush his skull. The air around her was pungent, strong and sweaty, but not unpleasant. More like a warm, old blanket; comforting.

"You look too thin," she said, slicing the fruit with a blade and tossing him half after removing the stone. She had far too many fingers, some almost the length of his forearm. "Where are you from? Ten?"

"You mean the Tenth?"

"You look like a Tenling. Were you thinking of diving in?" She sat back. "Almost did it myself, once. Not to escape, mind you."

He turned to the water again, understanding then that she was a prisoner here, too. "They'd really eat someone?"

"Lost a couple of prisoners on the last crossing," she said, snapping her half-peach between snaggled teeth and swallowing it whole. "Specially bred, you see. The nobility didn't want to have to start spoiling their lovely ships with gantries and cages and things once the war started, so they filled the whole lake with flesh-eating fishies to discourage anyone from jumping off."

Lycaste took a dainty bite of his unripe fruit, smelling her musk on it. "They bring a lot of prisoners like me this way?"

"Prisoners, slaves, soldiers. Not on His Excellency's private ship, though; and never at this Quarter." She gave him an appraising look, taking another peach out. "You must be someone special."

He took the new piece she offered him. "Not really."

The Melius put aside her book, *The Fabulous Escapades of Dorielziath and Scundry*, and looked him full in the face. He guessed she was thin for an Asiatic—not that he'd seen many Jalan barring the odd huge sailor stopping off at Kipris when he was a boy—with a wiry mane of curled white hair that framed her chin like a beard.

"I wouldn't say you're my type, so don't go getting ideas, but you're handsome for a Southerner. Don't be all bashful, you know you are. Is that what they're doing now, kidnapping pretty boys for the amusement of noble ladies?" She shook her head. "I can't pretend to like Twolings, no matter how much I may love my naughty little charge."

"You're her nanny?"

"Clever, too, this one. Throw in some wit and I'll let you wed my daughter."

"Oh, I don't have much of that."

Her large foreign eyes looked into his. They were kind, creased with care or laughter. "Never mind. My son was one of those funny boys. Not a looker, not like you, so he had to make up for it elsewhere. The fool got himself noticed, though, and they deported him. No idea where he is now. Slaved, perhaps, or sent to the Westerly Provinces." She sniffed and looked out at the twilight, the mountains almost invisible now. "Wouldn't wish that on anyone, even those doing the treating."

Lycaste shuffled closer under the weak light of the lantern, cold stars beginning to twinkle above them. Sounds of dinner and song continued from the top deck, the musical scrape of cutlery, crystal clinking.

"What will you do when you're free? If the war ends?" he asked her.

The giant shrugged, pulling her blanket closer. "Depends on how it ends." She hesitated, looked down at him. "Aren't you cold?"

"Not really. My skin changes."

"I forgot. All you lot with your special skin."

Lycaste tucked his knees under his chin, listening to the invisible water churn past. "I'm not like these people."

They docked at a shape in the darkness among the slap of waves striking an unseen jetty. Looking up, Lycaste saw faintly lit sections of wall, and across the water another distant island burning tiny wobbling reflections into the black fjord.

They led him without restraints across the broad wooden jetty to a recessed gate in the bulk of the massive wall. The Intermediary knocked gently but urgently on the woven metal of the gate, suddenly illuminated by a kindling light above their heads. Lycaste could hear music coming from the far shore of the other island, drifting vocals accompanied by instruments. The two weren't supposed to blend—even Lycaste, from his brief study of music, knew that—but the combined sound was beautiful and sad nonetheless, suddenly reaffirming why he had been taken all this way. He stepped back a little from the gate, attracting vague attention from the Secondling.

The door opened with the rasp of a multitude of locks and they proceeded through into an unlit, low-ceilinged chamber. Once inside, the music vanished. The person who had opened the door for them remained at the front, apparently unconcerned with Lycaste's presence.

The floor changed from boards to stone as they arrived at a glowing antechamber. Lycaste ran his hand along the delicately patterned wall, granulated and pocked like the substance of egg-shells, reminding himself that it was still just a house, and these were just men. Smaller, more refined, perhaps, but men like he was.

In the long room their guide stopped the procession to examine whatever it was he had let into his home. Lycaste was pushed to the front. Their escort was a boy, not yet twenty, but he was unmistakably Callistemon's brother. Lycaste met his eye long enough to see the familiarities. The boy nodded, announced something swiftly to the men in High Second and then led them deeper into the labyrinth of chambers. Now that there was light, Lycaste could see the ornamentation of the place: painted statues and busts, sweeping murals that outshone Pentas's best efforts, even the walls here were carved-relief stories running from left to right like writing. Inlaid in the stone were shimmering lines of pinstripe colour. He reached out to touch them but was swiftly rebuked by the Intermediary. They crossed a hall that opened into the night, revealing the first few feet of a sculpted garden. Two bright stars, very close together, shone above the hedges. *Cuprum* and *Stannum*, the elements most common in the Menyanthes jungle.

At the next doorway, Callistemon's brother stopped and waited for them, a tall door standing open. The guide looked at Lycaste one more time, taking in his thin, hairy extremities on the way up to contemplate his face, and gestured for him to enter. The door closed behind him, a snicking latch sealing any hope outside.

Lycaste patrolled his new quarters with the unease of someone expecting a long-overdue practical joke. Was that it? They were going to leave him alone? He reminded himself it was the middle of the night, so the rest of the household was most likely asleep. He'd have until morning to settle in.

At the far end of the room stood a bell-shaped, man-sized cage with its hatch ajar. Lined up against both walls were more busts, though as he made his way past them, Lycaste noted the similarity in their dainty features. Callistemon's family. On a plinth at the entrance to the cage stood one last disembodied head, painted black. He had to climb into the cage to see the face. It was his victim, immortalised in stone. Lycaste noted the angle, the position. He was supposed to contemplate the deceased while he rotted in his cell, perhaps weep for mercy as Callistemon looked on. He looked around, considering moving the plinth back against the wall, his mind weighing the possible consequences. He decided to leave it, sitting next to the wall and staring at the back of the statue's head.

If Sotiris had not abandoned him after all, if the Immortal had some plan to find him, then he had best do it soon. Lycaste had no idea how it might be done, or why Sotiris would want to go out of his way to do it at all. There was no favour he could offer in return, no reward he could give that was likely to interest a man who'd lived for twelve and a half thousand years.

Then there was Jasione. If he didn't escape he would never see her again. He expected, though, after a moment's solemn consideration while he looked at a fat bust of what he presumed was Callistemon's mother, that he would see all three of them here, at whatever trial he was being prepared for, forced to give their accounts as he had his. What nonsense would Silene invent to save herself? Lycaste shook his head, wondering if Jasione was here right now, in Callistemon's old home.

Moving his gaze to the next statue, Lycaste fancied he heard sobbing. It was a small, lonely sound coming from somewhere deep in the labyrinth of hallways beyond his room. He stood and went to the panelled door, pressing his ear against it. He was thinking of trying to find a drinking glass somewhere to see if it would amplify the sound when the door opened.

Another Callistemon look-alike entered, though he was much older than the last. Perhaps the elder brother the Plenipotentiary had once mentioned.

"I am Xanthostemon," said the broad man in accented Tenth, presumably because he thought Lycaste wouldn't understand anything else. He pointed casually at a bust Lycaste hadn't come to yet, his own. The man's skin was very yellow, with a whitish tinge around his palms and lips. He looked like he might be reaching his century. Xanthostemon walked over to the cage and checked inside.

"Penstemon said you were fair, handsome." He looked over his shoulder, eyebrows raised. "Penstemon—the one who brought you here, my younger brother."

Lycaste waited to see what the man would do while he stood awkwardly by the closed door.

"We read your . . . *note*," Xanthostemon said, opening the cage aperture a little wider and leaning on it. "It would be best—and for your own safety—if you got used to your new home." He pointed at the cage. Lycaste stared stupidly at him, looking for the trap. "There's water inside for you," the man said, waiting.

He shuffled forwards and climbed in.

Xanthostemon swung the cage shut and left the chamber, the distant weeping drifting through the momentarily open door again. Lycaste sat cross-legged and looked at Callistemon's face. It was a perfect likeness, if a little idealised. The man's curls had been scruffier, even when he'd made an effort before dinner, and his neck had perhaps not been so heroically muscular as that. He stretched to see the thing better, observing the chipped paint around the nose and chin where it must have been dropped or thrown. Perhaps it was rage rather than sadness he was hearing through the carved shell-layers of the walls.

The trial required him to be alive, he remembered Rubus telling him that, alive enough to answer the flow of simple and perhaps predictable questions that the Intermediary had assured him would be posed. His head might necessarily have to be left in a reasonable condition, but little else. He examined the bucket in the middle of the floor, stirring its water with a shaking fingertip. No gold flecks. He smirked even as he trembled, thinking he ought to complain and tell them he was used to finer stuff.

Everything but his head, and maybe his heart, was surplus to understanding and response. He took stock of his arms as if seeing them for the first time, his long skinny legs, bony knees sticking out like bolts. His eyes drifted between his thighs, absently cupping himself as he visualised some of the depraved things his vengeful gaolers might wish to try on him.

A key turned in the lock. Lycaste removed his hand guiltily from his groin and hid it behind his back. One by one, a pallid collection of people entered the chamber. Penstemon and Xanthostemon pushed past and directed them to a perpendicular bench with carved animal feet that Lycaste had assumed was ornamental in its ridiculousness, and the three women sat to examine him. The elderly lady dabbing at her eyes with a shining piece of silk was clearly the matriarch, Callistemon's mother. Her body was mercifully mostly folds, making her look more like some rotund weeping slug. The overpowering smell of cinnamon that had accompanied them into the room was most likely coming from her hair, which was powdered and piled into what must have been the latest fashion. Wedged on either side of her were two daughters, one of them monkeyish and sickly looking, as if she hadn't seen sun all year, the other rather attractive, if only by comparison. Lycaste studied them in return through the bars since he had nowhere to hide, a caged and wary animal. He could see Callistemon in all of them, five sets of his victim's eyes staring at him.

"What a poor, bedraggled creature," declared the mother softly in Plain Second, her voice hoarse. "I see no beauty in it, I don't care what everyone's saying."

The fairer daughter was looking intently at him. She stood from the ottoman, stepping closer to the cage.

"Cassiope," murmured Xanthostemon.

She glanced back at her brother, who was standing by the doorway. "I just want to see him properly."

Lycaste watched the sway of her hips and the lines of her body as she came to the bars, meeting her small eyes as she looked up at him. Her hair, bunned and curled like her mother's, was an unpowdered burnished gold.

Cassiope ran her gaze over his face and neck, casually dropping it to his lower half and up again. "I don't think they exaggerated, Mother," she said, angling her head slightly back towards the bench. "You must admit, he's very . . . unusual."

Lycaste let his eyes drift across her, taking in the small, pale nipples and blonde down that wandered south of her navel, hair so scantly suggested that it might not be there at all.

"They say you killed my brother for a woman, Cherry," she said quietly, so nobody else could hear. "That's what they say. You must have loved her with all your heart."

Her hand slipped something small and slim and white out of her bunned hair. Lycaste only noticed after a moment that it wasn't white, but reflective.

"That was the trouble with Callistemon—he always got what he wanted."

She snarled and thrust the blade between the bars at Lycaste's midriff, stabbing as far as she could before he could react. Xanthostemon's arms appeared swiftly around Cassiope's to drag her away from the cage. She struggled and swore, twisting to spit at Lycaste. Her brother swung her off her feet and carried her out in screams of fury. The other daughter scampered to follow, panic-stricken, leaving Penstemon and his mother in the chamber.

Lycaste put his hands to his stomach, watching the blood well between his fingers. It was deep, the wound stinging somewhere far inside him. Already he could feel the pain beginning to take root at the end of the cut, though the bleeding had stopped. His knees gave way as the mother approached, dabbing her dry eyes occasionally with the silk, her son following closely behind, a small smile stretching the unlined skin around his mouth. With Penstemon's help she manoeuvred the black bust of Callistemon until it was against the centre of the cage's door, looking in at him. Lycaste rolled to watch them, clutching his wet stomach, the burning agony doubling with each heartbeat, as if the knife had been dipped in something caustic. Perhaps it had.

When she had finished, the fat lady looked at him once more, then dropped her handkerchief through the bars. She shook her head and took her son's arm to leave.

Lycaste tried to roll himself towards the bucket, but something inside him was snipped, broken. It felt as if a giant pair of garden shears were cutting him in half every time he twisted his torso, so he stopped, lying and listening to the waves of pain pulse through him.

"*Sotiris*," he whispered to himself, eyes squeezed shut.

A convulsion caused him to press too hard on the wound, reopening it. Lycaste cried out, clamping his teeth together and groping for the silk handkerchief, jamming it into the hole in his belly. Darkness settled around the edge of his vision, mischievously darting this way and that. Gradually it won more ground until it grew bored of the game, and the lights went out.

Elatine

The small, sturdy bridge across the water looked like the best option, the booming detonations still coming from farther down where the lake broadened. The crossing was undefended save for a cannon some distance off, the walled city of Yuvileiene still standing guard between the bridge across the narrowest point and Elatine's attacking regiments. Sotiris strolled along, trying to enjoy the autumnal chill, watching the dark blue waters course alongside the banks. He had swapped his Utopian feather cloak for one of the lighter, verdigris-weathered Dongral coats of armour, actually pleasantly cool where the holed plates allowed air to circulate.

He crossed the bridge, noticing a company of Dongral—the legion dedicated to defending the borders of the Second—walking briskly towards him, probably with the intention of manning the heavy gun on the bank he'd just left. Sotiris passed to one side, letting the tall Melius breeze past. He sat for a little while on the stone wall of the bridge as one of them stopped to look back, the blind spots in the Melius's mind hiding Sotiris with room to spare. The Amaranthine hadn't been seen, merely felt, like something glimpsed out of the corner of your eye. The Melius stood for a while, unconvinced, and then sheepishly hurried after his companions.

He remembered, as he sat, the bridge he had crossed in his dream. He felt the rough growthstone between his fingers, his shoulders tense. What he had done to Lycaste was beyond reprehensible, perhaps one of the cruellest things he had ever done to another person—even if they were of a different, arguably lesser species. But it was all he could do, all he could think of doing, that might save the Firmament from what he saw when he slept. *No* Amaranthine had ever before gained the ability to infiltrate another's dreams; it was unheard of, unknown. But Sotiris's instincts had told him enough already—that Aaron was no Amaranthine. Wherever the Long-Life now resided, almost certainly west of here in the grand capital of the First, he wore the appearance of a kindly, middle-aged and anonymous fellow, betrayed only by eyes that could not decide on a colour when the light touched them. Sotiris had no idea what Aaron's true self—whatever lurked beneath that bland and accommodating façade—might really be, but he was determined to find out. And poor Lycaste was to be his bait.

He gazed over the plantations towards the city, hearing the thud of heavy guns as he removed his helmet. He'd have to remind himself to put it back on once he'd crossed the battlefield, for random shells remained considerably less susceptible to trickery than the Melius who fired them.

The battle, though still in its infancy, *was* spectacular, in its own way. The gleaming city, pinkish against the miles of plantations from which it rose, was only being struck lightly so far, the cannon on the far hill more interested in the massed troops dug in among the palms. There, across the fields, huge fanned bursts of smoke smudged the whitish sky, brown clouds drifting with the brisk wind before the crack and thunder followed across the air. He could actually see the shells, incredibly fast, arcing and slamming into the fields, and wondered how many were hitting their targets.

Sotiris scanned the fretting city, seeing twinkling guns and troops crowding the ramparts, looking for a way around that wouldn't involve wading through the shallow trenches of the plantation. In an hour or so, the regiments camped in their temporary paper city on the far line of hills—themselves just a thicker line in the smoky distance—would be moving forward to engage the foot-soldiers as their guns targeted Yuvileiene itself. Sotiris wasn't sure how effective the soldiery of this strategy was, but Elatine's luck wasn't failing yet. He'd fought across vast tracts of eastern jungle to get this far, the fingers of his legions finding the last soft spot into the rural fringes of the Second here at Yuvileiene. Sotiris got the sense that many of the outlying Provinces had held out only long enough to convince the First of their loyalty, great swathes exhaling in relief at last as Elatine's legions marched through, triumphant in the conquest of their new territories. Of course he'd heard of the atrocities, but Sotiris had chosen to believe they were greatly exaggerated. He needed this army; turning a blind eye here and there was all that would secure it for him. For the hundredth time his thoughts returned to Aaron's offer at the café, the promise he had made. It was in those subjective dream-moments that Sotiris had begun to fear his own weaknesses, and to strengthen his resolve.

He stood, fastening his wide helmet and considering the possibilities of waiting out the battle here, on the bridge. It might take a day or two for the army to finish its siege, and Elatine would likely be getting drunk on his success in the ruined city by the time the paper encampment had been relocated to the far bank. He decided to get it over with, before any major skirmishes started and while the warlord's head was still clear. It would be more dangerous to leave for the encampment now, but the feeling that time was somehow running out was returning to him.

Once on the other bank, he spotted a large heap of ordnance stacked in the sun-browned grasses. Shells twice as long as he was—relatively liftable for a strong Melius (and light enough for their giant Jalan adversaries in Elatine's army on the hill to pick up one-handed)—were laid out ready for use, the first fallen leaves already having drifted into some of the gaps between their tubing. The gun on the far bank had its own piles of ammunition, so these must be meant for something else that he hadn't seen, unless the Second had given up supplying weapons at all now to its outlying regions. He wouldn't be surprised.

Sotiris looked around for any sign of troops and began carefully tipping the ammunition down the bank into the river, leaving the largest shells until last. They wouldn't budge, so he walked off a fair distance into a line of oil palms at the edge of the plantation, then turned back to look at the piled shells. He concentrated, watching the sun blink on the faded blue casings until a spark leapt from one of the metal surfaces and danced away into the grass. He gritted his teeth, rubbing his hands together absently. A complicated-looking hinge popped at the back of one of the shells at the top of the stack. It clattered away, some more parts falling out after it. Sotiris frowned. They were useless, too old to explode properly even while the materials inside them were being frantically agitated. Elatine wouldn't need much of a helping hand against the Second after all.

Voices began drifting through the trees. Sotiris turned and walked east, jumping across a pungent-smelling trench trap disguised with rushes. A thought occurred to him as he came upon the outer walls, avoiding a line of armed Melius carting some equipment quickly along a painted line between the orderly foliage: land-mines. They had grown in popularity as the war progressed along with other, more desperate measures as each outer Province fell.

Sotiris followed the curve of wall for a couple of miles, climbing mossy lumps of rubble and hillside into which the city was built, dodging encampments of refugees who had not been allowed inside the walls and platoons scrabbling on the rocks, passing crates of ammunition up and swinging their crude Howitzers out to watch over the surrounding fields. Every few minutes, Melius and machines clattered past him, seeing nothing, the roar and crackle of artillery softer and then louder as he found himself facing the hills again.

He set out across the browning fields, stopping to rinse his mouth when he came across an irrigation trench. A body further down had spilled its brains into it, but that hardly mattered. Around his feet the ground had been freshly dug, little mounds indicating where he shouldn't step. Sotiris tested his theory, as well as his damaged confidence in his own powers, turning back and staring hard at one of the earthworks. A small metal cylinder leapt from the ground like a coiled spring, smoke and bent nails popping from its casing. It landed with a disappointing tinny clank on the pile of nails, a desultory flame flickering from its shredded side and dying. Sotiris stared at it, beginning to see just how quickly Elatine might accomplish his goals.

He moved on, coming across a line of Secondling soldiers dug into some churned-up earth defences. Sotiris noticed that some of them clutched small Prism weapons in their hands, crudely manufactured spring and lumen rifles with Melius blades soldered to the barrels. Others further down carried simple pikes and curved rapiers, poorer servants, no doubt. The troops he stepped over were lying on their bellies, guns sighted off into the palms, waiting. He listened; the barrage had stopped.

Sotiris paused and stood with them, smelling the breeze, watching light and dappled shadows pierce the haze beneath the canopy of plants. He was in exactly the place he didn't want to be. Once again he imagined the ludicrous nature of fate; dying in a strange field surrounded by massive yellow men, men who would have scared the living daylights out of anyone he'd known in his youth. He looked down at them, uncomfortable and reeking in their battle costumes. The beasts coming for them were the really frightening ones, the ones he could count on being on his side.

Sotiris resumed his walk, ducking through some palms and running north, curving until he began to see the giants working their way through the foliage, their huge bodies bent almost double among the squat trees.

He stopped, taking in the sight. The Asiatic Melius, the Jalanbulon Regiments, were truly a sight to behold: the closest thing to trolls the Old World possessed. He slid through their ranks, studying the huge, muscled jawbones, the hooked yellow teeth peeping from loose lips. Their eyes, set darkly in shaded sockets, were the size of melons, their great grey hands equipped with seventeen fingers each, all different lengths. Most of the Jalanbulon wore plated suits of scaled, painted iron, scratched and dented from nine unrelenting years of war.

As he passed through them, he saw an especially large Jalan, naked but for the cloak of black silk around his gnarled shoulders. He carried no weapon. The display was designed to insult the minor aristocracy holed up in the city, to illustrate the punishments for their greed. Should the sacrificial Melius die today, Sotiris knew, the instructions were to leave his body and all its carried wealth on the battlefield as a final statement. Nobody among the Asiatic armies was permitted to claim what he wore, the generals of Elatine's army deciding the message of the act more important than apparently giving away funds to the enemy.

The weapons the Jalanbulon carried were also various Prism implements, probably looted from collectors of Firmamental antiquities in the lands the armies had pillaged. He stood still for a while, feeling them moving all around him, listening to them muttering to each other in a blend of languages, checking their weapons and unclipping things from their armour. He stole to one side as the guns on the hill roared into life again, booming overhead, standing with his arms delicately extended to let them pass. A barbed weapon hanging from a soldier's back snagged his light armour and almost dragged him along, but the metal plate snapped off before Sotiris could fall. Soon he saw a point where he might exit the columns and dashed breathlessly between the muscled legs into a calmer patch of the plantation where machines and equipment were being assembled and carted to positions on the hills further south.

He reached the crest of the hill, ducking as a gun slammed a shell over his head towards the city, a belch of earth and dust caking him. The huge copper machines were much more impressive than those the Dongral Legions possessed, and he went a little way over to sit and watch them fire while he caught his breath. Shells were loaded to one side and wound into the body of the gun on a circular track, a spring mechanism sliding them inside. It meant little lifting was required, despite the obvious strength of the gun-crews. Carriages of ordnance stood nearby; they would be loading shells into the night. Sotiris wondered who'd paid for it all.

The wind was much colder now, sucking away at his sweat-free skin beneath the layer of grime, each roll of thunder from the battery of guns on the ridge vibrating in his bones. He looked out to the city, its highest levels disintegrating under the pounding of the cannon. Spires were falling from the shearing walls and obliterated masonry, shafts of slanted smoke obscuring the lake entirely to the west. Fires from incendiary rounds had already begun to ignite the plantations, sweeping with the fresh wind nearly to the water's edge beyond the city. Sotiris shook himself, getting up unsteadily and covering his ears. The Jalan manning the Howitzers noticed nothing as he passed the line of guns and walked along the makeshift causeway into the paper city, which lay about a mile beyond the rise, steady lines of troops marching along the road.

Inside the barbicans of the paper city the barracks were already being folded away. He walked the wide streets, stepping to one side for an inebriated legion of relief troops. They rolled and staggered, turning a corner and heading for a tavern before it could be packed away. Across the open passage hung rows of spiked iron cages, like the sort of things that used to contain birds. Inside he could see tiny naked creatures, all mouth and teeth. They appeared even more naked than they were, attempting to cover themselves with their hands when they saw him. He stooped and looked in: Vulgar soldiers, their bodies bruised and bloody from torture. The little white things whimpered up at him, drooling like animals as they clung to the bars. Sotiris noticed their swollen, starved bellies protruding from racks of gnarled ribs. One of them tried to say something, but Sotiris put a finger to his lips, passing in some food he kept close in case of hounds or wolves. The Prism were banned from the Old World by edict of every Firmamental Emperor since the Most Venerable Biancardi took the throne of Gliese in 10,214, but Sotiris knew that the Firmament could no longer stop the occasional incursion. The Old World, once the sacred kernel of the heavens, was now an unprotected wilderness.

He stepped between some shabby-looking western captives pulling a roll of papery material to one side, exposing some stairways leading up into the body of the mobile encampment's main keep, and ascended them. The notion of an origami fortress looked at first glance rather unwise, and Sotiris could see why so many of Elatine's adversaries had thought they were being terribly clever in attempting, repeatedly, to burn it down. He grabbed a folded section of wall as he went, rubbing it between his fingers. The whole surface area of the material was laminated in some way, immune to rot or damp or flames. It took half a day to set up and the same to take it down, the whole thing easily portable. He'd heard tales of it being moved during previous campaigns; it took one hundred particularly strong Jalan with a great set of wooden beams stretched between them. The pile of material resting on the beams apparently looked like a vast stack of envelopes as it travelled about the Provinces behind the marching armies it sheltered.

Sotiris made his way quickly and quietly through some paper reception rooms at the top of the multiply folded, reinforced steps, following his intuition to a narrow bridge between the two sections of the keep. As he walked, he changed the rhythm of his step and straightened his posture, visible now to anyone who might pass, knowing that there would be no more guards from here on.

Elatine, the great commander and tactician, was at his sink finishing his morning ablutions, a process Sotiris had forgotten all about. Lacking the bull strength and muscle tone Sotiris had seen in the marching army below, the tall Jalan was washing his face slowly with a towel of plain white linen as Sotiris made himself known.

He paused, the cloth still covering his wide, toothy mouth, locks of long, wet hair swept back.

"Amaranthine."

"Commander Elatine."

Elatine's huge eyes watched him standing there, closing as the cloth passed over them, his surprise well concealed. "Come to tell me to desist?"

Sotiris went to a chair and sat, exhausted. "Not at all."

Elatine put down the cloth and looked at him in the mirror. "Make yourself comfortable." His voice was comparatively high for such a large specimen, standing almost three times Sotiris's own height.

Sotiris planted his helmet on a cushion beside him and looked up at the wooden frames of the simple apartments, noticing their unscrewable joints. A large golden lionhound snoozed belly-up on the rug. The huge, simple bed in the next room was tousled, recently slept in.

Elatine noticed him looking through to the bed. "I woke late. My legions need no more instruction."

He looked over at the mottled, reflected face of the Melius. "You do as you see fit."

"Good. So, what have you come here for? I've received my silk."

Sotiris raised his eyebrows. "Silk?"

"This very day by messenger. You bring more?"

"Ah—no, I'm afraid not."

"Well, I shan't be returning it, if that's what you're after." The giant scowled at him. "It was unusual to receive it that way."

"It was?"

Elatine watched him suspiciously. "This last month, my allowance has been delivered in the form of raw supplies every night, by the roads. Now my legions must be allowed rights of *reapage* at every city they come to." His eyes fixed Sotiris's. "They will have no less, you understand."

Sotiris spread his hands magnanimously, trying to think quickly. "You must take what you require."

"Very well," the warlord grumbled, picking up a razor by the side of the basin. "Your fellows forget how stretched my supply line has become." He nodded at Sotiris. "Tell them that, will you? I shan't be amused if the mistake is repeated."

"Of course," said Sotiris. "And what of those who brought the silk?"

Elatine glanced at him, razor poised at his chin. "Tortured, for information. Traps are sprung in this way, delivering unasked-for gifts and the like."

Sotiris nodded as he watched the sleeping lionhound's legs twitch. Silk, the Old World's most precious currency, remained so due to the mystery of its manufacture. The Melius naturally had no appreciation of the extinct moths from which it came, or of the berry trees necessary in their cultivation. Amaranthine pilgrims to the Old World brought it with them by the sackful, travelling in comfort among the Melius even when disguised, either through subtle suggestion or near total invisibility. Perennials, who cared less for lugging possessions, often tricked their huge hosts into believing they had received quantities of silk when they had been given nothing. Such practices were technically illegal by the charters of the Firmament, but no younger Amaranthine could by law challenge his elder, and so wizardly deceptions went unpunished.

Sotiris studied the Melius's gigantic frame as he shaved, thinking now on whom among the Amaranthine might have been supplying the warlord. The letter in the castle. It could only have been the vanished Perennial, Yanenko. Could he possibly be alive still?

The war in the east had progressed more rapidly than anyone had ever expected, burning its way through the outlying Provinces and into lands that had been held for centuries without question of revolution. Though few had expected them to come as close as the Fourth, the Vaulted Lands had ruled that the commander's Eastern legions would halt upon reaching the Greater Second, with no assistance or mischief allowed from any Amaranthine on the Old World that might encourage them to progress further. As the Asiatic front drew closer to the Central Provinces, this edict was strengthened until it had become punishable first by excommunication from the Firmament and ultimately by death. The Amaranthine—the few thousand who still understood the stakes they played for—were fearful of any Prism breed gaining a foothold on the Old World, understanding that the chaos of war in the Provinces would provide a perfect distraction for anything wishing to slip in unseen. They had deemed a continuous monarchy—that of the First—the most efficient way to warn of any such encroachments, no matter the ruthlessness with which it treated its own citizens. Sotiris depended now on Elatine's will to continue in the face of such an edict, to take what he thought was rightfully his.

"I would be in a position to offer you more, should you consider my terms, Commander," Sotiris said to the man's broad, grey back.

Elatine shaved carefully while he considered the Immortal, dragging the foot-long blade to a stop beside his hooked nose. "I'm sure you might." He began to make rapid strokes beneath his nostrils. "But I do not discuss terms."

Sotiris noticed how poor the Melius's Unified was. He could have switched at any time to Twenty-Second, Elatine's mother tongue, but had little interest in making things easier for the man. Amaranthine were spoken to in their own language; it had always been so.

"The treasures would be substantial," he said, more slowly and clearly.

Elatine turned from the mirror to look at the Amaranthine, massively brooding. "You did not hear me, Immortal. I do not negotiate. Talk is for people who doubt their own strength."

Sotiris straightened a little from his hunch, eyes narrowing, gratified at last to see uncertainty cross Elatine's face.

"I meant no offence," the commander added, rinsing the blade in the clouded water. "I know what you would ask of me—it has already been asked by a hundred advisors, a dozen Provincial princes. Even one or two of *your* kind, Amaranthine. I have not fought tooth and claw through Firstling protectorates to stop at the gates, an inch from total victory, only to turn and slink home. But I have been given little choice— I disobey the *Firmamental Edicts*—" he twirled his huge fingers as he said the words, imbuing them with mock mysticism "—at my peril. You know this. The silk is a very fine and much appreciated gesture, but it cannot change what your people have decreed."

Sotiris sat back a little. "Would you follow *me*, if I could guarantee your success?"

The Asiatic stared at him, the razor still clutched in his hand. "I can think of little you might bargain with."

Sotiris nodded pensively, running his hand along the rough, striped weave of the cushions. "I could give you the boy-king."

Elatine smiled at last, wiping his face and going to pat the lion-hound. "A bold guarantee. Too bold. Not even your competitors dared offer me Lyonothamnus." He shook his colossal head. "What is it you want, Amaranthine?"

"I want nothing more than to see you crowned before the Autumn has waned, Commander, and to know the Provinces are at peace."

"Ha! I am quite sure." Elatine sat opposite Sotiris, leg stretched out, one great toe engaged in massaging his pet. A broad grin had begun to split his face. "By what new conditions can you give the brat away? Assassins have tried, and failed, to bring him to me many times already."

Sotiris shrugged. "I have a little bird in my employ, one that sings more sweetly than any other. Now that he is caged, the Lyono-thamnine Court won't resist gathering to see." He sat back, looking at Elatine.

In truth he had no guarantee that the famously slippery and constantly moving royalty of the First would assemble to see Lycaste, but it was all Sotiris had. The Melius's beauty—obvious when Sotiris had first set eyes upon him—was indeed extraordinary, even from the perspective of another species, but that did not guarantee him an audience with the sovereign Lyonothamnus, let alone the First Court. Sotiris hoped in the meantime that Lycaste would be safe, whatever happened, but could not even be certain of that.

"What does he do?" asked Elatine, his smile vanished. "Perform tricks?"

"Just know that they will be there," Sotiris replied, "in the Sarine Palace, from the middle of the Octrate Moon. Vanquish the Second, as is your destiny, and I shall see that your entry into the noble First lands goes unhindered."

"The Octrate is almost upon us. Mistakes are made by rushing in, Immortal," Elatine said. He grunted humourlessly. "Besides, what certainty have you? Why should I trust my forces to the word of one, even one such as you?"

"Because I have arranged it, Lord Commander." Sotiris brought the smile back into his eyes. "The Firstling Royal Court will be there—you have my word."

Elatine's great concave ears flattened slightly as he regarded him, his hand toying with the razor. "I'm no fool, Amaranthine," he said slowly. "There is more going on at the Sarine Palace than you let on. I *know*—the Skylings have described it to me. Someone has dared to challenge the Firmament, someone powerful, and you wish to brandish my legions against him—is that not the truth?"

Sotiris did his best to hide his surprise as the warlord looked at him accusingly. In the Asiatic tongue, the Skylings were creatures from myths and fables, dwellers from the worlds above. Aside from merely capturing lone Prism, Elatine also appeared to be in communion with one or more of their kingdoms.

"You see, the simple tactician knows more than you realise," Elatine continued, staring earnestly at him as he stood. "Perhaps I'll retreat to my new capital at Vanadzor to watch your heavens crumble. How would you like that?"

Sotiris smiled wearily, looking up at the looming Melius. "By all means, enjoy your successes. But know that greatness will ever elude you if you do." A butterfly caught in Sotiris's stomach as he heard the echo of Aaron's own words to him.

Elatine continued to stand above him, his face grave. Suddenly his trollish features softened in a surprisingly gentle laugh. "Never fear, Amaranthine. I may still hear your terms, but give me time to think on it. My emissaries say Goniolimon Berenzargol, the Secondling Prince, waits for me at Elblag Second, upriver—I can only think he wishes to prove his loyalty to King Lyonothamnus and his court." He shook his huge head with a smile. "They say the boy-king still cares more for toys than conversation, let alone remembering individuals from the simpering masses who must crowd him each day." He sat back down, still shaking his head. "When I was that age I worked the fields with my brothers. I knew nothing of luxury."

Sotiris indicated the room, his good humour returning. "Nor do you now."

Elatine snorted approvingly. "I was pleased, when I reached the Second, to see that my spies had not exaggerated. Each aristocratic family owns their own galleon. Every one." He smirked, turning up the corners of his wide lips. "It is always a welcome sight to see such wastefulness in one's enemy." He regarded the Amaranthine, pointing a thick, many-jointed finger. "They are waiting because they think themselves too noble to suffer. Provincial conventions decree that I must spare their lives, taking only the wealth I find and disseminating it, let alone stop at the borders of the First. Think of it—men who would have shot at me only the day before, and we're supposed to sit down and *dine* together, discussing the weather, passing salt. Well, I tell you, Immortal, they're in for a shock."

Sotiris watched the lionhound stretch luxuriously, his thoughts returning for a moment to the swirling flurry of snow and that colossal, misted interior. The bellow of fury and terror he'd heard still seemed to echo somewhere, as if locked away in the paper walls. He wondered if the vision of the man that confronted him each time he slept watched his every action, too—if he was here in this origami chamber with them at this moment.

Elatine had been observing him sink into daydreams. "Am I boring you, Amaranthine?"

He shook himself internally, forcing some speed into his thoughts. "So we are agreed? You will not slow your advance?"

"I will follow your lead," Elatine replied, "if everything is as you say, and if my funds are improved somewhat for the trouble."

"Of course."

The warlord looked at Sotiris like a man about to bargain once more. The Amaranthine knew the look well. "You could sweeten our deal with a miracle, if it pleases you. I haven't seen one since my very first meeting with your kind."

Elatine meant the Amaranthine Scrophularia, a locally famous madman in his home Province, who had cast off his skin in a rainbow flutter and declared himself immortal, an aboriginal man of the Old World, come to recruit Elatine to save the people of the Twenty-Second. Scrophularia, or Francesco Di Paolo as Sotiris had once known him, was now safely tucked away in a Utopia on the eastern shore of the Black Sea, totally unaware that the war he'd started still raged.

"What would you like?" Sotiris asked warily.

"Anything. Something to amaze me."

Sotiris glanced around, standing from the cushions. "You say the material of this camp is indestructible?"

Elatine nodded.

The Amaranthine took a breath and swept his gaze across the wall, looking down and mentally dividing the ground between himself and the waking lionhound. He stepped away.

A line of black began to form at once in the laminate, bubbling and spitting, the substance separating like a gangrenous wound. The hound jumped up, barking ferociously at the hissing floor.

Elatine yelped with delight, clapping his gigantic hands and prancing away from the damage. "Enough! Stop!" He laughed, dropping to a chair while the lionhound paced, growling at the sizzling floor. "How? You must tell me, how can you do this? How is it done?"

"Did you become frustrated with magic shows as a boy?"

"Ah, but this isn't magic, I know that much."

"It is very hard to explain." In truth it wasn't, but Sotiris had no wish to tell the Melius he would never live long enough even to begin to see the changes in his body that would lead to such abilities.

Elatine shooed the aggravated lionhound out of the way to look at the cooling floor. "Can you heal? That is something I've always wanted to know."

Sotiris shook his head. "I have limited control. Building requires more skill than destruction, as I'm sure you of all people understand, Commander."

The warlord nodded impatiently. "But you grow more powerful, more potent, as you age?"

"Yes."

"And you are truly very old? Many thousands of years?"

"Almost too many to recall."

Elatine touched a hand to his rump. "I have this problem, you see. It has plagued me since I left the Seventeenth. Acid, scalding bowel movements, pain when I sit down. Don't suppose you experience such things, do you? You Immortals cannot feel anything, I hear."

Sotiris sat again. The man could talk to himself all day. "It's your diet, I expect."

"My what?"

"Eat softer, more fibrous foods."

Elatine laughed. "Fine, you joke, I was wrong to ask. My fleshdoctors agree it is troubled thoughts, the pressure of command. I will listen to their advice, I think."

Sotiris put a hand to his brow.

"Anyway," the Melius continued, his wide eyes gleaming from the fits of laughter, "it is a curse, is it not?"

Sotiris looked up. "Immortality? Oh, yes." He knew precisely where Elatine was going with his questions.

Elatine paused, looking to the window almost casually. "But how did you become this way?"

Sotiris wished he could have some water for his mouth. "I was part of something a long time ago. There were hundreds of thousands of us. Now only a few remain."

The warlord paced to the bedchamber, choosing his words. "*Is* it attainable? Be honest with me, Amaranthine, I must have honesty."

There. They always asked. "Anything is attainable," he replied.

"Be careful," Elatine said, smiling, his vast grinning jaws gummy and shark-like, "I could take some hope from that, were it suggested to me by any normal person."

Sotiris glanced up at the horrific parody of a man staring down at him. He knew Elatine would gladly kill him for the gift of Immortality, were that the way to gain it, and reflected on what a poor choice of title it was. The Firmament was woven of jealousy, an envy that burned in every hominid race, even on the Old World. "I told you, it's a curse."

Like the man his legions were marching to confront, there were plenty of things the full extent of which Elatine didn't need to know.

The truth Sotiris chose to hide from him was simply that the more you lived, the more you needed to keep doing it. Enlightenment came to Sotiris as simple pleasures—a tug of wind, the slant of evening light, a deep breath in cold, clear air. The alternative to such a convivial state became increasingly unthinkable with each passing year. Immortality didn't drive you mad, as people had once assumed—not for a while, anyway—and the loneliness did not become unbearable every year you lost a friend. Not one person (at least not among those he'd known) had chosen suicide after their first turbulent five hundred years or so, when the idea is still fresh that you're doing something unnatural, that you've made a mistake. Passing that milestone, the thoughts in your head slowing, all lusts and hungers receding, tended to make one realise that *Life*, pronounced in a firm upper case, had more to show anyone intrepid enough to keep sailing across its waters. Sotiris's Greek roots helped him relate to the metaphor, his own life passing from tiny island-speckled seas into deep, cold oceans that appeared to stretch forever. And they *did* go on forever, or near enough to it—that was guaranteed; it was one's own state, however, one's body, the little ramshackle boat you used to sail through the storms, that would let you down in the end.

"I understand now why some people say it is hard work carrying on a conversation with an Immortal," said Elatine, stepping closer to inspect him. "You haven't chosen this moment to die on me, have you, Amaranthine?"

"I'm sorry—were you saying something?"

"I was asking where you will go now."

"Oh, here and there. Perhaps I'll see you at your coronation, Commander."

"I'm sure you will," Elatine replied with a wry smile. They both watched the lionhound as it began licking itself with wet slurping noises. Its testicles would shine with a mirror finish by the time it was done with them.

Elatine went back to scratching his hound. It rolled over in anticipation, one leg trembling, a large brown eye lolling in their direction.

"Why not stay a while, Amaranthine? I like your company, and we could use you here at the front."

"You hardly need my help, Elatine. Besides, there are things I must do."

"What sort of business does an Immortal get up to? Do you have friends to visit?"

Sotiris shrugged, standing again. "Something like that."

The city by the lake was a column of darkness some miles across, the smoke torn and slanted towards the mountains by the fresh wind. Lines of fleeing Secondlings swamped the far roads, some mounted, others pulling clanking wheeled houses as fast as they could. Inside the city seething armies fought, the small pops of detonations still coming from somewhere inside the walls as messenger birds wheeled and dipped against the cream sky. Sotiris was thinking of Zigadenus, the anointed poster boy of the First and Elatine's old nemesis, as he made his way along the hilltop to the distant road that spanned the tea-coloured water into Elblag Second. He'd heard nothing but praise for the dead man, from both sides of the war. Lenient and merciful, he apparently had an eye for beauty both great and modest. He would have let the city be.

The dream he'd had in the Utopia was to be the last of their strange meetings, he felt sure of it, even though the offer still went unanswered. In the darkness that came with each blink, Sotiris saw the cathedral-space with its blood-red walls, the snow melting as it drifted inside from the strange, timeless night. Now he could feel Aaron waiting for him just beyond those mountains: a presence almost as tangible as if they were walking side by side. He thought of Tussilago, the Melius servant who'd rowed him across the small, buoyant sea, and his warning that Sotiris might not return.

Sotiris pulled off his helmet and dropped it in the weeds by the roadside. Bilocation was not possible this far from the Old World's magnetic poles, and attempting it might well ruin his mind before its time. He would have to settle for a fast stroll, perhaps climbing aboard a moving convoy should any take his road. As he walked, he tried to come up with something he could whistle to buoy his spirits on the walk ahead of him, but couldn't think of a single song. His mind was blank for a moment, totally empty, even his name a passing mystery.

As the emptiness left him, he reflected it was not the first time that had happened today.

Zeliolopos

By the time they'd realised that the fleet of ships wasn't after them at all, the *Wilemo Maril* had already dived right through them, dispatching hundreds of the Prism vessels in silent sparkles among the hanging blooms of mines. The thousands of unknown ships were running scared like Old World schools of fish evading a predator, the storm of glinting, swirling craft parting around the *Wilemo Maril* to form a glittering metallic tunnel five hundred feet across for the privateer as it spun. It was impossible to work out what class or manufacture of Voidships they were, let alone who owned them in the handful of seconds it took for them all to pass by; Maril could only glimpse flashes of whirling light through the reopened porthole shields, two thousand twinkling shards of glass falling past them in a silent blizzard. The privateer banked sharply away from the sun as it found itself in open vacuum again, light filling the tipping windows, the master-at-arms now upside down and trying to clip himself in the wrong way round as the ship's gyroscopes feebly found their gravity. He managed at last to regain his seat, officiously brushing himself down and checking his holstered pistol self-consciously as a few stragglers in the shoal of unknown craft blinked across their path in chrome flashes.

Maril listened carefully to the damage reports still coming in as the rolling decreased. Substantial loss of hull plating, a few broken bones among the crew and an antique cabinet in the scullery lifted and smashed to splinters by the temporary loss of gravity; he tapped the master-at-arms on the shoulder to listen in—that cabinet had been Jospor's pride and joy, hefted aboard during a raid and varnished once a month thereafter.

The captain closed his eyes, breathing the fish-scented darkness inside the nested shells of cockpit and padded helmet, considering what precious few choices they had. The last of the mysterious fleet of ships blipped one last time on the radar and disappeared, heading out of the system and back into the Firmament. It would still take the *Wilemo Maril* five hours to pass the remaining planets of Tau Ceti; five hours of slowed manoeuvring, constant readings and range reports. Lifting above the forest of Zelioceti Kingdoms would lengthen the journey as well as instantly expose them to whatever was on their tail, an encounter he knew they could not survive in open space, and yet negotiating his way through might prove equally perilous. He sat back, thoughtful, ignoring the high-pitched queries on the communications. Encountering that fleeing shoal of ships had been infinitesimally unlikely considering the enormity of the blackness around them, like meeting your best friend in a crowd of trillions. He could only assume, however much he might not wish to, that there were many more shoals like them rushing away from Tau Ceti.

Away from the Investiture and into the Firmament, he thought, his gloved fingers intertwining.

The privateer curved on Maril's command towards the shadow of the system's first ruddy gas giant, Zeliomoltus, passing its largest moon AntiZelio-Formis. The hazy magenta globe rose to starboard and grew swiftly in the lateral windows, its pink atmosphere thrown into contrast by the dark brown churning thunder of its parent world's nightside. He took in the brushed swirl of cloud-tops wrapping the luminous moon for an instant, attempting to recall which Zelioceti Kingdom owned it, before returning his attention to a mewling chime and the whitish-grey sweep of the long-range wave projection.

Images were a luxuriant expense. The privateer possessed only one optisocket, its ten inch viewing hole cracked and taped. Maril leaned forward in his seat to study the tiny image. A black swirl like a miniature hurricane had pierced the haze in a torrent of eddying sonar read-outs and was closing directly on their position. A mournful cry like wind in a gully preceded it, the rear antennas mapping the shape as best they could while it screamed towards the privateer.

"Is that—?" He leaned backwards, trying to take it in.

"Schooner class, Captain," said the master-at-arms. "Thirteen lengths, tetraluminal, by the looks of it."

Maril stared at the dark swirl as it descended upon them, parting the solar winds like spray. "Violent, please, Ribio," he said to the pilot.

The *Wilemo Maril* swung a harsh, engine-crumpling about-turn above the moon, flipping the privateer in a haze of frozen soot and firing off at an angle, the ferocity of the conflicting forces grinding the captain into his seat. As they swung away, a snap of whitish silver burst like a bullet across the horizon; a schooner—as the master-at-arms had predicted—long and cruelly pointed, though some miles off, swooping on where it thought it would find them. The speck of their attacker dwindled in an instant, but the echoing trace of its fabulously rare tetraluminal motors remained repeated and augmented inside the darkness of Maril's heated helmet. After a moment, the communications reported in, relaying information Maril had already guessed. It was the Lacaille Nomad they'd encountered on Steerilden's Land. It had found them by some means after a month of erratic flight and was closing again on their position.

He slapped the Vulgar-Wulm pilot's shoulder. "Zeliolopos, Ribio." Ribio nodded his unusual crossbreed face, banking the controls while the other pilot unfurled the sun chart on his lap. The sand grain colours of thousands of visible stars began to blend to chrome, moonlit silver as the privateer picked up speed again, edging into the superluminal.

Maril unbuckled the master-at-arms' belt. "Jospor, with me."

The captain waited for his second to follow, grabbing at the handholds on the side of the cockpit to pull himself out. He took the nearest ladder to the forward battery compartment, already able to feel the heat from the recently fired heavy cannon radiating through his thin—and probably useless—Voidsuit, which he had not yet tested in open space. Once inside the dark compartment, he paused, watching the gaggle of small, naked Vulgar steadily pouring ladles of water over the sizzling guns. They noticed him and paused in their work, one knocking over his vat in a fit of clumsiness.

"They're cooled enough—be ready to fire all batteries," he announced, stepping to one side of the gushing water and turning back to the gangway, reaffirming his reputation among the crew as a captain of few words. The master-at-arms, bumblingly resplendent as he fitted his stolen Quetterel helmet, caught up with him at last. They approached the ladder together through the fog of steam.

"We'll be overtaken," Maril said to him as they climbed down past huge wooden lockers piled with tins and supplies. "Fall back the moment we are."

"What if they aren't interested in boarding?" his second-in-command squeaked in reply.

"We'd all be dead by now if they weren't—"

Just at that moment, the lockers flew open under a heavy jolt, scattering their cargo down the shaft. Maril and the master-at-arms ducked as barrels and cans and heavy sacks thudded past and knocked them from the ladder. They fell together to the bottom of the shaft, Maril striking his helmet against the scullery hatchway with a crack. Gallons of water, presumably from the vats in the forward battery, came pouring down the ladder shaft after them, splashing the banded iron and wood of the floors and running in a river into the scullery. Helped by Jospor, the captain climbed blearily to his feet, the crude internal systems inside his helmet apparently dead or frozen, and stumbled through the water into the scullery. The walls and floor were trembling as frying pans and pots fell rattling into the torrent. Maril was struck again on the side of the helm, but waved the master-at-arms away and continued on. An oaken dresser shed its load of iron plates as the ship received another battering, each blow to the hull rippling through Maril's body with the adrenalin of a real, tangible slap. The water was coursing into forward operations, and by the groaning of the hull Maril could already tell that his privateer had taken a crippling shot. He grabbed Jospor once more and sent the master-at-arms back the way they had come, dragging his boots through the water as he tried to run to operations and swearing softly inside his battered helmet.

The water followed him, flowing between his legs and almost knocking him over. Maps and sun charts floated, washing past him as he stooped to enter the capsule. The squabbling Vulgar crew were busily trying to shut off the electrics in the chamber, but so far with no success. They wailed and scattered as sparks and flame erupted suddenly from some equipment they were working on.

"Voidsuits on!" he yelled, as loudly as he could so that his voice would carry from the dead helmet, and as the flapping crowd of Vulgar made their way to their bunks to find their suits, Maril glanced around, pushing on through the soggy mass of charts and scattered equipment.

Another trembling bang shook the *Wilemo Maril* as he made it through to his quarters, sending him crashing into his desk. The water had drained off into a side corridor, where it ran gurgling to the site of the damage somewhere at the rear of the privateer, possibly in the aft superluminal compartments. An unusual breeze was tugging the loose papers and maps in his chamber so he slammed the door, pulled off his helmet and searched the mess for his ceremonial sword and pistol, locating both on the rug under a pile of books and a tipped globe of the

Firmament. He went to the shelf and flicked open a golden case, collecting a gloveful of shigella-poison-tipped bullets before clipping the pistol into its holster and tucking the rapier into his leather bandolier. As he did so, he caught sight of his reflection in the greasy, gilded mirror that still hung on the wall.

His gaunt, pale face was stern, eyes creased with worry, long eartips grizzled and bent with age. Where his weak chin sank into his neck, a few whiskers of Vulgar beard, white and bristly, had grown over the last month or so—his attempt at appearing distinguished. Now, in a rattling ship under siege, such affectation looked weak and stupid, perhaps the traits of a sightless vanity that had succeeded in getting them caught after all. Maril glanced back to the eyes of his reflection, the sword weighing heavily against his hip. *If I'm to lose this fight—if it is to be my last, then at least it'll be quick.* Such was the blessing of Voidfaring, he sometimes mused, that in death there simply wasn't time to lament one's mistakes.

He wrenched open the door against the strengthening gust that was trying to pull it shut again and stamped out into the passageway just as the whole privateer rolled at forty-five degrees. The strips of lighting wire that followed the curve of the passage had begun to dim, so as he braced himself he fumbled for his suit lights, still swearing softly and continuously under his breath while he clipped the unresponsive helmet back on.

The enormous planet they were aiming for—Maril was sufficiently experienced in the maintenance of his own Voidship to realise that they were no longer in full control any more, their progress across the system more akin to a thrown rock than anything resembling powered flight—held within its thrall a string of forty-three moons, many of them separate and ancient kingdoms in their own right. Plunging to one at random would be their only chance of survival, where with luck they could evade the attentions of the Nomad and make repairs. The captain understood—as would any of his crew possessing knowledge of the Zelioceti, the local Prism—that even if they did manage to set down on one of the moons, their troubles were far from over.

He slid the handful of bullets into the bandolier, dropping one as another slap shook the hull and watching it roll away before he could bend to catch it. Another blow dislodged the piping from the bulkhead around him and he ducked as it clattered into the passageway, spilling sewage and filthy water across his suit. Wiping at his forearms, Maril could feel his ship slowing. Vague forces from which the privateer was supposed to be protected were compressing the hull like an accordion.

He ran at a crouch, trailing his gloved hand along the corridor's wall until he got to the junction at the privateer's central passage, the walls boarded with slats that had served as beds for the extra crew he'd hired on Drolgins. Figures huddled in their worn blankets in some of the bunks stared down at him in the weak, flickering light. He thought of saying something to them, but there was no time. He steadied himself and ran on, slamming into the scullery ladder at the end of the passageway as the ship rolled again, his sword rattling against the riveted iron panels and almost getting jammed in the grille of a radiator column. He pulled his pistol free as he prepared to climb, kicking aside smashed barrels that had rolled and plunged down two levels from the larders.

By now the privateer had begun to pitch from one direction to the other, more hits hammering the fuselage and likely deforming the hull. Maril held tightly to the ladder's rungs, his small body swaying from side to side, and clawed his way up into the scullery. The cooks were trying to salvage what was left of the supplies, dodging falling crockery and waving away smoke pouring from the clogged ovens, taking no time to stop and acknowledge his presence when they saw him.

The cannon began firing before he reached the forward battery, the privateer still weaving and banking. Popped shell casings like barrels sprang and bounced from the rear of the guns, flipping into piles that rolled with the motion of the ship. Maril jumped over a spinning casing and ducked against the roaring heat, swinging quickly into the cockpit beneath the battery chamber. Nobody turned to him as he fell into his seat, their eyes fixed on the blazing image ahead of them.

Pieces of wreckage illuminated by popping blasts of light tumbled and whipped past almost too fast to catch, the afterglow staining Maril's eyes a muddy, streaked blend of colours. Ahead of them the Nomad traded fire, veering and twisting and spinning, as the haunting, glorious bulk of Zeliolopos—the largest of Tau Ceti's gas giants—swelled rapidly before them.

Amid the bolts of light, Maril could see that the schooner had been modified, with large-calibre guns now ruining the sleek lines of its exterior. Its pristine outer paintwork had been similarly despoiled with a bold new insignia that was hard to miss.

He mouthed the word before he said it, knowing how ill the crew would take it despite those who sat with him in the cockpit knowing full well by now who their pursuers were. The insignia blazed across the Nomad's sides was of three pan-Prism fingers stencilled in red. A famous warning, known and feared all across the Investiture. *The Bult.*

Maril and his crew were being hunted by cannibals.

The privateer's cannon reloaded and fired into the curve of the Nomad's hull before it could release countermeasures, smashing away a flurry of protective plating. The schooner swerved, discharging a round of glittering, explosive-tipped needle rounds that the *Wilemo Maril* twisted to avoid, the sudden force jamming Maril's bones into the side of his suit and squeezing his face up against the inside of his helmet. The schooner was trying to slow, flaring retro engines as a snowstorm of shattered plating spattered the privateer. Maril saw his chance, tearing open his visor plate.

"Full battery!" he screamed into the forward compartment above them, unclipping his belt to lean back as far as he could. Twelve guns situated in a halo around the bulge of the cockpit bellowed into life, shredding the rear of the Nomad with a flash that blinded them all for the best part of a minute. When their eyes had adjusted, they saw that the schooner had managed to deflect only one shell, the material of its hull sloughing away like shed skin, white-hot and sparkling.

"Make full speed, Ribio," Maril said, unclipping the jaw of his helmet to feel his bruised chin through the beard. He peeled a chart from the wall, turning it this way and that and ripping it in the process. "Anti-Zelio-Coriopil," he said, tracing the concentric red lines with his shaking finger and tapping a red dot the size of a full stop.

The privateer swung beneath the sleet of debris and outdistanced the Nomad once more, sailing like a broken leaf in a hurricane towards Zeliolopos.

The giant planet was nine times the size of Jupiter, banded with fourteen hundred atmospheric belts of turbulence; all but one subtly different shades of green and gold, the last like a blood-red paper cut across its lower middle, speckled with lighter storm systems. The *Wilemo Maril* plunged on towards the swirling current of the storm until the details of its flowing clouds became visible, coiled and wound around a central gaping eye. To Maril it looked like a filthy, deep wound on the verge of turning septic, a rancid, infected crimson gash on such a vast, violently beautiful wall of colour. The privateer angled slightly while the tempest grew before them and eventually lost its form altogether, the miniature blotches of surrounding storms taking on their own sublime intricacies. Maril knew that each of the hundreds of weather systems that rolled around the giant eye were themselves bigger than the Old World, wider even than any of the moons that circled the planet. He looked into their dirty red sockets while he listened for the return of the stricken Nomad, his thin body still trembling every now and then inside the suit, and thought of all the ships and souls that had lost their way inside those storms over the centuries. He would not make the same mistake.

As if in confirmation of his cunning, a speck rose to port, doubling in size with every heartbeat. The cockpit crew strained their damaged eyes, the pilots leaning forward. Maril sat back at last, listening to the ragged coughing of the master-at-arms and the similarly ill-sounding grumble emanating from somewhere in the superluminal compartments.

The dot was as large as his outstretched thumb now, a hot, salty glob of viridian suspended like a teardrop against Zeliolopos's tawny golds, greens and reds. The moon, AntiZelio-Coriopil, was almost entirely ocean but for a chain of islands circling its equator—it was to them that he and his crew would fall. Maril knew little of what lay there besides information gathered from drinking songs, notably the *Songs of Lopos*, many of which he knew by heart. He did not sing—of course—but he deigned to sit and listen while his crew relaxed in whatever port they found themselves in, tapping a finger to their carousing if the drink got the better of him. He knew the soldiers called his finger-taps "the Marillion waltz," and smiled secretly at the thought.

The green globe's faint string of islands became minutely visible and his smile stiffened, the feeling returning to his bruised face and battered limbs, still reeking with the film of sewage that had leaked from the pipes. The privateer began to judder as it hit the moon's thick atmosphere, soft as smoke where the shadow formed its crescent.

Maril flicked a switch, broadcasting through the only remaining internal channel.

"Men: scuttling drill. Secure yourselves where necessary." The pilots busied themselves in the front seats. Jospor turned to him, thrice buckled. His helmet stayed on, so that all Maril saw was a faded reflection of his own worn face peeping from its layers of Voidsuit.

"Wilemo, you are sure of this? We might still have some strength— the damage crews are not done reporting in. There may be a chance of reaching AntiZelio-Slaathis."

"I am sure," he said, hinging up the jaw of his helmet. The internal workings looked reinvigorated, if still weak, as glowing, stolen Amaranthine automation lit up to either side of the faceplate. The moon became red in his helmet display, criss-crossed with symbols and representations of weather fronts. Jospor's suited body flashed X-ray through the chair, his bones jumping out before the wavelengths of the helmet's vision settled. "Descend," Maril's voice said clearly into the other helmets in the cockpit, their mumbled assent reaching his ears as if they were sitting beside him, and the ship began to fall.

The green moon grew, its face wriggling across the windows as the privateer fought to remain level. Rivets rattled in their sockets, the plastic of the portholes to Maril's side whitening with the smashing strain. He watched with dismay as his beloved Voidship took steadily increasing injury, the cockpit itself feeling loose in its housing beneath the forward battery. The tip of the nose, just visible beyond the hazing windows, was glowing and loosing sparks that splattered the view.

The whole ship kicked upwards suddenly, jarring their bones, and the Nomad roared beneath. It fell in a scream from the radars, which had failed to anticipate its approach, spinning sideways for a moment before them and breaking in half above the clouds in a ruptured burst of flying pieces. The pilots of the *Wilemo Maril* shrieked, grappling with the turbulence of the enemy ship's descent, and bounced through the flying white-hot debris and smoke trails. Maril saw the piece of shredded hull gliding towards them in his suit vision, its probable trajectory calculated and drawn across the view. Warnings flashed at the bottom of his sight, displayed with a multitude of arrows and excited Unified exclamation marks. The debris darkened the window, blocking the view of the entire moon. The helmet screamed in a tinny, synthesised voice, strobing the oncoming piece of hull in case he hadn't noticed.

"Battery!" he shouted again, spittle dampening his bristly beard, just as the white trails of a dozen shells slammed from around the cockpit.

The piece of hull detonated into a thousand glowing shards, the splinters whickering past the cockpit in a blooming star of grey smoke tails. The *Wilemo Maril* dived through, the window hazing in one corner where wreckage had struck it. More thunks and bangs signalled their descent through the comet trail of debris from the Nomad, a ragged hole appearing in the nose where something had shot through it. Maril watched his Voidship begin to unravel, the rivets popping at last from the tip of the nose and pinging away, plates of metal loosening and flapping and tearing in the gust of their fall. The green sea, hot and smooth like a worked slab of sun-baked jade, tipped to meet them.

"Cut them," he said to the pilots. The nose disintegrated, battering the forward windows as it spun away. The growling superluminal engines screamed once and were silent, only the shriek of a foreign wind coursing past and catching on the angles of the ship, all flaps and wings now extended to increase drag. Maril crossed his padded arms over his chest, hearing the moaning ship losing its momentum. Pieces of the enemy Nomad still rained through the haze of lemon-yellow sky in spears of black smoke, dashing white into the hot sea, the main bulk having already scuttled somewhere behind them.

Jospor flicked off the last of the electrics, turning in his seat. He clapped a salute, followed by the pilots. "Captain."

Maril nodded back, his eyes drawn once more to the wall of emerald green rushing towards them.

Trial

"Wake up, Lycaste." The words were spoken just before the water hit his hot, dry skin.

"He doesn't look too good."

"Better than dead. Cassiope made a grave mistake."

"He'll live out the festival?"

"One hopes."

"Then that's all that matters."

*

He'd been dreaming of Jasione. But it hadn't been a normal dream, more like the one he'd had in the field of purple plants that day, terrifying and surreal. Lycaste opened his eyes; the pain in his stomach had spread, throbbing, to his back and sides, and there was a bitter taste in his mouth as if he'd vomited nothing but bile while he slept.

In the dream he'd rescued her and they'd gone back to Kipris Isle together, starting a family and growing old. It had felt real enough, but not as happy as he'd have wished. Silene had been there, begrudgingly accepting her mother's choice and tormenting her new siblings. Lycaste had to pay her to keep silent, eventually granting her a yearly stipend until he died. The silken money he gave her always came from a hole in his stomach, caked with drying blood.

The children were the only happy part of the dream: two, no, three girls. He was glad they weren't been boys. They were beautiful.

Lycaste tried to touch his stomach, flinching at the tenderness along his entire torso. At some point the cut had burst again, a slug-trail of blood marking his fevered progress across the floor while he slept. He felt weak, light-headed: the only part that wasn't entirely unpleasant.

A reception had begun outside the door to his prison chamber, its rising volume and music not unlike what he'd heard on the far island. Perhaps a hundred voices conversed and laughed in High Second beyond the wall, broken by clinks of metal or glass, occasional shouts and intervals of raucous hilarity.

The door opened carefully to avoid prying eyes and Xanthostemon slipped in, closing it gently behind him. He came to Callistemon's repositioned plinth and stared at it thoughtfully, obviously unsure how it had moved, and pushed it over to the wall.

"Can you walk?" he asked, gazing into the cage.

Lycaste cleared his dry throat and tried to sit up. "I'm not sure."

Xanthostemon opened the door of the cage, putting a hand delicately to his nose. He squatted beside Lycaste and peered at his midriff. "You're swollen. Here." He took Lycaste's arm and hauled him to his feet. It took a while; despite his emaciation, Lycaste was still over a foot taller than the Secondling.

"Thank you," Lycaste said through the pain. The smallest kindnesses felt magnified these days.

"You've nothing to thank me for," Xanthostemon said plainly, without looking at him. "We'll see you pay, but not before the trial. Our sister would have caused us great shame had she succeeded." He glanced up at Lycaste. "So give no thanks."

"All right."

Xanthostemon remained looking at him. "I . . . I can begin to understand how it may have been, why he died. But do not count on mercy you shall not receive." He handed Lycaste a small crystal glass that he'd brought in with him. Lycaste took it and peered at the rapidly dissolving little pearl sinking to the bottom.

"Drink. It will keep you awake if the pain gets too much."

He drank, gagging. After he'd finished, Xanthostemon led him through another door Lycaste hadn't known was there, a recessed alcove behind the line of busts. It took them to a narrow hallway inlaid with more of the coloured stripes.

He was made to wait in a circular stone room, unadorned except for an ornate trapeze dangling in the centre from a hook in the ceiling. A ghostly white chameleon hung by three of its limbs from the jewelled perch. Its ruby-red eyes were mounted in sockets that swivelled at him inquisitively before moving on, as if dull guests infringing on its valuable time were an all too regular occurrence. Lycaste limped to the wall to investigate the coloured stripes to see what they were, confirming his suspicion. It was money, of all the highest denominations, implanted in shining lengths along the walls. He was impressed, despite everything, and smoothed his finger over a piece to find it was buried some way beneath the surface, entombed in the resin-like depths of a superior form of translucent growthstone. The lizard strained and clasped the perch with another limb, hanging feebly upside down while it decided what to do next. A long tongue slithered from between its lips and travelled wetly across one eye.

The door, itself also lined with the silken money, reopened and stayed ajar. Lycaste found himself looking out across a terrace of exquisite geometric hedges and fountains lit by the last of the day's pink light. Milling about and waiting to be seated were dozens, perhaps hundreds, of people, glowingly yellow and patterned with tawny stripes of primary colour. A semicircular dining table faced him, at which a few were already seated and finishing some kind of dessert course.

Lycaste glanced at them the longest as he made his way stumblingly into the garden while Xanthostemon looked on. They were the oldest-looking men and women he'd ever seen, elders undoubtedly now beginning—or ending—their last years of grace, though he doubted any of them were even a fraction as venerable as the Amaranthine he'd met in the Utopia. Certainly they had to be older than Elcholtzia. Their skin appeared to have slid from their hollow cheeks and down to their necks, as if the pull of the world could only be resisted for so long, and their eyes were dull and yellowed. Hair was scant between them, the last of the light gleaming from bald heads and shiny, lined brows. It was what he would look like one day, if he ever made it.

The elders ate slowly, directing their drooping eyes about them until some ripple of conversation brought everyone's attention to Lycaste's arrival. He crossed his arms about himself, the waves of pain growing stronger again, and scanned the attentive audience, seeing first Hamamelis and then Melilotis, who smiled and waved cheerfully. Melilotis mouthed something Lycaste couldn't quite catch. Callistemon's sister Cassiope, his would-be executioner, was conspicuously absent among her family, who were seated at either end of the elders' table.

Beside her empty seat a small gold man slouched alone, uninvolved in the conversations that flanked him, almost as if nobody could see him. He stared straight at Lycaste without expression, as someone might absently watch a pot of water boiling. Lycaste held Sotiris's gaze but the man didn't respond, taking a sip of what looked like wine from a fluted goblet and swilling his mouth. Nobody appeared to notice when he spat.

Xanthostemon took Lycaste's arm and directed him to a veined marble seat, solidly throne-like, where everyone would be able to see him. When he was settled, his hands still pressed to his throbbing belly, the audience's conversation diminished to a whisper, some perhaps taking in the wound across his stomach, others more enthralled, no doubt, by his appearance. An elder in the middle of the table raised a sagging arm to the assembly as a sheaf of papers was put in front of him by a secretary with extraordinarily coiffed auburn hair. He stood shakily from his chair, propping himself up with a cane whilst waving away the attentions of the secretary, and turned to the assembly.

Lycaste watched Sotiris. The Immortal was running a fingernail along the marble tabletop and investigating its tip, not looking at the elder as the rest of the crowd applauded. Melilotis and his father stood, applauding particularly hard and attracting disapproving looks from the front table.

The elder waggled an arthritic finger for silence, stooping over his cane. Lycaste saw a misshapen little person on a leash under the table grab at some of the old man's dessert and scurry back into shadow beneath.

"Dignitaries and Plenipotentiaries, youthful and old," he intoned, not in High Second, but First. Lycaste peered into the crowd but they all looked the same, yellow and small, ducklings before a mallard. If there was a Firstling in there, he was carefully hidden.

"This evening we process, by the Lyonothamnine Enlightenment of the First and her daughter the Second, the actions of . . ." He strained his eyes at the top paper when the secretary passed it to him. "*Licasse*, of the . . . Tenth Province, dishonourer of the noble House of Berenzargol."

The elder paused for a sip of wine. Lycaste looked for Sotiris but his seat was vacant, as if he'd never even been there. None of the yellow people had even looked at the Amaranthine since Lycaste had ascended his stone seat. He felt cold for the first time, the pain shooting up his spine now, making him wriggle in his chair. The drink he'd taken was supposed to simply keep him alert, but he was starting to feel everything now. It hurt everywhere.

"During these harrowing times," the elder resumed, "when we must remind ourselves with certainty that justice shall soon find us triumphant, it does our realm great credit to be seen to continue in all splendour, to serve as a barrier against the creeping filth, this wicked *Elatine* and his Jalan plague, that seeks to scale our walls."

The crowd roared with approval, standing and applauding loudly. The elder waited patiently, acknowledging them. The little bone-white fellow beneath the table helped himself to more of the leftover dinner, glancing furtively around and up at Lycaste before withdrawing.

"Perhaps in time, even the Third shall become to us as we are to the First, loyal and obedient in all things, the scales of power dipping for the weight of the worthy." His stooped form, theatrically challenging, surveyed the garden. "But until that time, we must toil in the work that the First has given us, glad in the knowledge that these trials only serve to conjoin our great Provinces further." He smiled, to more applause. "Now then, to business." His thickly hooded eyes regarded Lycaste.

"It is imperative that the Southern species are not encouraged to believe that they may do as they wish, that their masters are not hindered by something as trifling as geography in carrying out the venerable First statutes—" he raised his voice and turned to the audience again "—statutes we *all* live by here, with gratitude and humility as Second to the sovereign state. It is you privileged few, nobles of regard, who have been invited here to decide the nature of our response, and have done so graciously this very evening."

Cheers while the grizzled man held his hand up once more, visibly exhausted from his speech. Lycaste's eyes widened as he thought about what the man had said. This was just a display, perhaps for any Firstlings present. His own judgement had already taken place.

"Owing to the evident difficulties Southern Cherries have in remembering simple instructions, let this be their lesson for the day. If you would all be so kind as to remain after drinks, we shall hold the festival of this desecrator's punishment then." He sat slowly, easing his flabby body back into whatever chair hid behind the grandly heaped table.

Before the applause died, Hamamelis had risen quickly to his feet. At his gesture the claps subsided, not, Lycaste guessed, from respect but out of surprise. He knew approaching embarrassment when he saw it. The cadaverous Intermediary cleared his throat and inclined his head in an even more theatrical display of submission.

"My dear Scabiosa, the effect of your words is matched only by their incisive and modest brevity, always distinguishing you as an orator of unique power from whom we can all draw inspiration." He pointed to his chest. "I myself make speeches of similar proportions to my Second-beloved family so that they might learn to condense their more grandiose thoughts into morsels that signify the utmost consideration and wisdom."

Hamamelis's deep-set eyes searched the table for a moment, but his creative well had run dry. He took a breath during which he might accept acknowledgment, but the audience was silent. He straightened, the emaciation of his frame making him appear even more elongated among the shorter people in the audience. Lycaste imagined himself standing there, taller even than Hamamelis by another hand or two.

"I am well aware that it is not my place in this garden court to pass any judgement along with my betters, and that my sons and I are here only to provide another story of this wicked Cherry's wrongdoing. That is of the murder of my promising and gentle son Leonotis, which has so far gone unmentioned."

Scabiosa, leaning backwards to see Hamamelis, exchanged glances with the other elders at the table. One old man had gone to sleep.

"Indeed?" He sifted through the papers. His secretary pointed to a footnote.

"I . . . I merely present our case so that it may be recognised and our part acknowledged," Hamamelis said, bowing again.

An excruciatingly thin elder inclined his head. "Your *part*?" he screeched in a rasping voice. "It is my understanding that you and your esteemed family allowed the Cherry to escape. Has this court been misinformed?"

Hamamelis looked at Lycaste with alarm, as if hoping for a contribution. "We did the best we could—"

"And—" the elder glanced at the assembly "—it is my understanding that you had no idea of the Cherry's previous crimes. Are we misinformed in this matter as well?"

"I had my . . . my suspicions," Hamamelis stuttered, glancing at the crowd. "He claimed to be Callistemon's servant and that his master was lost. Our family was held in high regard by the Plenipotentiary during his life. Having known him, I found this unlikely."

Xanthostemon, still seated, raised his eyebrows with amusement and whispered something to his sickly sister.

Hamamelis bridled. "It was *my understanding* that something was amiss. My sons and I have suffered as greatly as anyone here."

The crowd didn't like this. Lycaste watched several hands lifting with questions. Scabiosa, the elder who had first spoken, shook his head and eyed Callistemon's relatives. "Sir, you may sit. If I am not mistaken, you have already been rewarded for your pains. You were granted execution rights for the three who sheltered him. They have now been put to death, yes?"

Lycaste had been ripping at a grubby and trembling fingernail with his teeth while he listened, trying not to bite too deep whenever the pain grasped at his innards. He took it from his mouth and stared stupidly at Scabiosa, then at Hamamelis. The court had fallen silent for a moment, expectant.

Hamamelis nodded. "That is correct."

"Well," said the elder, "then you have extracted the modicum of revenge owed to you. The law here is identical to that of the Seventh. Those of *position*, sir, are awarded the satisfaction in events such as these."

Hamamelis appeared unable to think of anything further to say. Melilotis noticed Lycaste's slack-jawed expression and smirked. He mouthed something again. Lycaste caught the last word. *Alone.*

"But Scabiosa, *please.*" Hamamelis remained standing, inviting groans from the back. "Punishing them was no honour, at least not the honour you make it out to be; we want a say in this!"

Uproar. The sleeping elder awoke with a start, blinking. Scabiosa covered his eyes as abuse erupted around him.

"You embarrass yourself, *go-between*!" shouted an imperious-looking lady to a chorus of agreement.

Scabiosa waved his hand weakly at the front table. "Xanthostemon, would you take the Cherry out?"

Xanthostemon helped Lycaste down and ushered him back into the lizard's chamber, closing the door quickly behind him again. As it creaked shut, Lycaste heard raised voices as the Secondlings took their turns berating Hamamelis.

He sank to the stone floor, legs skidding out and splaying like a dropped puppet, his stomach starting to bleed again, bright in the white, acerbic light of the room, the naturally talented coagulants in his blood apparently giving up. It couldn't be true. They were lying to get a reaction out of him. Somehow they'd known about his feelings for Jasione; Hamamelis must have found out.

The chameleon had seemingly only moved one limb during the shambolic trial. It paused with another raised as Lycaste fell to the floor, caught in the act and now considering its next move even more carefully than before. Its red eye twitched at him, waiting. Lycaste scrabbled to his knees, wetness coating his lower half, and crawled along the polished floor to the recessed door. The creature hissed, flinching and raising spiny white hackles. He felt as if a blunt stick were being forced through the length of his guts, spitting him. Drops of blood followed Lycaste through the door and along the passageway to the chamber where his cage stood.

"I'm sorry."

Lycaste started blearily, his hand pressed to the seeping blood. Sotiris was sitting opposite him on the decorative couch, between the family busts.

"They were lying, weren't they?" Lycaste gasped, sinking closer to the floor. "They lied about Jasione."

The Amaranthine took too long to answer. "I'm sorry, Lycaste," he repeated. "They didn't lie." He went to Lycaste's side, gently taking his shoulder and turning him so that he could see the wound. Lycaste began to sob, lightly at first, but soon he found he couldn't catch his breath. His body started shaking, his head swimming.

"This isn't something that's going to get better, is it?" Lycaste asked, at last taking a breath and grimacing as the pain grew nearly unbearable. His voice had become a shuddering growl of effort. "That blade was dipped in something. Tell me the truth for once."

Sotiris was feeling his stomach, finding the tender parts from the way Lycaste winced. "Stay very still, even when it hurts," the Immortal whispered, still pressing. Lycaste saw the man's small hand was covered with bright, shining blood.

After a moment Lycaste felt the subtle thud of blood in his ears build to a roar. His heart stuttered and pounded, working the blood faster and faster. Pain came and went, leaping through his innards and quieting again only to spring up somewhere else. At first he thought he must be dying, here and now, and marvelled in the revelation that death was not some cold and steady thing but energetic and disorderly—even chaotic. It didn't feel so bad, he reflected as he lay there, puzzling at the swarming pins and needles. His stomach warmed, as if he were lying face down on hot sand, losing all feeling. Sweat sprang out all over his face and back, the tides coinciding with a soft tugging sensation inside his stomach. He strained his neck to check that the Amaranthine hadn't physically pushed his hand into the hole in his belly, but Sotiris was sitting silently, staring at Lycaste, his arms folded.

Just as the heat became almost too much to take, it died away. An empty, gnawing hunger remained where the pain had been only moments before. Lycaste felt his belly carefully, taking some time before sitting up and looking at himself. All that remained of the wound was a pink, cruelly hook-shaped scar a few centimetres above and to the right of his navel. He prodded it, expecting it to burst open again, but the skin was firm, shiny with new growth. Sotiris looked on solemnly. Lycaste pointed at his stomach, unable for the moment to frame his question.

"How . . . ?"

"It hasn't finished healing, so don't pick at it." The Immortal smiled softly. "And try not to get stabbed again."

Lycaste sniffed his bloody hand, the metallic scent confirming he had been wounded, at least at some point, and shook his head dreamily. Sotiris's palms were still red.

"You took your time about it," he croaked, crossing his legs carefully in case he ripped the seam open again.

"Even I have trouble getting onto some guest lists."

"The owl? Garamond's message?"

"You did well to last so long, not to try and escape."

"I certainly thought about it." He swallowed, realising how hungry he'd become in such a short space of time, and how sad. "So we're leaving now? I just want to get out of here. Please, let's just go."

The Amaranthine's solemn look returned. "I can't let you do that yet, Lycaste."

He stared at him in exasperation, his grief darkening to something else. "What?"

"Something is happening. It's bigger than both of us, any of us. I need to you to stay here for the moment."

Lycaste uncrossed his legs and stood, towering over the Immortal.

"You're leaving me *again*? After what they did to me?" He wanted to shake the Amaranthine, to throttle the ridiculously enduring life out of his petrified neck, but glared miserably at the floor instead, eyes crumpling. He went and sat, looking at the busts through a glimmer of tears. "They killed her, Sotiris. They'll kill me, too." In his mind's eye he saw her colouring bashfully into that of her flower. *It doesn't matter. What you may or may not be. That doesn't matter to me at all, not one bit.*

"You won't be harmed again, Lycaste. I have seen to it," Sotiris whispered, coming over to sit at Lycaste's side and placing a small hand gently on his shoulder. Lycaste wanted to shrug it away, rip it off and throw it across the room. He had the strength, perhaps, Sotiris's wrists were very narrow. But he let the hand stay. Without it, he had nothing.

He sensed Sotiris breathing softly beside him and speculated detachedly on how the Immortal still needed to do what they all did, to breathe, how he was no better or more efficient at it after so many thousands of years of life.

"Lycaste," he said gently, "there's more. Just after you left, Scabiosa decided to compensate Hamamelis further, perhaps just to shut him up. His sons have been granted permission to make their way to the Tenth."

Lycaste sniffed and cleared his throat. "What for?"

"To punish the people there, your friends, for their complicity."

"Complicity?"

"Knowing, and not telling anyone."

Lycaste let the Amaranthine's hand slide from his shoulder, shuddering slightly at its delicate weight. He could hardly picture his old friends any more.

"I've sent word. They'll be protected when the time comes."

"But . . . you're leaving me now? Going somewhere else?"

Sotiris stared at his hands, lingering on the edge of the long ornamental bench. "Yes. I must."

"We'll see each other soon?"

"We will. I promise."

Silence. Lycaste waited for more, eventually turning back to the patch of shadow the Amaranthine had been sitting in, but he wasn't there any more.

The door to the half-glimpsed hallway stood open. He saw Penstemon watching him through the crack.

"Who were you talking to? Who are you going to see soon?" he asked, stepping cautiously into the room. He had an ornamental, rather rusty-looking ring pistol on one finger, pointed roughly in Lycaste's direction.

"Nobody," Lycaste replied meekly, beginning to climb back into his cage. There was a word Eranthis had taught him once, when something was all just your imagination. A figment.

"No, no, you don't have to be in there any more," Penstemon said, pointing the ring squarely at him now. Lycaste stared at the weapon, beginning to raise his hands.

Xanthostemon burst into the room behind his brother, slamming back the door in a rattling cacophony. He threw Penstemon against the wall, pinning his hand and disarming him with one swift expert move, and shouted a torrent of quick, gabbling High Second, shaking the ring furiously. Penstemon came to his senses and grappled him, grabbing it back and aiming at Lycaste. He fired, the angle of the shot flicked upwards by a blow from Xanthostemon, who grabbed Penstemon by elbow and shoved him to the wall, knocking a plinth sideways.

Lycaste stood slowly, the blood pulsing in his ears and beneath the thinned skin around his scar. There was no pain anymore, only a growing, restless strength. He watched them fight, suddenly no longer afraid. The brothers looked so small, so weak to him now. He hated their puny voices and faces. He hated them all.

He picked up the bust of Callistemon with ease and advanced upon them. The brothers hesitated against the wall, their eyes registering the enormous Melius's new healthy state and the clean pink mark on his waist. He gripped Xanthostemon by the hair in one swift movement, feeling a surge of power on top of the ravenous hunger, and threw him to one side, the ring clattering off towards the cage. Penstemon cowered, covering his face as Lycaste brought the plinth up and smashed it down across his shoulder, roaring in inarticulate rage and despair. Callistemon's head went spinning through the open door, chips of stone flying from its extremities. Lycaste rounded on Xanthostemon, who was crawling for the ring, and kicked him hard in the ribs, pulling him by his ankle back towards his moaning brother in the corner. Penstemon quailed and hobbled for the door, his arm looking loose, perhaps broken. Lycaste followed him out, still dragging Xanthostemon, the wash of euphoria dulling only slightly when he saw the Firstling standing in the hallway, one of the man's monstrous Asiatic escorts apprehending Penstemon. He dropped Xanthostemon's leg, hearing the knee crack on the hard, patterned floor.

"You must be Lycaste." The childlike, white-gold person smirked, signalling his guard to release Penstemon and see to the boy's crushed arm.

Xanthostemon moaned. "He's all yours, Envoy. Get him out of here."

The Envoy directed the second of his giants to attend to Xanthostemon. He inspected Lycaste's healed knife wound as he came closer. "Ah, that is good. I'd begun to worry you were seriously injured."

"Nothing serious," growled Lycaste, considering his chances against the huge guard. He knew he could get a grip on Penstemon's neck before they could stop him, perhaps finish the job.

"That is good," the Firstling repeated, his strange eyes flicking to the scar once more. He looked up, dipping his head gently. "Well, now that you're well enough, I'd like very much to invite you to dinner, Lycaste."

Iro

He looks at her, seeing her face as it was before she became immortal.

"You can't even set foot on the shore?"

Iro shakes her head, looking down to the warm planked deck they're both sitting on. The elegant sailing boat he saw her on the first time is now moored in the middle of the harbour, majestic under the beating sun.

"I must stay at sea now, Sotiris."

Sotiris glances to the harbour's edge, where the specks of small figures wander about their daily business. His eyes travel to the café, but he cannot see Aaron. He and his sister appear to be alone together.

"I could sail this boat to shore myself."

She puts a hand to her brow. "You mustn't do that. *He* will not allow it."

"Does he speak to you?"

Iro closes her eyes, shakes her head again. "Let's not talk about him."

He takes her hand gently, prising it away from her eyes. Her skin feels somehow insubstantial, his fingers sliding from her own. At last she looks back at him, managing a smile before her eyes crinkle with tears. She looks quickly off to the cerulean water.

Sotiris tries to take her hand again. "What must I do? Tell me what I can do."

*

"I need your answer, Sotiris."

He blinks. Aaron walks past his chair, setting the coffee down him-self this time. There is a round cinnamon biscuit balanced on the edge of his saucer, like an absurd bribe.

"Why?" he asks. "Why ask anyone to rule in your stead? Why should you care what happens to the Firmament?"

Aaron sits down to his own cup, blowing on the black surface of the coffee before taking a sip. For a moment, Sotiris sees something reflected in the ruffled liquid, a monstrous shape, but then it is gone.

"I have my reasons. If you refuse me, your Firmament shall be torn down by the Prism and Iro will be lost to you for ever."

"Torn down?"

Aaron sighs, draining his cup. It is clearly still very hot but he doesn't even wince. "I know everything about the legions marching on me. This Commander Elatine of yours is vain and stupid. He will not succeed—but even if by some chance he does, the Prism shall not hesitate to follow."

Sotiris pushes his coffee cup to one side, staring at the surface of the table. "Permit me one more question."

Aaron shrugs irritably. "Go on."

"My friend, Maneker. That wasn't him I spoke to, was it? He was never there. It was just a part of you."

The man-shape stares impassively back.

"What have you done with him? Locked him up somewhere? Killed him?"

"Your answer, please." He points at the sailing boat in the harbour. Sotiris stands from his chair to see. There are Melius aboard—Firstlings, judgeing by their gleaming yellow skin. The one at the stern pulls up the anchor, hauling it over the railing and onto the deck. Another strides up from below with Iro struggling and screaming in his arms. Sotiris tightens his fists, glaring back at Aaron.

"Your answer, Sotiris."

Embassy

The islands speckling the fjord were closer to blue than green, with boats and ships crossing lazily between them. White and pink towers peeped from among the wooded hills to look out over the frigid, crystalline-blue water, where plump reddish trees sheltered barges and jetties around the base of the far spires, their leaves beginning to fall and blow twisting out across the lakes. With daylight the Second had become peaceful—when looked at from the safety of the First—as if everything Lycaste had experienced the night before was nothing but a dream. Between the grassy slope Lycaste stood on and the water's edge was an invisible border known instinctively by all those who lived in these lands, the small gatehouses that punctuated the woodlands representing the closest thing there was to a wall between the two Provinces. He was safe; he had the Envoy's assurance of that, but it would take more than a morning's unbroken sleep in a luxurious bed to convince him of it.

"You know my name," said Lycaste as they climbed up the slope towards a thicket of sighing trees. "What's yours?"

"Just call me Envoy," the Firstling said brightly as he walked beside him.

The embassy rose into view, the giant parent of the building where they had just breakfasted together, a geometric edifice that might have been sculpted by a pair of huge flattened hands. Green flags of the First fluttered from spires rising above its cupola, snapping against the light grey sky.

"Do you live in there alone?" Lycaste asked.

"Yes, most of the time."

"All that space, just for one person?"

Envoy gave the monolith only a fleeting glance, returning his gaze to the islands. "In the First there is too much space. You get used to it, you begin to crave it when it is denied."

They walked across the summit of the hill to where a small cultivated forest sank into a trough in the land, hiding the towering embassy from them once more. Bluebells brushed Lycaste's ankles and Envoy's shins. The woodland was not like the Menyanthes; the foodless trees appeared to have been planted for aesthetic considerations only, pleasing the eye at every turn as the Firstling guided Lycaste through them. Envoy explained that he didn't come here much, having grown bored of the garden's limited size, but that it gave him new pleasure to be able to show it to someone else, someone as *wild*—if he didn't mind the adjective—as Lycaste. Lycaste walked and listened and looked, understanding more than he'd expected thanks to the unexpected plainness of the man's First.

Envoy admitted to Lycaste how he actually enjoyed being away from the capital, finding his new life—clearly intended as a demotion for some past misdemeanour he hadn't yet revealed—quite enthralling after the confines of the Lyonothamnine Court. Lycaste's eyes followed the Firstling's mouth while he spoke, noticing the small, pointed teeth that peeped between his lips with each word. A carnivore's teeth.

They came to a gap in the trees that revealed a glittering river valley and a grand house jutting into the lake.

"The house of Goniolimon Berenzargol. Where you were staying."

Lycaste looked at it with more interest. He hadn't seen much on his journey out of the estate with Envoy that night. "That's Callistemon's father?"

"Mmm. He was due to return for your trial but the war has kept him east, I believe."

"It was me the brothers were fighting over. Penstemon didn't want you to take me."

Envoy shrugged. "He's just a boy. He will learn his place in things."

Lycaste nodded, as if he understood. He stole a glance at the man's body as they walked side by side. The image from Silene's book had been no exaggeration. The Firstling's golden body was proportionately that of a child: smooth and undistorted by the type of masculinity Lycaste understood, yet strangely beautiful, as if made for dancing or some peculiar acrobatic sport.

He noticed Envoy looking at him and cleared his throat. "I heard the war, when I came here from the Utopia."

"Loud, isn't it?"

"Like thunder."

The trees opened up to the edges of the embassy gardens, the air dampening. Lycaste noticed how grey the clouds had become, like old linen, and the trees moved more restlessly in the wind than they had anywhere else he'd been. Once the landscape dulled as a passing cloud obscured the vague light, and Lycaste felt an imagined chill pass through him.

"Well, we're secure up here," Envoy said. "There are Protocols, things made clear by those to whom the boy-king listens. Even if Elatine succeeds in the Greater Second, the First shall endure." He laughed quietly to himself and sighed. "Listen to me—I'm sorry, Lycaste, we talk about the war up here like we discuss the weather, you must be very bored of hearing about it."

Lycaste shook his head. "No, I know so little about it all. We are safe from them? The Asiatic?"

"Quite safe. My own guard are loyal, raised from infancy here at the embassy."

Lycaste looked about, always hoping to see one of the giants following them through the woodlands, but he and Envoy appeared to be alone. He still couldn't believe he was safe from the Berenzargols simply because of an ancient border only visible on maps.

"I still don't think I understand, Envoy." He pointed stupidly at his face. "You took me away, delivered me from those people—even though I had been tried and found guilty—because of how I look?"

Envoy smiled broadly, nodding at the apparent ridiculousness of the situation. "Because of how you look, Lycaste."

Lycaste couldn't help but smile back. "And they—Callistemon's family—had no choice but to accept your decision."

The Firstling shrugged modestly. "Oh, not my decision. My instructions came from higher up, from court. Do you understand? From His *Enlightenment*, Lyonothamnus the Second himself."

Lycaste took a moment to digest what the Firstling had said. "What would the king want with me? I was famous in the Tenth already, he could have come to see me then."

"Indeed? Well, you're famous in the First now, a different thing entirely."

They were back in the garden again, passing ornamental bushes and scampering serving finches. Lycaste turned to watch them run, smiling. A light drizzle floated in the grey air. Envoy stretched, yawning silently. Lycaste glimpsed the teeth again, tiny white triangles against his golden skin.

"You mentioned coming from the Utopia, Lycaste. I heard you were there for quite some time?"

"A little while." Lycaste felt less at ease when the man asked him questions in return.

"How did you find *them*? I heard they are all quite mad—is that so?"

Lycaste shrugged. "Have you never been?"

"Well, I did the grand tour, like most First men. Dutifully introduced myself to my ancestors and strolled the ruins of Olimp and Terziyan. All very lovely, but I found their company understandably lacking."

"Well, then, you've been there—you've seen them."

"Most were mad, in a way." He glanced at Lycaste, creamy eyes narrowing. "But they're not *all* like that, are they, Lycaste?"

He looked blankly back, waiting.

"It's all right, this isn't an interrogation." Envoy leaned forward. "I've met one, too, you see."

Lycaste put his hands behind his back stiffly and continued walking, sensing Envoy wished to stop a while or sit.

"You are most privileged, Lycaste," the Firstling continued, lengthening his stride to keep up. "These particular Amaranthine only appear to people for a reason, you know."

"And why were you honoured so?" Lycaste asked quickly, unwilling to slow his pace.

"I still don't know."

He finally stopped and turned. "How did you know about . . . ?"

"About you?" Envoy grinned, eyes flicking to Lycaste's stomach. "I was at the show trial. That injury you sustained was clearly fatal. I'd already written to tell the king's secretaries that he would be disappointed, and had to hastily recall the letter." He reached out slowly, hesitantly, towards Lycaste's scar. "It appears you have a guardian angel. They make themselves known only if it is their desire, never by accident. Was he among us, then, at the trial?"

"Perhaps. Perhaps he's here now."

Envoy assumed an expression of mock fear, glancing about the garden. His face softened to a smile. "You won't need him here."

Lycaste glowered at him. "You give me your word?"

Envoy reached to place a hand on his arm. "You are *absolved*, my dear fellow. Didn't you realise? When the king requests one's presence, puny Second noblemen see to it that they obey. That was Pentemon's mistake, but you taught him better than I could, didn't you?" He laughed.

Lycaste laughed, too, his tension seeping away. He'd never have imagined it possible, that the ordeal could somehow end this way. "I was sick of people telling me what to do."

"There comes a time, doesn't there, when one puts one's foot down," the Firstling agreed, smiling up at him. "For what it's worth, I'm proud of you. They are a *nasty* little family, those Berenzargols. Too much influence for such an ignorant bunch."

He stretched again, looking out to the embassy. "And now I have to leave you for a little while. The lodge where you slept this morning is yours until your departure. It's been a pleasure, Lycaste. I'm glad to say, after meeting you, that the interest shown in you by the First is justi-fied." He smiled toothily. "Would you come up to the embassy dining room for main supper tonight?"

Lycaste shrugged. "Do I have a choice?"

"I find you too fascinating to leave to dawdle in the grounds. Please, you'll enjoy it."

"Fine."

"Good. I'll come and collect you end of third Quarter."

"Farewell, Envoy."

"Until then, Lycaste."

Normally people said dusk. Dusk was a perfectly reasonable and unam-biguous measure of the Quarter. It was still daylight when Envoy came for Lycaste, and he wasn't at all hungry yet. Together they walked, chat-ting politely, through the dimming woodland to a path that flanked the embassy, crossing a bridge over a clear stream and entering the building through a high, open arch.

Lycaste caressed his beard as they walked beneath the arch, feeling how soft his usually wiry hair had become. The necessarium in his lodge was extraordinary, equipped with pools of scented water and coloured oils and a retinue of servants on hand to wash and dry him. Lycaste had shrugged them off at first, unnerved by the attention, but had gradually relaxed.

Envoy watched him stroking his beard. "Did you try the fragrances? I smell nothing on you."

"Fragrances?"

"In the room adjoining the water-chamber, on one of the shelves—a row of bottles. They are scents, aphrodisiacs and such."

Lycaste had no idea what *aphrodisiacs* were. "No. I'm happy just to be so clean."

For much of the day he'd been wary of dropping his guard in the luxurious household where he was staying, looking up sharply whenever a serving bird entered, expecting to see one of his many enemies come for their revenge. How times had changed; he'd once been shocked to hear that Elcholtzia possessed locks. To calm himself, Lycaste had sifted through the library of books the lodge offered. New things moved on metal pages so thin they were nothing but rectangular shavings, bendy to the touch. If he turned his head and concentrated hard he could just make out quiet whispers coming from somewhere in the metal, almost inaudible in the oldest of them.

"Supper's nearly ready—would you like a drink first?" asked Envoy. They had entered a naturally lit, high-ceilinged reception room elaborately crusted with dangling stalactites of sculpted stone that looked out over a view of the waterways of the Second. The grey-brown clouds above the far mountains were daubed scarlet where the sun hit them, and both men stopped to look. Lycaste accepted a drink without noticing, touching the bitter liquid to his lips with a nod. To his right stood a massive globe half his height. He wandered over to it, glancing at the Firstling to make sure it was all right to touch.

"Can you see where we are?" his host asked from across the chamber, coming to examine it, too. Lycaste ran his fingers with exploratory hesitation over the green and gold painted surface, looking in vain for his home coast. He ducked down to one side, eyes following the contours of the mountains, finding it hidden by his knee. The Nostrum Provinces. North-west across the continent lay the broken spear-tip of land they stood in now, smashed into westward-drifting islands. Lycaste stood back, trying to take in the whole thing. Over his head the land changed as embossed and gold-tipped mountains rose beneath his fingers, leading into a continent of strange colours and names. Its edges were blurred and hardly marked, save for an S-shaped appendage almost on the other side of the world.

"It's so big," he whispered, scanning the scrolls of city names and tiny painted capillaries of river systems.

"I can't move it," said Envoy, "not even with both hands."

Lycaste spread his arms, hands flat against continent and ocean, and pushed as the Firstling stood back to watch. Very slowly the sphere turned. Parts of the world he knew nothing about slid by beneath his elbow. A crescent of land appeared as the globe stopped, multiple round bite marks like craters decorating its edges.

"*Ban-klosh*," Lycaste read, bending once more to follow it south. "Have you been here?"

"No, no. Never."

He walked back around to locate the First and Second. "Have you travelled much?"

Envoy gulped his drink and went to get another from the table. "The East is another world. Lyonothamnine ambassadors who travel there don't return. Some flippantly suggest that's because it's a paradise, but there are certainly more morbid conclusions one might draw."

A bell sounded in a far room. Lycaste straightened, wondering with mild alarm if anyone else would be joining them. Envoy clapped his hands together excitedly. "Supper."

Whoever or whatever had rung the bell wasn't present when they arrived at the richly laid table. Lycaste stood by it until Envoy had chosen a seat and offered the one at his side.

"So that we can talk without having to raise our voices. I hate raised voices, don't you?"

"It's an awfully big table for just the two of us," said Lycaste, looking around nervously. He thought he saw a shadow move in a doorway.

"That's the butlers. First laws demand that they remain unseen while we eat. For privacy. Start, go on."

Lycaste looked down at a bewildering selection of ceramic cutlery arranged in a circle around his plate. Even to a Melius accustomed to six meals a day, there appeared to be an unnecessary amount of everything, including napkins. He took two and spread them on his knees, which banged up against the underside of the gilded table. Envoy opened a case by his glass, taking out a fragrant red stick and offering one to Lycaste. "Perfumed spitette?"

"I'm sorry?" He took a stick and sniffed it, trying to crumble it in his palm.

"No no, here." Envoy reached across with a candle, lighting the end. He showed Lycaste what to do, puffing some smoke in his direction. It smelled delicious.

Lycaste stuck it in his mouth, waiting for something to happen while he watched the tip burn with crossed eyes. He took a breath experimentally, feeling the fragrance tickle his throat and lungs.

"I like this," he said through his teeth.

"They heighten the senses, perfect before a large supper."

Lycaste continued to puff away as he was poured another drink, watching the alcohol fill the goblet. It was almost, but not exactly, the same shade of blue as Jasione's colour, the one she'd shown him. He stared at it for what felt like a very long time.

"Try it," said Envoy, noticing his hesitation. Lycaste took a sip and grunted. It was very strong.

"No, you drink it all in one go. Like this." The man slugged it back and screwed his eyes shut animatedly.

Lycaste smiled and did the same, enjoying the familiar burn as the alcohol touched his throat and warmed his stomach. He put the stick back into his mouth and let the flavours combine, forcing his thoughts away from the course they were taking.

Envoy was a lightweight. He began to giggle as they talked of earthly things: the increasing storms and rains, the foetid smell of overripe bloodfruit. Lycaste matched the Firstling's drinking, feeling more at ease, remembering that Impatiens used to claim he could drink the most because he was the biggest of them. A pang of regret chimed inside him when he thought of his old friends. At least Sotiris had said they would be protected, whatever happened.

Envoy circled back, as Lycaste knew he would, to the topic of Amaranthine visitations. As they ate course after course of food prepared in every conceivable style and fashion, not all to his liking but some very delicious, Lycaste insisted the Firstling tell his own tale of his dealings with the Immortal, still not ready to reveal too much.

"It is a rite of passage, of sorts, for any First man to be visited, or at least to suggest that they have been visited—I'm not sure how truthful all the accounts are. Some don't ever receive an audience and are darkly respected for their honesty if nothing else. I *was* visited, I assure you. Anyway—" he waved his hands together, as if expecting Lycaste to interrupt, "—it is an accepted truth that the men of the First are closer in form and mind to the Immortals than any other species of people, and as such we have a special bond with them, you see. They work with us, help us, guide us. The world—*this* world—is sacred to them, you understand, the jewel of their Firmament—their name for the heavens—and our rule is accepted. Through them we learn about the Satrapies beyond our own, the *solar system* and such, and the further stars they call their homes." He paused, his train of thought lost. "Where was I?"

"Your visit."

"My visit. Yes. You know they can telegraph themselves?"

"I don't know what that means."

Envoy paused, staring at his finger as it tapped the tablecloth. "Have you not wondered, Lycaste, how your friend can do what he does—where his magic comes from?"

Lycaste shrugged, waiting expectantly.

"They are so old, you see, that their *minds* have changed—it would happen to all of us if we lived long enough, apparently." He grinned, pointed teeth twinkling in the candlelight. "The hemispheres of the thinking organs, apparently, are not naturally precocious at magical things, but become talented if left to stew for thousands upon thousands of years. It was something they only discovered when they started getting old enough. Teleportation, telekinesis, pyrokinesis, all that sort of thing." His childish face grew mischievous as he stretched to peer at Lycaste's stomach. "The case in point being your little accident, Lycaste. With age comes power. Our guardians cannot be challenged, that is what I'm saying, and that is why I believe our position in this frightful war is unimpeachable."

"You think they're on your side in this?"

The Firstling hiccupped into his drink. "Of course. They are at the king's ear, you may depend on it."

Lycaste couldn't believe what he was hearing. "The Immortals support the First?"

"Of course. They are our direct ancestors, we their children." The Firstling took another drink, looking immensely pleased with himself.

Lycaste considered the man dubiously, noticing little resemblance between him and Sotiris besides the Firstling's willowy figure. "Envoy," he said tentatively, "can I ask you something?"

"Please do."

"Do *you* hate Cherries?"

Envoy regarded him, mouth slightly open, spiked tips of his teeth glimmering in the gloom. He moved slowly closer. "Of course I don't, Lycaste. How could you think such a thing? Look." He scowled with concentration, fighting through his drunkenness. "Some things must happen, people must be appeased. Do you understand?"

"I think so."

"These decisions are never personal. It is regrettable, the situation you find yourself in." He looked up at Lycaste tenderly. "I am very taken with you, you know."

Another bell rang, startling them both. Dessert was ready.

"This is very special, now," said Envoy, rising from his seat and placing a warm hand on Lycaste's shoulder. "Excuse me."

Lycaste waited, sipping wine and looking up at the ceiling while he thought on what the Firstling had said. The ceiling's minutiae were carved to very exact standards, as if by a shaped template and not guiding hands. He let his eyes skirt the beautiful accumulation of shapes dreamily. Precision was attainable in growthstone, but not a goal. Perhaps this wasn't growthstone at all, but something even more sophisticated.

Envoy returned and placed a large plate in front of him. On it was a subdued-looking, thoroughly alive bird. It glanced at Lycaste in recognition. One of the Glorious Birds that had captured him in the Utopia.

Lycaste stared at it. "I know this bird, Envoy."

"Yes. If I'm not mistaken, it tried to remove your eyes."

Lycaste pulled his head back, remembering.

"The First requires you whole," Envoy said, sliding a curved knife from the tablecloth. The bird looked at Envoy with bland acceptance as the Firstling sawed into a shaved area in the bright plumage at its rear. Lycaste closed his eyes and set his drink down.

"I didn't ask for this, Envoy," he muttered, turning his head away.

"This bird was bred for the Firsts' table, Lycaste. All of them were. Do not fear—it is an honour for them." He took a ceramic fork with two long tines and removed the sliver of pink, bloody meat, holding it towards Lycaste's plate. "Try some. Nothing compares to mature, living flesh."

Lycaste winced. "Why doesn't it make a sound?"

"Would you prefer that it did?" Envoy took the piece for himself. "This isn't a test, Lycaste, you don't have to try it. But you'd be missing out."

Lycaste watched the bleeding bird with fascination. It looked sleepy. He reached out slowly with his fork and snagged a small piece from the cut, pulling it free. Keeping his wine close to hand, he put it in his mouth, tasting blood and fat, slippery like fish. It was fragrant, as if flavoured by all the fruit it had eaten in its life. *Living flesh*.

Envoy watched him closely, passing him a new wine. "Try this with it."

Lycaste took the cup, suddenly realising what was in his mouth and wanting to be rid of it. He fought a gag and drank deeply, finishing his host's wine, then sat very still until he was sure it would all stay down.

The Firstling cut away a few more pieces until the bird's eyes closed completely. "It's enough for me that you tried it, thank you. You need not eat any more." He draped a white silk napkin over the bird, shrouding it entirely, and pushed the platter away from them.

Lycaste took a large drink and pulled his eyes from the shroud, which had begun to move again slightly. "What happens to me after the king has seen me, Envoy? What then? Will I be allowed to go home?"

Envoy fell silent, staring into the darkness of his wine. "I was afraid you'd ask that, simply because I don't know the answer. It may be that you can; the boy-king's attention span is . . . fickle, at best. But your fame will keep you in the public eye well past that time. You are as free as you may ever be, Lycaste. Learn to embrace it, enjoy your state. From now on you're going to find life a lot more comfortable."

Lycaste could hear his new self as it phrased the question, a ghostly future image of a man not so cursed by shyness settling in the same chair he sat in now. "Perhaps I'd refuse. You never know."

Envoy's smile returned. "Well now, that would be even more unwise than murdering a Plenipotentiary, so we mustn't speak of it. I beg you to trust me in this, Lycaste. I am a sincere man." He refilled Lycaste's cup with the diminishing wine and pre-emptively plucked the stopper from another decorative jug. "This is good, isn't it?"

Lycaste looked around him and out into the night, suddenly beginning to giggle. Envoy's smile broadened. He slid to the seat closest to Lycaste and filled a couple of fresh cups, adding something from a reflective bowl near the centre of the table. Lycaste looked at the purple leaf bobbing in the pale drink, wisps of strong colour leaching from it, and bellowed laughter. They put the drinks to their mouths in unison and sipped. What would his old friends think of him now? Worldly wise and supping mind-altering substances with a powerful man of the First; Impatiens would be climbing the walls with jealousy.

Envoy stood groggily and held a finger up with mock dramatics, leaving the room. Suddenly music began to drift in, as if a hundred voices had been waiting next door for his command. He returned and moved slowly about the room, dimming lights with a languidly twirled finger.

"Your looks, Lycaste," he said abruptly as he came near. "Do they make people jealous?"

Lycaste thought about the question groggily, wanting to get up and dance. "Yes. No. I'm not very good at . . . reading people."

Envoy sat down again, his face very close to Lycaste's, eyes searching his. "Do people treat you unfairly sometimes? As if you have been gifted with a natural talent, something they don't have?"

"I suppose. Sometimes."

"There you are, then. But it is not always a gift, is it?"

"Never." Lycaste shook his head and frowned as the man placed a hand on his thigh.

"I wish you could spend more time here, with me, Lycaste."

He stared at the man. The drug was taking effect, he knew, but he found himself wanting to agree. The room drooped and sagged, its lights dimming even more. It felt like they were in a quiet corner of a crowded space, surrounded by revellers.

"Aren't you happy here?" His friend's eyes grew large, beautiful.

"I am, I am. I like it here."

"You're happy with me?"

"Of course. You've been kind, when few else were." He thought suddenly of Sotiris, how he'd forgotten to thank the Immortal for saving his life.

"I see much in you, much that I admire. You have charmed me, Lycaste."

They took each other's hands, Lycaste's huge fingers enfolding Envoy's completely.

"I wish you could stay," the Firstling said regretfully, gazing up into his eyes.

"Tell them to let me, then. Can't you tell them to let me?"

Envoy laughed at the desperation in Lycaste's voice, suddenly nuzzling his chest. "Dance with me."

Time skipped in a yellow-golden blur, infused and infected by the hundreds of soft voices. As it slowed, Lycaste found himself holding Envoy tightly. The man looked up, his face very close.

Lycaste glanced around suddenly, worried for an instant that someone in the crowded room might see, but they were completely, shockingly alone. It was very dark. He pulled away and looked at where the other man's hand had ended up.

"What's the matter?" His companion's voice was very small.

"Don't," said Lycaste thickly, putting the Firstling down. "I don't want that. What's going . . . ?"

"Don't worry, Lycaste."

"I'm not worrying." He stepped away and clung to the table, abruptly aware with a hideous vertigo where he was, so far from home, as if nothing had really happened in the intervening time since he'd left the Tenth. It had all been a spell, a trick. He lurched for the door. "I'm going to bed now, Envoy."

"Lycaste!" the man called after him, but he was already passing the globe, ready to negotiate the broad stairs. At their top he gripped the wall, staggering sideways like a crab as the room blossomed in and out of focus. He vaguely heard his name drifting from above, but lurched on down to the archway at the bottom.

The night was very dark. Trees sprinted past, their long fingers striking his face. Many times he fell painlessly, rolling until he could stand again. From the depths appeared the spark of light from his lodgings, far, then close.

Departure

Something apart from the pain made him open his eyes. There was someone outside. He shuffled to the high windows and looked out, squinting against the whitish First light, but saw nobody.

Lycaste went to the impressively stocked larder and drank some sweet water from a silver jug, large chunks of the night before perfectly blank in his memory. Feeling a little better, he went to examine the fruit trees in the courtyard, but breakfast was still a nauseating thought. He sat on the table, his head in his hands, listening to the twitter and warble of birdsong, a word here and there interspersing the nonsense. He looked around at the artful nihilism of the chamber, beginning to remember something about dancing. He didn't know any ladies here. Perhaps it had been a dream. Across the room the bed, huge and opulent in crumpled white silks, beckoned to him. He staggered back to it, sure he'd heard something again, too tired to care. He climbed in, scooping the cool material about him as he felt the throb of an enormous headache begin its business behind his eyes.

The hard, cold edge of a blade slid across his neck.

"Good morning," said a female voice in his ear. "Look at you, sleeping in silk. Thought you'd got away with it, did you?"

Lycaste opened an eye. Cassiope, his victim's sister, bent over him, sweating and trembling.

"Those two halfwits from the Fifth couldn't get in, but they send their regards." He tried to raise his head, despite the ache. She pressed the knife against his throat until he thought it would break the skin.

"Stay down, foolish Cherry, that's what this means."

"Cassiope." A different voice. Envoy. Lycaste suddenly remembered the previous night.

The pressure lifted.

"What's the point?" Envoy's voice from behind them both was stern, like Lycaste had never heard him. "Lycaste is ours now. If your sow of a mother had truly wanted justice, she would not have sold him to me."

"You say that like she was given a choice, Tagetes."

"She was welcome to refuse." Lycaste heard him walk to the bookshelf. "But all choice carries a chance of penalty. I know you're a little light at the moment, waiting for the First to cover your debts—I understand, really, I do. But you'd be ripping the precious walls of your house down in no time to get at all that boastful silk if it weren't for Lycaste."

Sure that the knife was no longer near his throat, Lycaste inched his face around. Envoy—Tagetes—was flanked by his two Asiatic guards, massive and grotesque, all watching Cassiope as she stood by his bed.

He turned his face back to her, seeing finally that she had the knife to her own throat now.

She began to cry, the blade trembling at her thin neck. "You say you understand but you *don't*! None of you damn Firstlings do!"

"Drop it," Envoy Tagetes said, one of the guards advancing slowly towards her, his thick, oddly jointed arms extended and ready. "Drop it and we can forget the whole thing."

Cassiope hesitated, looking at Lycaste with brimming eyes, and tossed the knife down. She tried to run from the chamber but was intercepted by the second Asiatic, who held her tightly with one great fist.

Lycaste sat up in bed, feeling his neck and watching as Envoy went to her. The Firstling took the dagger handed to him by the guard and looked at it.

"In difficult times like this, the First can't stomach disobedience— I'm sorry, Cassiope." The girl's eyes widened.

He brought the blade across her exposed neck, left to right. She jerked, legs kicking in the stiffened grip of the guard, her spraying throat gurgling. A whistling sound came from the slit as she tried to draw breath.

Lycaste pulled the covers closer, watching her spasming body, her bulging eyes meeting his. Envoy casually handed the knife back to the guard and turned to Lycaste.

"Bred for the First's table, Lycaste."

Lycaste pulled his hand free from Envoy's grip at the ship's steps. Tagetes looked pained but let him go. He turned only when he was at the top of the gangplank and surrounded by fascinated courtiers.

"It was an honour, Lycaste," Envoy called up to him.

Lycaste stared at him but didn't reply. He stepped backwards into the throng of people, all asking him questions at once, until Tagetes and the dock he stood on were finally lost from view.

Tenth

None of the Melius people they'd met on the way were listed; the maps were too old, the lands towards the strange southern coast unsurveyed since Wintering 14,551, apparently—almost a hundred years before.

It shouldn't have mattered; the brothers knew where they were. But it did matter. It mattered to Melilotis—it gave the tall, distorted people they questioned every few days the opportunity to lie to them.

He left his brother and cousin next to the late-afternoon fire they were preparing by the dirt road, the air alive with cicadas, and climbed a steep hill rough with olive and fruit trees to look out over the sea. The Mediterranean Nostrum, visible at last, days after the map had promised. He'd not seen the Southern Sea since he was a boy. It looked the same shade of warm, inviting blue, even though they kept saying the weather was changing. He thought the astronomers said such things just to keep people listening. It was what he'd have done, faced with such a thankless life of study and reflection, a stack of ring books and globes instead of women to keep him company through the night.

The Southern Cherries here had put up a good fight. They had spirit, sufficient to withstand the kind of pain that could winkle out secrets from a pampered Second man. But Melilotis had been customarily adventurous in his work. It wasn't so difficult. Mental agony required less fuel, like a fire built from rotten logs; you didn't have to aerate it, nurture it so much. Tell them horrible things and usually up from nowhere sprang what you wanted in the first place. He'd found out what he needed to know.

He called Ulmus over, looking out across the sea while he waited for the boy. Melilotis was well aware that his cousin had no taste for the things he'd seen done on the way and knew that once he was home the boy would become what simpletons referred to as a *kind man*, perhaps softer still once he took up his duties as Intermediary. As far as Melilotis was concerned it was a weakness—perhaps even cowardice—that made people appear good. He didn't think that should be something to aspire to. His father thought differently. Hamamelis wanted a stable, successful heir. Someone boring, that was what he'd meant.

"Look, Ulmus." He pointed as his cousin arrived. "The sea."

The boy nodded, barely interested.

"We're here now. Not long till we can go home."

"How soon?" Ulmus asked him, pulling at a green olive on a branch but not removing it.

"Soon." Melilotis didn't like the boy's tone. "Remember, this is for Leonotis."

The boy thought for a while, brushing the leaves away from his face. "And for that Plenipotentiary."

"Yes, but especially for your cousin. Never forget that, you hear me?"

Ulmus bowed his head, pulling the olive free and turning away. Melilotis took his arm. "Say it, Ulmus."

"For Leonotis."

He nodded, looking the boy up and down coldly. "Fetch Cladrastis for me."

He waited for his brother and studied the view, seeing how the edges of the great forest they'd travelled appeared to stop suddenly at the crest of the next rise. The lonely road they'd taken had been in good repair, indicating use of some kind every now and then, but as far as the brothers knew, they'd had it to themselves for the last four days.

Still, something whispered at the edges of the forest whenever night fell, so subtly at first that it was almost nothing, a coastal wind tickling his ear. Melilotis had remained unconvinced, even when his own name came breathing from the palms, until Ulmus's and Cladrastis's fears together had overwhelmed him. He'd encouraged his brother and cousin not to show their terror, but to laugh back at whatever was calling their names each night, all three howling at the dark trees until the voices stopped. But whatever it was never ceased for long, watching and waiting until the brothers were coiled together on the verge of sleep around their dying fire, then beginning again. The night before, he'd jerked awake—remembering that someone had once told him it was your body thinking it was dying—to see a pair of pale eyes widen and vanish, whipping back into the undergrowth. Tonight they'd build the fire high, making camp in the middle of the road for once. Only time would tell whether he'd be able to sleep.

"I can see the sea, can you see the sea?" sang Cladrastis as he came through the olive trees towards him. He placed a hand on top of his brother's head, taking it away quickly. "You have greasy hair, Meli. Why do you have such dirty hair?"

Melilotis pushed a hand through his hair irritably and pointed at a path that wound down the hills past a sloping, wind-shaped dwelling, small in the distance. Its structure was clearly designed to reflect light down the path to a hidden garden like his father's out-houses. He had no interest in that, knowing from his map that the place they sought lay in the crescent bay about four and a half miles south of there.

"We start out tomorrow, early. Not tonight."

Cladrastis stared at him. "Why wait?"

"It'll be dark before we're halfway there."

"Tonight looks clear."

"Dawn," Melilotis said firmly.

Cladrastis shrugged. "Ulmus doesn't want to sleep here any longer, he keeps asking me when we're going." He scratched his elbow sheepishly. "I don't either, Meli."

Melilotis shook his head, wishing he could slap his brother without starting a fight that he'd probably lose. "Listen to yourself. I used to look up to you. When Ulmus gets to keep what he wants from those houses—*then* he'll be glad he came."

Cladrastis feigned a punch, making Melilotis flinch. "The ladies, you mean?"

He pushed his brother's hovering fist away wearily. "Exactly."

Chapel

"Please state your names, clearly," the hard-faced Amaranthine called Von Schiller asked them in Unified. His voice rang through the high-ceilinged chapel like a bell.

Corphuso looked at Ghaldezuel. The Lacaille had changed into a shimmering peignoir of blue and gold, his little slippered feet poking out. His white, long-eared head was bare in the Lacaille ambassadorial custom, and Corphuso was surprised to see that Ghaldezuel had some sparse dark hair growing at the back. He was younger than the Vulgar had imagined.

"Ghaldezuel Es-Mejor, Op-Zlan-Lacaille," his captor said confidently into the huge space, his eyes fixed on the middle distance. Corphuso could see no one but the stooped Amaranthine in the chapel. He opened his mouth to say his own name, but the Lacaille continued, "This is my captive, the builder of your gift."

Von Schiller stared at them a little longer before beckoning them forward. Corphuso gazed in wonder at the ceiling, the insult forgotten when he spotted the intricacies of the Prism worlds depicted there. As he looked, he wondered that the detail was not lost on these people—it was well known that Vulgar eyes were better than Amaranthine, and he could barely make out the smallest brushwork himself.

"I trust you had an uneventful journey?" the Amaranthine asked as they approached.

"Reasonably," replied Ghaldezuel. He did not look at all intimidated by the Immortal. "I was most impressed with my reward. Am I to thank your master in person?"

The Amaranthine's eyes narrowed, but he inclined his head and stepped back. "The master is here with us," he said quietly.

Ghaldezuel folded his arms and looked around, turning at last to Corphuso. Since their journey began, it had mollified the Vulgar somewhat to see that Ghaldezuel appreciated his intelligence; more than once he had asked the architect's advice over that of the soldiers at his command.

Corphuso shrugged in response to Ghaldezuel's glance, shuddering as a chill passed through him. The air appeared to darken.

"*Two hominids*," said a voice all around them. It filled the space up to the ceiling, its words crisp and precise. Corphuso heard the voice in Vulgar, guessing after a moment that perhaps Ghaldezuel heard his version in Lacaille.

"Yes, Long-Life," Von Schiller whispered beside them. "They have brought what you wanted."

"*Both* things?" the voice said loudly, critically.

The Amaranthine looked sharply at Ghaldezuel. He nodded.

"Both, Long-Life."

The voice did not reply. Corphuso felt the tiny blond hairs on his arms and neck rise. Suddenly there came footsteps from behind them. They turned to see a man, clothed simply in Amaranthine apparel, walking slowly towards them.

"I will have them here," he said, his face appearing to grow from nothing in the shadows. Corphuso still heard the words in Vulgar.

There was a pause as Ghaldezuel tried to work out exactly what was being asked of him. "Our cargo? You wish it brought here?"

"Yes," the bizarre man said thoughtfully, glancing to Von Schiller. "Now."

Ghaldezuel looked at the Amaranthine beside him. "Shall I . . . go and send word?"

"Go now, yes," replied Von Schiller simply. "Leave the builder here with us."

Corphuso gulped, staring at Ghaldezuel in the hope that he would deny the request, but the Lacaille nodded and excused himself, walking quickly across the chapel to the doors.

"This is the designer?" the master asked Von Schiller as he circled Corphuso, taking in every aspect of the Vulgar. Corphuso hated it, looking back to the man as he arrived before him again.

"What is he, precisely?" the man asked.

"He is *Paranthropus Vulgarii*, Long-Life, of the pale Harboldt breed. Common within the Firmament after the Ninth Era."

The man appeared to think about this. "What was the other? Not the same, I think."

"*Paranthropus Lacaille-Colensis*, a Zalnir blue. Also common to the Firmament and Investiture. They are closely related races, sharing a recent ancestor with the Pifoon, also."

"Tell me about yourself, *Vulgarii*," the circling man said to Corphuso. "How did you think up such a thing?"

Corphuso could feel himself sweating as he tried to choose which language to speak. He opted for Unified. "It was an accident, really, a stroke of luck."

The man, the Long-Life, nodded. His vague, pleasant eyes flicked to Von Schiller. "I am indebted to you, *Vulgarii*. I have waited so very long for your accident to occur."

There was a knock on the chapel doors and Von Schiller turned. Corphuso noticed that the Long-Life's eyes remained fixed on him.

"My gifts are here," he said softly, the smile spreading on his face.

Barge

"Look at him!" the Secondling jeered, tightening his yellow fist on the cane and grinning to the ladies. "Won't you fight me, Cherry? Are you too afraid?"

The man, portly and rather tall for a Secondling, gave Lycaste a flick with his stick, standing back to watch his sport's reaction. Lycaste growled and glanced among the circle of gaily coiffed people on the deck of the river barge. Some of the ladies looked afraid of him, others laughed, but few could pull their eyes away.

The attention had made the gentlemen on board jealous, and they had begun deliberately knocking and nudging Lycaste while the first drinks of the afternoon were served aboard the sailed barge. He was no longer tied or chained and had made the mistake of lashing out at one Second man, shocking the giggling ladies into silence.

"Come on." The chubby Secondling tapped him again with the cane. Lycaste's arm was beginning to sting. He could see the man would lose face if he carried on tormenting Lycaste without effect—some of the women had already spoken up and told the Secondling to stop being so cruel. They clearly thought Lycaste defenceless despite his size. He looked into their pinkish eyes, knowing that most simply wanted to see a drop or two of blood spilled, perhaps not even caring from which man it came.

"Fight! Fight me! Pitiful excuse for a man." The Secondling whipped him once more, jumping back slightly in case Lycaste decided to try and grab him. Lycaste sighed, rubbing his arm and glaring at the Secondling, who sneered up at him.

"Ooh, look, he's getting angry!" He turned to the crowd. "Who wants to see me teach this Southerner a lesson? Eh?"

Some inchoate cheers came from the back, probably from the man's group of friends, but most were still staring silently at Lycaste. Women whispered to each other behind their hands and smiled.

"Fight!" the Secondling screeched, swinging his cane at Lycaste's head. Before the blow could fall, Lycaste snatched the cane and snapped it in half, taking both pieces and hurling them at the shocked man. The ladies all stood back, the deck of the barge suddenly silent but for the sighing of the golden trees that lined the riverbank and the tug of the sails in the breeze.

Lycaste roared and shoved the man to the deck. The onlookers took a few more steps back. He paused as he stood over the trembling Secondling, looking around. Men were pushing to the front of the crowd, some carrying even longer canes and staves.

Lycaste stared to the bow, where brightly coloured flags trailed like fishtails in the warm river wind. He had already reflected upon boarding that even if he did jump and make it to shore, the barge—slowly travelling upriver to the next distant outpost of the First—had now looped back into Second waters, where he would no longer be free. No matter what happened, he had decided to try and stay aboard.

"Don't let him jump," he heard one of the Secondlings say as they approached, and Lycaste stepped back. The shivering man at his feet crawled past the wreckage of his expensive cane and into the safety of the crowd, which parted slightly for him.

Lycaste took a deep lungful of air, his crimson fists curling, and roared as loudly as he could at them. He spread his arms and flexed his feeble muscles, baring his teeth. The Secondlings hesitated, their sticks shaking. Finally they nodded to each other cautiously and continued their advance. Lycaste growled and lowered his head, seeing no option but to meet them head-on. The sticks were sharp-ended but not thick, and without them the smaller Second men were nothing. He charged the crowd.

His shoulder connected with someone and he shoved them aside, reaching for the nearest outstretched staff but failing to catch it. The man holding the cane swung it and knocked Lycaste on the head as he turned and grabbed another of the Secondlings by the throat, lifting him clear off his feet and throwing the man overboard. The women, their various pets and many of the men had stampeded to the furthest end of the barge where servants cowered, or climbed a mast to get a better view of the fight.

Lycaste spun, his fist finding someone's face before it was seized and weighed down by two more. He deflected another blow to his head with his free hand, pushing the spike of the cane aside and kicking out. The men surrounding him ducked and jumped back, but not before someone behind grabbed hold of his other hand. Lycaste struggled like a fish in a net, throwing the men who had been holding him backwards, and shoved the closest of them towards one of the masts. The Secondling's head hit the wood with a thump and he fell.

Lycaste wasted no time, whirling on the other and snapping his arm like a dry branch. The man screamed and staggered while the crowd gasped. As Lycaste turned, he felt the spear-tip of a staff pierce his leg and drive into the muscle. He snarled, ripping it free and twirling it by the bloodied end like a sword. He'd only ever practised sword-fighting on the beach with Impatiens, but knew the basics of blocking well enough to fling away a poking stave and whack the man holding it.

The Secondlings fell back, breathing hard. Blood ran from some cuts and grazes, but Lycaste knew they would wear him down before too long. He rumbled another threatening snarl, his breath labouring from him, and retreated towards the bow.

Houses had begun to pass by on the riverbank, and as he glanced around, Lycaste saw that people had come to their grand steps to watch. They were screaming and shouting, but their voices were too small and distant to be heard across the wide waterway. He looked back to the Secondlings, realising that their attention was now directed towards the people on the bank as well. Almost everyone, even some of his attackers, had stopped to peer over the railings, leaving Lycaste temporarily forgotten.

Lycaste allowed himself another moment to turn and stare. The people on the steps were carrying items and furniture in their hands. Smoke was pouring from one of the buildings as the barge drew alongside it, and Lycaste could just make out screaming from within. Suddenly a huge mounted Asiatic galloped from the entranceway and down the steps towards the people, who dropped their possessions and ran for the river. The armoured Jalan soldier raised his scimitar—a six foot blade, extravagantly coiled at the tip—and beheaded the slowest young man to a gasp from the watching crowd.

The Asiatic pulled the mount around—an animal Lycaste had never seen before—and watched the barge as it sailed past. Lycaste saw someone fall from the smoking window into a crumpled heap beside the Asiatic, and the soldier looked up for a moment at the other Jalanbulon who had come to the window. Lycaste scanned the riverbank for the rest of the group of Secondlings that had escaped from the giants, but they had melted into the trees along the bank, their exquisite furniture abandoned.

The barge continued on and soon the ruined house was lost from sight, but there were further signs of disaster upriver. People—mostly children—ran parallel with the bank, weaving through the trees as they glanced behind, unaware that they were running into another regiment of the Jalan pursuing them. Nobody on the barge said a word to stop them, all of Lycaste's attackers now stunned into silence. Houses burned, their reflections staining the muddy river, while dusty silhouettes of fleeing people and animals scampered before the flames. In one building with very tall chimneys, a group of Asiatic were flinging goods from the windows while they drank, and at the next house they had chased a petite Secondling lady from her hiding place and were wrestling her to the stone courtyard facing the river. The entire barge watched in silence.

A mounted legion of Jalanbulon cantered and splashed through the reeds at the base of the river house and past the ravaged woman. They stopped to look back, some of the soldiers dismounting so they could take a turn with her while the others, still astride their peculiar black beasts, turned in their saddles to watch the barge passing.

Lycaste noticed the people on the barge with him whimpering and trying to hide behind the railings under the gaze of the Asiatic soldiers. He met the eye of the glitteringly caparisoned Jalan captain himself, mounted on the finest of the beasts. For a moment, the giant might have looked puzzled, perhaps wondering what a red Tenthling was doing alone among such high company. The captain said something to the soldier beside him, who quickly unshouldered his strange rifle, took aim and fired into the crowd on the barge. Lycaste flinched, ducking and running for the boat's port side. He risked a look behind him at the people screaming and thundering across the deck, rocking the entire barge. An elderly yellowish woman with a pyramid of painted hair took refuge beside Lycaste at the port-side railings, staring up at him plaintively. He hesitated, finally extending his hand. She took it, and he lifted her under her arms and dropped her carefully over the side into the water. As he checked behind him once more, a bullet whined past and chipped splinters from the wooden railings. Lycaste lifted a leg over the smashed rail and jumped.

For a moment there was no sound besides the roar of water in his ears, and he struck out under the river's surface, heading in the direction he hoped would take him towards the opposite bank. When he finally surfaced, his lungs feeling as if they were about to split at the seams, the barge had sailed past and he was exposed to the Jalan on the far banks. They continued to fire at the barge—where people still milled and screamed, a few plunging overboard—but none of the Asiatic stopped to survey the water. Lycaste followed the progress of the sailing boat a moment longer, noticing holes appearing in the sails and flags. A small fire had started to engulf the bow, smokeless in the warming afternoon. He headed for the other bank, seeing no sign of the elderly woman he had helped.

At the riverbank, an orchard of underripe bloodfruit ran down to the water. Lycaste pushed aside the tall reeds and headed for the trees, smelling the sweet smoke that drifted from the pillaged houses on the other side of the river. He stumbled into the orchard, aware that bullets were finally making their way across to him and rustling through the trees—the pops of their firing arrived at his ears a little later—but he was too far away for them to hit him. Nevertheless, he heaved a sigh of relief as he dumped himself over a grassy, tree-lined levee, rolling down into another orchard. When he reached the bottom, he lay quite still, listening for a while before standing to a crouch. The wound in his leg still throbbed but had closed up. He looked around. The land here was flat and wooded with fruit trees, interspersed with groves of red flowers taller than he was. Through the rapidly moving clouds a glow of sun poked, drifting and dimming a moment later.

Some even more opulent but tightly packed dwellings appeared between the trees as he ran, his breath leaving his body in torn gulps, but they were all locked up and deserted. In the maze of ornamental gardens he found more furniture and valuables abandoned, their owners presumably long gone, as well as heaps of silk that drifted in the wind and collected at the base of the trees, some blowing like coloured rain across the gardens. Lycaste stopped for a second to look at it all, but decided to keep moving. These people had seen fit to abandon their wealth, so it couldn't be of much use now.

At the sound of galloping hooves he paused, ducking behind a tree. The rapid clop of shod feet didn't sound like the beasts the Jalan were riding, but still he remained hidden, peeking between the branches. The clattering grew louder, and Lycaste began to see soldiers mounted on zeltabras coming through the trees. The first of them slowed at the abandoned gardens and houses, pulling the reins to halt the animal while he surveyed the scene. They looked to Lycaste like some elite type of Secondling regiment. Their silver helms fluttered with shimmering feathers of blue and green and gold—undoubtedly from Glorious Birds, Lycaste thought—but when the rider at the front pushed up his visor, Lycaste saw that the face beneath was more white than yellow, with small, childish features. Firstlings.

The closest rider glanced into the trees. Lycaste held his breath, but the man's gaze moved on. It was only after the soldier had patted the striped mount and urged it on that he remembered he was coloured again to match the fruits and berries. More cavalry followed through the trees, pausing only briefly at the abandoned dwellings. Lycaste watched them all charge through the trees, the man at the rear blowing into a horn. He shivered at the haunting call, wondering if any of the Firstlings he'd just seen would make it away from the river alive.

Lycaste moved through the trees cautiously, ears straining for any more galloping hooves, but the forests were silent save for the leaves' swaying and whispering. At the distant sound of cantering he swung behind a tree again, waiting as a small armoured man arrived in the clearing at the edge of the gardens. The man stopped, sitting very still atop his zeltabra, which lowered its head to the flowers and began to munch experimentally. The figure leaned on the pommel of the saddle and glanced in Lycaste's direction, finally flipping up the faceplate.

"Didn't I tell you not to get stabbed again, Lycaste?"

He stiffened behind the tree—it couldn't be. "Sotiris?" He poked his head out from behind the cover. "What are you doing here?"

"Saving that pretty face of yours, among other things."

Lycaste glanced into the forest on both sides, then jogged up to the mount. Its eyes widened and it stepped back. "You can't go that way," he said, pointing. "They've taken the river."

"Yes." Sotiris trotted the animal expertly in a tight circle. "I've brought you one of their harsants to ride." In the woods, a little way off, he could make out a dark shape tied to a tree.

It did not look at all startled to meet Lycaste, and he supposed he was a good deal smaller than the giants it was used to taking. The horned animal shook its shaggy red mane, its huge, glossy shoulder muscles rippling. It looked a little like an ocsin—the ones they sometimes used to plough the rocky fields on Kipris. It lifted a long, tufted tail and deposited a heap of steaming dung as he climbed atop it.

"You have ridden before?" Sotiris asked.

"Once or twice," he said uncertainly. It had been just the once.

"Good, then let's be away." Sotiris kicked his spur into the zelta-bra's flank and it galloped into the forest.

"Come on, then," he said to the harsant, patting its hard rump. It grunted and ambled after the zeltabra, picking up speed as Lycaste saw the sun shining through the trees ahead.

Preparations

"Reginald, you look distraught," Holtby said, breaking from the mur-muring crowd with a cup in his hand. He offered it to Bonneville. "What-ever is the matter?"

"Nothing, nothing," he said, looking in surprise at the cup as his reverie broke. "I'm just so very affected by the plight of the poor First-lets we oversee." Bonneville gazed at the preparations from the rain-streaked window and composed his face. Across the wet lawns, rows of huge guns were being uncovered. Their damp sheets, heavy with mois-ture from the brief rainstorm, fluttered in the gathering wind.

"I believe the term is *Firstling*," Holtby replied, joining him at the warped glass. "The complexity of their language renders the former rather rude, I'm afraid."

Bonneville shrugged, touching the water to his lips. By microbial standards it would be teeming, unclean to the point of hazardous, but it could not affect him. He found the taste of First water rather pleas-ant—like iron, or blood—and reflected occasionally that it was perhaps the flavour of some pathogen new to the world to which the Melius were similarly immune. He imagined forcing it on a Prism creature and observing the effects.

At the bottom of the stairway a large, ungainly group of yellow-white Melius, their skin bleached to appear lighter than they actually were, was jostling through the crowd of Pre-Perennials, the armoured soldiers at the rear of the procession bowing liberally whenever they chanced to touch a corner of cloth or small, delicate hand. At their front strode the forward general, one Filago, son of the late Zigadenus and now Protector of the First. The thin Melius bore the fantastically ugly features of the severely inbred, his nose long and protruding, his chin sloping to a wattle of flesh dusted with the stubble of days preparing for battle. His skinny legs were coated with brick-red mud, sloppy from the rain. Bonneville noticed with vague amusement that some had smeared the Immortals' finery as the Melius passed. He took in their looks of consternation before his gaze returned to the new Protector's face.

"I still don't see why he bothers," he whispered to Holtby, hand at his mouth; Filago's Unified was said to be superb.

"Bothers?" Holtby looked at him, his soft face irritatingly earnest.

"This," he said, inclining his head to the window of the grand house and the teeming field of weaponry and troops beyond. "The Second is breached already—why defend the indefensible?"

Caleb Holtby looked down at the Protector, something like admiration creeping into his voice. "I believe he does it out of love for his Province, as his father did before him." The younger Amaranthine gulped, hesitating at Bonneville's silence. "One supposes."

Bonneville felt a laugh building inside him, stirring the weak, inert currents of his blood. He wanted to scoff, not just at Holtby but also the majestic stupidity of the mingled, gaudy freaks who chattered and plotted in the great hall at the foot of the stairs.

"I think you read too many stories, Caleb," Bonneville muttered, spitting back into the cup and studying the crowd forming below.

At the Melius's side, stooped and shrouded in heavy finery that caught the candelabra light with silken flashes, was Zacharia Stone. He was the last of the Perennials to remain in the Second, the others already on their way out of the Province by mounted escort or Vulgar clipper. Bonneville wondered if his continued presence was intended as a show of bravery, doubting the Perennial would stay longer than the Protector's dinner later that evening. Also with them, but maintaining a respectful distance, were two Prism ambassadors, the Honourable Filch of the Zelioceti and his ally Princeling Elumo, heir to the Vulgar moon of Stole-Havish. The Princeling's intense blue eyes locked on to Bonneville's, then turned back to the Zelioceti ambassador.

They came to the stairs, talking quietly, many sets of Pre-Perennial eyes following their progress. The Zelioceti Filch was robed in bold swathes of red, trimmed at the high collar with thick black fur. His rosy proboscis, almost as grand as that of a Melius, drooped to tickle the black buttons dotting the garment all the way down to his pointed slippers. Bonneville did not look at him long, having always found their faces unsettling, and instead took in Elumo's shimmering blue evening wear. Stole-Havish was a famously filthy and dangerous place, one of the few Vulgar Kingdoms that hadn't contributed soldiers to the Volirian Conflict and as such had been pointedly overlooked when it came to rewarding the victors. Its ruling family, a squabbling, incestuous dynasty of Vulgar only loyal to Filgurbirund when it suited them, had finally found their coffers running low and pledged themselves to the assistance of the Amaranthine. Bonneville had found Princeling Elumo, who had little to do but wait for his sickly uncle's death, a most agreeable prospective partner in business. The group paused on the steps, looking out at the preparations. Again, Bonneville met the Vulgar Princeling's eye.

"You will remember Pre-Perennial Bonneville," Stone said, indicating him to Elumo. The Vulgar gave a sharp nod and returned his attention to the guns. The Zelioceti Filch stared for longer, then whispered something to the Princeling. Outside, across the gardens, the hazy sky was turning to evening. Bonneville could just see spires of the city rising below the house walls, a flock of white birds scattering in the middle distance and disappearing behind a cluster of bell-towers. At the base of the city, a ruined bridge from another era stretched halfway across the valley floor into the temperate jungles of the Inner Second. It had been reinforced and turreted for nearly five years in anticipation of Elatine's advance and was now patrolled by Filago's elite Firstling cavalry. Once the dinner was finished and the important Amaranthine safely across the border, the Protector would make his way down to the front to await his father's old foe.

Bonneville looked at the Melius now as they were introduced, his hand suddenly enveloped in the Protector's gnarled fist. It was ever a courtesy to receive the Amaranthine handshake, but Bonneville hated performing it with these giants. He pulled his hand away as soon as was tactful.

"You will stay with us, I am told, while we hold the city," said Filago, his accent almost perfect. He had been educated in the Sarine capital, no doubt familiar with the Amaranthine and their ways since childhood.

"If you will have me, Protector," Bonneville replied.

"I will have you as long as you are prepared to stay." He smiled, a little sadly. "It will not be an easy victory, but I am confident we shall withstand a siege, should it come to that."

Bonneville smiled back.

"Shall we view the estate's readiness?" enquired Stone, pressing a hand gently against the Protector's back and guiding him to the high doorway on the landing. Thirdling servants, gangly and pumpkin-coloured, scrambled to open it.

They stepped out into the garden, the air heavy and humid after the shower. White birds strutted on the lawns while Vulgar and Secondling troops walked between the enormous cannon and five-legged tanks on loan from the Zelioceti. The tanks, painted in vibrant reds and yellows like everything in the Zelioforce, were being tested on the lawns, churning the grass into troughs of wet soil as they lumbered about, smoke curling from their wide, ungainly rears. Some Vulgar mechanics ceased their tinkering with a tank and stood to attention at the Princeling's passing.

"Our allies the Zelioceti are generous beyond measure," said Elumo, patting Filch—almost a foot taller—on the shoulder. "My kingdom will remember this kindness."

The Zelioceti ambassador grunted, inspecting a cannon as they passed. "Stole-Havish need not return the favour immediately."

Bonneville could barely understand him, hearing only the tone of sarcasm in his nasal voice.

They stooped to walk beneath the legs of a stalled tank, the under-hatch hanging open, and came to the garden walls. Bonneville turned briefly to inspect the house, gazing as innocently as he could up at the steepled roof. A Vulgar Voidship, *his* Voidship, had come to rest between the smoking chimneys, its dark guns aimed out over the city.

He glanced back over the walls, his gown billowing in the rising air. The majestic city of Vilnius, streamered with the smoke of cooking fires and flocking messenger birds, had become one giant encampment. Tents fluttering with the green banners and sigils of the First occupied the pale streets and rooftops of the citadel all the way down to the ruined bridge at its foundations, where cannon larger than any seen in the last ten grand conflicts stared into the valley. Mounted Melius rode clopping through the arches, parting uneasily around wandering groups of tiny Vulgar and Zelioceti. The city's huge orchards, its cellars and store-rooms and larders, had all been plundered by decree of the First, and soldiers ate in circles around glowing fire-pits as they waited for night to fall. Across the valley, misted with the rising steam of the recent rain, the forests screamed with animals.

Bonneville stared out at the scene, doubt settling over him. The city was ready, waiting for the fight to reach it. He glanced quickly at Elumo, but the Princeling was moving on with Stone towards the ramparts where Vulgar soldiers nursed spit-roasted weasels over a fire. Above them another Voidship hove into view, extending pale rubber sails as it cut its engines and dropped with a groan towards the grand house at the top of the citadel. They watched the rust-speckled vehicle land on the lawn, the sails bending against a wind that churned the fires in their pits for a moment and caused the soldiers to look up.

"Where were you born, Amaranthine?" asked Filago suddenly, appearing at Bonneville's side. He swept back his hair in the wind as they approached the ramparts.

"Where?" He looked up at the Melius. Nobody had asked him that question in centuries. "Far from here. You would not know the place."

"Try me," the Protector said, his manner friendly. Bonneville could see why he was liked and was suddenly intrigued.

"An island in what is now the Westerly Provinces."

Filago grinned. "I had thought so, from your face. Ingolland? Or Yire?"

Bonneville laughed, forgetting for a moment the landscape below him. "Between the two. It was then called Wales."

The Protector mouthed the word thoughtfully. "I do not know that such a land exists now. It would be part of Ingolland, I suppose."

Bonneville looked at him a while, remembering himself. "Yes, well, places change. I will never see it again, and do not wish to." He shook his head and strode out to the edge of the rampart, trying in vain to catch the Princeling's eye once more. More drops of rain carried on the wind as the day darkened.

"I think your new king will be pleased, yes?" someone said. Bonneville glanced down irritably. It was the Zelioceti, Filch. He was standing on tiptoes at the wall, his furred gloves behind his back.

"Yes, I daresay."

"We hear things about the Amaranthine king, you know." The ambassador looked up, his strange eyes staring. "The oddest things. They say he will not touch things, not even if they are clean and placed before him. They say he casts no shadow."

Bonneville moved away from the rampart, unsure what the creature was getting at. He pulled out a beautiful timepiece dangling from a chain within his robes and looked at it. "You must not take rumour to heart, Ambassador Filch—please excuse me."

As he made his way to the house among the long-legged tanks he glanced back, but the Zelioceti had resumed his stroll of the wall, Filago falling in beside him.

There *was* a way—quite a simple method, in fact—to kill a Perennial. The trick, of course, was getting close enough. Bonneville studied the departing group of Prism and Melius as he arrived at the door, wondering if he truly had missed something. Something they'd all missed. The Long-Life would be well guarded in the Sarine Palace, likely the very last place to face the threat of Elatine's encroaching legions. He might survive, of course, perhaps to be ransomed if the warlord discovered his significance, but such eventualities would by then be beyond Bonneville's (or Sovereign Reginald Iestyn Bonneville, Potentate of the Vulgar Monarchy of Filgurbirund and Sundry Lands) concern.

He tapped on the door and waited for the servants to open it, scenting the smoke on the wind. It was a pleasant smell, one of his favourites, and yet so often accompanied battle and death. Once inside, he went up the stairs, following the lines of embedded silk to the Pre-Perennial chambers.

Within his room, Bonneville exhaled slowly and shakily. His bags, leather-strapped satchels, were in their usual hiding place in the frame of the mustily palatial bed. The dinner was not for a few hours yet, another session of pointless entertainments while he watched the huge people guzzling their way through course after course of mostly living flesh. It seldom occurred to mortals as they went about their necessary processes what a profoundly disgusting sight they were. He would make sure to toast Filago and his painted generals, to wish them well in their defence of the First and all it stood for.

"Eat heartily," he said to himself under his breath as he rechecked his bags, his brow creasing with impermanent wrinkles as he heard the first of the cannon roaring into life.

Long-Life

Twelve Lacaille soldiers had wheeled in the two huge chests, one buckled and bolted and clearly of Vulgar make, the other golden and gnarled, like a huge metal walnut. Feeling the familiar pang of jealousy, Corphuso watched them unsnapping heavy buckles and locks to reveal the shape that had dominated his life for so long, flapping away the embroidered covering to expose the gleaming bulk of it to the chapel.

The Long-Life stood some distance away, a shadow in the depths, gazing as if he had waited for this moment his whole life. For all Corphuso knew, he had. He looked again at the bizarre man, thinking him the most interesting Amaranthine he had ever seen. There was something feral in the way he spoke and acted, and the growing indistinctness of his face and eyes made the Vulgar's head swim. His pale, veined hands hung limply at his sides, the sleeves of the anonymous gown he wore dangling to the thumbs. It was only then that Corphuso noted that the man's shadow did not quite match his figure, as if it were merely a cut-out shape arranged to give the impression of solidity. He felt his heart hammer inside him.

Ghaldezuel appeared to be unperturbed by what was happening, but Corphuso knew better. He had studied the Lacaille knight long enough to recognise the creeping nervousness now descending over his face, though he tried to hide it.

"Worried, Ghaldezuel?" he whispered, as casually as he could.

"Worried?" The knight affected surprise. "Why ever should I be worried? I am about to inherit the jewel of the Firmament, Corphuso."

"Do you have any idea what's about to happen?"

Ghaldezuel stared at him. "Well, they're . . . he's going to—"

"What is in that other case? You don't have any idea, do you?"

Now it was the Lacaille's turn to smile. "Just wait, Corphuso. Calm that racing intellect of yours and watch. I promise, it shall be quite a show."

They watched the Long-Life as he walked slowly over to the machine, stopping to inspect its colossal coils and loops. Unlike everyone else who had inspected the Soul Engine, Corphuso was interested to see that the man made no attempt to touch it, though from the way he was studying the device, it appeared that he might have some inclination of its workings. He looked tremendously, almost deliriously excited for a moment, then glanced directly at Corphuso.

"Yes, *Vulgarii*, I see now what you've done. I see how it might . . ." The Long-Life shook his head with apparently genuine wonder, his eyes wide. Suddenly his gaze shot to the second case of Amaranthine make. "The other one, *now*."

The golden Amaranthine-made chest was removed from its wheeled mount after much struggling and positioned on its side by the Lacaille soldiers, who glanced around nervously as more Perennial Amaranthine slowly filtered into the chapel. They stopped to stand in a circle, silent, waiting. Corphuso looked between their eternally young faces, wondering if this was to be his last day alive.

The Long-Life straightened, his jowly visage contorted with excitement, and went to the case.

The Lacaille soldiers glanced at Von Schiller, who nodded briskly. The whine of the case's hinges filled the quiet chapel.

Corphuso strained to see over the flowing, frosty mist that coiled and rose from whatever goods the case protected. Inside were two separate compartments of burnished, worked gold, each filled with some indescribable object still wreathed in fog. Everyone leaned in to watch, some of the closest Lacaille trying to wave away the mist.

As soon as they had confirmed the cargo, the Perennials walked forward in unison, each grabbing a Lacaille by the arm and pulling him back. Only the Long-Life and Von Schiller remained standing near the chest.

"There you are, withered thing," the Long-Life said to the object in the left compartment, his head tilted down to it, apparently lost in reverie. As he did so, the whiff of the chest's contents reached Corphuso's nostrils and he flinched. Ghaldezuel grimaced and put a hand to his nose.

The indistinct man turned to Von Schiller, who bowed.

"Do not be offended, Florian, that I did not choose your body as my new vessel." He gestured at the objects in the case, still seeping vapour. "These were my old masters. My mind, everything I was, was built to their own templates. Why tailor a fresh suit when you have one already?" His expression became slack and vacant as he regarded the case. "Now you shall see, Florian, how it is done." He looked over, an afterthought. "*Vulgarii*—you must come and watch."

Corphuso was pushed to the front, to Ghaldezuel's considerable amazement, by one of the Perennials. He found himself standing next to the Long-Life and looking down into the second case, the sharp stink wreathing his body.

At first he couldn't understand why they had come so far, endured so much, to bring nothing but the skinned carcass of some kind of animal with them. He bent closer, suddenly forgetting the presences around him as his eyes unravelled the form. A lonely paragraph from his expensively erratic education made itself known at the back of his mind.

The mist cleared around the twisted form, revealing gangly, taloned arms scattered with wiry blue plumage. Its chest was bony, concave where the ribcage met the stomach, svelte as a racing hound. The hips were distended, the scarred legs and gristly feet quite obviously reconstructed by some surgical procedure. Between them curled a gaudily plumed tail, forked at the end. He looked to the head.

It was almost alive, the eyes—their pupils horizontal red slits decorated with a corona of marbled white iris—bright with shock and pain. But he knew it was dead. He knew it was dead, because he knew what it was.

It was a dinosaur.

The snout, crooked and sharp like a patrician nose, could not conceal the cruel snaggle-teeth that poked at angles between its fleshy lips. The nostrils were huge and flared. Around its scrawny neck was a mane of iridescent feathering that tapered to the collarbones. He staggered back, at last beginning to understand. In the next compartment of the case was a Voidsuit, or something that appeared to be for the same purpose, but a fantastically advanced and beautiful example of one. An elegant bulge of cream material, it was tufted here and there with protrusions and wisps like the feelers of a moth. It had hinged open in places to display an interior like a sound-proofed chamber, all spears of soft red foam. Running along the surface of the spikes were veins of white machinery as fine and delicate as the membranes of a leaf. He opened his mouth slightly, astonished that such beauty could have swaddled such ugliness, trying to grasp how and why he should be seeing what he was seeing.

Corphuso noticed Ghaldezuel looking at him as he moved back. The Lacaille had known, but didn't fully understand. He turned to the Long-Life and gazed up at him in wonder, the man's vague face framed by the whirls of painted figures on the distant ceiling.

"You said they built your mind after their own." His lips trembored as he spoke. The Long-Life regarded him silently, his predatory eyes merging in and out of focus. Corphuso composed himself and continued, "They *made* you. But you are not one of these things. You were—you *were once*—" He stopped himself mid-stammer, quite sure for a moment that he was about to embarrass himself with his foolish assumptions, but he had to know. "You were a machine, weren't you? You belonged to these creatures."

Von Schiller moved to take Corphuso's arm but he resisted, staring into the apparition's eyes. "You're a ghost. A machine soul. Like Perception, the device made by the Amaranthine." His eyes widened. "This is why you need my Shell. What happened—how did you die? Were you destroyed, too? Is this all that's left of you?"

Another Perennial grabbed him by the wrist but he struggled out of the grip. "What are you planning to do? Why become mortal again?"

"Corphuso!" Ghaldezuel hissed, trying in vain to step forward. "Calm yourself!"

But Corphuso could see now the culmination of his mistakes as it lay there on the floor of the chapel. He had caused all of this. *His* invention had awoken this ancient power from its aeons of slumber. He looked across at his precious, glittering Shell.

He moved as swiftly as he could, reaching for and grasping the closest Lacaille's pistol. He ducked, steadying himself as Von Schiller grabbed him, and aimed at the Soul Engine.

Vilnius

Sotiris wrenched the zeltabra around with some difficulty. It panted, striped flanks coated with yellow pollen and blue sap, wild eyes straining to turn and glimpse the towering city at Sotiris's back. The Amaranthine pulled at the reins again, his face suddenly an image of fury, searching out Lycaste as he followed behind.

"Faster!" he shouted, his voice deep and instantly commanding. Lycaste slapped the harsant's rump as hard as he could, finally joining the Immortal at the field's edge.

Sotiris patted the zeltabra and turned to face Lycaste. His ancient eyes were bright in his grimy face as he extended a gleaming, metal-encased arm and pointed.

Where the forest of bloodfruit ended, the hill dropped towards a river valley wreathed in smoke. The light, fading quickly in the humid afternoon, could only just pick out the rusted bodies of war machines and their riding passengers as they swarmed in the forested valley. A great bridge spanned the river at the valley's bottom, stretching beneath a colossal gateway set into huge curtain walls already beginning to crumble under the siege. As Lycaste watched, a shell struck a section of the wall, erupting in a huge bulging mushroom of smoke that rose to drift on the wind, the echoing crump of its impact only just reaching his ears. A cheer, glottal and full-throated, rose from among the screams and roars in the dim trees of the valley.

Lycaste looked up, following the turreted ramparts and streets of the city as they wound to the crest of the canted hill it had been built upon. Clouds glowered over the topmost buildings, appearing to touch the spires.

"The city of Vilnius," Sotiris said. "Last outpost of the Second Province." Lycaste thought he looked worn, a man accepting defeat. He studied the dirty Amaranthine as Sotiris sat astride his mount, even the dainty Firstling armour dangling from him like a boy in adult's clothing. Lycaste did not want to end up like this: twelve thousand years on and still tired and filthy and scared, leading some idiot descendant around behind him. He looked back to the fury of tiny specks crowding the bridge—Secondlings defending their land—thinking on how many chances the Immortal were given to suffer anew.

"Ready?" Sotiris asked, taking up his reins.

"Bilocation, Elumo, is one of those phenomena that is quite impossible to describe to those who've yet to achieve it," Stone said, sitting back in the chair with a satisfied smile and listening to the rumble down below.

"It is the product of a gradual settling of the iron particles within the brain, a process that takes many thousands of years."

"Until they are aligned into a certain pattern," supplied the Princeling Elumo, somewhat doubtfully. His glass rattled on the table and he put out a stubby little hand to steady it.

Bonneville looked at the rings on the Vulgar's fingers: thick wedges of precious metal spotted with stones. Since his youth, the thrill of stealing had been like a drug to him; he would take those rings for himself one day, when the Princeling was no longer useful to him.

"Exactly, Elumo. The alignment is transitory, we are sure, possibly shifting to another pattern within a few millennia that will be of no practical use—certainly not for faster-than-light travel. It may be that we require our ancient fleet again before too long, and the further support of our dependable allies, the Vulgar."

"How do you know when you are able to do it?" Elumo asked, waving away the pleasantry. His other hand remained at the ready in case the drink shook again.

"It always accompanies other physical, and often detrimental, changes—the inability to keep time, a lack of awareness of one's surroundings, but also a swelling of the innate powers of the mind."

"Are you not afraid of these changes?"

Stone looked at Bonneville for the first time. "Ask Reginald here, he is yet to experience them."

Bonneville smiled, performing a little shrug for the benefit of the Vulgar. "It is our curse." He took another sip of his wine and washed it around inside his mouth.

The three were drinking Vulgar alcohol as a courtesy to the Princeling, who apparently refused to drink anything else. It was impossible for an Amaranthine of any age to get drunk, but Bonneville could already feel the strong mixture burning his gums slightly.

The Princeling took out his helmet briefly to check the time. He had changed from his shimmering gown into a beautifully made Void-suit in preparation for leaving. Bonneville glanced at the inside of the helmet as it was returned to the chair.

That was supposed to be the signal.

Elumo remained seated, staring at his hands, a smile forming on his small white mouth.

Bonneville looked to the door, waiting for it to burst in. He had taken no chances; beneath his waistcoats he wore a plate of treated iridium, plundered from the tomb of an ancient Amaranthine.

The door opened slowly, a couple of silent Vulgar soldiers entering to stand behind the Princeling, the tips of their pointed helmets only just reaching the arms of his high chair. Stone's eyes remained fixed on the table, his hand cradling the cup of Vulgar wine.

The realisation that he had been betrayed came to Bonneville slowly. He felt the smile dying on his face.

Lycaste swore again and again beneath his breath, his hands squeezing the reins. He kicked and the beast galloped on, swerving through a plume of smoking wreckage as a shell landed nearby.

Sotiris waited, circling the screaming zeltabra, his hand outstretched as if to shield his eyes as he stood in the stirrups. When the harsant was alongside, he put out his hand to catch Lycaste's reins and swung one leg over the broad upholstered saddle.

Lycaste shifted, the Amaranthine's metal toe plates scuffing his shin, and they cantered on. The terrified zeltabra skittered away across the bridge through the flames.

"Now!" Sotiris screamed, kicking his metal spur. The beast charged sideways along a crater in the stone, their teeth rattling with the impacts of shells slamming into the bridge. High above, the city of Vilnius Second burned.

Lycaste—even among the encompassing, deafening bombardment of cannon-fire and hand-to-hand battle on the bridge—could hardly take his eyes from the metal monsters that ripped and wheeled across the skies. The *Voidships*, as Sotiris had called them. He closed his eyes at last, gripping the harsant's neck, and let Sotiris do the steering.

They flashed through the heat of a flaming tank, Lycaste's eyebrows and beard singeing, and landed among a legion of thirty or more Jalanbulon directly engaging the small Firstling cavalry units with pikes and sabres. Amid the throng, an armoured Asiatic had hold of a Zeltabra's hind leg. He roared and swung, unseating the Firstling soldier and snapping the animal's limb, the beast's scream made silent by the huge, reverberating noise all around.

A Jalanbulon turned as they approached, raising his rifle. Sotiris leaned past Lycaste and stretched out his hand, engulfing the giant in an instantaneous blast of white flame that poured soot from its blazing tips. Three nearby Jalanbulon began thrashing and roasting in the heat given out by their burning comrade, whose armour pooled and bubbled amid the rubble. A shell followed through the smoke, bursting from a gun emplacement on the parapet, and once again the Amaranthine opened his palm, dissolving it into a molten bloom of falling sparks that showered the bridge ahead. Lycaste ducked his head through the coiling, rolling heat of another fallen war machine, the harsant bouncing madly as it galloped. It knocked a Firstling down, crushing him with a sickening crunch of bones, and slammed a Jalanbulon furiously to one side, the Asiatic rolling and clattering where his metal armour bit at the stone.

A single, concerted bombardment suddenly lit up the edge of the bridge nearest to the city walls, shattering one side into the river below and dumping the chaotic crowd of hundreds of fighting Melius a hundred feet into the water. The harsant adjusted, swerving away from the shattered stone edges where troops still crawled and dangled, maimed and mauled by the bombardment, leaping a regiment of standard-bearing Firstlings and thumping to the ground amid a shattered tangle of spiked wire. It howled, stamping the wire down, but was snagged. They twisted, turning the beast as best they could while Melius thrust pikes and spears at them through the coils of wire. A sharp edge nicked Sotiris's chin, flinging blood across Lycaste's arm, and then they were free, the burned skin on his legs ripping away. Lycaste stared at the Immortal blood, astonished for a moment as they cantered on. Sotiris extended his hand while they shook off the last of the wire, sweeping a host of charging Firstlings into nothing but a slanted column of sparks and ash. Blood streaming from cuts across the harsant's own flanks flicked into their faces with each bouncing gallop.

Lycaste looked up as a formation of the metal ships thundered overhead. They loosed rounds of erratic projectiles and angled away, the pale evening sun catching their coloured fins and strakes like glittering fish. He followed the trailing smoke of the flying mines until they encountered the walls, some blooming away in falling fragments of light before they could impact, others detonating and hurling stone far into the sky. Lumps of wall began raining down upon the throng of troops, smashing into the bridge. Legions and battalions stared upwards to watch the fleeing Voidships being overtaken by others of a different, even more threadbare design. Lycaste gaped in wonder, watching them tangle in mid-air. Tiny black specks—the strange men who made the Voidships—were slinging hooked ropes to leap between the craft as they rolled and twisted, many falling to their deaths. One of the vessels, the largest of the initial squadron, was suddenly blown in half in a lightning burst of flame and hurled detritus, screaming downwards to strike the bridge in an erupting fireball. The blast swept upwards from orange to black, engulfing the city gates and the hundreds of troops defending it.

"Grab the damn reins, Lycaste!" Sotiris yelled, the barbed elbow of his suit scraping past Lycaste's own. He did as he was told, pressing himself as low as he could into the harsant's back. Sotiris stretched out a hand as they approached a lumbering tank, its guns swivelling in their direction. As they galloped past, the Amaranthine reached and snatched up one of the shocked little creatures that were climbing about on it, swinging him in an arc by the end of his helmet and depositing him roughly in the saddle facing Lycaste.

Lycaste stared at the creature and it stared back, huge blue eyes wide in its pale face.

"Vulgar!" Sotiris shouted, lifting his faceplate, "You will take this Melius into the city and to the House of Gellesh. You will *not* stop to engage Lacaille, you understand?"

The little head nodded, glancing uneasily back at Lycaste. "Yes, Amaranthine," it squeaked in Unified, "the House of Gellesh."

The harsant swerved again, the flames of the downed Voidship rumbling across their path. Sotiris took Lycaste suddenly by the arm. "You remember my instructions?"

He stared back into the Amaranthine's eyes for a moment. "I do, but I still don't understand why you won't come with us."

"Just do as I say and all will be well," Sotiris said, sliding down his faceplate. With one hand still on the reins, he pulled the harsant to a stop and dismounted quickly, slapping it hard on the rump with his gauntlet. As they raced through the smashed wreck of the guttering Voidship, Lycaste tried to look back, but Sotiris had already disappeared in the pall of smoke.

When they were through, Lycaste and the creature regarded each other dubiously, both ducking under a sudden volley of shots. The Vulgar glanced around and shook his head, muttering.

"You know where this house is?" Lycaste asked in First, taking in the intensely foreign look of the creature.

The Vulgar twisted in the saddle and unholstered a side arm, twining a length of the reins around one arm. "We have to get through the city first, Melius—just steer this thing while I shoot."

Lycaste pulled on the reins, directing the stumbling harsant through another bank of smoke. Up ahead a pulverised section of the city walls, charred black and scattered with burning bodies, spilled out towards them. They climbed the huge blocks of smashed stone, clopping among stunned, half-dead Secondlings shuffling and coughing. When at last a wounded soldier thought to raise his weapon, Lycaste spurred the beast on, galloping up into the flaming city streets.

"What are you?" he asked as they cantered, dodging running troops and tents.

"Just *steer*!" The little man aimed and fired at a doorway, blowing it to splinters. "Through there!"

Lycaste yanked the reins and the harsant went smashing through the house, knocking furniture and screaming Secondlings out of the way. They emerged in an ash-settled back garden stacked with supplies, ploughing through the boxes of fruits and meats and on into the next house.

"Where—"

"Short cut!"

Another two houses later, they emerged into an empty street, sheets of ripped linen flapping around the pommel of the saddle. A group of Firstling soldiers in polished silver armour strung with long green standard capes rounded the corner, stopping when they saw the animal cantering towards them.

"*Jégeresső a Vulgáris, jégeresső azt Első!*" the little man shouted in High Second as they swept past. Lycaste looked back to see some of the Firstlings cheering. *Hail the Vulgar, hail the First.*

The streets narrowed as they ascended, coiling in a corkscrew fashion up the cone-shaped hill of the citadel. The guns at the top fired in stuttering bursts, their voices louder as the harsant climbed higher, but Lycaste could also hear the shouts and screams from below, where the Jalanbulon had made their way into the city. Secondling citizens scrabbled across the streets before the harsant, clothed in whatever makeshift armour they could cobble together from pans and plates and pots. They yelped and scattered at the animal's approach, and Lycaste found he was enjoying himself despite his fear.

The thundering of monstrous engines came suddenly from above. Lycaste looked up into the raging evening clouds to see more of the elaborate Voidships screaming down upon the citadel. Bursts of repelling fire pulped the closest of them to a fireworks display of glowing cinders, the others banking away.

"Ha!" screamed the little man in First again, almost falling from the mount. "Not so easy!"

He swivelled to face Lycaste as they clattered through one last empty encampment of colourful tents and up to the gates of the mighty house. "What happens now? Who are we looking for?"

"Just get us in there," he grunted, urging the beast up some stone steps to the gardens. He found that he'd become quite a proficient rider since leaving the forest with Sotiris, barely half a day earlier.

The Vulgar shrugged. "Very well—you'll have let me know who I'm allowed to shoot at, though."

The harsant clambered, grumbling, over the lip of the garden wall and onto the sunken lawns surrounding the estate, now strewn with smouldering pieces of the Voidship that had dared to attack the house. A column of guns, each of their barrels longer than three Melius men, pointed to the darkening sky or looked out over the bridge. Some clearly exhausted Secondlings plated in old-looking cuirasses were loading shells and ducking as they fired. Two five-legged tanks painted a lurid orange were still waiting, un-crewed, at the edges of the path to the house. Lycaste led the harsant to the edge of the wall, the animal panting and coughing, so that he could look out while they remained hidden from the house. The bridge, far below, had been almost completely destroyed, with only one or two connecting paths of stone remaining between the craters and towers of rising smoke. Massed troops still swarmed upon it, bottlenecking at the crossings, their voices like the distant roar of a waterfall. He watched a few being picked off by snipers higher in the city and retaliating fire from below. Down at the ruined gates the battle raged amid the decimated carcass of the Voidship. Heaving crowds of Jalanbulon and Firstlings struggled and shot at each other, the First soldiers outnumbered and surrounded. Lycaste's eyes moved to the city streets where shots rang out among the white stone buildings, many already gutted by the fires. Some mounted Jalanbulon were cantering back down to the aid of their comrades at the gates; it would not be long before they had the city. Over the dark, misted jungle, the Voidships were massing again, the throaty rumble of their movements cutting a low bass note beneath the crack of shots and the boom of shells.

The Vulgar sat up in the saddle. "Quick now, Melius, they're coming back."

"My name's Lycaste," he growled, looking up to the grand house. "We'll have to leave the harsant here."

"The what? Oh." The little man seemed to consider dismounting on his own, finally turning and raising his arms impatiently.

Lycaste set him down, wiping his hands with mild disgust, then dismounted himself. He stood on tiptoe to look over the inner wall, taking in the Voidship stationed at the top of the building. "Around the side, there are some outhouses—probably a necessarium. We could get in there, couldn't we?"

The Vulgar shot him an inquisitive look, and Lycaste wondered once more what he was doing with such a strange little person. "A necess—?" the soldier began to ask.

"A place where you, you know . . ." Lycaste mimed a squat.

The Vulgar's eyes widened and he looked away. They were modest people, apparently. "Yes, yes, that's enough." He sighed, pushing back his spiked helmet. "Come on, then."

Lycaste kicked open the necessarium door, the Vulgar soldier sitting atop his shoulders with his rifle poised. The house kitchens were deserted and bare, with nothing but crumbs and empty sacks scattered across the vast oak tables. Long windows let in the last light of the falling dusk but were too high to see out of. He looked over to the three huge hearths, their fires still stoked and roaring.

"All right, Melius, let me down," the Vulgar said, swinging his little legs.

"*Lycaste*. My name's Lycaste."

"Yes, yes, Licasse, very good—let me down now."

Lycaste grabbed the soldier by the foot and dangled him upside down. "What's my name?"

"Lycaste! Lycaste!" the Vulgar screamed, his helmet clattering to the floor.

"Good. And what do I call you?"

"Huerepo! Huerepo Morimiel Vuisse! At your service!"

"Pleased to meet you," he grumbled, setting the soldier down.

"How dare you!" the Vulgar spluttered, sweeping his wiry hair back from his reddened face. "You wouldn't like it if I did that to you!"

Lycaste smiled as he investigated one of the larders quickly. He'd not eaten a thing since his dinner with Envoy the night before.

"I've done my job, you know. I got you here, like the Amaranthine asked. He didn't say anything about being dangled upside *bloody* down!"

"All right," said Lycaste through a mouthful of starchfruit. He stared at the peculiar person—apparently from some unimaginable place beyond the sky—marvelling for a moment at how poor both of them were at spoken First. "Do you know the inside of this place?"

"No, I don't. Why should I?" Huerepo slung his rifle across his shoulder and peeped over the edge of the table in search of his helmet. "Now, if it's all the same to you, I'll be on my way."

Lycaste's ears twitched as he took another bite of the fruit. He grasped the Vulgar by the end of his rifle and hurled him into the larder, closing the wooden door behind them and covering the struggling little man's mouth.

Through the crack in the door he saw a Firstling dash into the kitchen and stare wildly about. His armour looked blackened and burned, his face bloodied. "There are tables!" he shouted in Second, grabbing the edge of one and pushing it further into the room until it slammed up against another.

"Here! Here!" yelled more voices, the thundering of their metal boots reaching the kitchen. Lycaste saw perhaps a dozen fully armed Firstlings and Secondlings swarm into the chamber, suddenly remembering the last time he'd been trapped in a cupboard. The soldiers rushed about, sweeping the sacks and crumbs from the surfaces of the oaken tables before dragging more of them together.

Others came in, their faces stained with filth and gore, their pinkish eyes haunted. They were hauling something that scraped along the flagstones. It was too low for Lycaste to see.

"Clear some space!" an authoritative voice shouted and the soldiers fanned out, exposing an armoured Firstling body being lifted onto the pushed-together tables. The body's cuirass had been bent and hammered by some huge impact, and Lycaste saw that pieces of it were embedded in the Firstling's torn-looking face.

Huerepo muttered something, struggling, and Lycaste reluctantly removed his hand.

"*Filago*," the Vulgar whispered.

Lycaste didn't know the name, but he kept his mouth shut, watching a Thirdling fleshdoctor bending over the man and fiddling with shaky hands at the clasp of his case. The Firstling soldiers in the room paced and muttered, some glaring at the doctor. The Secondlings looked too numb and shocked to care. One turned to the larder, his yellow face expressionless, and began to try to open the door.

"Staunch!" the fleshdoctor announced as a spurt of blood splashed him in the face. "I need linen!"

The Secondling turned back and went to the table, blocking the bloody scene from view.

"We can't stay in here," hissed Lycaste.

"Why not?" whispered Huerepo. "There's no way out."

"There must be!" He looked around in the darkness of the larder.

A tall Secondling soldier clad in a huge banner cape, muddy and bloodstained around the hem, rattled into the doorway. He raised the visor of his plumed helm and stared in horror at the scene on the table.

A general who had been pacing up and down stopped to regard him. "Goniolimon?"

Lycaste pushed his eye to the gap again to see the man, his heart thumping. Goniolimon Berenzargol, Callistemon's father.

The Secondling came to his senses and looked round at the general. "Skylings, FirstLord, in the grounds."

The Melius on the table moaned as the fleshdoctor extracted another shard from his face, dropping it into a mixing bowl with a clink. The Firstling general glanced grimly at the high windows, taking Goniolimon by the arm and leading him over to the larder door.

"Listen carefully," he said in a whisper. "Take Protector Filago to the roof. There was a Vulgar galleon stationed up there—with any luck it may be there still."

"What do I tell—"

"Here." There came the rasp of metal on metal. Lycaste peered through the gap.

"It contains two hundred length of silk," said the general, lifting a chain over his head and passing it to Goniolimon. At the end of the chain dangled an intricately wrought pendant. The Firstling checked over his shoulder and opened the complicated clasp for the Secondling to see.

"The Vulgar won't refuse you."

"I won't flatter you by saying I'm disappointed, Reginald," said Stone, looking up from his wine.

Bonneville stared into his eyes, his body very still. He could do nothing but picture how he looked to the Perennial. An eroded, antique memory of the little priest's house in Colwyn Bay flittered through his mind, rain battering the roof tiles. *This is what happens to boys who steal.*

"You think you're the only one who tried to assist the Jalan?" Stone's eyes narrowed for a moment. "Elatine will bow to us even when he reaches the First." He glanced at Elumo. "We did not imagine he would have such eager help, however."

Elumo rose from his seat, not looking at Bonneville. He put the drink down. "You come to us with lies, Sire Bonneville, financing our enemies behind our backs."

"I never lied, not to you!" Bonneville blurted. Stone's eyes widened in fury.

Elumo looked at him at last. "The Lacaille schooner you spoke of, the Nomad Class? A figment of your imagination, I think. Because of you, thousands of my men died above Mars-Gaol, and the Lacaille now hold the Satrapy."

"Enough of this, Elumo," Stone said, shaking his head. "This one roasts tonight—there's no point trying to make him see sense."

Bonneville could feel himself shaking as they looked at him, no longer trying to quell it. "It was the truth," he implored, looking into Elumo's eyes. "The delivery of the Soul Engine was—"

"I will not hear any *more!*" Stone roared, thumping his fist on the table. The air filled with static, snapping from the silken fibres of Bonneville's cloak. Elumo stepped back, a fearfully expectant look suddenly crossing his face.

Stone hesitated, his eyes suddenly flicking to the darkening window. Elumo turned, too, the helmet clutched in his hand.

The guns on the lawns were firing into life, making their glasses jump from the tables as if animate. Each throaty boom shook through Bonneville's innards, and he was gratified to see Elumo flinch. Stone went to the window cautiously, peering out into the twilight, while Elumo made to leave. Bonneville saw his chance.

"*Here!*" he hissed, opening his palms and extending his will into the chamber. A scorching blast of air engulfed the space, invisible but for the shimmer. The walls peeled as Stone's body withered and crumpled, loosing ash as the window blew out. Elumo, slightly further from the source of Bonneville's rage, was blasted to his knees, the skin of his face melting and separating. Bonneville let him scream, watching with a trembling excitement as the eyes in his unsightly Vulgar head burst, the sockets fuming, before delivering another blast of heat that blew open the door and set the corridor aflame.

He crunched over to Elumo's burning body and stamped his heel onto one of the ringed hands, putting out the flames. He bent quickly and tore three of the rings from the denuded fingers—one was pliable to the touch, on the verge of melting—and stuffed them in a pocket. He stopped to inspect some crisped Vulgar skin that had come off in his hand before wiping it carefully on the ruined wall. Just one more thing they'd never suspected—that he might have lied, oh so slightly, about his age.

He left the remains of the inner dining chamber, where moaning Vulgar guards still rolled about the smoking floors, and scuttled through the still-undamaged grand hall, noticing that some Secondlings were already engaged in ripping down the precious, fabulously intricate tapestries. Bonneville stopped in the candlelit chamber, eyeing them warily. They noticed him and paused in their work.

"The roof," he said, as loudly and resonantly as he could, "is that Voidship still there?"

"I believe so, Amaranthine," said one in faltering Unified, bowing fearfully. "Follow me, if it pleases."

The soldier took him along the passageways of the grand house, pausing at some service doors and directing him through. Bonneville could hear the fighting spreading within the house, and several Thirdlings brandishing fire-tongs and curtain rails ran nervously past.

"Up here?" he asked, pointing to a spiral stair rising at the end of the linen chambers.

The Secondling hesitated for a moment, directing his eyes at the floor. "Take me with you, Amaranthine." He raised his head. "Please! I would be loyal and true, the finest servant there ever was!"

Bonneville stared at him, snorting a laugh, and jogged for the stairs. The Secondling followed. "Please, Amaranthine!" He reached out a hand to grab Bonneville's cloak.

Bonneville turned and lashed out, his fingers missing the Melius but the force of his rage igniting the man's hair. The Secondling yelped and beat at his head. Bonneville ran on, not looking back.

He took the polished growthstone steps three at a time, sure he had missed his chance. With every pounding heartbeat his certainty that it was all for nothing increased. At the top of the stairs he paused for breath, leaning against the cold stone. The passage was built for a species of person much taller than he was and the wide steps had been especially tiring to negotiate. He looked up. A locked wooden trapdoor was all that led to the roof from here. Bonneville grabbed it, melting through the metal in a few seconds, and thrust it open.

The evening air ripped through his hair, almost blowing him back against the trapdoor. There among the spires of the house was the Vulgar ship, its engines thrumming through the metal tiles of the roof. Across the spires, Vulgar and Lacaille fought, the tiny goblin men swearing and grappling, some slipping on the tiles and falling. Bonneville recoiled as a white Lacaille crashed to the roof in front of him, a flaming hole puncturing its chest. More were firing on the Voidship's open hatch and the Vulgar just inside, hammering the metal hull until it had begun to glow and deform. The ship, trying in vain to pick them off with its light nose falconets, flared its superluminal engines like an animal in danger, bursting liquid green flame across the rooftop and deafening all closest to it.

Bonneville ducked back into the trapdoor, his hands at his ears, and leaned against the stone.

He rocked his body, eyes compressed shut, understanding finally what the Long-Life had achieved. With the Treaty of Silp sabotaged and the Vulgar and Lacaille at each other's throats again, Aaron had ensured that no two Prism empires could be used against him. Perhaps he'd even known of Bonneville's plot all along, waiting until the moment the Shell was being transported—and at its most vulnerable—to seize it. There were no deals now, no loyalty. The Lacaille, just like their sworn enemy the Vulgar, had been thrown against each other, their forces employed to the hilt in a war created just to distract. Anything to keep the Long-Life's enemies at arm's length for the small amount of time he needed.

The door rattled as something tried to pull it open. Bonneville flinched, his gaze darting back down the stairway.

He ran, steadying himself against the wall with the tips of his fingers as he heard them come through. Sounds of clattering boots followed him. He missed a step.

Bonneville felt the slip before it had fully happened, his feet swinging out from under him, arms pinwheeling to find a banister that wasn't there. His last full realisation before his skull burst on a stone step ten feet below was that he'd just done a small, wet and totally miraculous fart in his underclothes.

Lycaste and Huerepo emerged from the larder into the dim kitchen. The logs on the hearths had burned down a little, filling the chamber with a haze of smoke that mixed with the scents of sweat and blood.

Filago had been moved into the upper chambers on the pretence that he needed rest to recover, while the others had filed out to guard the entrance to the lower hall. Only Lycaste and Huerepo knew where the Lord Protector of the First was really being taken.

"That galleon on the roof," he said to Huerepo, peeking around the corner of the arch and into the staff antechambers. The sounds of fighting outside were explosive, yet the corner of the house they were in still felt relatively quiet. "Do you think you could . . . fly it? Make it fly?"

Huerepo shook his head, dumping the contents of his many pockets so that he could fill them with fruit and cheeses from the larder. Lycaste saw that the Vulgar had been carrying a few books on him, but they were all printed in some angular, foreign text. "I've never flown anything before, you might as well ask a Melius—" His expression became suddenly sheepish. "Apologies, a Vulgar saying." He looked wistfully at one of the books he'd discarded and then back at Lycaste's nakedness. "No pockets," he muttered grumpily and threw it into one of the fires.

"What was that?" Lycaste asked, checking again through the archway.

"Just an adventure book," Huerepo replied, a touch defensively.

He considered the soldier a moment. "So what *did* you do? Before today?"

"Pump operator. I lived on a tanker in the Sea of Winth until I was drafted."

"You speak our languages well enough."

Huerepo performed a little bow. "First shares some similarities with Vulgar, but thank you, all the same."

Lycaste nodded, motioning the Vulgar to the doorway. "I don't think it's going to get any quieter than this. Let's go."

They made their way across the linked chambers and into the under-hall, pausing behind pillars and curtains whenever troops—usually increasingly ragged-looking and skinny Secondlings and Thirdlings—ran past. Lycaste noticed that some had empty sacks with them, perhaps heading for the kitchen larders. When the group of Melius were almost at the kitchens, the sound of smashing glass stopped them in their tracks. The first of them screamed and fled in the other direction, followed shortly after by a small, thin creature quite a lot like Huerepo, except its face was a slightly less angelic shape and its eyes smaller. It snarled and produced an unpleasant-looking pistol, firing into the crowd of running Melius.

"What's *that*?" hissed Lycaste.

"Op-Ful-Lacaille," the Vulgar said. "Infantry. Those cannon in the garden must have been taken care of."

Ten more Lacaille joined the first, those at the end of the procession emerging from the kitchen unpacking themselves from bulky rubber suits with ropes and strings attached. They threw the padded orange inflatables down on the ground and continued on, sniffing the air around them with curiosity and gabbling together in a foreign tongue.

"Can you understand them?" he asked Huerepo.

"Yes. They're looking for a Vulgar prince who is here."

"A prince?"

"Princeling Elumo. I've heard of him. They'll try and ransom him when they find him, I imagine—probably something just for themselves, not on anyone's order."

They followed behind the yammering Lacaille, ducking once as a firefight broke out with some better-equipped Secondling soldiers. Shots and bolts of light slammed around the under-hall, smashing chunks out of the stonework and setting fire to one of the huge wooden beams that arched into the ceiling. Lycaste was not surprised when the last of the Secondlings tried to run. The Lacaille brought him down, laughing as he screamed.

"The Amaranthine told you where to find this man?" asked Huerepo when they were sure the Lacaille had moved on.

"Upstairs somewhere, in one of the prison chambers."

"One of them? How many are there?"

"Just *help me*, will you?" Lycaste sighed, spotting a passage that appeared to lead upwards. "He'll come and find us when it's all over, I'm sure of it."

Transformation

Ghaldezuel had hung back as the foolish Vulgar started to run his mouth, partly in the spirit of self-preservation—finely attuned, he liked to think—but also out of simple curiosity.

He had, of course, been aware of his cargo's preserved contents— one of the two beasts left over from another age, some millions of years old and surely inestimably valuable—but only recently learned of their significance. They were *Old World* history, nothing he usually concerned himself with. People– early *Hiomens*—found the creatures long before his race had even come into existence in the Firmament, and as such their importance had faded over the millennia to little more than an archaeological footnote relating to a forlorn and for-gotten planet, a place where horrors still roamed. He had considered holding on to the precious corpse should the deal turn sour, knowing it would be worth a fortune to the right Amaranthine buyer, but this

Aaron the Long-Life struck him as being a dangerous, unpredictable sort of Immortal.

So he had waited, and listened to what Corphuso had to say to the Lord of the Amaranthine, his long ears straining to hear the import of the babbling Vulgar's sudden revelations. Something about machines and ghosts, monsters and mistakes. Ghaldezuel knew enough about the fabled prospect of machine intelligence to state happily that such a thing did not exist—or if it ever had, it was made and destroyed swiftly by a more powerful lost generation of Amaranthine, the Decadents, people the Immortals never spoke of. What all this had to do with a stinking, mummified cadaver more than seventy million years old was beyond him.

He watched Corphuso disgrace himself until he could take no more, sure it would somehow impact on the Lacaille and their handling of the precious goods. That was when he tried to stop the Vulgar inventor himself.

But he was too late.

The gun had melted into a sparkle of liquid drops before Corphuso had time to pull the trigger and splashed across the bronze floor of the chapel like a thrown jug of water. A spell cast by one of the Perennials, eager to demonstrate his loyalty—and perhaps his powers—to the master. Ghaldezuel watched Corphuso stare slackly at the mess of molten metal in his hand, no doubt unable in his shock to feel it burning into his skin, and then rush recklessly at the Long-Life, screaming incoherently. He disappeared within the shadowy folds of the man's robe as if he had run through a waterfall, the material parting around him momentarily and flowing back into place.

Everyone in the chapel held their breath.

Aaron looked down at himself calmly, stepping to one side. Corphuso was nowhere to be seen. The Lacaille soldiers glanced at each other but held fast, and Ghaldezuel, his own shock notwithstanding, was proud of them. Even the Perennials were glancing surreptitiously around the chapel, unsure quite how the trick had been accomplished. Ghaldezuel watched their faces for any sign that this freakish show was for his benefit, but the Amaranthine looked genuinely mystified. It was as if the man was nothing but a projection, some trick of the light.

"Now, to business," Aaron concluded smartly, sweeping his robes around him and stepping towards the circle of Amaranthine. "Would you?"

Two of the Perennials, one immensely fat and bejewelled, the other sallow and lean like a caricature, approached the corpse in its glistening vat. The fat one had upon his hands a pair of fine damask gloves. He stooped over the chest, eyes going to the petrified monster's face before delicately gripping it behind the neck and around the legs, as one might carry a bride. Ghaldezuel, of course, would never have a bride, but he had seen the process at Lacaille wedding ceremonies as a child. Awful, deceitful affairs. A waste of precious years.

The thin Perennial lifted the ancient Voidsuit—apparently as light as air—from the second compartment and passed it to another. The Amaranthine who took it regarded it with fastidious reverence, holding it at arm's length and gazing up at the painted ceiling.

Ghaldezuel returned his attention to the Immortal carrying the body. At a word from the Amaranthine, the Lacaille soldiers heaved the Shell onto its side, the embroidered gold tapestry falling away with a thump. Aaron watched intently, stepping around the action to get a better view, his clothes floating like a spot of oil dropped in water. Ghaldezuel finally noticed the man's shadow and felt his skin crawl.

Candles were being lit at the end of the chapel as darkness fell beyond the windows. The procession of the corpse did not take any heed of them, and Ghaldezuel observed the huge Melius standing to watch. Among them, nothing but a spectral face in the gloom, he spotted the boy king surrounded by his entourage, totally ignored by the Amaranthine. It had grown too late for anything else to matter, apparently.

The fat Perennial took the body to the Shell, its tufted tail trailing and arms dangling, and turned, waiting. The Long-Life nodded slowly.

In the candlelight the Shell gleamed like a polished musical instrument, all coils and tubes, the body nothing but a limp husk of shadow cradled almost tenderly in the Perennial's arms. They watched him consult the thin Amaranthine before fitting the creature into an enlarged hollow in the machine's belly, pushing it delicately until it was in an upright position. The other Amaranthine shook his head and pointed, and the two stood there before it, their shadows long in the candlelight.

Ghaldezuel managed one last smirk at their weakness, their indecision. It was a trait they hid from the Prism at all times, but he had bought himself a seat at the table now and they cared not for his opinion. At last they saw how it was done, the Long-Life pacing around them like a caged animal, his shadow appearing to take on different forms. As soon as Ghaldezuel noticed it changing, he averted his eyes, not wanting to see. Some things were just too odd to be glimpsed, and he planned to leave this place with a clear head. The others' faces brought his eyes back, however, and he was startled to observe that beneath the man's dark robes the silhouette of a shaggy-coated wolf paced, its tongue lolling. It seemed to look up for a moment, and Ghaldezuel raised his eyes to find the man observing him.

The body was apparently correctly inserted, though Ghaldezuel could barely see. In the vast space, only the candles on the far side of the chapel had been lit and everything that faced him was in darkness. He had seen enough to know that the creature's jaws had been distended and placed over a tubular orifice somewhere at the machine's centre, as if to blow up a huge balloon.

He was thinking of Corphuso, and where in the world—or elsewhere—he might have vanished to, when the rustle of every Perennial stepping back filled his ears. Aaron the Long-Life was standing very still, head tilted to the ceiling, his eyes apparently closed.

The change began with his clothing, which lightened and withered to a tight-fitting gown of some ancient fashion. The body beneath was at first slender, too narrow for the man's jowly head, then suddenly portly. In an eyeblink the clothing changed again, dappling with stripes, spots, cravats. Jewels and chains grew and died, the stones popping like sores across his chest and belly. Each caught the meagre light, totally real in their twinkling reflections. They disappeared beneath the swelling of collars and lapels, then ruffs, fur and dark, greasy armour. The serene expression on the man's face never changed, even while a hurricane of movement crawled across his body. A cape flapped and twisted about him, dissolving immediately into wisps of colour. It was replaced by a larger hooded robe, which again wrinkled and fell away. Ghaldezuel began to see now that the clothing was becoming simpler and less ornate, the textures rougher. Buttons erupted and healed while the colours settled into an earthy blur.

Finally the process stalled, strobing, at a coarse wollen cloak, loose and hooded. Aaron opened his eyes to look calmly down at the shadowed block of the Shell, and disappeared.

They watched, and they waited.

The Shell stood alone, the body somewhere inside it, its shadow trailing almost to his feet. Something twinkled on the floor under the scintillating candlelight, but it was only the melted, hardening globules of Corphuso's weapon.

A noise, like the scratching of a tree-branch on a windowpane, began somewhere within the shadows. It stopped just as Ghaldezuel was replaying what Corphuso had been saying in his head, trying to make sense of it all. When it began again it was louder, interspersed with a shallow moaning like a cold, lonely wind. As the chapel grew blacker and the noises resumed, Ghaldezuel felt the hairs all over his pale skin rising. A shiver rippled through him beneath his new Voidsuit.

Suddenly a scream like nothing he had ever heard ripped across the chapel floor from the dark interior of the Shell. The instrument shook as the bawl of pain grew louder, and a few Perennials stepped forward uncertainly.

"Most Venerable?" the fat Amaranthine asked in an unsteady voice, hurrying to the side of the Shell. Ghaldezuel saw a clawed shadow whip from the depths of the dark block and strike out at the Perennial. He gasped and retreated a few steps.

The screaming of a voice never before heard by hominid ears dwindled and finally stopped altogether. Muffled grunts and groans suggested the thing was trying to extricate itself from the chambers of the machine, but the Amaranthine remained at their positions, fearful of the thing's talons.

Ghaldezuel had had enough of this. He snatched a candle from its table at the corner of the chapel and lit it, making his way slowly towards the dark block of shadow. Nobody tried to stop him.

The light touched the Shell as he held the candle high, dancing reflections back into his eyes. It was empty.

He bent, suddenly very glad of his costly Voidsuit, and peered into the hollows. The trembling light from his candle illuminated a cave of dark, shining blood. It must have come from the thing as it awoke, from some unmended old wound. His eyes went to the bronze floor, examining the thin trails of darkness that wove around to the other side of the Shell, the marks already smeared with his bootprints.

A rasping breath tickled his ear.

Ghaldezuel swung around, the flame flickering and snuffing out. Red, reflective eyes glimmered at him in the gloom.

"Of all the strange things . . ." he muttered, staring into the darkness at the horizontal slits.

"Come away now, Lacaille," said Von Schiller, moving to stand beside him. "You did well."

"What happens now?" asked Ghaldezuel, first to Von Schiller, and then into the darkness. "Am I to be released?"

"Released?" said a high, chuckling voice. The eyes came closer, something brushing against him in the darkness. He looked down to see a shadowy clawed finger touching the metal of his Voidsuit. "Not just yet." The creature's speech was like a blade dragged across metal.

"Why not?" he managed, his hands slippery within his gauntlets. "What could you possibly want with me?"

The thing—Aaron, he supposed it was still Aaron—pushed past Von Schiller, a gnarled shadow. It hobbled towards the Amaranthine carrying the suit, pausing to cough and retch violently, one thin arm bracing itself on the bronze floor. Ghaldezuel saw the black silhouette of its stomach straining, the ancient muscles tightening, only their contours touched by the candlelight. But nothing was coming up. If what Corphuso said was true, the ghostly form Aaron had once been had never experienced physical processes, and all this would be new to him. To *it*.

Ghaldezuel looked on in wonder, his own circumstances forgotten.

It lurched closer to the light. The scars that striped its back and flanks were deep, unhealed, the shiny glue obvious where the edges of the greyish skin had been pushed back together. One had reopened and dripped wherever the creature walked.

Dilasor, he thought, trying to recall the pictures of what they were thought to look like. Part of him realised the thing that coughed and spluttered before them was no more a Dilasor than if Aaron had chosen to inhabit Ghaldezuel's body and then call himself a Lacaille. It was nothing but a corpse, suitably formed to accommodate the artificial being that inhabited it. He stepped a little closer to see what it was doing.

Aaron's new form had taken the exotic Voidsuit from the Amarathine, who shrank back into the group to watch. It examined the folds of cream material, pulling and prodding until the fronds that dangled from the suit began to stir. It raised a leg awkwardly, as if in incredible pain, and stepped in. The suit closed around the leg with a sucking sound, searching and rising over Aaron's new clothing of wrinkled flesh. As it spread to reach the head it became engorged, like a giant maggot trying to swallow something far too large for it, until all they could see was a struggling white blob.

Ghaldezuel and Von Schiller glanced at each other.

The suit crumpled back in on itself, vacuum-forming around the beast's contours while it stood there, still visibly coughing and gagging. Extra limbs, alien in their structure and digits, sprouted to either side of the arms and the head bulged with blisters.

The form became still. Two black eyes emerged in a moving churn of some kind of surface ink, widening and appearing to register the people around them. Aaron straightened his long back, stretching his four arms and clacking the claw-like extensions with obvious relish, his crippling pain apparently gone. With a flourish of his white tail, he turned back to Ghaldezuel, the black discs on his face suddenly huge.

"I must go to Gliese," its new, confident voice boomed. "*You* will take me there."

Ghaldezuel hesitated until the white-suited form came to stand before him, the black eyes—formed from thousands of minuscule moving dots, he noticed—gazing steadily into his own.

"Aid my transcendence, *Galdess-uel*, and you shall live for ever."

Prisoner

The upper chambers were all bedrooms of a sort, with tousled beds and the remains of a great deal of hasty packing. Rich clothing that could only be of ancient Amaranthine manufacture lay scattered on the floor of one of the rooms, as well as opened satchels, their contents strewn across the floorboards.

Lycaste and Huerepo paused at the entrance to the chamber, looking at the scene, hearing gunfire raging throughout the lower reaches of the house. Outside, in the grey darkness, the city had reignited and Jalanbulon surely stormed the streets. The Lacaille they had been following had succeeded in locating a hiding enclave of Secondlings. Their cries echoed down the stone hallways.

"Must be one level up," said Lycaste, stepping into the room to inspect a sheathed sword leaning against the hearth. Its basket hilt was almost rusted away.

"That won't do you much good," Huerepo muttered, watching Lycaste draw the blade to inspect it. The metal was pre-growth, holed and pitted with rust, likely to snap if he tried to use it for anything. "Here," the Vulgar said after some thought, passing Lycaste the second of his pistols, "take this."

Lycaste looked at the tiny gun, accepting it reluctantly. It was of a sleek, foreign design not used in the Provinces and did not even appear to have anywhere to stow the projectiles. He wished he'd managed to keep Chaemerion's ring.

"Where's the firing latch?"

Huerepo looked up. "Firing latch?" He took it and held it out in front of him. "Finger here, aim like this." The Vulgar passed it back, watching Lycaste try to replicate the actions and shaking his head.

Lycaste returned the gun, pointing at the rifle slung over Huerepo's shoulder. "How about that one?"

Huerepo reluctantly handed it over. "This was a gift. Don't *break* it."

They took the hallway back to the steps, Huerepo walking in front. Lycaste cursed occasionally as he glanced behind them, continually having to shorten his stride for fear of accidentally crushing the small person underfoot. At the foot of the steps leading up to the prison chambers they found a body slumped at the door. From the look of the streaks of blood that marred the coloured walls, it had rolled its way from another floor.

"Looks like an Amaranthine," said Huerepo, turning the corpse as much as he could with his boot. The face was youngish, its bloody forehead caved in and split by a colossal blow.

"Do you think a Jalan did this?" Lycaste asked nervously, staring as far as he could up the spiral stair.

"A fall, more likely," whispered the Vulgar, bending to look at some small, shiny objects that had come to rest alongside the body.

Lycaste saw him pick up and inspect the rings in the weak light that suffused the narrow space. "Look at these," he said, passing one to Lycaste. "They were made for Vulgar royalty—see the imprinted seals?"

Lycaste took one and peered at it, far more concerned about the possibility that there was a Jalanbulon on the loose somewhere in the upper reaches of the house. He returned the ring, thinking of the giant old woman, the nanny he'd met on the galleon to the house of Berenzargol. At least they weren't all bad.

"Don't mind if I do," Huerepo said, taking off a glove and slotting all three onto his white fingers to admire them. "Real crimson diamond, red as your skin," he whispered, eyes suddenly wide. "Check his other pockets."

Lycaste looked in disgust at the soldier. "You do it! I'm not touching a dead Amaranthine."

"Fine." Huerepo sighed theatrically, stuffing his pistol into Lycaste's hand and rummaging through the dead Immortal's blood-soaked clothes. The Vulgar sniggered suddenly, lifting a handful of soft-looking pink jelly. "Found some of his brains inside his undershirt."

Lycaste recoiled, cursing.

"Maybe they still contain his powers," Huerepo said thoughtfully, appearing to genuinely consider taking the glob of offal. "Might fetch a pretty price." He shook his head, glancing at Lycaste and dumping the brains on the stone step. "Don't look at me like that, Lycaste. But it's true that they don't rot—we wouldn't have had to worry about the smell, at least."

Lycaste handed back the pistol irritably. "Come on, I'll go first this time."

A tangle of dead Amaranthine lay on the decorative floor around one of the cell doors, some with their faces burned away to the bone. As Lycaste watched, a bolt trembled and flew off the door, bouncing across the floor towards him, where dozens of other bolts were scattered. He saw that the whole metal door had been sealed closed with hundreds of rivets across its face. Only a few of them remained now.

Lycaste and Huerepo raised their weapons as the last three bolts whizzed off, watching the foot-thick, specially coated door crumple and dent and finally shear from its hinges to crash onto the floor.

A tall, slender Amaranthine was standing inside the open cell, his thin underclothes pulled around him for warmth. Lycaste took in the hollow cheeks and curved blade of nose; it was how Sotiris said he'd look.

"Hugo Hassan Maneker?" he asked diffidently, the rifle tipped downward.

The Amaranthine checked among the bodies, kicking some over to see their faces. He cursed, glancing at Lycaste warily. "What?"

"I was told to come and find you. I'm a friend of Sotiris's."

The Immortal regarded at him with renewed interest. "Sotiris is here?"

Lycaste looked at Huerepo. "I don't know. He said he'd meet us when he could."

Maneker pulled a cloak from a victim, shaking it out and draping it around his shoulders. "I must find him."

"He told me to take care of you until he met us again."

The Amaranthine looked sharply up at Lycaste, then down at the Vulgar. "I don't think that will be necessary." He made as if to pass into the hallway, and Lycaste put out a hand.

Maneker rounded on him, the skin on Lycaste's chest suddenly smarting as if from an invisible slap. "I do *not* require a Melius and a Vulgar to assist me!" The air appeared to prickle with extra density between them. "I thank you both for your loyalty to my friend, but you should have left for safety a long time ago."

Lycaste rubbed at his sore skin, squaring his shoulders. "He is *my* friend, too, Sire Maneker, and I will not disobey him." Huerepo glanced up worriedly.

The Amaranthine hesitated, the hint of a smile crossing his face. "And where would you take me, given the chance?"

"There is a galleon on the roof," Lycaste said, astonished at his sudden bravery but determined to hold his nerve. Huerepo shook his head and muttered, stamping into the hallway to check for Lacaille.

Maneker appeared to think, glancing among the dead at his feet. "I have been in this cell for many months. What has become of Zigadenus? He's retreated to the First I suppose?"

Huerepo glanced back, sensing Lycaste's confusion. "He fell, Amaranthine, at the Battle of Vanadzor. His son has succeeded him, but . . ." The Vulgar fell silent a moment, regarding the rings on his fingers. "I could barter our way aboard the vessel, if it came to it—this single stone will be worth more than the entire Voidship."

Maneker stared at Huerepo, straightening his back. "It is an odd pair you make. I'll go with you to the roof—to see what there is to be seen, if nothing else."

Lycaste turned to Huerepo, his skin still smarting. "Do you want a lift?"

"A *lift*?" Huerepo's face twitched with embarrassment. "Of course I don't want a bloody lift."

"All right," Lycaste said dubiously, eyeing Maneker. "I don't expect Sire Amaranthine will wish to slow down for you."

The Vulgar glared at Lycaste, his face reddening. "Yes . . . very well, pick me up."

They passed the body of the fallen Amaranthine once more, Maneker pausing only for an instant to look at the man.

"Did you know him?" Lycaste asked.

Maneker did not reply, pushing ahead up the spiral stair. His breath, thin and wheezing, laboured as they climbed higher.

"How was he?" asked Maneker suddenly. "Sotiris, I mean. How did you find him?"

Lycaste shrugged, though the Amaranthine couldn't see the gesture as he raced ahead. "He was himself. Strong. He saved me."

"Saved you?"

"I had been . . . wounded. I was dying. Sotiris healed me."

Maneker looked back, into Lycaste's eyes, but did not stop. "He didn't say anything about a dream? A recurring dream?"

Lycaste tried to think. "Not that I can recall, Amaranthine." He was determined to be on his best behaviour, despite the exhilarating thought that not long ago he had been prepared to fight an Immortal. He chided himself again for being so foolish.

"You were dying?" Huerepo asked from atop his shoulders.

"I think so."

Up ahead, Maneker snorted. "Where is this roof?"

They came to a smashed trapdoor in the ceiling, the lock melted, wind and rain whistling through the gaps in what remained of the wooden door, accompanied by the sounds of the battle raging all around the house and possibly atop it. Maneker was already opening it, and, before either Lycaste or Huerepo could protest, the Amaranthine had made his way out onto the roof, the door slamming closed again.

"Throw me up before you climb out," Huerepo said. Lycaste nodded and gingerly pushed open the trapdoor. Huerepo scrabbled from his back and dived out into the rain, the trapdoor slamming shut again.

Lycaste glanced back into the gloom towards the way they'd come, hearing the smashing of crockery and the overturning of furniture in the grand chambers of the prison level. He thought of the rusted sword, leaning against the hearth. There was still time to run and hide, perhaps wait out the battle for this place for a chance to slip away. He pushed his hands through his oily hair, turning in a slow circle as conflicting fears pushed him this way and that. Up there was a ship that might take him to safety, but also to his death. *Should have left that ring with the dead woman and slipped through the gates*, he thought, pacing the narrow hall. He shook his head, groaning. *Should have gone home to Kipris, that's what I should have done.* The vertigo returned for a moment as he thought of how far he'd come in less than half a year, how much he had changed. Lycaste stopped, looking up at the trapdoor. But he hadn't really changed at all. Still he whined and sulked and trembled at the thought of what might come to pass, fearful of anything he did not know. He ground his teeth, rubbing his hands, hearing the bellowing of war above him as it rattled the wooden door, droplets of rain swirling through the holes and dampening his face. This was the World, not the tiny cove he came from. This was life.

Lycaste took a deep breath, suddenly finding that his entire body was shaking violently, and opened the door.

The Voidship was gone, the space it must have occupied filled instead by blistering flashes and carnage that slammed and vaporised every shadow on the roof. Lacaille were crouched at the crenellated battlements around the spire, firing down into the smashed roof as Vulgar swarmed and shouted. Many of the Lacaille dead had fallen and rolled, jamming among the black tiles and creating cover for the Vulgar. In the night around them, Voidships thundered past on high parabolas, blowing the little people over with each strafe.

Maneker stood—like a Melius hero from one of Lycaste's strip serials—in the middle of it all, his back to the trapdoor, his loose clothes flapping around him. Lycaste climbed up and crouched, a new light forcing him to shield his eyes. The Amaranthine had raised his arms above his head as if beseeching the blustery moonlit clouds. His hands directed a floating, coiling snake of fire, its ends branching away from the Immortal's fingertips. Lacaille and Vulgar alike fell silent for a moment, entranced by the white fire. Lycaste watched it stretch out across the roof and into the night, looping and closing around a passing Voidship. The ship's hull squealed and burned away in a bright sparkle, dashing its contents across the spire and incinerating many of the Lacaille who had been watching. Huerepo crouched and fired into the mess of remaining Prism on the other side of the roof, the replying shots smashing into the tiles he was hiding behind and splashing their molten pieces towards Lycaste.

Lycaste ran, throwing himself behind Huerepo's cover, his feet stinging where their thick skin had made contact with the glowing wreckage. Maneker melted two Voidships that were bolting straight towards him, their glowing hulls swinging into each other and merging in a sloppy embrace. Lycaste glimpsed the chambers inside one of the vessels liquefying, their occupants already nothing but white-hot embers. The two ships fell as one, spearing through the southern face of the grand house in a glittering explosion that knocked over everyone but the Amaranthine.

Below, on the blackened grass of the sculpted lawns, Lacaille droppers loosed their bouncing salvos of padded troops and vehicles, all protected by the same rubbery orange material. White shock troops were unpacking themselves chaotically from their orange inflatables and harnesses as the tanks rolled forward, firing into the lower halls of the house with barely a pause.

On the far side of the roof, the view dropped away to darkness. Zipping points of light that were either Voidships or their released munitions swarmed over the river valley and invisible remains of the bridge, some blossoming into explosions, others turning and darting elsewhere. Inchoate shouts and screams and booms drifted up to them, only to be torn away by the keening winds.

Through the ragged silver-green clouds they could hear the bellowing of something far larger approaching them, a kraken parting the vapour. Lycaste looked up as the shape loomed over them, turreted, gnarled, built unlike any of the other things he had seen over the course of the long day. It hovered, jets roaring, whipping and billowing Maneker's stolen robes about him. A mandible-like rear door swung down, extending jerkily to become a fluted ramp and revealing a gathering of fantastically suited Jalanbulon troops. They were flanked by anatomically unusual, slightly larger Prism people of a kind unknown to Lycaste, some dropping to one knee and sighting their rifles on Maneker. The tall Jalan commander at the front of the group was suited in complex white armour much like a scaled-up version of the sort the Lacaille wore. He stepped forward onto the wobbling ramp, long hair buffeted by the ship's howling downthrust, and pointed a gauntleted hand at Maneker.

"Amaranthine!" he called out in a surprisingly high voice, "Enough of this! The Second is lost!"

Whatever speech the commander had prepared was interrupted by sudden falconet fire from a fleet of smaller Vulgar balloon ships, their men dropping on ropes from the floating craft. The unknown Prism vessel twisted in the air as it was fired upon, spilling the white-suited Jalanbulon and his generals into the blackness. Lycaste, Maneker and Huerepo watched the tumbling figures for a moment before the tiles they stood on were also struck, crumbling and hurling them over the edges of the garden and down to the city walls.

The moonlit stone rushed past, Lycaste's stomach thrown around inside him as he tumbled, Huerepo clinging to his neck and choking him. From nowhere a hand found his, gripping tightly. Maneker took Lycaste's other arm, the three falling together now, wind rushing in their ears and eyes, the view swinging and roaring. The grip on his hand tightened and the whole world began to slow down.

He opened his eyes, seeing the great belly of the unknown ship fall past, turgid black smoke pouring from its exhausts. Tiny men dropped and spiralled languidly around them like sycamore seeds, everyone appearing lighter than air. The white Jalanbulon roared as they fell— Lycaste found he could hear them quite clearly—some striking the city streets below and bouncing, others swept away in the throwing-knife blur of passing Voidships beneath. A weight from behind and above struck them, squeezing them together, and he turned to look into the huge eyes of the Prism-suited commander as he grabbed at Maneker's sinuously fluttering cloak.

Time slowed seemingly to a lifespan in a single breath. Lycaste watched the Asiatic's great jaws contort in the twisted grimace of a scream. Beside the glowing moon a new light flickered, burning and warming until the darkness of the night receded. A curve of land like the inside of the world began to show through the moonlit clouds, all the falling bodies fading away in the new light like stars at dawn. Lycaste gaped, his eyes tracing the rivers that slithered between the emerald roots of mountains, their twists glimmering silver like streams of mercury. A new wind, powerful and cold, suddenly clawed at his hair, his chest, his face. He opened his mouth and it filled him, drumming his cheeks and drying his tongue. And then the old world that he knew was gone.

The great house crumbled and fell, illuminated in a spiralling froth of sparks. The spent fires of fallen Voidships allowed Sotiris to see some of the stones as they tumbled from the citadel's peak, thumping the ruins of the walls and streets on their way down to the city gates.

He patted the snorting zeltabra. It, too, had raised its long head to watch the structure fall to earth. Sotiris could already hear the beginnings of revelry from the ruins, but the silhouettes he saw dancing around some of the distant fires were not those of Melius people, the voices not those of the Old World. The *Prism* had won this battle, they held the city now. Elatine would treat the loss of Vilnius Second as a personal slight, likely placing a bounty on Sotiris's head for his treachery. It would have to be a very large sum indeed, Sotiris reflected as he toyed with the leather reins. Assassinating an Immortal was a job few in the Investiture would entertain.

He allowed himself one last chance to consider what would happen if she wasn't real, if Aaron had lied to him all this time. The Long-Life had somehow used a version of Maneker that he'd found inside Sotiris's head—surely he could have done the same with Iro. Sotiris scowled, the night air chilling him slowly beneath his Firstling armour. She *had* been real, he'd felt it, nothing like the image of Maneker he'd met at the dream port all those months ago. She had been frightened. The thought of her still out there somewhere, terrified and alone, brought the sting of tears to Sotiris's eyes once more. He would find her. He would save her.

More detonations echoed from the remains of the house, one last stand by some harried group of Secondlings, perhaps even Jalanbulon. Sotiris swept the thoughts from his head, his face suddenly hardening as he took in the vague lights of the burning city. Sending Lycaste to find Hugo Maneker had used what Sotiris knew was to be the last of his charity. He sincerely hoped they were safe, and that his Immortal friend gave Lycaste every advantage in his quest to return home, but they were now beyond his concern. The Provincial battles were over, the war for the Old World itself now only just beginning. All that remained was to take what he had been promised.

His black messenger owl from the Utopia came fluttering to land on the pommel of the saddle. It swivelled its face to look up at Sotiris, its round eyes catching the spark of the flaming city.

"You found your friend?"

"I did," Sotiris said, pulling off one of his gauntlets to caress the bird's feathers. "You need not report to me any longer."

The owl twitched. "No? What of that Melius?"

Sotiris smiled kindly at it, suddenly unsure of what exactly the bird was referring to. "Go home, you've earned it."

"As you say, Amaranthine," the bird replied uncertainly and after some hesitation. It tensed and leapt from the saddle, disappearing silently into the night.

Sotiris did not watch it leave. His gaze came to rest on the gauntlet he'd removed, now lying limply like a metal spider in his bare hand. He didn't remember taking it off.

"Amaranthine," he muttered, slipping it back on and flexing his fingers. The word sounded like it might once have been familiar to him, many scores of centuries before. He searched again, his eyes tracing the reflected fire on the polished gauntlet's surface, and found nothing.

Return

They'd been expected. He didn't quite understand how, not yet, but the devious Southerners had known he was coming. An uneaten breakfast spread on the grass was attracting the attention of the bolder wasps while the Cherries sat and watched him.

Melilotis counted quickly. One man (looking distinctly odd, as if something large and hungry had chewed on him in the not too distant past), a small boy and three ladies, as promised by that rat Ipheon. Someone was missing, another man, older and fatter—unlikely to pose a threat. If he were hiding somewhere, they'd sniff him out sooner or later.

Melilotis strolled into the sweet-smelling orchard and gave the three women a gleaming smile, his eyes settling on a prettily familiar face, the younger-looking of the twins. She was swollen with child. He cocked his head.

"Now, why do I know *you*, pretty lady?"

She frowned, and then he knew. *Ah!*

Her white eyes widened.

The taller of the sisters, equally attractive in an older sort of way, took her by the shoulders defensively. Melilotis smiled, looking her up and down.

"What is it, Meli?" asked Cladrastis, smiling sheepishly like he'd missed a particularly obvious joke. Ulmus lingered worriedly behind at the fringes of the garden.

The older sister tried to take the girl inside, standing her up unsteadily, but Melilotis held up a hand.

"Cladrastis, keep them here." He fished quickly in the satchel at his side and brought out the spoked ring, slipping it on for all to see, while his brother grappled with the girls.

"Pentas, isn't it?" he asked her. She began to cry.

"Look at you." He pointed at her stomach, creeping a little closer. "Not mine, I think? Been seeing some Cherry behind my back, have you?"

He reached out his hand.

"That's enough of that," a deep voice murmured behind him. Melilotis turned, finding himself looking up into the eyes of a gruff, bearded Melius with a pot belly. In his crimson hands he held a long antique rifle. "You'll want to take that ring off, I think."

He glanced at his brother, who had the two women in his grip.

"Let them go," the Cherry—Impatiens, he presumed—growled, raising the rifle slightly.

Cladrastis looked at Melilotis, the women squirming as he tried to hold them.

"Don't you dare, Cladrastis," Melilotis muttered, scrunching his fist. The ring felt hard and sharp pressed against his palm.

"Look, the Plenipotentiary was alive," the crippled Cherry said, "we didn't kill him—he died from some illness. We buried him not ten days ago at the end of the beach."

Melilotis didn't look at the man who had spoken, but stayed facing the plump one. "Is that so? Then you have nothing to worry about, good people." He shrugged. "Just show me where he lies and we can be on our way."

"You give us your word?" the fat Cherry grunted, the rifle still aimed.

"Of course!" Melilotis grinned. "Cladrastis," he said, without looking at his brother, "let them go."

"Meli?" The man gripped the women tighter. "Are you sure?"

He sighed. "Do as I say!"

The fat Cherry's eyes twitched to Cladrastis. Melilotis brought the ring up.

"Impatiens!" one of the women screamed.

"How have you been?" Melilotis touched Pentas's hair tenderly, curling a lock of it around a finger and laughing. He slid a hand to her swollen stomach. She looked as if she was about to faint. "I thought about you a lot, you know. What are the chances, eh?"

He glanced around at the other people, then finally at the body in the grass.

"Go inside with my brother," he told them, directing his gaze at the crippled man, his family huddled around him. "Or the little boy gets to see your insides, too." He cracked a smile at Pentas. "I think I'll go for a walk along the beach." He grabbed Pentas's limp arm. "I'll take this one with me, she can show me where Callistemon is."

"No you won't!" Her sister screamed, lunging forward in Cladrastis's grip. Melilotis pointed the ring at her wide eyes, his fingertips almost touching her lashes.

"Come on, then, you lucky girl," he said to Pentas. "Do what you like with the other one, Cladrastis. Let Ulmus have a go when you're done."

Melilotis wiped his mouth as he led her stumbling down to the beach. Pentas's legs finally buckled and he caught her, dragging her the last of the way over the pebbles towards a patch of sand. He paused, sweating, wondering why he was trying to make her comfortable; the pebbles would hurt more, and he *liked* it when they made noise. She whispered something through her tears.

"What was that?" he whispered back, admiring her body as he pushed her down, the ring still pressed to her slight neck. She was just as firm and toned as he remembered her, despite the pregnancy. He was excited; he'd never done it to a butterfly with a baby inside her. "Did you miss me? I bet nobody's given you anything like it since, have they, pretty lady?"

She sobbed the word again, turning her head away.

"*What*?" He had to bend his head to hear. "*Jotroffe*? Calling some other bastard's name? While you're with me you've got to say my name, pretty lady, say *Melilotis*."

She shook her head, eyes shut. He laughed, settling atop her and smoothing one hand down the side of her waist, breathing harder. "No, Melilotis. Come on, say it."

Melilotis took himself in hand but didn't feel ready yet. What was wrong with him? He was excited enough, damn it. After a moment, he sat back on his haunches to look at her dispassionately. She'd stopped crying and lay with her eyes closed, pulse ticking against his two fingers at her neck. He grabbed her breast with some force, trying one last time to feel something, but nothing happened. It was as if someone had castrated him without his noticing. He glanced slowly back at the grass-topped dune, unsure, sensing eyes on him from somewhere. He didn't feel like it—which was strange, because he *always* felt like it. What he really felt like, though it was very odd indeed, was going for a walk.

But that wasn't right. There was nowhere he wanted to go. He looked past Pentas to the extraordinarily green water lapping at the pebbles. A swim would be perfect, it was so hot. He might see how far he could get; the sea here was beautiful. The feeling of being observed suddenly returned, much stronger this time. Someone on the shore was staring at the back of his neck; he didn't like it.

Cladrastis abruptly ran past laughing and plunged into the waves. Melilotis called out his name in alarm, sure there was something his brother was supposed to be doing instead, but he was damned if he knew what it was. He stood, taking his fingers away from the girl's neck, and watched his brother swim out into the hot water of the cove.

Cladrastis had the right idea. Get away from the beach. He threw the ring down on the pebbles and ran out into the sea, almost tripping against the force of a swell, finally letting himself fall forward, tasting the salt rush into his mouth.

"Cladrastis, wait!"

His brother had swum far out already, the top of his head bobbing above the green. Melilotis swam a little and turned back once more. On the shore stood a small, strangely proportioned man, different in shape from anyone he'd ever seen, even a Firstling. Next to the figure was someone he thought he knew. It looked like Ulmus, but his little cousin somehow dwarfed the man at his side. Ah, well, he'd see them after his swim; he had to catch up with Cladrastis.

Melilotis turned in the water and kicked, trying to raise his head to glimpse where his brother had got to with every breath, but he could no longer see him. He slowed and swept his arms to bob upright in the waves.

"Cladrastis?"

The lime cove was empty all the way to the cliffs ahead, where the water darkened, making him shiver just to look at it. Glancing back, the distant sunny beach was empty once more.

It was as if he was the only person in the world.

Melilotis smiled slightly, raising his face to the strong sun. He ducked under and resurfaced, wiping the stinging salt out of his eyes clumsily with his knuckles while he squeezed them shut.

There was something moving down there, something he'd seen just before closing his eyes, a shadow glimmering into lightness. And a sound, lilting, almost like a song.

EPILOGUE

Perception

The old man unfastened his wrapped bundle of belongings and turned to face the sun. He had come twenty miles, he reckoned, since starting out this morning in the ice-carved valley at the edge of the flats, and could still easily make out the foothills of the mountains rising from the haze behind him. The sun warmed his creased brow, the heat of it glowing through his eyelids. The Most Venerable Sabran smiled, opening his mouth as if to drink in the warmth, and laughed a little to himself. After a while he sat, the pebbles of the cold, flat shore crunching beneath his weight.

"Yes?" He busied himself unwrapping his belongings while he listened to the voice at his ear. He searched quickly for his old wooden cup, taking it out and wiping it with the edge of his robe.

"Your kin? On the Old World?" He sat up, turning to his side as if someone were sitting there on the shore. Sabran nodded absently, leaning to dip his cup in the cold, clear water of a rock pool at the edge of the pebbles.

"You? Bound to this place?" He laughed gently, taking a sip. "And I thought all this time you stayed for the pleasure of my company."

Sabran swilled the water around in his mouth, spitting quickly and dipping the cup again. As he reached over the pool, its reflections darkened for a moment, revealing a hunched shape beside him. He looked up sharply. "What?"

The wind keened across the shore, stirring his hair. Sabran shrugged, looking back into the pool at the grey form. "So he is free now, what of it? He will not come *here*."

He listened, eyes searching the water. "Thresholds? I don't—"

The whispering in Sabran's ear grew loud, as if all the voices of the barren world—for there were indeed many—had chosen now to speak. The Most Venerable clutched his hands together as he listened to the parliament's fury, kneading them against something other than the cold.

"There may be one who could help," he said through the din. The voices fell silent.

"Yes." He smiled. "A spirit, like you, but made by Amaranthine hands. We called it Perception."

Acknowledgements

This book has been a big part of my life for some time now, and there are an awful lot of people I'd really like to thank for putting up with me while I've bored the pants off them all these years, firstly:

My dear old long-suffering parents, Bob and Janet, with all my love. Tony Pemberton, also long-suffering, thank you. My beautiful Steph, the sweetest, kindest of beans. My agent and friend Andy Kifer, who must certainly know by now that he's The Man. My lovely editor Simon Spanton for taking a huge chance and Lisa Rogers for her clever, patient and occasionally hilarious copy-editing whilst wading through so much nonsense. Also, of course, Gillian, Marcus, Sophie and all the brilliant chaps at Gollancz, Night Shade and the Gernert Company. It's been an absolute pleasure.

Some dear friends: the mighty Nick Wade, whose pen wrote the first five notebooks, Joss Cole, gentleman beta reader, Marty Jackson for all the swift halves, Helena, Booboo, Mikey and the Callinicos family (including Jessie) for all the sass, Lee and Kirsty Ambrose-Smith for my first review ("I've got no qualms with it"), Giddy for the cigars and pirate stuff, the Gomersals for a hell of a lot more than I've ever properly thanked them for and Tishy and Gary, who convinced me to give it all another go.

Not forgetting everyone around the world who looked after me while I wrote: the wonderful Rita-Rita for loaning me her home and shiny new laptop (which I still have for some reason, oops), Steve and all the Dolans in Australia, my Germans: Maria, Yula, Steffi and Johnny out in Berlin, Robert and Ilsa at Metropolis Gallery for employing such a bloody useless assistant and David and Karen at the Geelong tea house for all the free drinks. Thank you all.

Tom Toner
London
April 3rd, 2015